Tommy's Girl
Parts One and Two

By LM Morgan

Copyright LM Morgan
All rights reserved

2021 Edition

Cover art by LM Morgan
Cover photograph courtesy of Bigstock and Deposit Photos

ISBN: 9798466414042

LM Morgan

Tommy's Girl
Part One

By LM Morgan

Copyright LM Morgan
All rights reserved

2021 Edition

License Notes
This is a work of fiction. Names, characters, places, and incidents are the products of the author's imagination or are used fictitiously. Any resemblance to actual events, locales, or persons, living or dead, is entirely coincidental.

Tommy's Girl: parts one and two

WARNING
Please note – This book is a thrilling crime story and is not suitable for those under 18 years old.
There are numerous severe triggers and intense scenes.
This book is dark. There will be moments you won't like and people you will hate. Know this before you go in…

DEDICATION

For Brian.
My Mr. Dark and Dangerous

ACKNOWLEDGMENTS

This book could never have happened without the superb help and advice from two wonderful ladies, Gemma, and Sal. Without your guidance and support, I might never have decided to go for it.

PROLOGUE

Piper

This is not a tale of romance or of love and passion with all the sweet and fluffy that comes along with it. This is a warning. A lesson.

There are two sides to my story.

Firstly, I fell in love with the most fiercely passionate and darkly obsessive man I'd ever met. He swept me off my feet and loved me so much he would do anything to make me his. It was wonderful in so many ways.

But, on the other hand, I also became the object of a monster's affections and paid the price for his love. I loved and hated it in equal measure but learned one thing for sure.

I'll never be the same again…

If you're ready, follow me into the darkness. To where there is no light at the end of the tunnel.

Only Tommy, and the various sides to him.

***

Me? I'm a professional actress. I am allowed to say that because I went to drama school and because I was one of the lucky few who has made a living in 'Tinsel Town' as a full-time actor.

I have played almost all the more modern roles out there in the various film industries and also put on a Victorian dress and recited Shakespeare like the best of them. I've donned a set of combats and trained my body hard to play an army girl in a zombie horror flick. I've mastered languages so I could speak them effectively in whatever movie required it, and I've learned to play more than a few musical instruments. I can even perform dances and martial arts to a decent degree. But really, I have always been given a role to play and lines to read, and that's it. I'd go out there and do it and somehow, I've managed to do it well enough to keep being asked to come back and make more movies. Any actor's dream, I guess.

To be honest, I was happy with my modest fame and proud of my accomplishments. I'd not yet been the leading lady or the sexy starlet, but was okay with that…

Well, not really.

Don't get me wrong, it was what all actors wanted in the long term. To be the big name in bright lights. To be adored and screamed at by our stalker fans. Okay, maybe not quite that much, but I'd certainly had my share of fan boys and girls who made what I had accomplished all the more worth it. They were the ones who bought the movie theater tickets and DVDs, and if they kept wanting more, I endeavored to deliver it.

Things were going so well for me I could only hope it would continue. All that was missing was that coveted starring role to land at my feet, along with the man of my dreams, to sweep me off them. Yeah, a girl can dream, but in seriousness, the only thing I could imagine was me continuing my journey up the fabled ladder. If only I could find the right role to push me into proper stardom. To cement me in the halls of fame forevermore.

The only way I knew how was to take on something out of my comfort zone or to immerse myself in a role so deeply that I would transform for it—both mentally and physically. I wasn't sure I was ready to pile on the pounds for a role quite yet, but I did become intrigued by the extreme practices some people in my industry had studied. I began looking at the techniques outlined by the likes of Stanislavsky and his fully immersive methods but wasn't sure I could be serious enough about the realism needed to properly do it any justice. I didn't fully understand how or why someone would want to perform in such a way. What did it add on-screen? How did it differ from what I'd normally done while starring in my roles?

I yearned to know more. To meet one of those strange creatures and study them. Learn their methods and try to implement it in my own work.

And then I met one and my entire world was turned upside-down. I can never forget when I got to work with a real method actor for the first time. Tommy Darke. He shattered everything I thought I knew about acting in a matter of days and proceeded to set about a sequence of events that would change my life forever.

For better or for worse…

ONE

Piper

I was getting ready to begin shooting my newest movie about a famous crime boss and his antics, set in the nineteen-twenties, when it began. Tommy Darke was the star. He was playing the role of George Ward, AKA 'The Boss.' I was playing the role of doting wife to a character named Ronnie who had been George's top henchman, played by the gorgeous Bradley Thomas.

Bradley and I had worked long hours together in the build up to shooting to ensure we had our roles fully hashed out. We'd get together and practice our lines while growing more confident with one another in readiness for the relationship we were getting ready to portray on the screen. It was going great, and we both readily admitted that we had a natural chemistry I knew was going to work really well once shooting started.

We'd both been sure to attend the numerous workshops put together by the producers and of course the screen test shots in the run-up to filming, but every time the cast got together, Tommy was a no-show. We were warned not to expect an appearance, but every time we had one of the writers or producers step in to read his lines, it surprised me.

It became apparent I wasn't going to meet our leading man prior to shooting, but at the time, I figured I wasn't that bothered. All I cared about was getting to grips with my own character, and then I could figure out how to work with the illustrious Mr. Darke. There were a couple of steamy scenes ahead for Brad and me I'd have to get comfortable with, but mostly mine was the typical role of a woman of that era in her late twenties, even though I was much younger at only twenty-three. I was just another trophy wife. Playing the woman on Brad's character's arm while he carried out his work at the behest of his cold and ruthless mob boss.

In our sessions, I'd come to trust Brad and his ability to lead me through the given dialogue and scenes. I relied on him in the same way I did any other co-star I'd had in the past, but I like to think I also supported him, too. That he felt comfortable working with me.

There were some darker parts later in the movie I still had to work through, though. Scenes depicting when things started to break down for Tommy's character, George, and even a sex-scene for him and me, and I had to wonder what it was going to be like working with him. I'd seen his photos and watched some scenes from a couple of his most recent movies in a bid to understand what I'd be working with, and there was no denying he was every inch the heartthrob who could pull off the role of gangster and loveable rogue with ease. But of course, he had his own way of doing things so hadn't so much as responded to one of my emails. I had no idea how, but I knew that with him as our leading man his method acting approach would dominate how the entire movie would be made and there was nothing myself, the other actors, or the production team could do other than tackle it one day at a time.

So, I arrived at the studio on the first day of shooting and located Bradley and the other actors by the set. After greeting them all and introducing myself to the very few people I didn't already know—mostly smaller parts and extras as I'd made a point of reaching out to everyone I could beforehand—we got chatting, and that was when I was warned to expect the unexpected when it came to our leading man. I was right. Tommy had purposely stayed away in the build-up to our final run through, and I soon discovered why. He really was, as his reputation had dictated. One of those strange but also renowned method actors. A rare breed of artist and I didn't know what to envisage. He had prepared intensely for the role and apparently believed he truly was George Ward the kingpin and head of the Ward family mob. A ruthless gangster and dirty dog, our lead character was about to embark on a journey of both incredible highs and epic lows before finding the error of his ways in the arms of the right woman, his leading lady. She was being played by the beautiful and up-and-coming new face in Hollywood, Scarlet Rosen. Based on real-life events, we were about to portray the dark and intense story of a man at the top coming undone from the inside out. And Tommy was evidently going to live it for real. It was something I'd not yet experienced in the movie biz and had to admit; I was interested to see for myself.

We got to work and if I was honest, my initial opinion of him wasn't all that exciting. I didn't have much time with Tommy on or off screen at first, but while watching the first few scenes being shot, I couldn't deny he was beyond handsome. Inked up and stylish. Naturally rugged, no matter the shave and polish the makeup team gave him ready for the first shots, and his almost jet-black hair was so thick and coarse I could make out every strand even from feet away.

Along with all the others, I watched him working through scene after scene, but couldn't fathom how there were fundamentally two men inside that skin. Tommy and George. Like a split personality or something.

However, for the purposes of the movie he was only letting George come out to play, and I quickly realized I had no idea who the real man was underneath.

My first scene with him was a couple days' in and I caved when it came to being positioned beneath that intense stare of his. Tommy scared me, but I used that fear to add an extra layer to my own character. Penny was based on the real woman who, as the story went, had put up with her drunken nobody of a husband for years. She never saw Ronnie because of his job within the Ward mob, and while my research had told me she was reportedly strong and didn't take any shit from the men around her, I also made her a little timid. I wanted her to be real to the women of my time but also of the days in which the movie was set. She had to be relatable. To be soft when she needed to be because she knew the men in her life wouldn't accept being treated like dirt by a woman. But then I knew she had also been ready to stand firm if the need arose.

Tommy's character George was confronting me in the scene. After being guilty of simply ending up in the wrong place at the wrong time, Penny had suffered the brunt of George's wrath whether she had earned it or not and had bitten her tongue rather than give him the lashing he'd deserved. As her bestselling biography had told it, this was the pivotal moment when things began to change between them, but at the time she had done what any other woman would've back when men ruled the world, especially men like George Ward. She'd caved.

Tommy was standing over me like some huge beast, glowering at me menacingly, and I took it without batting an eye. I recited my lines as the script dictated and then backed off, just like I was supposed to. But he wasn't satisfied. No matter the script, Tommy continued to stare me down, adding a sinister layer to the scene that soon had my knees trembling. By the time the director shouted 'cut,' he'd plucked a real reaction from me, and I already knew this movie would be gold when shown on the big screen. Some things you just can't fake.

Tommy's gaze had penetrated me. Claimed me as his in some wild and feral way. I hadn't known why he'd done things that way until our next scene together.

For continuity purposes, we shot it right away while we were still wearing the same clothes etc. and so we moved sets and took our places. This was it, the scene when our characters were supposed to have a quickie in Penny and Bradley's kitchen. Following the script, I greeted Tommy at my fake doorway and pointed an angry finger at where Brad lay on the sofa, pretending to be asleep.

"He's passed out drunk, Mr. Ward. Nothing new there..." I said in my best Boston accent, before walking through the set of our apartment and George followed, closing the door behind him silently. "You wanna

15

leave him a message I can relay for the mornin'?"

"No, let him rest. I came here for you," he answered, following me to the kitchenette like the script dictated. He was supposed to apologize for having been rude and give me a quick one while I bent over the counter, which is exactly what we played out before the numerous cameras and dozen onlookers. It wasn't hot, but the job was done as far as the storyline went because our particular quickie wasn't there to give the viewers rosy cheeks or a feast for the eyes. It was just one of many factors at the start of George's downfall. The moment that was to become the facilitator for his descent into chaos because, as the story went, poor Penny was to become pregnant with George's child.

As the crime history books told, the two of them had then hidden the truth from his one true love, Josie, played by Scarlet, and from Penny's husband. But the secret would eventually eat George alive. The real George Ward then murdered his entire crew before slaughtering his wife and putting a gun in his own mouth. Penny's child was his sole heir and had then inherited her father's fortune before liquidizing his assets and disappearing, along with her mother's memoirs. She never resurfaced, but the story had. The writers had taken a softer approach to their movie, though, opting for both Penny and Josie to survive his brutality. But it was still to become an intense tale of death and sorrow. Something they were all hoping the viewers would go wild for.

We did twelve takes in total and not once did we deviate from the script. Tommy hadn't allowed it for a start, and by the end of that afternoon, we had fake kissed and fake fucked our way into getting better acquainted. Not that it made me like him any more than I had earlier that morning. He was still a closed book to me.

And that was the story of how I met Tommy. Nothing too crazy or sexy. No explosion of heat and lust. Simply a work relationship like any other. If anything, I was kinda into Bradley back then and we'd hooked up more than just a few times while working on the movie. It isn't unusual for actors to fool around behind the scenes, and we were both single so weren't hurting anyone by it. Our liaisons were a bit of fun and the chance for me to blow off some steam with a hot guy, but I wasn't the type to fall head over heels with a co-worker so we would have our fun and then both saunter off casually afterward. A no strings kinda fling. Just how I liked it. I still remember with a smile how he snorted cocaine off my tits one night before eating me out like his life depended on it. Bradley was fun and boy, did he like to fuck. (I guess I'll have to edit that part out before letting anyone hear this, but damn, he knew what he was doing in the bedroom all right.)

Now, back to the story at hand.

By the time the movie wrapped, so too had my fling with Bradley. There were no messy goodbyes. No spiteful, heated words. We simply stopped hooking up. Just another short-term fling that'd run its course. That was when I finally met Tommy. The real Tommy.

It was after midnight when someone came knocking on my door. I'd normally never even check it at that hour, but something made me go find out who could possibly be swinging by unannounced at that time of night. I lived in a secure area with guards and security and all that, so knew it shouldn't be some prankster or crazed fan.

Turned out it was Tommy. He told me he wanted to invite me to his house the following afternoon for a pool party. I was surprised by his invitation but accepted, intrigued to see the real him now that he was coming out the other side of his apparent immersion into the role of George.

I headed over there the next day and had assumed there'd be others there too but got a shock when I discovered we were alone. It was a party for two and I wasn't impressed. As much as he was charming and had fallen back in touch with his real self, I knew it'd take me a while to feel comfortable around him. To forget the character he had been portraying the entire time I'd known him and see the real man beneath the cold and intimidating façade.

"What am I doing here?" I asked, but he simply grinned and stalked back inside his huge home. Like the curious little lamb I hadn't actually thought I was, I couldn't resist following. I wanted to figure him out and knew this was my chance. Tommy led me out into the garden to where his enclosed terrace overlooked the City of Angels. Man, he had an amazing view. I was instantly jealous but did my best not to let it show. He'd earned it, after all.

"I need to detox. To cleanse myself of George," he told me, stripping down to his underwear by the pool. "I was hoping you could help me?" With a bend of his waist, his boxers were on the ground along with the rest of his clothes, and Tommy stood there before me in all his naked glory.

He had the typical movie star body with plenty of incredibly defined muscle and hardly any hair. His impressive cock stood to attention, but I pointedly ignored it. I wasn't there just to be another quick fuck and then leave. Or was I? I couldn't remember why I'd even said yes to coming to his house, let alone having ended up stood there before the naked Adonis if it weren't exactly for that reason. But I didn't want him to assume anything of me.

Tommy then dived into the pool and I found myself stripping off as well before joining him. For some reason we didn't get right down to the dirty deed I'd clearly been summoned to his home for. Instead, we swam and floated in his perfectly clear and temperate pool, laughing, and letting a strangely natural banter start to fly between us both.

He was funny. Far funnier than I'd picked up on during our filming, but I knew then how it was the real Tommy coming back through. By laughing and joking together, he was indeed detoxing. Ridding himself of the extreme role he'd lived and breathed during the few months previously, and it was an honor to behold. Something I'd never understood, and yet I could see the transition with my own eyes.

After our swim, we then headed for the hot tub where Tommy offered me champagne, and I readily accepted. He had some too, and we sat there with all our jiggly bits bouncing around thanks to the bubbles and making us laugh even harder.

"Who are you, Tommy Darke? The real you?" I asked him, sipping on my wine.

"I'm every character I've ever played all rolled into one," he answered with a sly smile. I giggled and shook my head. That wasn't enough, and we both knew it. "It's true. They're all still a part of me, somewhere deep down. But mostly, I'm the real me. They just exist in the one percent of my brain that lets them."

"Like voices in your head?" I teased, but my smile dropped when Tommy fixed me with a cold and hard stare. One that both terrified and excited me at the same time. As if I'd just hit the nail right on the head. He then shook off whatever emotion I'd stimulated in him and took a deep breath, as though steadying himself. I had to wonder if anyone had asked him those types of questions before. If anyone had wanted to know the real him, rather than just bed the star and go on their way with an epic story to tell their friends.

"No, not voices. They're more like urges. Parts of myself I opened up when I played each of the roles and then had to lock away again. Pleasures and forbidden desires I never knew I had until I was forced to tame them again."

"Well," I answered, sliding closer to him with a sultry smile. "If it's that hard, how about you don't tame them, within reason, of course? Just make sure they don't rule you. Learn how to own them while enjoying the spoils each forbidden desire brings you…"

Tommy's eyes flashed and his nostrils flared like I might've angered him by my comment, but he didn't say another word. Instead, he kissed me like he had no other choice but to have me. As though something else was driving him, something I had conjured within him. And, by God, was it the most intense and memorable kiss I'd ever had. Our on-screen kisses were nothing in comparison to this. Not even partway close. I lost all comprehension of time and space in his kiss. I didn't swoon or go all girlie, but I did lose myself in his kiss. It was unlike anything I'd ever known before. Like he was claiming me. Owning me. But it was also like I owned him too.

When we finally pulled away, Tommy stared at me like he was suddenly terrified. He backed away, and I took the hint, feeling oddly the same. Neither of us was interested in something big springing to life between us. We'd only been after a hook-up, but that kiss had been something else entirely.

I should've realized it when we'd spent the better part of an afternoon laughing and getting to know each other rather than letting off steam with a healthy game of hide the sausage. What was I thinking getting close to him and talking about the deep and meaningful? It scared me too, and I backed off just like Tommy had done.

I then climbed out of the hot tub and made some lame excuse about having to get home and was glad when Tommy didn't try and stop me. He watched my every move, though, and the desperate look on his face confused the hell out of me. I wanted to stay and sleep with him, but I had a feeling we would end up making love or some shit like that, and I wasn't prepared for it. Not in the slightest. The only time I had ever been in love before I had ended up with a broken heart and a lifetime of baggage. I wouldn't even talk about those days anymore, or the girl I had been while timidly following around the love of my life like some lovesick puppy. That person was long gone, and I was glad I'd come out the other side. Even a few years on, I had days when I crumbled. When I didn't feel strong enough, or when I heard his voice going round and around in my head telling me I wasn't good enough to become a proper actress. That I'd never make it.

So, like the modern-day woman I was, I threw my clothes back on and walked away, trying my best not to let it show how what'd happened mortified me. I drove straight home and took a hot shower, where I relieved some of the pressure Tommy had stirred in my core. But it wasn't sufficient. I needed to unwind and playing with my clit in the shower just wasn't cutting it.

After drying off, I poured a large glass of wine from the bottle I thankfully already had chilled to perfection in my fridge and then headed back to my bedroom, where I watched some porn and drank my wine while getting down and dirty with my eight-inch dildo. It sorted me out nicely enough, and I fell asleep feeling far more relaxed than if I'd tried to ignore those needs. Plus, I wasn't ashamed to partake in some self-loving when the need arose.

The life and times of the rich and famous, hey? Well, I could've done something foolish, like heading to a club and finding someone to scratch that itch for me. However, those stories almost always made the news, and I wasn't that kind of girl, at least not as far as my public persona went. I had worked hard to maintain my girl-next-door image and was squeaky clean, so I was determined for it to stay that way.

I slept late the following morning, dreaming of that kiss, and had to repeat my chosen method of release I'd used the night before, minus the wine and the porn. I didn't need it, anyway. All I had to do was close my eyes and I could see Tommy there in all his glory. I came with him at the forefront of my mind over and over, cursing myself each time I did, but then going back for more, regardless.

My manager, Janie, came over mid-morning to check in with me and I soon got back to my normal routine of taking the calls she'd vetted and her giving me the options for my next possible ventures. I was quite particular in not wanting to get pigeonholed in the movie industry, hence my variety of roles in the past, so I was pleased to find a bit of all sorts in her bag for me to browse. There was everything from an upcoming Western to a voiceover spot on an animated movie. I picked out a few I liked the idea of and agreed to look at the scripts over the few days that followed and let her know if I wanted an audition arranging.

Janie was great. She had been a lifesaver in the past and had shown me how much I could be worth if I just played things the right way. I'd still been auditioning for advertisements when she'd taken me on as a client, but now I had scripts being regularly sent my way in the hopes I would come on board. I had friends in the movie industry who trusted me to be professional and trustworthy with their characters. They recommended me to their producer buddies and directors, often asked for me to read for them. Life was good. Great in fact, and it was thanks to her in a lot of ways.

I was ready for my dreams to become an even bigger reality. All I needed now was that one big role. The chance to be the leading lady at last and hit the big time.

"Sure, I'll let Piper know. When do you need us back at the studio?" Janie's voice broke through my thoughtfulness. She was on the phone and I could see her making a note of something on her notepad. I didn't really have to ask what it was. Re-shoots were a common factor in filmmaking but was surprised when my heart lurched at the prospect of being back in the same room as Tommy again.

Was I excited? No, of course not. Probably just anxious. "They need you back in at the end of the week for a few re-shoots," she confirmed once she'd ended the call, and I nodded.

"Yeah, I figured as much," I replied, staring out the window at my backyard. I guessed I'd have to see him again, eventually. We still had all the promotional work to do on *Wayward* yet, which would include us flying all around the world for the premiers and interviews together. Things would have to normalize between us or else it would show, so I decided I'd pretend if I had to. I certainly wouldn't let my afternoon with Tommy put me off my game.

"Are you okay, Piper?" Janie asked, and I turned to find her staring at me. I realized I must look a mess. Probably a little lost and too wrapped up in my own shit to carry on our usual conversation. That wasn't like me at all. I was usually proactive and my ambition pushed me to jump from one project right into the next, hence why she had turned up with some new material right after me finishing filming *Wayward*.

"Yeah, fine," I told her, snapping back to the matters at hand. "So, what are we doing today?" I asked, eager to get Tommy Darke out of my head by whatever means necessary, even if it meant working night and day to distract myself.

TWO

Tommy

I barely slept a wink after Piper left. I'd wanted her right from the moment I'd first laid eyes on her on set but hadn't let George do the talking for me. It was one of my strictest self-imposed rules when it came to immersing myself in whatever role I'd taken on. It had to be me doing the talking when it came to personal matters, not my character. There had been times when I'd fucked my co-stars while still engrossed in whatever role I was in, but it never truly felt like me. More like I was watching from the sidelines while the character I was in did the deed for me. I always ended up feeling dirty. Used by both the chick in question and my character. As if he had betrayed the trust I'd put in him when I allowed him to overtake my thoughts and actions. Yeah, I know, not crazy at all.

Not with Piper, though. I'd waited until I was in the final stages of my comedown to approach her, and she'd clearly been surprised to find me on her doorstep, but I couldn't blame her. It wasn't like we'd grown at all friendly while on set. When she'd come and stripped off at my poolside, I'd been sure we'd end up fucking in no time. But then she had made me laugh. She'd responded to my banter with her own and had drawn me further out of my shell. Made me want her for more than just that tight body I'd glimpsed more than just a few times whilst we'd been filming.

And then she'd taunted my dark side, and something deep inside of me had salivated at the sheer idea of letting those forbidden desires come out to play. I'd almost caved. Those urges I always worked hard to quash had risen at her command and when we'd kissed, it'd taken everything I had not to throw her over my shoulder and take her inside. Usually that wouldn't have been an issue, but not that day. I knew I wanted to do more than just fuck her. I'd imagined my hands around her wrists, pinning her down on my bed. My handprint on her ass after I'd spanked it raw. My cock pummeling her like a battering ram and me not letting her leave until I was well and truly done with her…

Something told me she wouldn't have liked me all that much if I'd taken her body like that. She wasn't into that kinda thing. Not Piper. No, she wasn't like all those other girls.

Or was she? Had I just not taken her hints? Damn, I was bouncing back and forth between the two assumptions and couldn't convince myself of either. Maybe she was like me? Good on the outside while all kinds of bad on the inside? She'd called to that part of me like she understood it. As if she had dabbled in those dark urges, too. So maybe...

I knew I shouldn't have let her leave. I should have begged her to stay. Pleaded with her for one more chance. No scrap that. I'm definitely not the sort for the beg-and-plead routine. I should've downright demanded for her to take me the way she'd baited. Forced her to want me the way she'd made me believe she did.

Taken her every which way I desired, whether she'd agreed or not...

There it was again, that darkness. It swelled and called to me so much stronger than ever. As though conjured from the depths of my soul at her command. And now it haunted me. I couldn't rid myself of those thoughts, but I could ignore them. Yes, that was the right approach. I would ignore it all. The thoughts of Piper and her cute body. Those nipples as they'd bobbed on the bubbles in my Jacuzzi. That tight ass as she had sashayed away from me. So easy to forget...

"Damn it!" I screamed, and I threw my coffee mug across the room. This wasn't me. I didn't obsess over women. Never in my thirty years had I ever been left feeling like this after a night with a woman. Especially not when we hadn't even fucked each other.

I got the call later that morning to say we had to go in for re-shoots and that was it. Whether she wanted to or not, I was going to show her who was boss. Who had and would always have the upper hand. Piper wasn't going to play me like some fool. She wasn't going to win. I was a winner in all things, and this would be no different.

I would get back into character and do what needed to be done. And then, I would invite her back to my home and we would try the whole 'fancy a swim?' thing again. Next time, I'd have her spread eagled on the edge of my pool before she could so much as dip a toe in the water. I wouldn't wait. I wouldn't falter. I would take what I wanted and ask her to leave again, just like with all the other girls. I would do it to prove to myself how I was incapable of being ruled by a woman. To show I wasn't growing soft.

I spent the entire afternoon watching the interview tapes of George Ward I still had from when I was first becoming the man himself. It didn't take me long to get back into character because I wasn't fully out of it yet, but I enjoyed transforming back into the notorious mob boss. I remembered how I'd spent months learning his mannerisms and the inflections of his accent. But first, I'd researched his history. Plotted the timeframe and read every single biography there was on the man. I'd immersed myself in the world of gang culture and had spent days as a personal guest in one of Los Angeles's top gangs. My co-star, Scarlet, had been my fixation for weeks in the run up to our filming. I'd sent her gifts and cryptic messages. I'd spent hours on the phone to her as George and she'd indulged me. I was positive she'd used my quirks to help get her better acquainted with the character, too, and I knew for sure that by the time we'd started rolling, she and I already had the perfect connection. The right chemistry to portray the mobster and the woman he fell for. The one George put on a pedestal above all others. Even his own child.

THREE

Piper

I arrived back on set a little earlier than necessary and reacquainted myself with Penny over coffee with Bradley. It was strange how quickly you could disassociate yourself with a role once you were done filming, and I always felt the same way when heading back for any extra shoots or retakes. I should've learned never to step away from the role until the director gave me the all clear, but something inside of me always seemed to switch off the moment we wrapped. Like I'd washed my hands with the person I'd been playing.

Usually, I hated having to go back in, but this time, I found I didn't mind so much.

"There's only a few scenes for us to go over, Brad," I said, browsing through the notes I'd been given when I'd arrived. "Looks like we're getting naked again," I then teased, earning myself a salacious smile from my on-screen husband.

"Is that an invitation?" he asked with a wink.

I shook my head.

"Not today, big boy." I couldn't bring myself to tell him why, but I wasn't interested in rekindling that flame, even if only for one last stoke. I still couldn't get Tommy off my mind and wanted to sort things out between us, but I knew there wouldn't be any of that yet. Tommy wouldn't be there with us, George would. He and I had to re-do our sex scene too, but I didn't doubt for a moment that our heat wouldn't end up becoming a factor in the remaking of the scene. I knew I had to dull that fire in my belly for Tommy, to reduce the heat so that I could remain professional with George and not make a fool out of myself.

Yeah, it was going to be an easy few days.

After finishing up with the makeup lady, I tracked down the director, Bud, and asked him for a moment of his time.

"What's up, Piper?" he asked with a soft smile. I was glad he'd remained friendly throughout the filming process and I felt I could approach him, but I decided against blurting it out in front of everyone and ushered him to one side.

"I was just wondering if there was a problem with my sex scenes? I'm retaking two of them over the next few days and wanted to find out why?"

"Don't worry," he quickly replied. "I'm sorry. I thought it'd been explained already, but we've decided to make them a little steamier. The playback was ace, but we want more heat. To turn things up a notch."

"That would've been nice to know before now," I replied, but didn't dwell on it. These things happened. Bradley and I could do that, no problem, and I guessed I'd just have to play it however Tommy wanted to with the George and Penny scene. It wasn't like I could ask him to run it through with me.

"You'll do great," Bud told me, before stepping away to set up for the first retake of the day.

I could see Tommy across from me, his eyes on the ground as he paced in wait for the cameras to roll. He and Bradley were about to punish a couple of George's dealers for losing some of his gear, and I watched for a while as they filmed the scene again and again, getting the perfect angles and shots before eventually finishing up.

Bradley stayed bloody while Tommy wandered away, and I was given the nod by the director to get in place.

"Baby, what the hell is going on?" I asked as I opened the door to our fake apartment and Bradley stumbled in, trying to wipe the blood from his face and hands rather than let me see.

"None of your business, Pen. Now, be a good little wifey and run me a bath, would you?" he replied, shooing me away.

Penny saw red. I loved putting on my Boston accent and went for him, screaming and shouting as the script dictated about how he was the worst husband and I was so hard done by. Poor Penny. I actually felt for her, especially when Bradley turned on me, playing out the scene exactly as had been described in her memoirs. We'd both read the books based on her life countless times and rehearsed where we'd be and how we'd do it, and even I could tell we had some movie gold right there.

He pinned me to the wall with his hand around my throat, his face just inches away from mine, and with a vicious scowl that had me quaking in my vintage boots. "Run me a bath and shut the hell up, or so help me God, I'll show you the back of my hand!"

"Sure thing, Ronnie," I replied in an icily calm tone I knew Penny had needed to perfect over the years or else take a beating off her darling husband.

Bradley cooled it with the threats and I sidled away when he finally let me go. "Take a load off and I'll go run you a bath, baby. Dinner's in the oven ready for 'ya when you've finished soaking." With tears in my eyes I then practically ran off set behind where our kitchenette would've been if it were a real apartment.

"Cut!" called the director, and I looked up at Bud with anticipation. "Nice one guys. That was perfect. Bradley, do not smudge or ruin your makeup. We'll go straight into the bath scene…"

We both did as we were told, waiting patiently while they set us up for our 'steamier' sex scene. Penny and Ronnie weren't the main couple of the story by a long shot, but they had their part to play in the mobster's story and I was ready to get down and dirty to make sure Bradley and I had our moment in the spotlight. I'd been working out like mad for months for this very eventuality. The first takes had only been timid portrayals of their lovemaking. My most nude scene had been with Tommy in the kitchen, but not after this, I was sure.

"You ready?" Brad asked with a wry smile.

"Always," I teased before following the makeup lady back to the chair so she could touch mine up just a little and make sure the tattoo on my shoulder was well hidden beneath the thick stage makeup.

When I returned, the set was ready, and the team had just finished pouring hot water into a tub for Bradley to lie in.

"Action!" cried Bud, and I watched from the sidelines as Bradley removed his bloody suit and climbed in the steaming hot bath. He showed plenty of ass as he lifted his leg over the side of the tub. But then everything was once again hidden thanks to the strategically positioned bubbles.

I watched, waiting for my cue, as Bradley washed some of the grime away. He too had been working out and was flexed to perfection, and I was reminded again of the times we'd been together like this for real. There wasn't a thing wrong with the man as far as I could tell, but he still wasn't boyfriend material for me. I wondered if perhaps anyone was. Nowadays monogamy was hard to come by simply because of a one worded question. Why? Why should we dedicate our lives to one person? Why should we struggle or settle? Why make do when you could have it all?

I was ushered on set and then sauntered over to where Bradley was laying still, half immersed in the tub. He had his head back and his eyes closed. And as the amended script had told me to, I kneeled beside him and grabbed the washcloth, getting to work on scrubbing away the fake blood from his neck and chest.

"The doctor said there's no reason I can't get pregnant, Ronnie," I whispered gently. "He said we're both young and healthy. All's we gotta do is keep fucking and it'll happen."

Quick as a flash, Bradley turned to me, and his hand shot down my back and then over my ass. He lifted my dress and grabbed a handful of the cheek I had been holding, tense at the ready.

"Hold it," the stage manager whispered, and I knew they were taking a wide shot of Bradley and I in the preamble to our big scene. I began to pant gently, watching my 'husband' with a look that meant I was ready for him. "Okay, go. Slowly," we were ordered.

Bradley didn't need to be told twice. He grabbed the hem of dress and began to lift, revealing my panties and then waist, before finally reaching my chest when I leaned toward him. He then yanked the thin fabric over my head and tossed it to the ground.

He didn't say a word, but the scene was no longer what it'd once been. It wasn't Penny and Ronnie having a quickie, but a steamy scene portraying their love for one another despite his dangerous job and her carefree attitude that was going to get her in trouble later in the movie.

Following the stage manager's instructions, I then climbed up and into the water with Bradley, where I pretended to mount him. Thankfully, he'd kept his junk covered, and I too had a flesh-colored piece of material covering my bits, so instead of riding him for real, I simulated the moves we'd done together time and again.

It took hours, but we finally got the right shots and eventually found ourselves standing in robes by the heaters for what we hoped was the final time of the day. The water had been topped up again and again with fresh, warm suds. But I had to admit I'd had enough. I was wrinkly from the wet and cold despite the heaters.

I'd also ditched the cover that'd come unglued countless times in the water so was fully naked beneath my robe and surrounded by fifty or so crew members but didn't care. They'd seen it all by now.

"We've got it," Bud informed the pair of us, and I sighed in relief.

I turned to head back to my trailer when Bradley stopped me with a gentle hand on my arm. He then leaned in close to whisper in my ear.

"Seeing as you've been writhing on top of me literally all day, how about we finish what we started…"

I fixed him with a scowl. There wasn't any part of me that wanted to jump back into bed with him, even if I'd enjoyed how many times I'd elicited a boner from him during our afternoon in the tub together.

"Nice try," I replied, and knew I was being a tease, but I genuinely wasn't interested in going back there with him. I had other things on my mind. Or should that have been other people?

FOUR

Tommy

I wasn't meant to stick around all afternoon, just do my few extra shots and then leave while the others did theirs, but I didn't. I stayed behind and watched them. Watched her. Piper. Penny... Whoever she was. I was drawn to her and had these intense urges. Like she belonged to me.

I stood in the shadows as Brad dared to ask her to fuck him, but was pleased when she said no. She was mine now. Or she soon would be. We were filming together again the following day, and I was more than ready to lay my claim on her as either George or Tommy, even if it was in front of an audience.

I followed her home that night. I couldn't help myself and stalked her as she walked inside her house and turned on the lights. Watched from the shadows as she made herself something to eat and poured a glass of wine. She seemed so relaxed and at ease with herself that I became even more enamored.

Did she know I was there? I didn't think so, but I couldn't be sure. Part of me thought she had to know and was toying with me on purpose. Either that or she wasn't very observant. How could she not have figured me out? How did she not know the extent of my need to own her? Could she really be that oblivious? No, she had to know. Had to be ignoring me on purpose because she was waiting, too. Waiting for us to be together behind Ronnie's back. *Soon*, I promised her wordlessly. *Tomorrow*.

After just a few hours' sleep, I woke early and went for a run. I just so happened to pass by Piper's house on my way and I accidentally-on-purpose came to a stop so I could stretch out my legs and have a chug of water. I couldn't resist another peek into her home and slunk around the back to where I could see a light on inside.

Dear God. Not only was she already awake, but also she was doing yoga. Yoga! Her body was twisting and stretching out right before my eyes, and she was absolutely flawless. Utterly perfect. And all mine. I got hard within seconds of watching her and couldn't resist jerking off into her bushes. I left a piece of myself behind and she would never know it. She would never discover the secret voyeurism I'd started undertaking, thanks to her.

Piper and her way with words that day in my tub had left me riled, and things had only gotten worse for me since.

She knows, a voice in my head chimed. *She saw you last night and has seen you now. She's ignoring you on purpose because she doesn't want you to know. You need to teach her a lesson. Show her you mean business. Force her…*

No, that couldn't be it. Piper had no idea of my presence, and even if she had caught me, I still believed she wouldn't tease me or ridicule me for it. No, not my Piper. She was perfect. Kind and sweet in ways I'd never known a woman could be. She was going to be mine. Whether that was George or Tommy talking, I wasn't all that sure, but I knew it was true from both angles. She had two sides to her, just like me, whether she realized or not. Her dark side had played with mine, and now they were firm friends. Lifelong partners.

I arrived on set early and took my time getting dressed. George was meticulous in his grooming, and so was I. He always wore a crisp, tailored suit and tie, and so did I. When the makeup lady was ready for me, I watched my reflection rather than her. I saw myself transforming, delving back into myself, and letting George take control once again.

Welcome back, George, I thought, smiling at my reflection.

"They're ready for you on set, Mr. Ward," the stage manager then told me, and I was pleased to see he remembered to address me properly. I didn't want to have to tell him off again, like I had the first day of shooting.

Without a word, I followed him down the corridor to where a fake door awaited me. This side of the set was plain wood, but on the other side stood my prize. Her…

Knock, knock. I tapped gently on the wood and when it opened; I was greeted with the face of an angel. Her long blonde hair was tied up away from her face in a delicate knot and her pale blue eyes were dazzlingly beautiful thanks to the lighting on set, but I couldn't smile and greet her like something deep within me wanted to. I had to keep my scowl in place and deliver my lines. I had to play the bad boy first.

"Mr. Ward, what a surprise. Please come in," she said in greeting, ushering me inside her fake apartment. I did, but then hovered in wait for her to say more. Penny then pointed an angry finger at where my minion lay on the sofa, pretending to be asleep. "Ronnie's passed out drunk. Nothing new there… You wanna leave a message I can give him in the mornin'?"

"No, let him rest. I came here for you," I answered, following her through the living room to the kitchen like before. "I wanted to apologize for being rude earlier. It wasn't fair on you, Penny," I said, having to remind myself that was her name. I then leaned against the counter, watching her tidy up the fake dishes left on the sink.

"No need," she told me with a warm smile, which I then mirrored. I was supposed to bend her over the counter and have her while she was stacking the dishes, but I decided to do things a little differently. I'd been given creative license with the script thanks to my fully immersive ways, so I used it to my advantage, adding a little improvisation to the scene.

"Something smells good," I replied, adding a sniff for good measure. Penny faltered for only a split second and then caught up quick. *Good girl*, I thought as she pointed to the refrigerator.

"Meatloaf and mashed potatoes. There's leftovers if you want some?"

"That'd be nice," I answered, and then watched as she plucked some fake food from the fridge and tossed it in the oven. Thank God for thorough assistants and set designers. They'd luckily had everything we needed already in place for continuity.

Penny then bent over, giving me the perfect view of her ass as she continued to put the dishes away in a suspiciously low drawer. It was my cue again, and I didn't need to be told twice.

I reached forward, grabbed the hem of her dress and lifted, exposing the perfect, peachy curve of her ass. Penny let out a surprised yelp and stood up, which was when I pressed myself against her from behind and pinned her to the counter in front. I then pulled her to me, my hands around the tops of her arms. "Ronnie doesn't deserve you," I whispered in her ear, relishing in her compliance as she relaxed against me and placed her hands down on the worktop.

I was supposed to unbutton my fly and simulate sex with her from behind. I knew this. We'd done it numerous times during our other takes, but this time it was more than just the director's order to make things steamier, spurring me to do things differently. It was that inner voice again. That desirous fiend who wanted more than he was meant to have. He wanted to rip off her clothes and force himself inside her sweet cunt. It didn't matter their audience, he would do it regardless, and I was already hard just thinking about it.

Penny cried out again when I turned her to face me, and she then peered up into my eyes like some sweet little doe. The lamb I was about to slaughter. The innocence I was about to defile.

"George?" she whimpered. I shushed her and then captured her mouth with mine. We'd kissed during our previous scenes, but never like this. I wanted it to be the kiss to end all kisses. The supreme and the sublime all wrapped into one. It wasn't because I loved her, but because I needed her. I had to make her feel for me the way I felt for her. To desire me the way I did her.

Penny gave herself to me entirely. I felt the switch happen in her as she succumbed to me not only for the sake of the movie, but in all things. And damn if that didn't make me harder.

After pushing her up onto the counter, I unbuckled my pants and lifted her dress up. There was no ignoring my boner, so I concealed it beneath the layers of her skirt, hiding it for the sake of the censors while we acted as though I'd just slid myself inside of her. I rocked back and forth, feeling her heat through the cotton underwear that was the only barrier between us. Without that, I would've been in her for real, and she knew it.

Focusing back on the task at hand, I simulated sex while our bodies mashed together for real. I wrapped her legs around me and kissed her hard, making Penny moan and pant like she was truly taking me deeper and deeper inside of her. God, I wanted to. When I pulled my lips away and watched her with a dark smile, I adored the flush of her cheeks and how her perfect makeup was now smudged. Her hands were on my chest, pushing me away while also holding me to her thanks to her fingers being curled around the lapels of my jacket. So wrong but so right.

I carried on, not knowing when, or if, I should stop, when she suddenly sucked in a breath and held it. Penny's eyes rolled back and she let out a sigh but was otherwise still. Well, except for the throbbing I could feel against the underside of my still thrusting cock.

She'd just come for me, I was sure of it. That was the hottest thing I'd ever experienced, and it was only a second before I did the same. I spurted my jizz all over her stomach, still ever thankful for the dress keeping us covered from view of the cameras and let out a groan for maximum effect. Whether the onlookers knew the truth or not, I didn't care. I played my part and acted like I was done. I didn't let her go, though. I couldn't. Not after I'd just come all over her in front of twenty other guys.

Ding! Went the buzzer on the oven, and I gazed down at Penny with a smile on my lips and a glint in my eye.

"Dinner's ready," I whispered, eliciting a genuine laugh from her.

"Cut!" called the director, breaking the silence from the crew all around us, and I was forced to release my grip on Penny's waist. Someone handed me a bunch of tissues and I wiped her clean, but didn't draw attention to any of it, and was glad when she didn't either. After tucking myself back in my pants, I then covered her up and helped her down off the counter.

She was mine now. I could see it in her eyes. She knew it too, and I was pleased to see she wasn't planning on fighting it.

FIVE

Piper

Christ, what the hell was that? I thought, taking a moment to reacquaint myself with my surroundings. My legs were like jelly as Tommy helped me down off the counter we'd pretty much just dry humped one another over, but he remained the perfect gentleman as he waited for me to find my strength again. Had I really just had an orgasm live on set? Had he just shot his load over me while the crew watched and the cameras still rolled? The answer to both those questions was an unquestionable yes.

I was mortified, but also walking on air. It'd felt amazing, and we both knew it. I just hoped it looked as good as it'd felt. No one said a word to us as they rearranged the set in readiness for one extra scene Bud decided was going to be shot off the back of mine and Tommy's far steamier sex scene. I was glad for the few minutes to compose myself again, but I couldn't take my eyes off Tommy. Mostly because he couldn't seem to take his eyes off me, either. He looked at me like he owned me. As if some deal had been made by our bodies in that moment and he expected me to follow through on it.

I realized it wasn't Tommy who had claimed me, though, but George. He was still in character and had been the entire time. And that realization brought me back down from cloud nine in a heartbeat.

"I'm okay now, thanks," I said, side-stepping out of his hold. I then took a deep breath and walked away, and while Tommy looked disappointed, he let me. I could still feel him watching me as I headed to the refreshment table and downed a glass of water but didn't mind. I guessed in his mind, he and I were lovers now. He'd soon snap out of it once the re-shoots were over again and we could go back to our normal lives. When we could forget all about our intense attraction as Penny and George.

"Stay exactly the way you are now," the stage manager called to me. "Bud wants you both back on set in the kitchen but sat at opposite ends of the dinner table. George will be finishing up with the meal and he's gonna say something like 'we should do this again sometime,' to which you'll agree. Got it?" he asked, and I nodded.

We then acted out the scene as directed but kept it more improvised like we had the other scene. It worked somehow, and like I had before, I followed Tommy's lead.

Afterwards, we were sent off while they checked out the footage and were promised an answer within the hour whether they needed anything else. Rather than stay with the others, I spent the time on the phone with Janie to distract myself from the matter at hand. And the man ever present in my mind.

After lunch, Bud informed us he didn't need to do any more to the scene, and I was glad. It wasn't that I hadn't enjoyed turning things up a notch. I just felt like we couldn't necessarily recreate it the same way, so was glad we didn't have to start all over again. My body couldn't take it for a start! My clit was still a little raw from Tommy's rubbing while simultaneously also being swollen with the need to satisfy it with something more than a mere strum. Part of me wondered if Bradley was still around so I could take him up on his offer from the day before, but I knew that wasn't what I wanted. Not really.

I wanted Tommy. I'd tried to deny my feelings for him all week, but our session on set had cemented that desire for him inside of me. I'd seen him naked and in all his buff glory by his pool, but when I'd felt him push that thing against me, all my resolve had disappeared. If he asked me over again, I knew I would say yes. I also knew I'd probably jump his bones the minute we got behind closed doors.

All I had to do was wait for him to come back out of character, however long that might take.

***

I spent the next few days in turmoil. I woke up in the night fretting over the sex scene with Tommy. Had it ended up too erotic? Would it make me look bad? I began the age-old routine of becoming riddled with self-doubt and fear, and with an intensity to both I hadn't experienced for a long time. Not since my first few roles when I convinced myself I was a hack who didn't know what she was doing every damn time. I tried to tell myself it wasn't true. That the movie was going to be awesome, and I had nothing to worry about, but I couldn't get away from that sinking feeling in my gut.

I knew what had me all over the place. Tommy Darke. I soon came to realize that it might be because he was one of the most amazing actors I've ever met, and I felt like my acting didn't stand up next to his. He didn't just put on a costume and recite lines. He becomes the character, inside and out. I'd heard of method actors before but had no idea the depth of their role-playing until I'd worked with one for myself. Until he'd dragged me into the darkness with him...

Another week passed, and I still hadn't heard from Tommy. I tried everything to distract myself, but none of it was working. And to top it all off, I still couldn't sleep.

With a huff, I climbed out of bed and walked over to the window, peering down into my small yard below. I wasn't one for anything fancy, nor had I put much thought into renting my first home. All I'd needed was somewhere comfortable and safe. Home was where I kicked off my shoes, or so we'd always said. Deep down, I guessed I was still the army brat I'd been as a kid who could lay down roots wherever she went. I'd travelled the world with my parents and had recreated myself every time. Playing one role after another for as long as I could remember. I had been an actress my entire life, and it was no wonder I found it so natural now.

Something moved in the bush to the side of my house as I stared down while lost in thought. I was sure of it. I watched longer but saw nothing, so pulled my nightshirt around myself. Maybe I was imagining things. It wasn't like I was completely with it the past few days or had slept well at all. No wonder my mind was starting to play tricks on me.

SIX

Tommy

That was close. What was she even doing awake at this hour? It's the middle of the night and she ought to be fast asleep. I knew I should be too, but that was beside the point. I was a delusional deviant with a serious case of obsessive-compulsive-attachment with a woman I hadn't even slept with. I was allowed to be skulking around her house in the dead of night. It's what crazy people did, and I was pretty sure I was certifiable about now.

I was on the other side of the characterization and George was slowly slipping away, but this time he was clinging on for dear life. He didn't want to be locked back in his box, and it was driving me insane.

Forcing myself to go home, I took a shower and shaved for the first time in days. I then popped a sedative and flung myself into bed. Sleep came, thank God, but it was filled with images of her. Of me taking her properly over that counter while everyone watched. She was telling me no while guiding me inside of her, playing coy when we all knew she wasn't.

I woke up with jizz all over my stomach and groaned. How many times had that woman made me come? Far too many to count, that was for sure, and still not once had that load been shot where it was supposed to. Her cunt was still a mystery to me, and I was determined that wouldn't be the case for much longer.

When she left her house for the first time in days for a photo-shoot, I knew the studio had lined up; I went back to my spot at the back of her house. There, I watched the house, lying in wait, and eventually it paid off. Her gardener came around the other side and opened the back door while he replenished the vases with flowers for her and then headed around to the front, leaving it wide open.

I took my moment of what I considered to be divine intervention and slipped inside without a sound.

I stayed hidden until the gardener had tidied the backyard and then locked up again. Once the coast was clear and the house was silent, I then wandered around, looking at all of Piper's things. Her bookshelf was bigger than her movie cabinet, which surprised me, and I plucked a few of the most tattered titles from the shelves. They weren't the classics I might've expected someone who was trying to show off to have on display. But contemporary romances and even some science fiction. I approved of her choices and took a huge hint from her pick of romantic novels. Alpha males and billionaire bad boys galore. Each domineering and determined to take the leading lady as theirs, no matter the cost. That had to be what she liked about them. Each book was like the last in that same way, and I knew how it wasn't going to be a case of waiting to get her out of my system. It was quite the opposite. I had to have her so much I would get bored. We all got bored in the end, there was truth to the saying 'too much of a good thing.' I would take and take and take until I no longer wanted what she had to give me, and then I would walk away. Like the powerful men she fantasized about in her nightly reads, I would be forceful and courageous, while also showing her just enough of my softer side to let her believe I was still the good guy.

Was I the good guy? Really? I'd broken into Piper's home and was planning to have my way with her, use her up, and spit her back out again. That wasn't what good guys did.

George. I blamed George. Before him, I was a happy-go-lucky type of guy. Our banter and fun in my pool and hot tub were testament to that. She was also partly to blame, given how she'd stirred my inner darkness and lured it out. Piper wanted it this way. That was why she'd seen right through my façade and how she could possibly know what was lurking beneath the surface.

After a good look around, I decided to hide out in her guest room until she came home and then I'd surprise her. Probably scare the hell out of her too, but I hoped she was game. I needed her to be. Otherwise, things were going to get weird pretty quickly.

I laid down on the bed and closed my eyes, thinking about all the things Piper and I were going to do to each other. That was all well and good, but then whaddya know, the lack of sleep caught up with me and the next thing I knew, it was nighttime. Thankfully, with me having been hiding in her guest room, I hadn't been spotted, but I could hear her a few doors away. She was humming to herself as she climbed into bed and I cracked open the door, watching her from across the dark hall.

Piper was wearing just shorts and a cami. Her tits were on full display, nipples tight like rocks she was smuggling under her skimpy top. I longed to caress them but froze rather than step out of my hiding spot to go to her. She wasn't going to be flattered by my presence. She was going to be furious. I'd made a huge mistake in staying and regret washed over me. I could go to jail for what I'd done. She could ruin not only my life but also my career if she called the police.

When Piper then went into her en-suite, I took my chance to leave and scurried towards the stairwell.

I was halfway down them when I heard it. A sound that immediately stopped me in my tracks and had me turning back around. Before I could second-guess myself, I was climbing the stairs and walking into her bedroom. I approached the bathroom door and pressed my ear to it, my eyes closing as the sound washed over me. She was crying. Soft sobs permeated the wooden door and invaded me. One hitched breath at a time. I loathed that sound and suddenly wanted to make it stop by any means necessary.

I didn't know what to do. Should I run from her tears like I had with everyone before? No, I wanted to hurt whoever was responsible for them. To punch their face into mush. But what if the culprit was me? Hadn't I already suffered enough because of her?

I was so lost in the sound that when it suddenly stopped and the door was wrenched open, I forgot I was an intruder. I opened my eyes and watched as Piper jumped out of her skin and then began screaming, and all the while I was just stood there wondering what on earth could have her so afraid. That was when realization struck. I was the reason.

"Shit!" I cried, lifting my hands to tell her I meant no harm. "Please don't call the cops."

Piper suddenly stopped screaming and scowled at me like I'd shocked her more by my response than my presence in her room in the dead of night.

This was good. Better she be angry than afraid. Now, I just had to win her over and then we could get back to the real matter at hand. Me getting what I came for.

SEVEN

Piper

I opened and closed my mouth, undecided how to respond. I knew I should kick him out. That I ought to call the cops and the press, in fact call everybody and out him as the twisted pervert he clearly was if he was skulking around my house uninvited in the middle of the night. I wanted to be furious with him for invading my privacy, but I wasn't. I was oddly flattered.

Just moments before I'd been feeling so sorry for myself, I'd actually had a good cry. I'd convinced myself I was unloved, uncared for, and unwanted. I'd felt lonely beyond anything I'd experienced in a long time, and while the rational part of my brain knew it was just my insecurities still flaring up, I couldn't seem to convince myself those vile thoughts weren't true.

But then I'd opened the door and found Tommy standing on the other side. I think I'd shocked him as much as he had done with me, but I couldn't laugh about it. In fact, I still hadn't reacted at all, other than my initial screams in surprise.

Rather than tell him to leave or threaten him with prosecution like my brain was telling me I ought to, I decided to follow the urge in my belly instead. The need that'd been growing and growing despite my regular use of my battery-operated boyfriend. The desire to have him, once and for all. To have a night of passion like I'd been dreaming non-stop about.

I stepped forward, tentatively at first, but then I flung myself at him. Tommy was more than ready for me, and I was glad. He'd come into my home uninvited and we both knew why. I knew what he wanted and was more than ready to give him it.

He tore away my clothes and threw me on the bed, where I watched as he too tossed off every inch of clothing he had on and then lunged for me. He was rough and aggressive with me, and I loved every second of it. His kisses weren't delicate or full of gentle care. They were hard and consuming, as if he didn't want me to breathe. Or at least, he wanted to take charge of every inch of my body, including my basic functions and needs, so let me take breaths as and when he allowed it. I gasped and found myself lifting up on the bed, unable to take it any longer for fear of passing out, which was when he grabbed my hips to stop my escape and plunged inside of me with that rock hard rod between his muscular thighs.

I arched my back and caught my breath at last, and then could do nothing but lie back in euphoric ecstasy as he pounded into me over and over. He didn't seem to care for anything other than claiming me, but damn, I wanted him to. I never wanted it to end, even when I came for him, and thankfully he didn't.

Tommy knew I was coming, but he didn't so much as slow for me to recover and carry on. He continued to slam into me over and over again, and it never even occurred to me to tell him to stop.

We carried on that way for hours. Tommy was a relentless lover, and I had a feeling he too had a lot of pent-up attraction for me he'd been trying to fight. Something that'd come to overwhelm us both, but thankfully we'd been able to finally exorcise some of those demons via a night of passion, albeit thanks only to him for violating my privacy.

When we were both finally spent and my body was screaming at me to let it rest, I looked over at Tommy and took him in. He was beautiful, even with his obscure urges still swirling within him. I could see it behind his eyes, but foolishly wasn't scared. In fact, I think that was what I liked about him. He had a dark side. A dangerous edge that had me both terrified and tantalized all at once.

I checked the clock, and it was almost dawn. Shit. I figured this could go one of two ways now. We could snuggle and fall asleep in one another's arms and then wake up a few hours later to talk things through and figure out where our night of passion was going to take us. Or we could go the other way. We could continue our 'no strings' affair and otherwise not draw attention to the wild nights of passion we'd hopefully enjoy together time and again in the days to come. I opted for the latter, not being the sort to want a relationship of all the gooey lovey stuff, so rather than nestle myself in Tommy's arms, I climbed out of bed and plucked his clothes up off the bedroom floor.

"Here," I handed them to him, and found myself relishing in his surprise. "Time for you to go home, Tommy. Be sure and lock up on your way out," I told him, before disappearing into my en-suite for a hot shower. By the time I emerged, he had indeed gone, and a wide smile spread across my face as I climbed back into bed and nestled into the sheets that still smelled of him. Of us. I was asleep in an instant and had the best few hours' rest I'd had in weeks.

I was up and doing my late-morning workout when my cell went off. I'd just finished a wobbly tree pose, given my overall tiredness and the tenderness of my core, and so welcomed the chance to take a break.

Hitting speaker, I grabbed my water bottle and took a swig while Janie's assistant connected our call.

"I hope you're ready, Piper?" she chimed through the loudspeaker on my handset.

"For what?" I asked with a frown.

"To conquer the world, of course!" she squealed, making me laugh. I was glad to hear she hadn't meant anything else and forced my anxiety away. For a moment there all sorts of things had whizzed through my head. Had Tommy been spotted leaving my house? Had someone found out about us and blabbed to the press? I liked our liaison being a secret and wanted it to stay that way.

"What are you talking about?" I groaned as I wandered over to my living room window and peered down into the garden below. I had to stifle a gasp when I saw who was waiting for me down below, spying on me from the bushes. So, I had been right the other night. Someone had been there. He wasn't even trying to hide this time. He'd been watching me again and wanted me to know. To catch him in the act like I had the night before. My heart beat wildly in my chest, but I refused to so much as grin at him or register his presence in any way.

"The director loves the new scenes, babe. He rang this morning and said the first round of edits are amazing. Your chemistry with Tommy is apparently off the charts!"

I hummed in answer, thinking how if only she knew the half of it she might be speechless for once.

"That's great. However, I'll believe it when I see it," I told her, but couldn't fight my smile. I was shifting. Growing. And it was all thanks to Tommy. Whether this thing between us went anywhere or not, I didn't care, because I somehow knew that my life was about to change. "Did he say when we could watch a copy?"

"Not for a while yet, but he does need you in today for more photos. They've decided to do some extra promos with you as a featured character. Not only Scarlet," Janie replied, and I could hear the smile in her voice. This was good. Great, in fact. I wasn't the leading lady and yet I was being given extra limelight thanks to my on-screen performance. This could be the opportunity I'd been waiting my whole career for. The chance to get noticed by more of the right kinds of people. Those who could make my dreams come true by offering me a follow-up role as the star, or at least the co-star of my next movie.

Yes, I was getting ahead of myself, but it wasn't impossible to believe in it happening. All I had to do now was keep my reputation as a professional and trustworthy actress intact. I would be on time for every meeting I was asked to attend. I would work hard and do everything I could to make *Wayward* a success. And when it was, I would bask in my limelight, knowing I'd earned it. That I deserved the recognition afforded to me and then humbly accept an upcoming role as leading lady by those who had only considered me a supporting actress in the past.

"We need to make sure this works," I replied, knowing how Janie would understand exactly where I was coming from. What elevated me also benefited her in the long run too and I knew she was as big of a shark as any other agent in Los Angeles. She would fight tooth and nail for me if I asked her to.

"Oh, don't worry, sweetie. I'm gonna make it my mission to have your name everywhere people look. Your face on every poster. Just watch me…"

"Looking forward to it," I told her, and then changed the subject. I was eager to get off the call and back to my workout, only of a different kind. "When do they want me?"

I put my cell on the table and stared down into Tommy's eyes. We really were heading into dangerous territory, but I couldn't stop myself. I wanted to celebrate in the only way my body was craving. I pulled off my tight yoga top to give him a full view of my then naked breasts.

"I spoke with Sarah, who's the photographer's assistant, and she said sometime this afternoon. They haven't been able to get hold of Tommy yet as he needs to be there too." I smiled again, thinking if only she knew he was standing just a few yards away from me. But I wasn't going to reveal all. In fact, the longer he remained unreachable, the better, because that meant I got to have him all to myself.

"Okay, just send me a text with the time and place and I'll be there," I said as I removed my pants and underwear, standing fully naked just inches away from my window so I was on full show to my voyeur.

"Sure, I'll let you know," Janie answered, and then she ended the call. I continued to stand there for a few seconds and then I went straight to the back door, which I opened a crack and stalked away again.

I then bounded up the stairs and jumped straight in yet another shower, needing to be clean rather than sweaty from my workout before Janie's call.

When the cubicle was suddenly full, the body of my tall and broad lover blocking out the light from overhead, I began to tremble. He was silent but gave off a vibe so dangerous I had to consider whether what I was doing was even safe, let alone a good idea or not.

Tommy was coming out of a deep characterization that made him unstable and unpredictable, and I was egging him on. I was nurturing those dark edges of his personality rather than helping him extinguish them. He was meant to be detoxing, but instead he was stalking me. Lurking in the bushes. Breaking into my home. Fucking me like he wanted to both hurt and pleasure me, but as if he didn't know which one was the stronger of the two urges. And what was worse is that I was letting him do it rather than get Tommy the help he might actually need.

He took me from behind this time, parting my thighs and lifting me onto him while pressing me into the cold tile wall. My pussy screamed at first, stinging a little from our escapades the night before, but once he started to move, I was putty in his hands. Tommy kissed my neck and then licked his way down over my shoulder before nipping me with his teeth. I felt my body clench around him with the shock of his bite. It wasn't hard enough to leave a mark, but it was enough to make me squirm in surprise.

Tommy cursed, and I wasn't sure why, but then I felt him pulsating inside of me and knew. I'd elicited an orgasm from him with my movement, and I don't think he liked it. I think he wanted to control when and how he came undone thanks to me because it gave him the power. But not this time.

He withdrew and let his release wash away down the drain. I thought he was gonna put me down so we could dry off and head to the bedroom to start all over again, but instead he spun me around to face him and then dived back in.

His kisses on my lips were as forceful as they had been the night before. But this time, I was clever. Despite the water rushing down over us from above, I moved against him and took my breaths when I needed them, rather than when Tommy allowed it, and I knew he didn't like it. He liked holding my life in his hands.

When I was ready to come, he reached up and took my chin in his huge hand, forcing me to keep my mouth on his. He wasn't going to let me go, not even when I was crying out with my explosive climax, and I knew it was his way of regaining his control. Taking the power back.

When we were done, Tommy put me down, tilted his head up, and let the water cascade over his glorious body. He let me watch for just a moment. To take a mental picture. And then—just like that—he was gone.

A quick dry off and he was out the door, not needing to be told to leave this time. He went of his own accord, and by God did I enjoy watching him walk away, because we both knew this was far from over.

He'd be back again and our power play would continue, whether either of us liked it or not.

EIGHT

Tommy

My thoughts were running wild as I slunk out the back door and around the back of her house in my usual way. I was becoming far too comfortable with sneaking around Piper's property, and it scared me. But what terrified me the most was how far I was willing to take all of this. At first, I'd tried the 'normal' way of getting her attention, but I knew how things with her would never be normal. I couldn't stand it. Not after everything we'd shared these past few days.

I'd tried to walk away, but then my affection had come bounding back during our on-screen exploits. I'd somehow managed to convince myself it'd been an obsession borne out of our character's liaison, and I'd been so wrong I almost had to laugh. It wasn't George who was obsessed with Penny. It was Tommy, and he had an ever-ready hard-on for all things Piper. There was nothing I could do and, so far at least, no amount of times I could fuck that obsession with her away.

She pushed my buttons. Poked the hornet's nest deep in my soul. Piper had welcomed me into her bed, but she hadn't submitted to me for even a moment. No matter how hard I'd been, she'd wanted it harder. It didn't matter that I'd left her close to asphyxiation, she'd taken it without so much as a fight.

She was challenging me, and I'd be damned if I didn't rise to her enticement. But I was going to win. I always did. Piper had no idea how far I was willing to go with this. How deep my need for her was becoming. I could feel it scratching at my soul, making holes in the shape of claw marks in the walls I'd built around my heart and the darkness I knew was also in there. It was seeping out, slithering to the surface.

I was going back to her house that night. I'd already decided on it before she gave me a strip show and literally opened the door and let me in. To be honest, it didn't matter whether she let me in or not. I was going back there whenever I damn well pleased. And I didn't need for her to open the door as I could do so myself thanks to the extra key now hanging on the chain in my pocket. I'd stolen her door key on my way out in the early hours when she'd dismissed me rather than let me share her bed any longer. That'd been as sexy as hell, I had to admit, but she'd issued me with yet another challenge, and one I'd readily accepted. Getting the key cut was a doddle. Then it was back to her place to lie in wait for her to take a shower so I could put it back again. And the rest, as they say, is history. I'd put the key back on my way up to her room, still grinning at how she'd left the door open for me in invitation, anyway.

Was I under her skin as much as she was under mine? Yes. I had to be. Otherwise, there was no way she would continue with such a strange charade.

There was a buzzing sound that grew louder as I approached my car, which reminded how I'd thrown my cell in the glove box before heading to the house a couple hours earlier. I had a ton of missed calls and messages but deleted them all and sped away. An over exaggeration, maybe, but I wasn't interested in what anyone had to say. There was one thing I had to do before I could head back to reality. One stop I had to make so I could stock up on some essentials for when I went back to her. For when I made sure she knew who was boss in this little tryst of ours.

My cell rang again, being sent to my car stereo via Bluetooth, and I answered with a bark.

"Finally! Where have you been, man?" my assistant, Miles, asked.

"Fuck you, Miles. Just tell me what's going on," I replied. I wasn't going to tell him shit, and we both knew it. He'd been my assistant for years and had suffered through every one of my intense ups and downs. Like the time when I disappeared for two weeks and turned up at his apartment, looking and smelling like a junkie. I'd been living in a crack den the entire time and while I'd chosen not to get high myself, I'd watched the others and documented the stages of both their highs and lows. I'd watched people hire out their ass for crack, or worse, their disease-ridden cunts. There was no way I wanted any part of that, but when the time came to shoot the movie I'd been prepping for, I was more than ready to portray a man living from one hit to the next.

"They need you down the set this afternoon. They're shooting some pictures for promos and first up it's you and Scarlet, followed by you and Piper." Just hearing him say her name made me want to curse at him. He wasn't worthy enough to say it.

What the actual fuck was the matter with me? I shook it off and focused back on the matter at hand.

"Tell them I'll be there in an hour," I ordered him and then ended the call. There was plenty of time for me to get to the store and back before heading to the set. Even so, I pressed harder on the gas and saw my knuckles turn white against the black leather wheel as I tore off towards my destination.

NINE

Piper

After a midday nap, I awoke to my cell chiming on my bedside cabinet and found the timings for my afternoon on set. Janie was going to send a car for me in an hour, which was great. It gave me time to straighten my unruly hair that was now fuzzy from being washed and left to air dry twice in just a few hours.

I also applied some light makeup and pulled on a figure-hugging dress I knew any paparazzi at the studio would be pleased to get some nice shots of, but that would provide nothing revealing or embarrassing to the image I was still so determined to keep wholesome. My tan was perfect, as was my waxing, thanks to my regular visits to the beauty salon, so I made myself a coffee and relaxed while I waited for the doorbell to chime.

I smiled to myself as I sipped on my hot drink and wondered what Tommy was doing. Was he turning on the charm with Scarlet, or was he struggling, having to imagine me in her place so he could portray the devotion to her he was meant to? I hoped it was the latter, and when the driver knocked on my door, I greeted him with a wide smile and left the house with a spring in my step.

I arrived on set within a half hour and headed right on in, not needing or wanting any chaperones or direction. All I wanted was my chance to take the perfect photo with Tommy. My chance to shine and bask in some of his limelight while establishing my own.

While our fantastic artist Deana was still making me up, Scarlet came in and began changing into her own clothes, a sign they were finished with their photo-shoot. I almost asked her how it went, but didn't want to seem too eager, so simply offered her a smile when I caught her eye in the mirror.

"He's not as weird as he was while we were filming, but there's definitely something strange about that guy," Scarlet told me as she tied her sandals and then stood, smoothing her skirt and checking in the mirror that she looked presentable.

"Thanks, I'll be sure and handle him as best I can," I replied in a way that I hoped was non-committal and that also didn't show just how ready I was to be under Tommy's hard stare again. "Are they going with the dark and brooding shots?" I had to ask, and Scarlet nodded.

"Yeah. Don't think I saw him smile once," she said with a giggle, before giving me a wave and strutting off without another word.

I began to feel nervous. What was he going to be like? Would he be the man I'd let into my home for a stalkerish booty call not once, but twice now? Or would he back in character? Did George await me in the studio, and if so, what on earth would he think of me?

There I went again, acting like George was a real person, or at least as if he was someone other than Tommy. The same Tommy I had been fantasizing about day and night. That had to mean I fancied George too?

I was damned if I could figure it out.

Instead, once Deana had worked her magic, and I was wearing my finest vintage style dress, I pulled up my proverbial big girl panties and took a deep breath before pushing through the door that led to the studio where the camera had been set up.

I veered straight for the group of assistants and nodded to one of the runners I'd met the day before while shooting with Bradley.

"What's the plan?" I asked, feeling awkward suddenly.

"Tommy's just having his makeup touched up and then we're good to go. The photographer will direct you where and how to stand," she replied, which I could've already guessed, but at least she gave me something to do for thirty seconds. I was on edge and liable to start a random conversation with any passer by just to fill the time if I wasn't careful, so instead I walked over to where a plain black background covered the floor and wall. There, I waited patiently to get started and tried not to look too uncomfortable in the process.

I sensed him before I saw him. That sounds so cheesy, but it's true. I honestly felt the air shift, and the room suddenly fell silent. I remained rooted to the spot, staring at nothing, yet I couldn't tear my eyes away. I just knew he was going to have me in the palm of his hand the moment I peered into his eyes and wanted to fight it a moment longer.

Shit. I was falling. Not in love, but in lust. I was caving to every desirous thought running through my usually so sensible mind, but I couldn't stop myself from carrying on. I didn't want to.

"You're going to do everything I say, Piper. Is that understood?" his deep, husky voice penetrated me from just inches away from my left ear. I didn't know how he hoped to achieve such dominance given the way these photo-shoots usually went, but I was willing to give it a try. I'd never been the submissive type. However, there was something about Tommy's intense, sensual side that made me want to do as he commanded. To follow his orders and be his willing slave.

"Yes," I replied, almost silently.

"Good, now turn to the camera and show them what they want to see so we can get out of here." I did as he asked and found the team all silently watching us from behind the photographer and the numerous lighting umbrellas that'd been set up around the small space Tommy and I were stood in.

I was surprised to find the man behind the camera standing in relative quiet. Instead of telling us what to do and where to position ourselves, he instead gave Tommy a nod and then began snapping away. "Straight face. Stare down the lens. Pretend it's the day when I shouted at you. Remember how horrible I was…" it was Tommy giving the orders and ultimately, I wasn't surprised. He had an affinity for this stuff. Knowledge not learned or passed on by some wise mage but instilled in him through experience and a natural connection with the camera.

I followed his lead and did exactly as he'd said, straightening my face so that I could widen my eyes in fear. The snap, snap of the camera didn't distract me, but Tommy's closeness did. He was pressed against my back, his lips at my ear, and my breath hitched when his arms reached around and grabbed me around the waist. His hand rested over my stomach and I knew exactly where he was heading with his direction.

I placed my hand over his instinctively and closed my eyes, smiling ever so slightly. I imagined I was really Penny. How I was pregnant with a child that wasn't my husband's and yet still had to hope that things could work out all right for us.

Before I could think about our next move, Tommy had my hair in his fist, and he'd used his hold to turn my face up to his. I opened my eyes and finally caught a glimpse of him. Not George, but Tommy. He was there this time, and he was peering down into my eyes like a man possessed. On a mission to rule all or else lay waste to it rather than let someone else win.

"Excellent," said the photographer, still snapping away. "Hold it there and if you can give us a tear, Piper, that'd be great." He shifted position and began capturing our moment again. Tommy nodded in agreement with the order, and I summoned my tears on command, like all good actors could do. I let my eyes well and then blinked, releasing the perfect droplet down onto my cheek, where it rested for a moment before sliding down to my chin and then fell.

"I don't like watching you cry, Piper," Tommy then told me, and it came as a shock. Part of me had taken him for a probable sadist. One who wanted to dominate me violently using pain as well as pleasure. But then I thought about it properly. He hadn't hurt me, even while being a forceful lover. He hadn't spanked my backside like men had in the past or so much as pinched my nipples during our frolicking in the bedroom and then in the shower. His bite had been like it was more about shocking me rather than delivering me pain, and it was a realization I welcomed.

I felt myself curl into Tommy's hold. Wanting him to squeeze me tighter because I trusted he wouldn't hurt me. At least not physically. I had no idea how or why, but I had the distinct feeling he was about to mess me up in ways I would never see coming. Some of those forbidden urges of his he'd shown me were all about power play and control. He had to control me, or at least it seemed that way, and against all my better instincts, I wanted to let him.

We continued for a short while, but it felt like formality more than anything else. Covering all the bases set by Bud. But we both knew they'd got the perfect shots already. And what they didn't have, the team of graphic designers could easily merge together from a shot that was right. Even I knew I didn't naturally look as good as I did in the photographs created for movie promos and such. It was a given in this industry that the airbrush option was everyone's best friend.

When we were done, I stepped out of Tommy's grasp, but he pulled me back to him, pressing my back against his torso. My gaze shot around the room, checking who might be watching, but everyone was going about their business and paying us no mind. They each wanted to get home as well, no doubt so they weren't watching what we were doing, and I figured Tommy had known that when he'd yanked me back into his hold. "This is how this is going to work, Piper. When I speak, you listen. When I call, you come to me. Do I make myself clear?"

I wanted to tell him no. To go to hell and to shove his demands up his ass. But I didn't. Instead, I peered back over my shoulder at him and grinned. He wasn't going to get it that easily.

"Are you forgetting who it is you're talking to? I'm the woman who kicked you out this morning because I don't need hugs or kisses, or to fall at a man's feet to feel worthy. I don't need you to love me. All I need is for you to give me what I want," I told him, stepping away. "I'll listen. I might even come to you, but I'll do it on my terms, Tommy. Are we clear?"

He didn't say a word or move a muscle. No nod of approval or laugh of dismay at my apparent gall. No reaction at all. I wasn't going to beg or plead with him for one either, so I carried on walking away. I didn't need him playing games or calling the shots. I was stronger than that, and so I didn't so much as look back as I stalked off set.

I hit the dressing room and ditched my clothes, threw on my dress and sunglasses, grabbed my purse, and left the studio like nothing had even happened.

TEN

Tommy

I spent the drive up to the cabin in fits of both rage and laughter. The old me, or I guess the 'normal' me, found it funny that Piper and I could have such a strange and fascinating way about us. I loved the back and forth. The hunger we each had for the other, and yet the reluctance both of us had when it came to backing down. I found her entertaining in both a sexually gratifying way and because she amused me in general. I enjoyed her laugh and her smile. I wanted to make love to her all night long and make her scream in ecstasy.

I also liked watching her, even as she'd gone about her normal business, just... well, because.

And then there was the other part of me. A side of myself I was slowly beginning to get to know. One I had kept locked away for so long I'd forgotten how it felt to let him out. To let him be free.

Becoming George had been the key to opening the door, and yet it was Piper who had taken his hand and yanked him back into existence. That both scary and exciting part of me found her an amusing plaything. It wanted to have all of her until she had nothing left, and all the while craving nothing but her complete submission.

I had begun to obsess over her. To need her to want to give me everything and for her to give it willingly. To downright insist upon it. I knew there was also an undeniable urge in me to fuck her raw and watch her scream in anguish and beg for me to stop.

But not cry. Never cry.

Tears made me remember the reason I had locked that part of myself away for so long. Made me remember the tears that had broken me so long before. Seeing her cry would mean I'd done a bad thing again and I couldn't have that. I'd only barely come away unscathed the last time, and I couldn't allow history to repeat itself. Not after I'd been so careful to turn my life around and bury that particular past. I knew I had to tell her, but not the full story.

Only how it was my one rule. My one necessity.

I arrived at my destination and charged inside, where I took my purchases from a couple hours earlier and arranged them on the kitchen counter. I'd fantasized about this for so long, but never with someone specific in the role of the female. Not until Piper had come charging into my world and encouraged me to indulge in those fantasies. The unusual and, I guess, slightly depraved urges of mine. And now she was going to pay for it.

After everything was ready, I opened the curtains over the large bay window to reveal the glorious sunset, and the reason I'd bought the cabin in the first place. The San Gabriel Mountains had been the perfect choice of venue for my escapes to the woods. I could hunt and hike to my heart's content, or use it as a sanctuary where I could come to drink myself numb and play computer games or loud music all night and no one could hear me. No one even knew I was out there half the time, and the same would be for Piper once I let her into my secluded secret. The only difference was that for her visit, we wouldn't be playing games or listening to music.

Plus, there was only one thing I wanted to hunt.

Her.

And I was ready to receive her.

I took a photograph of my sunlit balcony and attached it to a text message on my cell.

Tommy:

I want you here with me, Piper. I don't care what plans you might have made or what bed you thought you'd be in tonight. Come to me. And clear your schedule. What I have in store for you will take more than just one night...

I added the address and hit send. And then the nerves set in. Would she come? Did she want to spend time with me the way I anticipated she would? I damn well hoped so, otherwise I knew she'd see my bad side in one way or another whether she wanted to anymore or not. The connection we'd shared so far had been intense, and she'd peered right into my soul. She had seen the real me and hadn't run from him. In fact, she'd invited him in over and over again.

She'd let me watch her. Let me fuck her. Not forced me away when I'd snuck into her home and violated her personal space. Those moments simply couldn't be undone.

The sound of my cell vibrating on the counter startled me, and I lunged for it. She was calling. Not texting back, but calling me, and I had to take a breath before answering.

"I'll be there by ten," she said, before I then heard a beep that signaled the end of the call. Yes. She'd chosen to be a good girl, after all.

Everything was falling into place perfectly, so now all I had to do was wait.

ELEVEN

Piper

I arrived at the address Tommy had given me, thanks only to my trusty navigation system. I'd never been up into the San Gabriel Mountains before but couldn't deny they were certainly beautiful. After parking beside his truck and cutting the engine, I took a moment to gather myself and have a look around.

The cabin seemed quaint but well kept, as though Tommy had someone who looked after it for him while he was home in Los Angeles, and I could see the balcony where he had to have taken the photo of the sunset.

The house was built on the mountainside itself and from this angle I could see that beneath the viewing area were great huge stilts holding it up amidst the trees. They looked sturdy enough, but I still cringed at the idea of stepping out onto it. I hoped I wouldn't feel too scared to walk out onto the wooden platform if asked to. I wasn't all that great with heights but thought how nice it'd be if I managed to watch the sunset the following day there. Preferably with a glass of wine in one hand and Tommy sat beside me.

I flushed hot in anticipation and wondered what awaited me inside. Was he going to try and dominate me? If so, would I let him? I didn't think I could and had failed in my attempts at being a submissive lover in the past. But he hadn't seemed that way. Tommy was downright paradoxical really, and I struggled to get to the bottom of his likes and dislikes when it came to the real him in real situations. He'd not hurt me and had said himself how he didn't like seeing me cry on set. Perhaps he was the submissive one and I would need to learn how to be a dominatrix for him? Maybe he wanted me to be the one to elicit whatever pain or pleasure he needed? Possibly it was neither. Not every relationship had to have a dominant and a submissive, after all. It stood to reason I was just another one of the sexually explorative women my age who assumed everyone had to have a label. It made things easier in the bedroom, yes, but in my experience, it was sometimes less exciting too. Lacking the surprise and the intrigue.

Tommy certainly had a lot of both of those though, and as I walked up the steps to the large wooden door, I found myself growing desperate in my need to see what awaited me on the other side.

He answered it without me needing to knock, as if he'd been waiting, watching me, and I enjoyed the idea of it. Like when he'd been skulking around in my garden, watching me like a man obsessed. I'd enjoyed that too. I'd liked having his eyes on me and had gotten off on knowing he was watching me so intently.

Tommy didn't say a word as he led the way inside via a huge, open plan living space and over to where a table sat in front of a bay window. He simply sat down at the head of the table and continued watching me as I ditched my jacket and overnight bag I'd come prepared with.

"What do you want me to do to you, Piper?" his voice thrummed through the air and hit me like a wall of heat. Damn, he was hot. Just the sound of his voice had me weak at the knees, and I didn't have to think twice about my answer.

I didn't falter, nor did I hesitate. I knew exactly what I wanted and wasn't afraid to tell him so.

"I want you to fuck me, Tommy. Like we did at my house last night and this morning. I want more of what we had together," I replied as I turned and wandered over to him.

He looked sheepish, as if I'd caught him off guard, and I cringed. Maybe that wasn't what he'd wanted to hear. But then why had he summoned me to his cabin in the woods? We weren't particularly well acquainted with cuddling or having a date night. The only real interactions we'd had thus far had either been in character or through hot and steamy carnality.

"I don't want that," he finally murmured with a scowl. I stopped in my tracks and gripped the back of the chair I had been about to pull out so I could sit down beside him.

Oh great, I thought. He'd brought me here to call things off between us, and I'd just gone and made things one hundred times more awkward. Tommy didn't want me. And why would he? I was a fool to think someone like him would be interested in me.

Yep, there I went with the shame spiral and the self-doubt. It'd been kicking my ass a lot recently, and it reared its ugly head again just when I thought I'd gotten over it.

Angry tears pricked at my eyes, and I turned away. I wasn't going to give him the satisfaction of knowing he'd hurt me. My nerves were shot, and I wanted out of there before Tommy could hurt me anymore. It was like my old boyfriend all over again. Before he could break me like he had.

"Fine, I guess I'll see you around," I replied, and was almost back to my bag when I heard his chair screech across the wooden floor. Before I could look back, he was on me. Tommy's hands were wrapped around me from behind, and one was clasped around my throat, pulling me back into him.

I let out a yelp, surprised by his outburst.

"See, this is why I'm fucked in the head. Too messed up to be trusted with you, Piper," he growled in my ear. "Before you, I was happy to fuck every which way I wanted and then leave. I was satisfied with everyday girls and their everyday cunts."

"But not anymore?" I choked back, my breath hitching thanks to his hold.

"No, not anymore," Tommy replied. "I wanted to see you hurting just then. I enjoyed watching the regret and shame cross your face when you thought I didn't want you. I've had those kinds of urges my entire life but have never felt close to giving into them. Not until you reached into my soul and played with my demons. Not until you brought them to the surface and made them feel special."

"When?" I asked through my hoarse breaths thanks to his hand that was still wrapped around my throat. "How did I do that? By not freaking out when I found you in my house, or was it when I caught you lurking around in my back yard?"

Tommy sucked in a breath on a hiss, his hold tightening ever so slightly.

"Way, way earlier than that, Piper," he whispered in my ear in answer. "I'm talking about that night in my hot tub when you stared into my eyes and told me it was okay to give in. To let those urges rule me. And I did. I am…"

"And ever since that night, what have I been to you? An experiment? A test to see how you like letting your dark side out?" I asked and then spun to face him.

Damn, he looked amazing. The cheeky party boy I'd met that night by his pool truly was no more. He had something wild in his eyes. Something dangerous. And he was right. I liked it.

"You're becoming more like an obsession. When I look at you, I don't see another girl for me to have my fun with. Far from it," Tommy answered, eyeing me up and down with those intense blue eyes of his. "There are two sides of me warring inside. One part wants to punish and torment you for the sheer thrill of it. It's like I need to see you suffer, Piper, but not because I want you to be in pain. I want it because, well, I want to be the one who makes it better. The person who licks your wounds and takes care of you afterwards."

"That's rather perverse, don't you think?" I said after taking a deep breath, trying not to show how much his words had gotten to me. "You want to be both my tormentor and my protector?"

Tommy's eyes dropped to the ground. And I had my first taste of what it felt like to do exactly what he had described—hurt him for the fun of it. But unlike him, I wasn't going to leave him thinking I wasn't interested in exploring the desires spurring to life inside of him.

It wasn't a fantasy of mine to see him hurting. I wanted him to soothe my pain, not for me to have to help him overcome his own, so I put an end to his suffering and grinned from ear to ear. "It's a good thing I'm a sucker for the perverse, isn't it?"

TWELVE

Tommy

Damn, that woman was sure making me work hard to get her where I wanted her. But, like the deviant I was, I couldn't resist her lure. I was enjoying the up and down. The back and forth. It was exactly what I'd wanted from a potential relationship with the only person who had ever made me want more than just a quick fling. Most of the time, women were lucky if they lasted more than a night. But with her, I wanted forever.

"I'll tell you how I envision this going and you can stop me at any time to negotiate, okay?" I asked, and she nodded but said nothing while the black pools of her eyes swallowed me whole as she awaited my proposal.

I was a glutton for punishment and waited, watching her a moment longer. Waiting to see if I saw any flicker of doubt on her perfect face. There wasn't any, only that continued immense stare. I don't think she so much as blinked.

I felt smothered by her. Like I couldn't breathe, but also as if I no longer wanted to. "All of this will stay between just you and me. Neither of us want anyone knowing what's going on behind closed doors, but I'm happy for us to eventually be outed as a couple should this play out the way I hope it will," I said, relishing in the flush of her cheeks when I mentioned how I was up for more with her. For us to be a real couple.

I surprised myself by wanting it too but reminded my wildly beating heart that it was still early days. We were in lust, not in love. This flame could burn out just as quickly as it'd ignited. "I want to make you squirm, Piper. To see you suffer and to humiliate you for my own enjoyment. I plan on tying you up and having my way with you however I see fit. I want to make you my slave. My whore. A prize only I am allowed to enjoy because you're too terrified to so much as look at another man, let alone allow him between your legs."

"You cannot leave a mark," she interjected, and I nodded. Our livelihoods counted on us being perfect and screen-ready at all times. It wasn't an issue. I'd already planned how I could be careful not to mark or scar her. To keep Piper's body in the perfect, pristine condition it currently was.

"Of course," I told her. "I'll ensure that you're safe from any lasting harm because that's the nature of this beast within me. like I said, I also need to protect you and to care for you. I'll save you from... me. I'll make you feel on top of the world again and then some, because that's where you belong, Piper."

"You promise?" she whispered, and I saw real fear in her eyes. Someone had made her feel bad before. Had humiliated and tortured her. But unlike me, he hadn't made it all better again afterwards. He hadn't taken away the bad and replaced it with so much goodness Piper had left his company feeling cared for. Feeling loved. She looked as if she might cry, and I recoiled, being reminded of my one condition. My only hard limit, so to speak.

"I promise," I said, making sure my voice was calm and even. "You have to trust me, just like I will have to trust you. Rely on me implicitly, to take what I need and then flip the switch inside of me so that I can give you what you need, Piper. The sex you spoke of, yes, but also much, much more than that. A connection. Perhaps even more." I stepped forward and took her hands in mine, kissing each palm tenderly. "I do, however, have one condition."

Her stunning eyes peered up into mine, and I could tell she was searching for something. Trying to guess what it was herself and I loved how she was trying to figure me out. Trying to get there first without me having to lead her to my truth, but she could never guess what'd happened to me years before. There was no way she would figure out the reason behind my need to both punish and protect, or my reasons for never wanting to see tears streaming down her pretty face.

"What is it, Tommy?" Piper eventually asked me, taking my mind away from the memories of my youth and the girl who had once ruined me.

"Don't ever cry, Piper. Never. If you do, the moment's over. There will be no making it better and no taking it back. It's my only trigger." She didn't actually seem all that shocked, and I wondered if I had given too much away earlier at the photo-shoot when I'd told her how much I'd hated seeing her cry. Luckily, I was still ever so slightly in George mode, otherwise it would've been days before I could've seen her again. Maybe longer. Even knowing they'd been fake tears had still churned my stomach and I guessed she'd somehow been able to tell how much it'd affected me.

Not wanting to go into any other detail on the subject, I turned the conversation back to the matter at hand. My proposed indulgence in all the things my immoral and devious side demanded in return for her well-earned aftercare. "Do you think you can do it? Give yourself to me? I want you to play a role for me. Become my captive, here in this cabin. Give me the chance to explore these desires of mine and then we can go from there. Continue on together…"

Piper seemed a little hesitant, and part of me wanted to get down on my knees and beg, but I simply couldn't allow myself to do it. I needed her to say yes all on her own. Not to coerce her. She had to be mine. Not only in the sexual sense, but in every way I could imagine. I had impulses only she could help me explore. Urges she had summoned that demanded she say yes, otherwise I wasn't against forcing her to stay. Making her see sense.

"Only if you promise me," she eventually whispered, stilling my frenzied mind. "Promise you won't hurt me, Tommy. Promise you won't take me for granted or leave me behind. I need to trust you before we can venture too far into the unknown, but it'll take time, so we need to go slow. I need to know you'll let me be what you need in my own time. That you won't get bored of me."

Oh bless her heart. My darling girl. So naïve and timid. How could I ever tire of her?

"I'll never get bored of you, Piper. Don't you see? I'd fix whatever's broken inside of you before I could ever break it anymore. I promise," I reassured her, and like that, I saw the decision to submit to me fill Piper's eyes before she even told me her finite yes.

This was going to be fun.

THIRTEEN

Piper

What the hell was I thinking? Tommy wasn't only completely inexperienced with this whole 'unleashing your inner desires' nonsense, but he was clearly using me as his test subject. It could all end seriously badly, and yet I stepped closer to him.

I said yes.

And then I let him strip me naked and cuff me to his bed.

He'd at least thought things through, or so it seemed. He'd bought the Velcro cuffs with thick banding so it wouldn't cut into my skin. There was bottled water by the bed, and the sheets had been freshly laundered. They were soft, as though ready to be slept on, rather than any of the awful deeds I'd imagined as Tommy finished preparing me and then climbed back on the bed to admire his handiwork. I thought he might say something, but he didn't. All he did was stare as he sat cross-legged on the end of the bed. I waited for whatever suffering he had planned for me, but he continued to do nothing at all. Nothing but stare.

Time passed slowly, and I eventually began to grow cold and tired of waiting. Impatient. I tugged on the cuffs, lifting myself higher on the mattress, but there was no give, so I twisted my arm in a bid to loosen it. Nothing.

Tommy grinned up at me from his position at my feet and his smile was so wide it reminded me of a comic book villain. Or at the least some kind of voyeur who chose to say so much through saying nothing at all. I watched him lean closer, his fingers rubbing his bottom lip as he saw my skin pucker like gooseflesh thanks to the chill.

In the minutes that followed, I went through a wide range of emotions. I'd initially felt excited and somewhat scared of what he had planned but was rapidly growing bored of his game. My boredom quickly turned to impatience and then frustration.

"What are you waiting for?" I eventually demanded, throwing a kick in his direction and missing, which only served to make me angrier. "Come on, Tommy. You said you wanted to watch me suffer, so make me suffer! Get it over with."

He turned and straightened his legs before climbing up off the bed, where he began pacing up and down, his eyes still glued to me. "Is this it? Is this your super plan? You're going to bore me to death?"

Tommy burst out laughing and I thought for a moment he might shrug his shoulders and tell me he'd been wrong. That after trying out his whole thing out he'd come to realize he wasn't cut out for it after all. But no.

He didn't come and untie me. He still didn't say a word. And he didn't hurry things up. I let out a disgruntled cry, surprising myself at how angry he was making me.

Like a petulant child not getting her own way, I then proceeded to throw a strop and even when it got me nowhere, I carried on, spewing profanities the likes I'd never said before. I was cold, bored, tired, and angry. My mouth was dry, reminding me of the water just inches away, but when I told Tommy I was thirsty, he did nothing. With that wild smile and a look in his eye that meant business, he simply continued to watch me squirm, and I began to realize what he was doing.

I was suffering. Not through pain or anything dramatic, but through my basic needs for warmth and nourishment having been taken away. He was starting slow. Like he'd said, I was now his captive. He decided when I ate and drank, not me. Tommy would decide when to warm me up and cover my naked body with a blanket or some clothes, and I knew nothing I said or did would affect his decision.

"Tell me what you need, Piper. How do you feel?" he asked when I'd finally calmed down and was laid on the bed, staring back at him with a scowl.

"I feel vulnerable. Tired. Thirsty." I curled my legs up against my torso as best I could to try and get some warmth back into them. "And I've come to realize I don't like being tied up."

"Why?" he asked, as he grabbed my feet and yanked my legs back down. Tommy then climbed over me and I instinctively curled up against him in spite of him having tormented me, desperate for his warmth.

"Tell me it's over now, Tommy. Please," I replied, but he shook his head.

"It's not over until I see how much you're willing to suffer to please me, Piper. You don't like being tied up. Why?" he asked again, and I let out a huff.

"Because it kinda makes me feel claustrophobic, if that makes sense? As if I'm trapped, and I don't like it," I answered, trembling beneath him regardless of the heat he was sharing with me.

"And why do you feel vulnerable?" he demanded as he climbed back and shoved open my legs, giving him a full view of my pussy. Normally I wouldn't mind, but he wasn't doing it to make me feel desired or wanted.

He wanted to push me to my limits before the switch could be flipped, and instead of feeling sexy, it felt all sorts of wrong.

I found myself wanting to get there sooner than later. Wanting this part to be over with so I could get to the good stuff.

"Because you aren't looking at my naked body as though you want to pleasure me. You're looking at me like you want to torture me," I replied, trying to pull them closed again, but he wouldn't let me. Tommy pressed down hard on my thighs, reacting to me exactly the way I'd expected. I decided to take things to the next level. To force him to go there whether he was ready or not, just like he was doing with me. "Get your fucking hands off me. I'm done with your games and I'm done with you, Tommy."

My words lit a fire within him I could see shining from the windows to his soul—his eyes. Something snapped in him, and it was my turn to grin as I watched Tommy struggle with how to handle my rejection.

With a growl, Tommy thrust two fingers inside of me and I cried out, writhing against him like a woman possessed. It was wetter than I would've thought after being more angry than turned on by his antics so far, but I couldn't deny his touch had me warmed up and desperate for more in a heartbeat.

"I say when you're done, Piper," he informed me, stroking his way in and out a few more times. "And it's not yet," Tommy added, removing himself and climbing up off the bed again.

I let out a garbled cry. I wanted to tell him I was sorry and beg him to come back and finish what he had started, but I knew this was all part of the game. It wasn't time to move on from the punishment side of things yet, so with a groan I snapped my legs closed and cursed at him.

Tommy continued his routine of torturing and then pleasuring me until I was fit to burst with all my denied orgasms. When he finally flipped that damn switch of his and thrust his cock inside of me, I exploded in seconds. It was too much. Too bad and yet so good. I had the best and most intense climax of my life.

"I hate you," I teased as I came down from my high and Tommy didn't reply. He simply unbound me and then lifted me into his arms before carrying me into the bathroom, where a steaming hot shower awaited me.

It felt so good to get warm again, especially when Tommy lathered me up and began washing me. Taking care of me like he had promised. Bringing me comfort and a sense of accomplishment for what I had given him.

"Let me look after you," he groaned, his hands running over my soaked skin while his eyes were closed. Like he was in some sort of daze. "Let me make love to you now, Piper. I need you to know how gentle and giving I can be."

I wanted that more than anything. We each rinsed off the last of the soap, and I shut off the shower. Tommy then followed me back into the bedroom, each of us dripping wet, but we didn't care.

"Show me," was all I said as I climbed back onto the bed he'd tied me to and pulled the covers up over myself in a bid to stay warm. Tommy joined me, and then he did exactly as he'd promised. He made love to me.

FOURTEEN

Tommy

I awoke the next morning with a human hot water bottle draped over my chest, but I didn't care one little bit. For the first time, I didn't want to sneak away and then make a run for it. I wanted to stay and hold her. To watch her sleep and greet her the moment she finally woke up.

She hadn't denied me one thing and even though we really had started slowly, she'd seen me for everything I truly was and hadn't run either. After me letting my fear stop me from indulging for so long, I'd finally opened up to someone, and she hadn't laughed at me or called me a freak. She had said yes. She'd let me torment her for my own pleasure and had reacted just how I'd hoped, even when she hated unleashing her usually so controlled anger.

That'd been my true undoing. Knowing I had the power to make or break her in those moments was exhilarating. To be able to unravel Piper's very many layers of calm and controlled exterior was a power I'd craved, and now I had it. I could've untied her at any point and apologized. Let her walk away. But I hadn't. And most importantly, she hadn't given up on me. Piper had trusted in me to deliver on my promises and I'd been morally bound to finish what I'd started. I'd adhered to the rules and flipped that switch when the right moment had presented itself.

It'd been perfect.

She'd been perfect.

There would always be a part of me that craved more, though. I could've watched her squirm all night. Seen her rage and scream. Watch her beg… damn, now that would've driven me over the edge. I might never have let her go if she'd turned fully submissive on me, but then again, that wasn't really what I wanted. I'd had a hundred women who had fallen at my feet and treated me like a God, but not Piper. She fought me every step of the way, and I adored it.

I always had liked a woman with a good deal of attitude about her.

I already wanted to take things to the next level. Like an addict, she had given me a high I craved more of, but I knew I had to fight my urges at least a little. I couldn't let them get the better of me. I ruled them, and not the other way around. I had to remember that.

Piper stirred and let out a soft hum in her sleep. She was adorable. Too adorable.

But I reminded myself how the cute little lady lying next to me wasn't cute or adorable at all. She was a slut who had let me fuck her anyway I'd desired. She hadn't cared while I'd defiled her with my filth.

"Whore," I whispered to her. "You're such a fucking whore, Piper. I'm gonna show you what I do to whores..." she was still asleep as I positioned myself behind her, the tip of my cock at just the right angle to take her again. I parted her lips, dipping my head inside.

"Not now, Tommy," she whispered groggily, pulling away just enough, so that I was no longer nestled in the perfect spot.

I felt like grabbing her and plunging myself inside, whether she consented or not. Like having my way no matter the consequences, but instead, I backed off. I did the right thing.

My good side won—this time.

FIFTEEN

Piper

I woke the next morning with the most amazing feeling in my belly. I felt, I don't know, happy? I certainly felt wonderful, put it that way, and knew it was Tommy who had helped make me feel that way. He'd let me rage on him when we'd been playing his game of the predator and his prey, and I had loved letting all my frustrations go. I hadn't held back. For the first time in forever, I'd let my words fly without a care for being the good girl. It'd felt good to offload my rage and I couldn't deny there was a huge part of me wanted more of it.

Tommy woke up not long after me, and he was beyond attentive to my every need. He made me breakfast and then we fooled around for a bit, which was lovely. I giggled and played coy while he teased me and bargained me into submission. We were acting like teenagers again and I was walking on air until he suggested we take a dip in the hot tub. This was my nightmare. I desperately wanted to join him, but the tub was out on that horrible deck, and my fear of heights came crashing down on me like a suffocating haze.

I went over to the glass door and looked out. I could see through the tiny gaps in the floorboards and down onto the forest below. They looked far from safe, and I was convinced they would break beneath my feet and I'd fall.

"How about a walk instead?" I suggested, trying my best to sound aloof. I wasn't sure he bought it, but Tommy agreed and then he grabbed us some supplies while I used the bathroom and got freshened up.

By the time I was dressed and good to go, he had the truck packed and indicated for me to jump in the passenger's side. I looked into the cab and pouted. "What happened to our walk?" I demanded, and he simply shook his head in response before jumping into the driver's seat and starting the engine.

I climbed in and fastened my belt, figuring we were still having fun after all, so I decided to be adventurous, and I let him decide on our next step. Tommy sped away and at the end of the long drive that led to his cabin. Instead of turning right for the highway, he turned left, taking us further up towards the mountain's peaks.

After a few minutes, he then turned down a dirt track. And I had to grab the handrail above me to stop from flying around in my seat. I giggled, watching him drive, and he couldn't hide his smile even though he was concentrating hard on the road ahead.

Tommy was dazzling, a true movie star, and I was smitten with him. I knew it.

When we came to a stop and he put the truck in park, I climbed out of my seat and over the center console so I could straddle him. He knew what I was after, and his pants were around his thighs and his cock free and pointing up at me before I could even get out of my clothes. He knew exactly what to do and with a grunt he had me down on him the second he'd spied that my underwear was out of the way.

I let out a garbled cry and tried to move, but there was no way he was going to let me take control and ride him. Not the ever present dominant force that was Tommy Darke. With my legs tangled thanks to my ineptitude at getting my pants off, he used them to hold me in place while he thrust up inside of me again and again.

It was heaven. Like a jackhammer pummeling up and into me over and over, while I was pinned against his steering wheel and could do nothing but lean back and take it as he fucked me hard. It felt exhilarating to let him take me like that. Like I was an adventurous teenager again, and we were parked up in the woods for some naughty alone time.

I loved it. The truck smelled like real forest pine, and the windows were steamed up just like in the movies. My senses were all heightened, and every element just added to my euphoric ecstasy.

Tommy was soon grunting while I was letting out those weird noises that were something between a groan and an, 'oh my God,' but neither of us cared what we sounded like. All we cared about was being together.

When I came, Tommy started pounding me harder. I figured he must be close, and that was why, but when he didn't stop and I came a second time and saw the wicked smile on his face, I knew why he'd done it. He'd wanted to make me climax for him over and over. Once evidently hadn't been enough and I didn't mind one little bit.

With a shudder and a moan, he then joined me in the release and stilled. I tried to climb off him, but still couldn't move. I couldn't until Tommy put me down and let me untangle my legs, so we simply stayed there while he composed himself.

When I was finally free, I grabbed some paper towels from the box on the dash just in time to catch the wetness trickling between my thighs. I'd always found it gross, but it was just one of those things I had learnt to tackle after a bit of fun in the sack. A lesson no one had needed to teach me about, but one I'd learned for myself when I'd become a woman and taken charge of my body during sex.

"Damn, woman. I thought we were meant to be going for a walk?" Tommy teased as he put himself away. I didn't answer. I just shrugged and offered him a salacious smile.

I was back in the passenger side and almost ready when he opened the driver's side door and jumped down and out of sight. Next thing I knew, Tommy had my door open and his hand stretched out for me to take.

I let him lift me down, like a gentleman, before groaning as I took in the trail ahead of us—if you could call it that. It was a proper mountain path with a steep incline. Not for the faint of heart.

"Tommy, I'm not cut out for a hike right now," I grumbled, but he took off anyway.

I figured I had two choices, wait in the truck, or follow him.

So I did the latter of course.

It was when I caught him up I realized he had more than just a backpack full of snacks on his back. "Not just a walk planned, I see," I said, indicating to the supplies on his shoulders. I could see roll mats and a small tent, so wasn't surprised when he told me we were spending the night beneath the stars.

I didn't mind, though. Growing up a military kid, I'd done all sorts of wilderness training over the years, usually for fun but sometimes for sport. Before I'd left home and headed for the bright lights of LA, I was one of the volunteers at the local school and would take the kids on bug hunts and nature walks over the summer or on weekends. I knew which berries were good and which mushrooms were even better. I knew how to start a fire from scratch and how best to tap water from a tree. Not that Tommy knew any of that, of course. He seemed to think he was teaching me a thing or two by having me come up the mountain alongside him, and I was more than happy to let him carry on. He didn't have to know everything.

After a few hours spent hiking, we reached the top of a truly scenic peak, and that was where Tommy decided we would make our camp for the night. Personally, I would've chosen a spot closer to the tree line, but I was still letting him take charge so just sat back and let him do his thing while I sipped on some water and ate some trail mix he'd handed me.

Tommy made quick work of it and seemed to have finished setting up the tent and our beds, but then he reached into the pack and pulled out one more length of rope. I eyed it curiously as he tugged on it, testing the strength. "What's that for?" I asked.

"I'll show you after dinner," he replied, setting up a small gas stove for us to boil some food on. He was utterly at ease with nature, and I knew he'd done this all a ton of times before.

I watched, mesmerized, as he then tore open some food packets and cooked us up a hearty stew. It reminded me of the ration packs my dad would bring home from work sometimes. Random meals all squished together, but that still tasted amazing because we only ever ate them when we too had been hiking for hours or working hard on whatever project he had us involved in. I closed my eyes, and the smell took me right back to my childhood.

"I like being here with you," I told him, forgetting where I was for a second, and whom I was with. I was in the company of either my tormentor or my protector, whichever one Tommy decided he wanted to be, so I knew I couldn't show any signs of weakness with him otherwise he'd pounce all over it, I could tell.

"If you like it so much, perhaps you'll let me make our night a little more memorable?" he enquired, and I couldn't deny being intrigued.

"How?" I asked as I cleaned up our dinner bowls and then packed them away. Tommy answered by getting up and walking over to the tent he'd made up for us to sleep in. He lifted the awning and beckoned me inside, so I wandered closer.

"Wait, no shoes," he demanded, and I rolled my eyes but still kicked off my boots before clambering into the tent. It was small and cramped inside. Not enough room to stand in, but our two roll mats and sleeping bags fit perfectly, so was more than enough. "Take off your clothes," Tommy ordered, breaking my reverie. I did as he'd asked and was soon kneeling before him, stark naked. He watched me for a few seconds and then went to the pack he'd stashed the rope away in.

I inhaled sharply. I didn't want to be tied up again and shook my head no, but Tommy reacted to my refusal by grabbing the back of my neck and forcing me down onto the pillow face first. And all with the biggest smile on his darkly handsome face.

I squealed and tried to fight him off me, but he was far too strong. It still didn't stop me from trying, though. The cushion muffled my screams and pleas, but I still writhed and kicked, trying my hardest to get out of his hold.

It was no use. Tommy had my wrists bound in seconds and then tied them to my ankles before I could so much as register what he was doing. In my panic, I tried to twist and pull at the ropes in a bid to get free, and what made it worse was how I was unable to see or speak thanks to the pillow, almost smothering me. It was torture and I couldn't stand it. And Tommy was clearly in tormentor mode because he was doing nothing but watch me squirm.

I forced myself to get a grip and turned my head to the side, where I breathed a sigh of relief when he brushed my hair out of my face, peering down at me.

"Please, Tommy. I don't like it," I begged. He shushed me and then ran his hands down my back, where he delivered a heavy-handed slap to one of my ass cheeks.

"I told you what I am. The things I want," he reminded me. "And you promised to deliver them, Piper. Don't let me down."

I didn't know how else I could play his game other than beg for him to stop. He wanted to torment me and he was doing just that, so I let out an angry moan and fought against my binds again. And then it dawned on me. He needed something else. Not begging or bargaining, but something far more primal. Something more vulgar and cruel.

"It's not worth the hassle," I demanded, feeling angry and ready once again to let it show. "You're not worth it. I fucking hate you."

I saw the rage flash in Tommy's eyes, and it felt good to elicit such a strong reaction from him. Two could play this game, and I was going to make damn sure he knew I was no weak little girl for him to toy with.

SIXTEEN

Tommy

I had never wanted to hurt a woman as much as I wanted to hurt Piper in that moment. A voice in my head was screaming for me to teach her a proper lesson. To punch and kick her into submission. Then we'd see who was boss.

Instead, I left her there to stew on her words and made a sharp exit from the tent so I didn't have to look at her any longer. I was liable to slap more than just her backside if she didn't bite her fucking tongue.

I zipped the entryway closed, locking her inside. Not that she could escape the binds, but I needed an extra barrier between us. She was calling out to me, saying she was sorry, but I could hardly hear her over the sound of the blood rushing through my skull.

My heart was pounding hard. My cock even harder. I ignored them both as I built up the fire and relit it, watching the sun as it began to creep lower on the horizon.

I was just about finished when I heard feet moving over the gravel on the trail above us. I could tell Piper had heard it too because she finally shut the hell up and I grinned to myself, thinking how terrified she must be of anyone finding her in such a predicament. I looked up and nodded, lifting my hand in greeting to the hikers on their way down the mountain, and then received two smile-and-wave gestures in return.

"Hey, are you Tommy Darke?" the first of the hikers then asked after he'd rounded the bend and reached the part of the trail we'd come off at. He was close enough to see me properly and seemed over the moon to have stumbled on a Hollywood A-lister in the mountains.

"Yeah, in the flesh," I replied and then grinned inwardly as he and his friend came off the trail towards me. God, Piper must be shitting herself in that tent listening to this, and I intended to make it ten times worse. "You heading back down?" I asked when they were closer, and the guy nodded. "Come and sit with me. You've got time before sunset."

They looked like all their Christmases had come at once and immediately dropped their packs before taking a seat on them to avoid the cold ground.

We caught up for a few minutes and the guys told me how they'd spent the previous two days scaling San Gabriel's peaks. They were evidently keen hikers, and I liked their style. In fact, I quite liked the pair of them in general. They were fun to talk to and seemed adventurous. Just like me.

Even though we were chatting away, my eyes kept darting to the tent, and I was imagining Piper inside cursing my name while trying her hardest not to make a sound. I wanted to push her further. Make her hate me just that little bit more. "Oh, hey. You wanna see something cool?" I asked, before letting them go finish their hike.

"Yeah, sure," the first one said, and they watched me as I went over to the tent and began unzipping the door just enough so that I could poke my head inside.

There she was, my little captive. Piper looked beyond terrified. Just as I'd hoped. But of course, she was out of sight to the others. Only I could see her gorgeous face and stunning nakedness. After all, it didn't matter that I wanted to push her; she was mine to torment and enjoy. Not theirs. It was all I could do to hide my smile, though, as I reached inside and grabbed my cell before closing the zipper again.

I then proceeded to show the guys some snaps from the latest movie on my phone before taking a selfie I promised I would upload the second I was back in cell reception range. The two guys were over the moon and thanked me profusely, which sure caressed my ego nicely. They could come around more often. No, on second thoughts I'd rather be alone with my girl and decided it was time they left. I wrapped things up, and we said our goodbyes before I sat by the fire and watched the tops of their heads disappear down the mountain. I also listened to be sure they'd gone before clambering back into the tent and began pulling Piper free from her binds.

She freaked when I'd untied her. I could understand it, but damn, she was hot when she was angry. I let her hit me a few times and spew curses my way, and then I'd had enough. It was time I dished out just a little bit more brutality. Or maybe a lot. I wasn't sure when I'd stop, only that at some point I'd flip that switch and all would be well.

I grabbed Piper by the throat and pushed her facedown onto the pillow again, unbuttoning my fly with my free hand as I did so. I then pushed my pants down my thighs and knees, eventually kicking them off into a heap at the end of the tent. Piper still resisted me, and I answered by pressing her face harder into the cushion. She went limp when I forced open her knees with mine, but it didn't matter that she'd finally stopped fighting me. I was taking what was mine, and nothing was going to stop me.

Piper was soaking wet, and I slid right inside without any need to coat myself in her juices for lubrication first. I almost came then and there.

"Were you ready for me, Piper," I groaned as I began pushing in and out. "You feel ready."

"Fuck you," she croaked in response, and I laughed loudly as I did just that. I pounded into her and Piper pushed back against me, her pussy clenching around my cock as I burrowed deeper and deeper into her. "Stop, Tommy," she then begged. "Please. I think I'm gonna pee!"

I didn't stop. Something about the entire scenario made me want it darker and more depraved. I wanted Piper to piss herself while I continued to hold her down and fuck her. I wanted to see the humiliation such an act would bring.

She came and her writhing and clenching were enough to drive me over the edge, so I joined her in the climax and then peered down at the sleeping bag beneath her. Damn it, she'd managed to hold her bladder, and I was uncannily disappointed.

As soon as I let her go, Piper threw on her shirt and flew outside into the darkness of the night. I yanked on my boxers and a jacket and followed her into the bushes where I watched as she took a piss. The longest piss in the world, without a doubt. It went on forever, but I was enthralled as I watched her let go. Mesmerized by the relief on her face as she crouched there, soaking the bushes beneath that fine behind of hers.

When it was over, I saw her do a little shake and began to laugh. Piper looked so silly it was endearing. So, I went to the tent and grabbed a roll of toilet paper I'd brought along for us to use. I then wrapped some around my palm, looping it over and over before ripping it along the perforated edge. She seemed surprised when I met her halfway between the tent and her designated toilet area and shoved my wrapped-up hand between her thighs to soak up any remains of her piss. "Don't, that's dirty," she squealed, trying to pull away, but I wouldn't let her. I felt the few droplets of pee left on her dirty cunt soak into the tissue, and grinned. I liked it dirty.

My tastes for her were getting darker by the minute, I could tell, but I also didn't care. I just hoped she was ready, because something inside of me seemed to sense we were only just getting started.

SEVENTEEN

Piper

After I was nicely dried up thanks to Tommy's weird way of helping me, I dragged the tissue paper over his knuckles and threw in our makeshift trash bag over by the tent before soaking both our palms in alcohol rub.

He certainly was an oddball, I'd give him that, and an infuriating ass for sure. But there was still so much that excited me about him. Something that made me want to push his buttons, regardless of knowing there was no remorse when it came to him retaliating if he was in one of his torturous moods. I was playing with fire and, even though I knew it was foolish, I wasn't afraid to get burned.

I grabbed my pants from the tent and slid my legs inside, already feeling the chill leeching into my skin and bones now that night had fallen. And then I climbed back into my boots and jacket. Tommy did the same, and I watched as he stoked the fire back to life and threw a few pieces of wood onto it to revive the flames. It wasn't long at all until it was blazing nicely and he sat down, beckoning me over with a soft smile. I went to him hesitantly. I had to know what I was getting myself into by approaching him, and I think he knew.

"Come here. Let me care for you, Piper," he told me.

I shook my head no. There was no way I could go for another round in the sack. I was beyond sore between my legs and felt exhausted and achy all over after having been tied up for the better part of an hour. Tommy held my gaze, his hand still outstretched in summoning. "I know what you need. Let me give it to you. Trust me…"

Did I trust him? I thought so, but then why was I hesitating? I think I needed to be sure that he'd flipped his switch, but Tommy was giving nothing more away. Against all my instincts telling me not to go to him, I went weak at the knees. His face was so gentle and calm. His tone of voice seemed sincere, and I ignored all my better judgments, telling me not to trust him. I put my faith in the man who had just moments before held me against my will and then fucked me while pinning me down by my throat. *Not like you didn't love it,* I reminded myself.

I went to Tommy and fell into his lap when he yanked me down, which seemed exactly where he wanted me. He then cradled me and wrapped his arms around my body so tightly I very quickly forgot all about the cold. All I could see was the concave at the base of his neck, and my forehead was tucked against his cheek. All I could smell was his heady musk, and I breathed it in with relish.

I was besotted with this dark and dangerous creature and knew it. No matter what he'd done, our moments like this made it all worth it, and I basked in his strong arms, expecting him to pull away again any moment, but he didn't. Tommy continued to hold me pressed tightly against him for what felt like hours.

He shushed me whenever I tried to ask him what was going on. All he let be said between us were words of adoration and love. He made me feel wanted and cared for again. Not remotely like a plaything he enjoyed tormenting or a quickie bit of fun. I felt like his one true love and knew I loved him in return, and all while neither of us spoke more than a few words.

Then and there, realization struck.

I was Tommy's girl now, and there was no going back.

Not that I wanted to.

After breakfast the next morning, we packed up the tent and started the walk back down to where Tommy had parked the truck. It didn't take us long, and while I didn't fret over it, part of me wondered what we would do if we came across any other hikers like Tommy had the evening before. Would we make some lame attempt at explaining why we were walking together in the woods? Would anyone even care? I didn't know, but part of me was intrigued to find out. I wanted to see what Tommy said and did if it happened. Whether he would put an arm around me and tell them I was his girl or if he'd play it cool and dumb down our relationship by telling whoever it was that we were just friends.

I didn't get my answer because we reached the truck without seeing another soul, and I climbed up into the passenger side with a sigh. I wanted to come right out and ask him if he'd considered it, but Tommy seemed so relaxed I didn't want to ruin the mood by making him have 'the talk' with me. I managed to convince myself that I wasn't one of those girls and wasn't going to cave just because I was having a girlie moment and forced it all away.

We reached the cabin after a short and quiet drive, and I was beyond glad to see the huge wooden building ahead of us. I needed to shower badly.

We headed inside and I helped Tommy unload the kit before hitting the bathroom. There, I locked the door and undressed before turning on the jets of the large shower.

I also checked myself over in the mirror and, true to Tommy's word, I didn't have a bruise or a scratch on me. Despite everything we'd been doing together and how aggressive his dark side seemed, no one who looked at me would be any the wiser. My clever lover knew his stuff.

As I climbed into the warm cascade from the showerheads above, I was reminded of my old life. One where I was timid and downtrodden. Where I had a man whom I adored but who never took care of me the way Tommy did, and I felt a lump form in my throat just thinking back to those days. I knew I couldn't pour my heart out to Tommy because I could never talk about Damon without breaking down and letting my tears flow. And that was the one rule he'd insisted upon. I was never allowed to cry in front of Tommy. For whatever reason, they were a trigger for him. And one I didn't want to have to test the theory on. I'd take his word for it, thank you very much.

And so, I cried into my hands, letting the water wash my tears down the plughole and out of sight. I felt lucky to have Tommy and happy that he loved me, but also terrified of losing him. I couldn't imagine ever wanting this thing between us to end, and even the thought of it broke my heart in two, making the tears flow harder.

Man, I was in serious trouble.

EIGHTEEN

Tommy

Piper was taking so long in the bathroom that I found myself growing more and more annoyed. What was she playing at? We had one more night together before we both had to head back to the city for work and she was wasting time primping and preening? I had a quick shower in the en-suite and as the hot water cleansed away the grime of our busy trip to the mountain, a thought crept into my mind. I wanted her at my mercy again, but this time, I was going to do it differently. No manhandling involved, just some good old manipulation.

I shut off the water and dried quickly so I could get started on the plan forming in my mind. The first step was simple. All I had to do was get her drunk. Out in the kitchen, I poured her a glass of wine and made myself a whiskey and soda using the teensiest bit of liquor. Just enough so she'd be able to smell it on me and taste it on my lips.

When Piper finally emerged from the bathroom, I plucked the glass by its stem and offered it to her with a dashing smile, reveling in the flush that instantly flooded her cheeks as she regarded me. My girl certainly was smitten. In all fairness, she enamored me, too. All she had to do was bat those lashes of hers and I wanted to bury myself so deeply inside of her she'd feel it in her navel. I wanted to be with her always and keep watch over her, day and night. I knew this now.

She wasn't free of me, and I hoped she accepted the truth of it by now—that she never would be.

I plied Piper with drink after drink while I had little more than a couple shots' worth of whiskey. I pretended to get drunk alongside her while we sat and chatted together, and I listened as she told me about her life before she'd moved to Los Angeles—as if I hadn't already done plenty of homework on her and knew exactly what army bases she'd lived in and when. Such a fool she was to let herself fall for the monster. But she loved it, I could tell.

I played along, but all the while I dominated her and everything around her. Using my body language, I made a point of physically overshadowing Piper, and before long she was showing signs of natural submission. She began mirroring my gestures and movements, even my facial expressions. When I took a sip of my drink, so did she, and when I smiled or frowned, I noticed she did too.

I went one step further and instructed that she sit on my lap and then didn't give her the option of moving into any other position than strewn across me. Only when she needed a top up did I move, but even then, she came along to the bar with me.

I had to keep her in my hands. To feel her and Piper was beyond complaint. She followed me and my black heart no matter where I went.

It wasn't long before my tiny love was blind drunk, and I decided to put on some music so I could hold her even closer. I decided on a slow, melodic track and pulled Piper to me, wrapping my arms around her shoulders.

A smile played on my lips as she slipped her hands around my waist, and I grinned back. So, she was still sober enough to know what she was doing. I wanted to rectify that. I wondered if perhaps next time I should pick up some sleeping pills to crush and put in her wine as well. That ought to do the trick in making her my slave. Mine to do with as I pleased, like a living doll.

The image of her glassy-eyed and out of it entered my head, and I grimaced. No. I didn't want that. I wanted Piper laid back with her legs open and her taking every inch of me while screaming, begging for more. Drunk and compliant would do nicely.

"You love me, don't you?" I whispered, and Piper hummed in response. That wasn't good enough. I pulled back from our embrace and peered down at her darkly. "You love me, don't you?" I asked again. Piper's eyes rolled up to look into my face and she swayed, thanks to the copious amounts of booze in her system.

"Yes. I love you, Tommy," she croaked.

"Why?" I demanded, suddenly needing to know.

She thought about it for a moment and then grinned. Her face lit up like the goddamn Fourth of July, and she giggled.

"Because you're weird, Tommy. You're so frickin' fucked up, but I love it, and I guess that makes me weird, too."

I had to laugh. She sure was right.

NINETEEN

Piper

I woke the next day feeling like death. I didn't know if I wanted to get up and hurl or just lie there a little longer and pray I kept my shit together. I sure didn't want Tommy to see me puke. God, how much had I had to drink? He'd kept up with my pace though, so I figured he had to be feeling as bad as me, but that didn't make me any better.

A shiver swept over me, and I finally opened my eyes to discover I was naked and had kicked off the bedsheets. Tommy wasn't there, so I quickly clambered to my feet and was just pulling on a shirt when he appeared in the doorway.

How could he look so damn good? I wanted to throttle him.

"Morning, beautiful," he chimed and then handed me a smoothie. "Drink this, it'll do you wonders." I did as he said while he watched me curiously, as though he were scrutinizing a piece of art or something.

"How much did we drink last night?" I asked once my glass was empty.

"A lot," he laughed before turning and heading back out the way he'd come in. I watched him go, not having the energy to move too much, but had to admit it felt good to have some food in my stomach.

Once I was feeling a little more human, I followed Tommy out into the lounge, hoping my hangover might not be so bad after all, thanks to his wonder-smoothie.

"I'm sorry if I was a mess," I said when I reached him. There weren't many blank spots in my memory, but I did remember chewing his ear off for a while about my issues with my parents and how hard some of the fresh starts had been. I didn't think I'd said anything about Damon and wasn't sure I ever could, at least not with Tommy. In many ways they were so alike, but at least Tommy treated me with kindness. At least he cared. Not like Damon, who had left me a shell of a woman by the time I'd finally had enough of his ways and broken free.

There were things I then suddenly remembered clearly from my drunken night the evening before. Moments such as him holding me close and telling me I was his. As if I'd needed reminding? I knew it in every inch of my heart and soul, regardless of what I'd tried to tell myself about being a strong and independent woman who didn't need a man in her life to know it was worthwhile. No need for validation. Yeah, who was I kidding? I needed all those things just like any other young woman, and luckily for me, Tommy was giving me everything, and then some.

He regarded me, watching as my emotions changed from up to down and back again in a heartbeat.

"You weren't a mess last night at all, Piper," he told me sternly. "Don't ever say sorry to me."

My breath hitched in my throat. How could he say such a thing? I began to doubt everything I'd thought I knew about our relationship simply because it felt too good to be true. Was he lying to me? Was I a fool for believing that this could work when we both knew there was darkness in him that demanded he torture me when it called to him? One that I had called forth from the depths of his soul and was forced to take responsibility for now that it'd come to the surface.

I had somehow come to accept how I needed to care for that dark side of his. To nurture it. Fool or not, I wasn't going to walk away, and we both knew it.

"Okay," I hummed and got the shock of my life when he crossed the room and pinned me to the wall behind.

Tommy gripped me by the throat, and I was reminded once again of his volatile tendencies that were mine alone to bear the brunt of. No matter my acceptance of it, I was still terrified at seeing the rage in his eyes and felt myself wilt under the pressure.

"Do you need me to teach you a lesson about just what you're worth to me?"

"No," I croaked, but he didn't hear me. Tommy was lost to his dark whims, and he dragged me toward the wooden deck without a care for how much I struggled against him. I was petrified of going out there and I realized he knew it. Evidently it truly was time I was properly punished. Tortured.

I knew what was coming before he'd even opened the door and thrown me out onto the damp wooden deck with a heartless thud.

He then slammed the door closed and clicked the lock. While all I could do was scream and beg for him to let me back inside, but I knew it was no use. I wouldn't be allowed back in until he said so, or at least not until he was finished with yet another of his awful games.

TWENTY

Tommy

This was it. The defining moment in my quest to have outright control over my darling Piper. I locked that door and lifted my arms above my head, leaning against the doorframe so I could watch her out the window, like the highest definition screen in the whole damn world.

She was hugging the outside of the door while screaming in pure terror, pressing her ass against the glass in a bid to stay as close to the actual house as possible. I was captivated. This wasn't my doing, but her fear of heights, and I loved seeing her fall apart. Part of me wanted to break her even more. To remove every shackle she had holding her down and leave her with only me. Perhaps save her, or better yet, torment her even more?

I could hear Piper sucking in hitched breaths, and my cock hardened at the sound. When she then slumped to the floor and curled into a ball like some wounded creature trying to protect itself, I let myself smile for a moment before booting the door to get her attention.

Piper looked up at me with venom in her eyes. She was beyond furious with me, and that was fine by me. All part of my new favorite game.

"Walk to the end of the balcony and back, then I'll let you back in…" I told her.

She looked to the edge of the deck and then back at me, shaking her head frantically.

"I can't, Tommy. Please just let me back in," she begged. I didn't answer. I simply continued to watch her process her options. If she did it, she'd be back inside and in my arms within minutes. Then I'd flip my switch and care for her. Make it all better again. I might even make love to her again. That was nice.

But first, she had to do this one little thing. Sadly for her, it was the one thing she was terrified of doing. I couldn't understand why, though. The deck was perfectly safe, and it annoyed the hell out of me that she had left herself believe otherwise. To not trust me and listen to her irrational brain instead.

She eventually stood, and I could see her calming her frantic breaths. I could then hear her talking to herself, urging her feet to move forward, and before long she took a tentative step onto the next plank. I could see her trembling violently, and knew it had nothing to do with the cold. It was actually rather mild out there, so I knew her shivers had more to do with her fear than any morning chill.

Well, at least she'd forgotten all about her hangover.

It felt like an age, but eventually Piper moved forward onto the next board, and the next. She made it to the end, touched the ledge, and hotfooted it back over to the doorway, which I'd unlocked and had open at the ready for her.

TWENTY-ONE

Piper

I ran through that doorway and straight past Tommy without even looking at him. I didn't feel elated for having conquered one of my fears. No way. I was still terrified of that deck, perhaps even more so now, and hated that it was him who had put me out on there to begin with. This wasn't fun anymore, and I wanted out.

I ran to the bedroom and grabbed my things, stuffing them back in my suitcase without any care for crumpling my nice clothes or whether my perfume leaked all over the place. I just needed to get out of there.

It didn't matter the promises I'd made both Tommy and myself about letting him torture me. He'd gone too far this time. I'd almost had a panic attack out there, and it was far from fun or exciting. It was downright petrifying. Thank God for my years of therapy and my ability to talk myself down now that I'd learned the best ways to overcome my heightened anxiety.

I felt ruined. Broken. This wasn't fun.

I was leaving.

Tommy tried to reason with me and he also tried to hold me, evidently ready to flip his internal switch, but I wasn't ready to listen or to calm down. I needed some air. Some space.

I grabbed my keys and headed for the door. Outside, I threw myself and my things in my car and pressed the button that ought to have switched the engine on. Nothing happened. I let out a loud roar in fury.

"Asshole!" I screamed, looking up to find Tommy watching me from the doorway with a smile. I wasn't going to give him the satisfaction of watching me walk back inside. Back to him. Instead, I climbed out and slammed my car door closed before I started walking back towards the main road that I'd driven up the mountain via. I'd hitchhike home if I had to. Anything was better than staying there with him.

I tried not to look back. Not to check if he was following me, but I couldn't help myself. Right before I turned a bend that I knew would leave me without sight of his cabin, I looked back over my shoulder and found Tommy continuing to watch me from the doorway. Still half-dressed and as calm as ever, he simply watched me walk away as though so sure I'd only get so far before turning back. I flipped him the bird and kept on going. All I wanted was to get home.

I talked to myself as I pounded the pavement. Calling myself an idiot and cursing Tommy and everything he meant to me.

Just as I was coming up to the main road, I heard a twig snap somewhere in the trees to my right and came to a stop. Was he there? No, he couldn't be. It had to be an animal or something. Tommy would've just come down the path if he wanted to chase after me, surely?

I kept on walking.

I could see some cars driving past the turnoff and picked up speed. I'd flag one down and say I'd broken down after a hike up the mountain. No one would need to know I'd been there with Tommy. Our secrets would remain just that.

Right before I reached the road, I heard another twig snap, but this time I ignored it. I immediately wished I hadn't.

Thick, strong arms enveloped me from behind and lifted me off the ground. I screamed, and my attacker put a hand over my mouth. I knew it was Tommy, but that didn't stop me from writhing and trying to break out of his hold. The last thing I wanted was to go back to that cabin. I wasn't ready for him to tell me he was sorry and try to make it up to me. No, sir. He needed to pay first. To beg me for forgiveness.

I jabbed him with my elbows and tried to kick, but it was no use. Tommy dragged me into the bushes and flung me against a tree, pressing into me from behind.

"You shouldn't have run from me, Piper," he groaned in my ear before releasing my mouth.

"I didn't run. I stormed away because you're an asshole who didn't deserve for me to stay."

He turned me to face him, and I thought for a minute he might slap me. He looked ready to strike, as if I'd hit a nerve.

"You need to let me take care of you," he said, but his eyes were still dark. I didn't trust that he'd flipped his switch and was going to be soft and kind. Plus, I was still too angry to want it. "I have to do both otherwise it won't work." He unbuttoned my pants, and I pushed him away.

"No," I demanded. "Not here, and not like this. It isn't love if I'm still hurting."

Tommy grabbed my hands and held them in one of his, still going for my pants with his free hand.

"Let me show you, Piper. It'll feel better after I make you see how much I love you," he pleaded, but I was having none of it. Tommy had gone too far this time, and he couldn't make up for it by fucking me.

"This isn't love," I repeated, but he carried on. He pulled my pants down a little and panic started to rise in my chest. I didn't want it. Not there. Not like that. The games were over, but Tommy was going to take something I didn't want to give him, and that wasn't going to be okay with me.

I felt my eyes well up in fear, and I knew what to do. What would make him back off and leave me be. I let the tears fall.

The moment he saw them, Tommy paled. He looked like I'd just torn his heart out and stomped on it, and he immediately backed off. I hated it, but was also glad I had been able to stop him before things had taken a direction we'd both have regretted.

Once I was free, I pulled my pants back up and buttoned them before I then stumbled away, heading for the road again.

"Wait," Tommy pleaded, and I was about to tell him to go to hell when I turned back and saw the agony in his eyes, but also the iciness. Like I had broken him, too. Good. "Take my truck," was all he added, throwing me the keys. I caught them and nodded but didn't thank him. There was no need, given how he was clearly responsible for my own car being dead.

I turned and walked away, hiding the fresh tears streaming down my face. They had already served their purpose, and I didn't feel the need to torture Tommy further by showing him them anymore.

My heart felt like it was breaking with every step away from him I took. The moment was far from anything I'd hoped for when I'd awoken that morning, and I knew it'd haunt me until the end of my days.

His aggressive touch.

That violent, tortured face.

Gone had been my gorgeous and cock-sure lover, and I had crumbled.

The walk back up towards the cabin was a hard one. I felt slow and exhausted. As if our altercation had completely taken it out of me. When I reached the two cars parked side-by-side in front of the cabin, I was glad to be leaving it all behind me.

I grabbed my things and jumped in the driver's side, and then I drove away without so much as looking for Tommy on the road back down. I drove like my life depended on it and reached home in record time.

I even left his car on my driveway, not caring who might recognize it, and ran inside, double locking the doors behind me. Without checking my mail or listening to my voice messages, I went straight up to my room, where I showered and then climbed into bed.

That's where I stayed for the twenty or so hours that followed. My phone rang a few times, and I could hear Janie's angry voice on the machine as she left me messages demanding to know where I was and if I was okay. But I wasn't okay, and I wasn't sure I ever would be. I couldn't face telling her or anyone else what'd happened, so I hid away. Locked the doors, closed the drapes, and blocked out the world.

My plan worked fine until I got an email directly from the PR team for *Wayward* outlining the press dates and commitments I was expected to attend. Janie had given up calling, and I soon knew why when she was banging down my door, so I flung it open and glared at her.

"I know, okay!" I demanded.

"No, it's not okay," she replied angrily. "Where the fuck have you been, Piper? You said a few days, and it's been over a week. I was worried."

I looked past Janie to my driveway, where I expected Tommy's truck to still be parked. I was surprised she hadn't asked me about it and got my answer when I saw my little soft top nestled in its usual spot beneath my tree. Tommy had brought it back and taken his truck away. When had he done it? Had he tried snooping in my windows to see what I was up to while he was here? If he had, it wouldn't have been a pretty sight, I knew that much. I'd hardly taken care of myself other than showering and scraping my hair back while either crying myself to sleep or eating everything I could get my hands on while watching TV. Yeah, super sexy.

"I've had a hard few days, that's all," I told Janie, who was still staring at me with what appeared to be a genuine concern in her eyes. "I... I kinda broke up with someone I thought meant something to me," I revealed, and Janie sighed in what I presumed was relief that I wasn't having some random meltdown.

I turned and went back inside but left the door open in welcome for her to follow me, which, of course, she did.

"We've all been there, babe," she said as she took a seat beside me on the sofa and looked around at my empty home. One thing I wasn't was a slob, so luckily my house wasn't in a state, but I still hated her seeing me like this, even if it was nice to have a shoulder to cry on. "Whoever he is, he's a damn fool to have lost you. What you need is to focus on work. Drive yourself forward rather than back and don't let anyone or anything bring you down."

I had to stifle fresh tears. Janie had given me that same talk a few years before, and I nodded. She was right, like always.

"What do you have in mind?" I asked with a smile and was glad she hadn't asked for more details regarding the source of my heartbreak. One thing Janie had going for her was she wasn't one to pry. She was no doubt dying to know who had broken my heart, but she wouldn't come right out and say it. If I offered up the details, she wouldn't refuse to hear the ins and outs, don't get me wrong, but she was a kind enough soul to see I was hurting and she wanted to help take my mind off the situation at hand.

"Well, if you'd just answered your goddam phone!" she teased before handing me her tablet. Open on it was a set of photographs that took my breath away. It was all I could do not to start crying again, but I forced the tears away. I focused on rebuilding my walls rather than let them come crashing down again.

The pictures were the promo shots Tommy, and I had taken together the few days previously. They were incredible. More than that, they were the perfect portrayal of heat and tension between two people.

George and Penny.

Tommy and Piper.

Two actors and their chemistry caught on camera for all to see. God, he was beautiful. I felt a pang of yearning hit me for the first time since I'd come flying through that patio door from the deck of the cabin. I didn't want to feel those things for him. To want him. And yet there I was, staring at his photograph like a lovesick teenager...

"These are amazing," I eventually whispered as I handed the device back to Janie.

"No shit," she replied with a wide smile. "They're going public during your interview with Tommy and Scarlet on the *Nightly Show* this weekend."

I wanted to feel excited or nervous about being live on television in front of millions of viewers, when instead I was still numb. I was desperate to care that the movie was getting some decent exposure and so too would I. To hope people would be excited to see it. I wanted to care about anything other than missing him, but all I could think of was that horrible yet remarkable man and how I wished he hadn't ruined things.

"Let's celebrate," I told Janie as I jumped up off the sofa and grabbed her hand. "I feel like going to a crazily expensive and exclusive club and dancing to music by bands I can't even pronounce the names of while I get shitfaced. What do you say?"

"Well... if one of my jobs as your ever-loyal manager isn't to keep you out of trouble on drunken nights out, I don't know what is," she replied with a grin, but I wasn't buying it. She wasn't just my manager, but my friend, too. I had known that for a long time and I also knew they were very hard to come by nowadays. I was going to make sure she knew I appreciated the hell out of her for turning up at my house and forcing me out of my funk and was going to start by taking her out and endeavoring to have the night of our lives.

Tommy's Girl: parts one and two

TWENTY-TWO

Tommy

When had I last slept? I wasn't sure. But sleep was overrated and unnecessary, anyway. Especially when I had an obsession that'd seemed to override every other need.

I'd been sneaking around for days and was glad I'd been keeping abreast of her movements when I saw Piper and her friend walk out of her house, both dressed up like whores. I followed them and pulled my truck to a stop while I watched the pair climb out of the limo they'd hired and head straight toward the doorman at one of LA's most prestigious nightclubs. The guy took one look at her and plucked that rope he was the king of to let her pass, much to the distaste of some of the people queuing to get in. But she deserved that kind of treatment. Piper had earned it. This town knew her name and showed her some respect, and all while I was utterly consumed by her. That damn woman had wormed her way inside my skin and then ripped her way back out again without a care for the carnage she'd left behind. I'd seen her tears and backed off, but it'd been more than that. Piper had broken me. I had puked my guts up in the bushes the minute she'd gone. I'd felt repulsed by the mere suggestion of her, let alone the sight of her, and had been glad when my truck had torn down the long drive and out of sight.

I'd then gone back to the cabin and taken a chainsaw to that deck. The hot tub was now in pieces, and the wooden boards carved up and thrown down onto the mountainside below. But I had still felt the same. Nothing had made me feel better. Not drinking myself into a stupor or watching violent pornography and even snuff films while jerking off so hard, I gave myself friction burns. The only thing that'd helped was watching *her*.

Sneaking glimpses from the shadows after I'd let myself in with my secret key while she'd slept.

Spying on her from the garden when she passed the cracks in her curtains during the day.

My poor Piper had looked like shit, and rightly so. I would've bet I looked like shit, too.

I toyed with the idea of going inside the club so I could watch her but decided against it. Someone was bound to recognize me or tip off the paparazzi, and I didn't want her to find out about me being so hot on her tail. Following her around like some lovesick puppy.

That wasn't what I was doing it for, though. I was doing it because Piper was mine. She belonged to me and had tried to get away, but I wasn't going to allow it. Didn't she know by now that she'd never escape me?

She deserved to be punished, and I wanted to find the best way to do it. But first, I'd known I had to do the reconnaissance work. To figure out her next steps by knowing Piper inside and out. Not only that but also by making her do what I wanted. By manipulating her. Controlling every aspect of her life, so she had no one but me. And then I would be there with open arms, ready and raring to pick up the pieces.

I would've been content to sit and wait for her out the front of the club, but then I noticed a group of guys being let inside ahead of the queue by the burly bouncer. I recognized the one at the head of them right away and felt my lips curl back from my teeth in a snarl.

Bradley Fucking Thomas.

I knew all about his history with Piper and how she'd been the one to put a stop to their liaisons rather than him. He was still interested. Of course he was, and my mind began to race with scenarios in which they rekindled that flame beneath the strobe lights of the club.

She was in there and still hated me and seeing Bradley might just make her want to do something to hurt me. Something I would make it my mission to make her regret. She belonged to me, and it didn't matter that she'd run away. I was happy to have to remind her of it sooner than later.

I drove back towards home and dialed up a few of my buddies on the way. They were more than happy to come and meet me for a night out at the club, and I had to smile to myself as I got dressed. I pulled on a tight shirt that practically creaked when I flexed my biceps and a pair of pants I knew I looked hot in. Two could play this game of cat and mouse, and I knew I would be the winner. I always was.

After looking at my reflection in the mirror for a few seconds, I decided I was good to go. Ready for Piper to fall at my feet and beg for forgiveness. More than ready for the paparazzi and the screaming fans to come and gawk in awe of me. For them to clamber over themselves to have a mere glimpse of me. The one and only Tommy Darke.

I didn't mean to be bigheaded, but I knew I'd get plenty of attention once I got to the club, and not just because of my epic stardom. I mean, I looked great. Who wouldn't want to come and fawn all over me? Gone was the scrawny young man I'd once been, and in his place was a toned and sculpted Adonis—if I did say so myself. I'd worked hard to develop the body I now had, and it hadn't come easy. The same was easily said for my good looks I'd had to endure a lot to attain. A secret nose job and an operation to bring forward what was once a weak jaw had left me with perfectly asymmetrical features, which was apparently what almost all women found attractive in a lover and had certainly gotten me my share of tail. The years of having fixed braces had then fixed my crooked teeth and of course there were the hours I spent at the barbers having my hair trimmed to perfection along with my designer stubble to thank for the rest.

Yep, I was a Hollywood boy through and through. I was one of them now. I did the work and was vain enough to dedicate every waking moment I had to my biggest asset—me. I had been accepted into the fold and I knew I could never leave. No part of me even wanted to.

I closed my eyes and imagined Piper. What was she doing? Probably drinking too much and dancing with that friend of hers I'd seen her go in with. Maybe they were talking about boys, and Piper was telling her about me. About how she loved it when I'd stalked her and had sneaked into her home to fuck her.

Damn, now I was rocking a huge hard on, just imagining those cheeks of hers flushing while she told her friend about our exploits. I grabbed my cell and pulled up one of my new favorite porn websites. One that catered to the ever so darker tastes. Within seconds I'd found the recording I was after, and I watched as the girl on the screen was tied up and humiliated by the man fucking her raw.

I was going to re-create this scene with Piper as her punishment for running away from me at the cabin. I unzipped my fly, gripped my cock, and began grinding into my hand. It was no time at all before I'd come into the tissue I'd plucked from the nearby box, and I let out a deep sigh.

Piper wasn't going to know what hit her when I got my ruthless hands on her again.

I got back to the club and found my friends waiting for me in the queue. The look on their faces told me they'd tried their luck with the doorman and had been told to get in line like everyone else. They were basically nobodies, so I couldn't understand why they'd even tried without me, but I hid my disdain. They were my cover, and I wanted to keep them sweet. But still, I didn't pluck them from the line. Instead, I just lifted my finger, telling them to wait. I'd handle it.

The doorman, Tony, and I went way back. He clapped me on the shoulder and grinned from ear to ear when I greeted him, as if he was surprised I'd remembered his name. We had a little bit of back and forth before I made it clear I wanted inside. The girls waiting nearby were calling my name, begging me to take them in with me, and while I smiled and told them they looked lovely, I didn't offer any of them a place at my side. They were starstruck whores, and I wasn't buying. Not tonight.

"Have you met my buddy Steve?" I asked Tony, who shook his head. I stepped back and hollered down the queue of people, and right on cue, my three buddies jumped out of the line and came toward us. "He's just started work on a remake of that old western movie you love…"

That was all Tony needed to hear. He ushered me and the other two guys inside and promised to send Steve in after he'd gotten the scoop on the movie he told me he'd grown up watching as a kid. I didn't mind ditching Steve if it got us inside quicker. I could've gone in alone, but I hated going in alone, so the two guys I considered more acquaintances than friends would do for when I made my entrance.

I walked in first and was greeted by a set of doors I knew all too well. This club had been a favorite of mine before I'd delved deeper into the craft of method acting. Before, I would've been there every week, but now my work took precedence. I immersed myself in whatever my upcoming role dictated, but not tonight. Tonight, I was just Tommy. Out on the town like old times.

The doors opened, and I was hit by a wall of sound and pure bass. There were strobe lights and lasers that lit the place up, and I soaked up the energy as we joined the sea of writhing bodies.

It thankfully didn't take long for me to lose the two hangers-on. One look at the talent propping up the bar and they'd sidled away ready to try out their best pick-up lines, and while I'd promised to join them after saying hello to a few people, I had no intention of finding my way back to them. They'd served their purpose.

I spotted Bradley right away and made a beeline for him. So far, it appeared Piper was nowhere to be found, but at least she wasn't hanging off him. So, for the time being, I was happy.

"Hey, Tommy," Bradley greeted me and I had to admit, he seemed more pleased to see me than I would've thought. It wasn't like we'd struck up a friendship while on set or anything.

I took a seat beside him and forced myself to smile.

"Hey," I replied coolly. "How's it goin'?"

"Good. Listen…" Brad said, suddenly looking sheepish. I frowned at him, wondering what he might be about to say. He stayed silent, so I ordered a round of shots from the barmaid and did nothing more than watch him patiently. Enjoying watching him squirm. "Well, I guess I usually make more of an effort to get to know the people I'm working with so wanted to apologize for not inviting you out for a beer or anything after filming. I didn't feel like I was working with the real you, if you know what I mean?"

The barmaid returned with our drinks and I downed one. My first of the night. It burned that sweet, sweet heat in the back of my throat, and I immediately took another. I watched Brad, feeling nothing but contempt for him.

Why would he think I'd want to go and have a beer with him? We weren't friends and would never be. And he was wrong about one thing. He hadn't been working with me. He'd been working *for* me. Brad was my underling. My supporting actor. Nothing more.

"Say no more," I told him as I reached for another shot. "And don't feel bad, man. I'm here with my friends, I just wanted to come and say hi. You're right, it's not the same working with me on a movie because I'm not the same guy when I'm on set. I was George, and he hated everyone." Brad laughed it off and shook his head, as if he couldn't even begin to fathom what I was getting at.

I wanted to throttle him. To punch that grin off his smug face. I opened my mouth, ready to tell him to get back in his fucking box, but then stopped myself just in time. It wasn't me thinking that. It was George.

I was about to shut up and run. To avoid my inner mobster, who seemed intent on making his comeback. But instead, I pushed those urges down. George was gone. I'd detoxed from him thanks to Piper, so why the hell was he rearing his head now?

Brad didn't even seem to notice. He was peering over my shoulder, and I saw as his eyes flashed with lust.

"Working with that one wasn't a chore though, was it?" he asked, and I knew before I even turned to follow his line of sight who would be standing not far behind me.

Piper. My Piper.

She was resplendent. A ray of goddam sunshine in my black world. She hadn't even seen me yet and still, I was burning with desire. I had to see her. To talk to her. Touch her. To fuck her. Discipline her...

When she finally saw me, I saw Piper's jaw clench and her eye flash with rage. Yes. That was what I was hoping for. I was still under her skin, but she just didn't want to show it in front of Brad. *Make me punish you, Piper*, I thought. *Make me have to hurt you. Break you. Own you...*

She sauntered forward with a cunning smile curling at her lips. She had a game to play with me, I could tell, so I let her come. Let her believe she had some control, when in fact, she had none.

I was going to make sure she knew it without any shadow of doubt before sunrise the following day.

"Well, if it isn't two of the hottest men I've had the privilege of working with," she whispered when she'd reached us, her voice low and husky. I then watched in awe as Piper licked her lips and came closer.

I didn't care who was in this club or who might be watching. I reacted to her presence. I stood taller and more commanding, dominating her and everyone else in this room. Or at least that was how I felt. Like a god. Someone she should worship and adore. One she should obey.

TWENTY-THREE

Piper

I should've run the moment I'd spotted him. I knew that. But I couldn't walk away a second time. I was still upset, but I'd been a damn wreck without him and knew he'd been right all along. I was his now. No matter the fight, I was still willing to put up to try and resist it.

Tommy was winning with every step I made in his and Brad's direction, and yet I could do nothing but go to him. He was the magnet, and I was a useless clump of metal, powerless against his attractive forces pulling me in.

It'd felt like a hundred men had come onto me in that club and yet none of them had made me want them. Not even Brad, who was staring at me the same way he had just a few weeks before when he'd propositioned me for sex after filming our bathtub scene.

And then there was the guy standing next to him who looked like he wanted to swallow me whole. Darkness and light stood personified before me. Two men who were different in so many ways.

How could I want the bad man? How could I crave him when he'd hurt me, and I knew he'd do it again and again if I forgave him? But I was powerless against his allure.

Weak.

His whether I admitted it or not.

"What can I get you to drink?" Brad asked me, but in all honesty, I'd already had enough.

"I'm good, thanks," I replied, and I came to a stop between the two of them with a coy smile. Without another word, I then raised my hands and cupped Brad's face before planting a soft kiss on his top lip. I knew he enjoyed it, but in all honesty, I was using him for appearance's sake. If I'd have walked up and kissed Tommy, it would've looked obvious that something was going on between us. If I kissed them both, I could argue I'd done it simply in greeting.

So, I then turned to Tommy and did the same, having to lift onto my tiptoes to reach him. He wasn't impressed at first, I could tell, but he soon softened and by the time I pulled away, his eyes were no longer dark and scary. They were like the deepest of oceans on a hot day and I wanted to get lost in them.

I swooned and sighed. "You're here…" I whispered so Brad wouldn't hear us.

"You're mine, Piper. Where else would I be?" he answered, so matter-of-factly it made me smile.

I wanted to cry. Why couldn't he always be like this? Why did I have to endure his cruelty first before I could have his softness? Why couldn't he just love and adore me, and that be enough? Why, why, why?

Some of our friends then found us and together we all danced and drank and then danced some more. By the end of it, I was smiling and laughing again. Enjoying myself and vowing to leave the past behind me.

Tommy was having fun, too. I could see it in his eyes. Maybe he wanted to go back to the night beside his pool too? To start over again and not make the same mistakes.

I hoped so.

TWENTY-FOUR

Tommy

There was no going back. Not now I'd cracked it. I knew exactly how to manipulate Piper and wrap her around my little finger. It'd barely taken any effort at all, really.

All I had to do was offer her the kind of love every woman craved. The doting glances and soft smiles. The promise of affection and lovemaking to come. For me to appear weakened by her was an easy role to play, and she lapped it up, believing everything I was portraying.

Little did she know of the things I still had planned. No one could know the depths of my depravity. Only her, and by the time she learned the truth, it'd be too late. It already was in many respects.

It was late when we all left the club, but the party wasn't stopping, so we shared a cab and headed for Brad's penthouse apartment. He'd opted for a central location rather than in Beverly Hills like Piper and me, so it made sense to take the party back to his place, and I didn't mind.

Brad hadn't failed to notice I had my sights set on Piper, so luckily, he'd opted to pursue her friend instead and we both ditched our buddies so we could make this a different kind of party.

We arrived and Brad delighted in showing us around his place and I had to admit; it was classier than I'd expected. Decorated with warm, neutral colors and he had nothing too showy. I liked it and could imagine myself living somewhere similar.

We grabbed some drinks from his bar and the four of us shot the shit for a while before he finally plucked up the courage to make the moves on Janie. She didn't need asking twice and practically had to drag him to his room, leaving Piper and I alone at long last.

She seemed shy with me for some strange reason, which I found amusing. Rather than put her at ease, I left the awkward silence hanging in the air. Watched as she tried to come up with something to say or decide what to do. I was entranced. An overwhelming urge to punish and command her came over me. My sweet little lover and her pale blue eyes that drove me wild. Her blonde hair was begging to be pulled. Her ass spanked. Her mouth stuffed full of my cock as I gagged her on it.

I watched her as she found the perfect spot on the sofa and beckoned me over to join her, which I did. I even smiled sweetly and nestled in close.

"Do you forgive me?" I asked, turning on the charm.

"Yes," she replied with a gentle smile. "And do you forgive me for breaking your number-one rule?" As if I'd needed reminding about those goddamn tears of hers. My blood boiled at the sheer remembrance.

"Always," I lied. She wasn't forgiven. Not yet. Not until I had forced her to understand that there would always be consequences for her actions. That she wasn't free to choose, only to be led.

"Maybe we can move forward and use what happened at the cabin as a lesson never to push each other so far again?" she replied hopefully. I hummed in feigned agreement, not really caring about anything other than getting what I'd come for.

"Take off your clothes," I demanded, having had enough of the talk. To my surprise, Piper did it without argument. When she was good and naked, I ran my hands over her perfect breasts and supple skin. "Good, now open your legs." She complied again, so I let my hand float lower down her body, where I found her more than ready for me. I gave her a little strum, but only for a few seconds. It wasn't time for her to receive pleasure. Not until the punishment was over and my torturous side had been locked back in his box.

I pulled my hand away and stood over her, unbuttoning my pants before releasing my dick. She stared at it longingly and I responded by slapping her directly across the face with it, like I'd often seen happen in the porn I frequented. My cock was rock hard and gave the most wonderful spanking sound as it made contact. Plus, I was sure it had to have hurt her cheek. Piper shot up in shock and opened her mouth as if to shout at me, which was when I shoved my dick inside and thrust it to the back of her throat before she could even utter a sound. The look in her eyes told me she was raging, but I loved it. Couldn't she see that it only made me worse when she gave me the reaction I'd hoped for? Didn't she know how perfect her hatred was in these moments?

As I then started fucking her mouth, I gripped her by the hair at the back of her neck and shoved her down onto me. Piper gagged and writhed, trying to fight me, and her resistance only made me thrust harder.

When I neared my release, I reduced speed and waited for the creeping sensation in my balls that told me it was time. Right before I shot my load down the back of her throat, I withdrew and replaced her mouth with my hand. It was barely two seconds before I was spurting my cum all over that pretty little face of hers. Piper was too busy gasping for breath and suppressing her gags to shield herself from me, and by the time I was done, my jizz was dripping from her face and hair in clumps of glorious white goop.

"Tommy…" she breathed but said nothing more. Piper knew not to test me.

"Don't move and don't speak to me, whore," I commanded as I stepped back, still admiring my handiwork. My art.

Another idea then sprang to mind, and I reached for my cell phone to snap a photograph and capture this moment forever. The moment for Piper was nothing. Used and defiled, she was just another whore. But it wasn't enough. I needed to humiliate her even more, so I looked around for inspiration and quickly found it.

I scribbled on a notepad Brad had on the desk across the room and then handed the sheet to Piper so she could hold it up for my camera. I half expected her to object, but I think she knew what would happen if she did. More punishments. More humiliation. Better to get it over with.

Click! The phone in my hand sounded, and I peered down at the picture with a smile. You'd hardly be able to recognize her. Piper looked disheveled, her lips swollen and her eyes red from where she'd screwed them up so tightly as I'd pounded into her mouth. She was still dripping with my cum like some sort of bukkake situation had just taken place, and in her hands was my scrawled note. *Please forgive me, Tommy. I'll never run away again.*

I snatched the note back off her and ripped it to shreds before tossing it in the trash, and then I handed her a wet wipe and gave her the okay to get cleaned up. Piper looked so sweet and innocent as she removed all remnants of the 'whore' I'd just defiled. Her makeup came off with the rest and I felt myself calming as I watched.

Relaxing.

Forgiving.

The switch flipped itself, and by the time she was done, I was on my knees before her, ready to show Piper just how much I'd missed her.

TWENTY-FIVE

Piper

"Tommy..." I whimpered, but he shushed me and shuffled closer on his knees. I didn't know what to think or how to feel. I'd spent the last few days believing we were over, only to have ended up with him at that club and now this? I realized I wasn't even remotely over him. In fact, I'd let him use me in a way no man had ever done before. Part of me felt violated. As if he'd taken something I wasn't ready to give, but then the other part of me was so glad I'd been forgiven I didn't care if I had to perform the same act over and over again for him.

But surely, he needed to be forgiven too? Why wasn't he saying sorry and making it up to me? And most importantly, why wasn't I demanding that he did so right away?

I knew why. Against all my instincts, I was letting Tommy be in charge. He called the shots. The boss didn't concern himself with the needs of his minions, or so I thought. He'd probably never apologize, and I knew I had to accept it.

"Let me take care of you now, Piper. I want to taste you," he said, his voice pulling me from my dark reverie. He then wrenched open my legs and pulled me toward him so my hips fell from the edge of the couch, my pussy completely on show for him. I tried to scoot back, but he held me tighter, his fingers digging into the skin on my thighs while he shook his head.

"No," I groaned as he thrust two fingers inside of me, and I far from meant it. God, it felt so good to be touched. It felt like it'd been more than just a few days, and I clenched around his fingers as he drove them in and out. Tommy responded by curling them forward, and I cried out as his fingertips hit my g-spot. "No, stop..." I moaned again but gave so little of a fight I knew it was clear I didn't mean it. Tommy refused, anyway. He latched onto my clit with his mouth and sucked hard, drawing it between his lips and then swirling around with his tongue. I bucked and arched my back, the sensation of his mouth on my core and his fingers still working their magic in that sweet spot deep within me making me crazy. He was relentless. There was no stopping or letting me go. No rest for the wicked, or so I thought. I cried out for him to stop, worried he might hurt me, but he refused me time and again, no matter when I begged. And then he fucked me like his life depended on it.

I woke up the next morning in a tangle of limbs sprawled across Brad's sofa. Tommy had me pinned to him, cradling me like his favorite stuffed animal, and the thought made me laugh. As if that man had ever had a stuffed toy in his life.

My breath against him made Tommy stir, and I watched as he slowly came around as well. He looked so gentle in the morning light. Like the kindest man on earth, and while I of course knew he could be kind, he could also be so dreadfully cruel. I had to wonder if I really could love both of those sides to him. Whether I could be okay with the punishment and cruelty because I craved the love and tenderness I knew would come my way once I'd appeased his dark side. And would one side always be able to make up for the other? Maybe I'd never know.

"Stop frowning, otherwise you're gonna need Botox," Tommy teased as he opened his eyes, and I immediately relaxed my face. I guessed I must've been frowning, so made sure to regard my lover with nothing but the reverence he deserved. I didn't want to upset or anger him after all. The punishment from the night before had been brutal and gross, but also hot and dirty, all at the same time. I didn't quite want a repeat of it just yet but couldn't deny I hadn't hated being mouth-fucked, even if I could still feel the bruises in the back of my throat thanks to his forceful thrusts.

"Morning, you two," Brad's chirpy voice plucked us from our morning-after reverie, making me jump. I grabbed the throw we'd been hiding under and wrapped it around myself in my haste to get covered up, my cheeks burning with embarrassment.

It didn't matter that Brad had seen me naked plenty of times. It wasn't appropriate now that we were no longer fucking each other. In contrast to my awkward reaction, Tommy didn't bat an eye as he stood and stretched. He was still showing his body off in all its naked glory as Janie came and joined us from the bedroom she'd shared with Bradley the night before.

"Holy crap, what a sight!" she cried, nodding approvingly rather than shy away and I had to laugh. Tommy simply offered her a wink and then grabbed his boxers and pants, which he slid on. I made a quick attempt of cleaning up the debris from our night of passion and then made a beeline for the bathroom so I could get washed up and dressed, as well as hide my shame for a few minutes before properly facing them.

When I returned, Brad had coffees on the go and Tommy was chatting away with Janie, telling her all about how he was indeed the mysterious guy who had broken my heart. I wanted to kill him. So much for us remaining a secret.

"You sure did a number on her, Tommy. What happened?" I heard Janie ask, and I smiled at her. She really did have my back.

"A misunderstanding. But when I saw Piper last night, I knew I had to make things up with her. It couldn't be the end," he replied, and then turned to offer me a kiss as I reached them.

"You made it up to me, hey?" I asked him in a whisper, and absolutely adored the dark smile he offered me in return. We both knew exactly who had done the apologizing, and it certainly wasn't him. I doubted it ever would be.

Maybe he truly was the ultimate dominant, and I just hadn't realized it before? I was becoming more and more subservient to his every whim without him having to ask or demand it of me. I followed orders and took pleasure in pleasing him. I loved seeing his smile and wanted more of his affection and attention. I wanted to be a good girl and receive the rewards only he could give me. Shit, maybe I was submitting to him.

"I'm happy for you guys," Brad said, as he put two coffees down in front of us and I thanked him. It was good to know there were no hard feelings. "But I'm guessing it needs to be kept a secret until the movie promo is done, right?"

I looked to Tommy for him to answer. In all honesty, I couldn't see the harm in coming clean about our relationship but wanted him to make the decision for the both of us. He was the star of the film, and I wasn't sure what angle he'd wanted to take during the PR time in the buildup to its release.

"Let's keep the news solely about the new film for now. We can come out about us when the time is right," he said, and I nodded. It made sense for us to be talking about the movie and not about ourselves in the upcoming interviews. The talkshow hosts wouldn't be able to help themselves, but we weren't going to be there to discuss our private lives.

"Speaking of which," Janie interjected, "are you guys both ready?"

"Yeah, I don't have many lined up until we hit the South American schedule," Brad answered first. "I've been asked to go down the angle of adding intrigue to the plot. Reveal just a little about how intense the story is and how we tied it to the real goings on between George Ward and his many foolish minions."

I saw something flash across Tommy's face when Brad talked about George and had to wonder what it was. Perhaps anger? If so, I couldn't fathom why. He'd told me himself how George was gone. Safely tucked away just like the other characters he had played over the years, so wasn't sure why Tommy would be angered by Brad talking about him with a hint of distaste in this tone. They weren't really the mobster and his henchman. The pair of them were simply two actors who I had assumed to be friends, but perhaps I was wrong?

Thankfully Janie and Brad had been chatting amongst themselves about what she'd been informed the producers wanted from me during the interviews. They were engrossed in their conversation, while I watched as a shudder swept over Tommy. And then, quick as a flash, he was back to his usual self again. Well, the persona he adopted for everyone except me, or so it seemed. His happy-go-lucky way and cocky grin were back, but when he turned to me, I saw the iciness in his stare. The sheer and total detachment.

"I have to go," he said. "I'll call you."

"Okay," I replied, offering him a smile I knew didn't reach my eyes. I couldn't tell what was going on with him, but I knew something was up. I just had to hope he might one day open up to me and reveal all. Even if it meant opening that Pandora's box inside of him that kept his demons at bay.

He left, and I sat watching Bradley and Janie talk for a while, offering a bit to the conversation here and there, but I was lost in my own thoughts again. Worrying about whether Tommy was okay and whether I should go and see him.

"I think it's time we went home too," Janie eventually told Brad, and while I was glad, I could tell he was a little disappointed to be saying goodbye. Maybe they'd had more fun together than I'd realized? Maybe even more than just a one-night stand? I knew Janie would tell me all about it when we got out of there, so I gathered up my things, checked I looked presentable enough, and then went out in the hall to call a town car, having chosen one I'd used numerous times before and trusted not to tip off the paparazzi.

When we got back to my place, I was barely in the door before Janie began spilling the beans. "Listen, I know you two used to hook up and, of course, that's fine by me, but I need to know something. You're okay with me sleeping with him, aren't you?"

"Of course!" I cried. I hadn't cared at all, if I was honest. If anything, it was nice to see how neither she nor Brad had been surprised by me and Tommy hooking up. It made me hope for the same reaction from the masses if and when we decided to go public with our relationship. "Tommy and I are really becoming something, so the stuff with Brad is ancient history. God, I remember thinking it was just gonna be a bit of fun between me and him. It scares me but at the same time I can't get enough."

"Yeah. I was going to ask you about him," she replied, her face turning serious. "I heard you two last night. Some of the things you were saying to each other had me a little concerned…"

I felt a wave of dread wash over me. What had we been saying? Nothing I could remember that would be too incriminating, surely?

"Like what?" I croaked.

"You were telling him no, but he didn't stop…"

Relief flooded my system. I let out a soft sigh and leaned closer to her, wanting Janie to understand and believe me when I told her my reply.

"It's just one of those things I like to do, you know, when in the throes of passion? He knows I don't mean it so keeps going." I had to admit, she did look relieved, and I was glad. The last thing I needed was for my closest friend to think I was getting into something dangerous or was out of my depth with Tommy. Well, maybe I was, but she didn't need to know that.

"Brad said the same when I asked him if I should come out and check on you. He said you used to do it with him too—"

"The less said about that, the better I think," I interjected, and Janie laughed.

"Yeah," she agreed, "but just as long as you're okay now and aren't in any trouble?"

"I'm great and couldn't be further from trouble, trust me." I wasn't sure Janie believed me, but then again, I couldn't be all that sure I believed myself.

TWENTY-SIX

Tommy

I slept for a while when I got home, and my dreams were full of her. They were dark dreams. Full of lustful drives and me succumbing to the violent urges I fought every day in my waking moments. I eventually woke with a raging hard-on that was clearly going nowhere, so I turned to my new favorite website. After logging into the members' only area, I sifted through the new recordings and found the perfect accompaniment to my afternoon jerk-off session.

My laptop screen went dark for a second before the file opened, with the image of a young woman being tied to a bed by her ankles and wrists. She was crying real tears. No one could fake those, so I turned my face away and waited until her captor covered her eyes with a black mask. Perfect.

"Perfect," he said, mirroring my thoughts, and I smiled. I knew exactly what I was going to invest in next. Behind a mask Piper could cry all she wanted, and I'd could ignore her. I'd be able to take things further than before and my one debilitating issue wouldn't necessarily be so much of a problem thanks to a mask that could hide it all away.

The punisher on the screen then whipped and beat the girl before my eyes. She wasn't one of those masochists who took pleasure in the pain, but evidently a real and everyday person who cried and pleaded for it to stop. But it didn't matter. He wouldn't stop, no matter what she did, and I loved it. I caressed my cock in one hand and began stroking up and down, tightening my grip every time she screamed. It was heaven.

When the man on the screen parted her thighs and stroked the woman's pussy, she tried to fight him off. But it was no use. He was inside of her a second later, pummeling hard. When he was done, he withdrew and came all over her stomach and then was right back inside of her, ready for more. After he'd come a second time, he then started beating her again, and I lost my damn mind watching her flinch and hearing cry out.

Pleasure and torture were working side-by-side rather than exclusive to one another. The concept of not just doing it once, but repeatedly in one sitting sent me over the edge. My eyes were closed, and I could envision

Piper at my mercy. The cries I could hear on screen were hers. The loud grunts of her tormentor mine. My hand was pumping hard on my cock and with a loud cry I then came into the tissue I'd had at the ready.

I knew what I had to do. But not yet. Piper was still getting over what I'd done at the cabin, so I decided I had to tread carefully. Bide my time.

I shut off the video and logged out of the website and deleted my browsing history for good measure before shutting down. As I lay back on my bed and stared up at the ceiling, all I could picture was Piper tied to that bed and me over her, punishment fucking to the sound of her screams.

I needed to get away from that fantasy rather than indulge it; I knew. Instead of jerking off again, I decided to go for a run. I went on my usual route and then doubled back on myself, detouring through Piper's neighborhood because I simply couldn't resist peeking at my darling girl. Perhaps I would find her in a compromising position worthy of severe punishment… A guy could dream, hey?

She was in her living room by the window doing her yoga routine in nothing but her underwear. Her body was curling and stretching in a stunning and obviously well-practiced set of moves, and I watched for a few glorious minutes. I couldn't go inside and take her, not in the mood I was in, so instead I crept away and hightailed it for home.

There, I found the front door ajar. I was sure I'd locked it when I'd left, but still went straight in. I wasn't afraid to confront an intruder and went inside to rather than head for the phone to call the security guards that myself and the other homeowners in our cul-de-sac paid handsomely to stop this very thing from happening.

I looked around the ground floor. Nothing looked out of place and there wasn't anything missing, so I went room to room in search of a clue as to who might've snuck into my home. As I rounded the top of the stairs to the first floor, I found my answer.

Soft humming was coming from the master bathroom. I could hear a bath running inside and saw steam slowly escaping from beneath the closed door. My intruder was taking a bath. How delightful.

With a wolfish grin, I crept closer, and knew who it was before I'd even laid eyes on her.

Regardless of the restraining order against her and the numerous times I had told her to leave me alone, my stalker had returned to me. Marina Del Rey had been obsessed with me for years and had become a joke to my friends and me. Someone I despised for being so weak and vulnerable when it came to her girlish whimsy. She was so desperate to please me and have me love her that she'd resorted to overly exaggerated declarations of love and adoration over the years.

I'd enjoyed the attention at first. Even the late-night messages on my cell when she'd begged one of the crewmembers on set for my number.

Then there were her numerous gifts and of course her being frontline in the crowd at all my red-carpet appearances. I'd thought she was harmless, but not when her adoration had turned to bothersome obsession.

The last time I saw Marina was when she'd broken into my home and tried to seduce me. I might've been desperate enough to fuck her. If only she hadn't crept into my bedroom in the dead of night and basically tried to rape me. After that, Marina was no longer considered just a harmless fanatic. She'd had to be stopped, and my efforts to remove her from my life had seemed to work. Until now.

I knew it couldn't be Piper in there, either. I was the one who stalked her and had crept into her home unannounced, not the other way around. Plus, I'd just been watching her so knew she was home working out and not in my bathroom getting ready to take a dip in my tub.

I turned the handle and stalked inside. Marina jumped right out of her skin and leapt to her feet. Her face was sour, as if she'd been expecting a fight, but as soon as she saw me smiling, she softened and beamed at me. I eyed her up and down. Marina was stark naked, and she liked having my eyes on her, I could tell. If only she knew how I detested the sight before me. Her tiny little tits were doing nothing to entice my flaccid cock, and neither was her scrawny waist and bare cunt. I was about to tell her to get the hell out of my house when she broke the silence.

"I couldn't stay away any longer, Tommy," she drawled. "The doctors tried to break me with their words and meds, but I couldn't listen or take them any longer. Not when I knew they were mistaken. My love for you isn't wrong, it's just different. Let me show you how much I love you. I'll do anything you want. Be whatever you need," Marina added.

She then fell to her knees before me, staring up into my eyes like a loyal, dutiful servant ready to do whatever her master commanded.

"Anything?" I enquired, my smile turning salacious.

"Anything..." she drawled, clearly aiming for seductive when, in fact, the sound had the opposite effect on me. However, there were some things she could assist me with.

A dozen ideas went through my mind. Perhaps I could tie her up and beat her? Re-enact any of the numerous violent porn movies I'd been watching of late? Piper would never have to know, and Marina could help me curb those desires welling within me that I didn't dare let loose on my main girl. I opened my mouth to speak and was about to command that she go to my bedroom and wait for me, but right at the last second, I changed my mind. If I fucked Marina, I knew I couldn't live with knowing I'd betrayed Piper. If I beat her and left her unsatisfied in the aftermath, Marina might go running to the gossip columns to sell her story and ruin me. My only option was to do as I had always done and send her away.

"Then leave and don't come back. If I find you in my house again, you won't like how I react." I stepped back and went to turn away, which was when I saw the flash of metal in the light and whipped back to face her. I'd expected a knife or something, but all she had in her grasp was a small shard of metal that looked like a piece from one of those crafting knives they used on set when creating elaborate effects in makeup.

"Please," Marina begged, holding the blade in the center of her wrist as though she might be about to slit it. "I need you, Tommy. If I can't have you, then I might as well be dead." Her hand hovered over the veins there, poised as though she might actually do it, and as I stood watching in shock, something inside of me exploded in intrigue.

I wanted her to do it. I wanted to watch. For the first time in all the years I'd known Marina, I felt desirous of her. Not of her body in a carnal way, like with Piper, but something else. Something entirely darker.

I reached out and put one hand under her wrist to hold the exposed arm steady, and the other on the trembling hand with the blade in it. Marina sighed in relief, like she thought I was going to take the blade away and change my mind about making her leave. Her foolish trust in me only made my dark heart beat faster.

Do it, a voice in my head demanded. *It'll look like a suicide.*

And so, I pushed the two together: the blade and her delicate forearm. She let out a cry as the metal pierced her skin and I felt her try to pull out of my grasp as if she was suddenly rethinking her promise to do anything I demanded, but it was no use. Her tiny body was nothing in comparison to mine and with no effort on my part at all, I yanked the blade up her inner forearm in one delectable and incredibly deep slice.

I then let go and with a shriek Marina threw the blade to the ground. We both stared at the cut for a second as her blood rose up into the groove and then began to pour out onto the floor. I watched in fascination as she processed what was happening and then cringed as she began to sob.

"If you can't have me, then you'd rather be dead, huh?" I reminded her, stepping away as she fell to her knees, looking paler by the second. "Then die," I whispered, watching her as my dark smile returned. "Die for me, Marina."

I thought she might try to save herself or run, but she didn't. Marina really was broken. Too broken to fight for her life any longer. She just stayed there on the ground, bleeding out, and breathed a deep sigh.

"Tell me you love me, Tommy. Tell me I'm beautiful," she whimpered, watching me through eyes that were growing steadily glassier.

"You're beautiful, Marina. Look at you." She followed my gaze down to the crimson pool forming around her and let out a dry laugh. "Thank you for giving me your life. I love you," I then said, and she smiled to herself.

Marina was still smiling when she slumped against the side of the bath and stopped breathing. I didn't need to check her pulse to know she'd gone. She was pale and floppy, unmoving, and all I wanted to do was watch her lifeless body sit there by my tub. I was in awe. Mesmerized by what'd just happened. Turned on by it.

I replayed the final moments of Marina's life in my mind. I'd done it. I'd made the cut that'd killed her, willing or not. I was a murderer.

And then it suddenly hit me. I was a murderer!

I ran to the toilet and threw up into it. What had I done? How could I have gone through with such a heinous act? I deserved to go to jail for what I'd made her do and knew I owed it to Marina to call the cops and admit to what I'd done.

But then again, maybe not. I wasn't that righteous. She'd wanted this, after all. I hadn't taken the life of an innocent. Why should I pay for what she herself had done?

After I'd finished puking my guts up, I cleaned my face and went out into the hall where I stood and stared out the window at the top of the stairs. It was dark out and I could see my reflection in it. I looked a wreck.

This is good, I thought. *Use it…*

I grabbed my cell from the bedroom and dialed up Miles. He answered after the first ring.

"Hey," he said.

"Hey, man. I need your help. Something's happened," I replied before I then proceeded to tell Miles how I'd come home from my run and found Marina dead in my bathroom. Yes, I was a murderer, but I certainly wasn't going to come clean. If there was a high road, I certainly didn't intend on taking it.

The cops arrived after Miles had come to inspect the scene for himself. He seemed convinced I was telling the truth and so had called the police, as well as my lawyer, just in case.

The first responders also came along, but there was nothing any of them could do other than wait for the coroner to arrive and do their thing. I gave my statement and acted shocked and horrified by what had happened, which was further proven when the forensics team found my vomit in the toilet.

"I couldn't believe what I was seeing at first, but when it finally sunk in, I was sick to my stomach. I'm sorry," I told the deputy taking down my story, but he waved me away.

"It's okay, a lot of people react the same way to finding a dead body. It's nothing you ever get used to," he said, and I nodded.

The police stayed for hours and by the time they left, I was exhausted. I showered in my en-suite and climbed into bed but couldn't sleep. Marina's death kept replaying in my head, but that wasn't what was keeping me awake. It was the questions. What if I'd missed something? What if they didn't believe my story and looked into the case a little deeper? Would they figure me out? Would I cave and tell them the truth? Would I end up spending my life in prison or eventually find myself on death row?

With a curse, I turned onto my side and grabbed my cell. There was a barrage of messages on there thanks to the police presence having tipped off the press so I'd put it on silent hours previously, but the most recent text was from the one person I knew could calm me and I was glad to hear from her.

Piper:
I can't stop thinking of you. Are you okay?

I hit the call button and put it to my ear, rather than text her back.

"Hey," her voice came through the speaker, and she sounded husky, like she'd been asleep.

"Where are you?" I asked, turning onto my back and staring at the ceiling.

"In bed, but I haven't been able to sleep. I keep thinking about what happened and whether you're okay."

"I'm fine," I lied. "She was someone who was unhinged and had broken into my home. I don't know why she did what she did, but I just hope everything's cleared up soon."

"Me too. When will I get to see you again?" she asked, and I heard her voice falter. Was she worried? Did she miss me? God, I hoped so. In fact, I damn right expected her to.

"Close your eyes and touch yourself, beautiful girl. I'm there with you. Can you feel me?"

I heard Piper let out a soft moan and knew she was doing exactly as I'd asked when she started panting and groaning. "Yes, that's it." I grabbed my cock and started to move with her. In my mind's eye, I could envision Piper lying strewn over her bed, rubbing her delicious cunt. I imagined myself standing over her to watch as she strummed on her clit, and when she began crying out in orgasm, I released as well.

"Tommy," she then whimpered, still panting. "Are you still there?"

"Yeah, I'm here," I replied as I cleaned myself up. I was about to tell her goodnight, but instead a moment of need washed over me and I asked her for something I hadn't needed or asked anyone for in a long time. I asked her to tell me it was all going to be okay.

"You're going to be fine, Tommy," she said. "That poor girl wasn't right in the head, and she did something foolish because of it. You're not to blame."

If only she knew the truth. I was to blame. I had murdered Marina and while I strangely felt no remorse anymore, I was still terrified I might get caught. No part of me was ready for prison or to lose the life I had made for myself.

"You're right," I eventually whispered back. "Thank you." I then said goodnight and ended the call before tossing my cell onto the bedside table. *So, Marina*, I thought. *We're going to keep this our little secret.*

I fell asleep quickly after that, my resolve to focus on self-preservation above all things helping to stop the voices screaming in my head.

TWENTY-SEVEN

Piper

Tommy ended up pretty much unreachable for days following Marina's suicide, and I hated I couldn't be with him. We talked on the phone plenty, but I could never quite figure out whether I thought he was actually okay or if he was just saying so. He seemed to not really care all that much about what Marina had done, and I couldn't understand why. I knew he wasn't heartless and yet every time I asked how he was dealing with things, he just batted my concern away like he truly didn't care enough to want to talk about what'd happened. I eventually figured it was all part of his coping mechanism and decided to stop asking altogether.

I spent the time reading through the script for the new movie I'd decided to audition for and used the alone time to practice my lines. Our promo dates were also rapidly approaching and while things had been rejigged a little to accommodate Tommy's crazy schedule, I was more than ready to get going with promoting *Wayward*. I was excited to see the end product too, and when I got the call from Janie to say the screener had arrived, I asked her to bring it right over. She was at my house less than thirty minutes later and we immediately sat down to watch the DVD she'd had delivered by courier just an hour or so before.

The movie began, and I watched as 'George' dominated the scenes with his intimidating way. That truly wasn't Tommy, and I understood at last just how different he became when playing his roles. There were snippets of the real him here and there, though. Looks and mannerisms that I'd come to know and love in him, but mostly he had been transformed. George Ward through and through. I watched in intrigue as my own scenes with Brad then came on screen and couldn't say I hated any of them. The bath scene had been shot well, and I didn't feel I was too exposed or the scene itself indecent. In fact, it was pretty damn hot, and I felt like it accurately portrayed the love Brad and I had tried to demonstrate effectively between the two characters.

And then came my sex scene with George. I had a feeling viewers were either going to love it or hate it based on their stances on infidelity and such, but overall, I felt like it was probably the hottest thing I had ever seen. By the end of it I was blushing, and I turned to find Janie looking a little flush herself. In all honesty, Tommy had some sex scenes with Scarlet that were way hotter than ours in a visual perspective, but something about what we'd managed to portray on the screen seemed more intense to me. Like it had truly been a wondrous and intimate moment between two people rather than something scripted or planned. I loved it but was also worried it might be too strong. That it could end up denting my reputation rather than improve it.

I waited until the whole movie was over before looking to Janie for her reaction, but I couldn't deny I was desperately anxious to find out what she'd thought about it. I was pleased. *Wayward* was far grittier than anything I'd worked on before and the intense scenes were explosive and exciting, while the romantic elements had ranged from sexy and smooth to hot and dark.

"So… what do you think?" I eventually asked when I could bite my tongue no longer.

"What do I think?" Janie replied, her mouth hanging open in shock. "I think this is the movie that's gonna make you, Piper. This is an incredible take on an age-old story of the gangster and the girl that's been done time and again, but you guys made it into something truly incredible. I felt like I was a fly on the wall watching real life rather than a storyline based loosely on facts someone sat and wrote at a computer one day."

I breathed a huge sigh of relief and wrung my hands. God, I hoped she was right. I felt good in spite of my fear of ruining my image, but Janie was right. The movie was great. I'd taken a risk and a calculated one too, but I had to believe it was going to pay off. That it'd be worth it.

"I'm shaking," I told her, and she put an arm around me.

"That's because you want this, Piper. You deserve it and I can't wait to see what everyone else's reaction is of this amazing movie."

I couldn't speak. I didn't dare to hope that this film coming out might just be the pivotal moment in my career but couldn't help it. There were so many things I wanted for myself and in life in general, but I felt like maybe, just maybe, I was finally on the road to getting all those things.

TWENTY-EIGHT

Tommy

I tried not to watch it. Like with all my work, I didn't like to see myself on screen, but this time was different. I was getting to watch *her*. To see us in our perfect scene atop that kitchen counter and I found myself enjoying all the parts Piper was in no matter of how obvious it was that she was still nothing more than one of the supporting cast members. Don't get me wrong, I thought of her far differently after our time together to when I'd turned up on set that first day, and I was sure the viewing public was going to think of her differently after seeing this movie too.

But then something snapped inside of me as I watched her fuck Brad in that bathtub. I know she said nothing happened for real, but could I ever really be sure? It looked real enough, and I'd heard the chatter on set about how they'd discarded their modesty covers and been bumping uglies all day long. I knew how easy it would've been for him to slip inside and for Piper to take a real ride. It wasn't uncommon at all, and I knew plenty of actors who got off on knowing they'd done it for real in front of not only the crew and other cast members on filming day, but then again to countless viewers who would watch the movie later.

Was Brad one of those people? Had he bragged to others about how he'd fucked Piper on camera and elicited an apparent climax while I had only rubbed her to orgasm during our own?

I had to know, but also to let him know he couldn't get away with taking what was mine. She had already belonged to me when they'd shot that scene, and violent rage simmered within me for long after their scene had finished.

I watched the movie till the end, but my mind was elsewhere. I was thinking of Piper fondly, but also remembering Marina's death with disgust. And then another thought kept creeping in around the edges of that distaste. What would I do differently if I had the chance? Would I make her death quicker or slower? More or less gory and gruesome? At first, I wasn't sure, but then I started to imagine not just slashing her one wrist, but the other too. Maybe I'd wait and watch the blood some more. I closed my eyes and imagined myself holding her arms high so the blood streamed down her arms and body, coating her in a sort of dark and vivid ink while the rest of the color faded from her skin. I thought about that over and over, never caring for the life lost but of how she would've looked if I'd only stopped and properly taken it in. If I'd thought to savor the moment she had given me.

That was when it struck me.

I could just try again.

Do it a second time and use the lessons I'd learned from Marina's death to perfect the second. But who would I choose as my next nominee? Not a Marina lookalike. She didn't turn me on in the slightest, but maybe a small, blonde beauty with a face naturally innocent and wide blue eyes…

She'd do nicely.

Just like my Piper, I would take her in my arms and kiss her, but unlike with my girl, I wouldn't fuck this one. I would kill her. And when it was all over, I would let myself into Piper's home and fuck her instead, whether she wanted me to or not, because even though she wouldn't know it, I would've just killed for her.

I fell asleep after a night spent all up in my head. Between my dreams of deviant murder and watching snuff films on my new favorite website, I had to have jerked off twenty times, but I didn't regret a thing or feel ashamed of a single moment of it. In fact, part of me wanted to share the euphoria I was filled with.

I considered going to see Piper and telling her all about what I'd done and still wanted to do. How I wanted to kill in her name. In my fantasy, she would smile and tell me yes—do it. The only thing stopping me was that I didn't really know if she would understand. I couldn't know for sure and decided that instead of turning my hand to murder, I'd focus instead on punishing her for not only what I'd had to watch on that screen between her and Brad, but also for her not being ready to hear my innermost desires. She owed it to me to be ready, and yet there she still was, thinking I even gave a flying fuck about that scrawny bitch whose blood would always leave its mark on my home.

I rolled out of bed and into the shower. It was time for me to finally leave the house and face the cameras for the first time since Marina had died in my tub. The police had already been by to tell me the case was closed, so I knew there wouldn't—or shouldn't—be any suspicion of me, but I still knew the questions would come. Everyone would want to know the story, so when I was dressed and ready, I took a moment to call upon a voice from somewhere deep within me. One I had locked away with all the others, but who was being unleashed for the time being to help me remain convincing in my lies. I stood in front of the mirror and softened my stare while I let my brows relax. I then took a few deep breaths and then cleared my throat.

"Mental health is something we should all talk about," I said repeatedly, trying out different sounds until I found a tone of voice I was sure would sound sincere. "Suicide affects everyone close to the victim and I can't deny, it hasn't been easy saying goodbye to Marina. I only wish she'd let me help her."

When my lines were rehearsed to perfection, I offered my reflection a wicked grin and then sauntered away. I knew I had it figured out. In the fucking bag.

***

The three days that followed were nothing more than a constant stream of interviews with people from magazines and radio shows or small-time TV stations. I said the same lines over and over. Answered the same questions over and over. The only thing that kept me sane was knowing that Piper was close by. Sometimes she was in the same room as me for joint interviews between us two and Scarlet and we'd all banter and chat away about *Wayward* like old pals. Other times, she'd be in another room giving private interviews and I could hear her laughing or shrieking in delight at whatever weird and wonderful things those interviewing her could come up with.

I was asked relentlessly about Marina but did the same thing each time—delivered my practiced lines and used that soft and gentle tone of voice I was beginning to hate. The interviewers lapped it up every damn time. Fuckwits.

After the main elements of smaller PR were done, it was time for the big ones. The chat shows with billions of viewers, or the comedy shows where me and Scarlet parodied the movie via skits and piss-takes. Piper didn't attend those. The producers had specifically asked for the two leading actors and no one else and I hated that she wasn't with me as I travelled from studio to studio, and even across the country for appearances in the cities of New York, Philadelphia, and Boston.

Piper was there when it mattered, though. Scarlet had just had surgery for some made-up disease she apparently had and was hit and miss as to whether she was well enough to do the appearances. I couldn't give any less of a shit about Scarlet and made that clear to the only person I knew wouldn't care—Miles. I often wondered if he was like me. He certainly had that same edge to his humor I did and when we were alone, our jokes often became so depraved in nature that I was sure I could see a glimpse of his darkness. But more to the point, he could also see mine. And yet, neither of us pulled away from our friendship, which was all the confirmation either of us needed.

I immediately informed Piper of Scarlet's lack of commitment and she had the forethought to be the first to offer to tag along with us under the pretense of being there solely for the benefit of the movie's PR should Scarlet be too poorly to feature on whatever show we were lined up to do. It worked and before I knew it, she was travelling right along with us. Deep down, she was just as devious as me, and I loved her even more for it.

It was manic, though. Every night we were both too exhausted to play any of our usual games, but we always shared either her bed or mine in whatever hotel we'd been put up in. It was the first time I'd ever truly made love to a woman, and for twelve nights straight we did the same routine over and over again. I didn't feel the need to punish her anymore, only to give and take as much pleasure as I was able, and I could tell she liked having things back to some semblance of simplicity between us. I couldn't get enough and would've been inside her for hours every night if I could. I tried, but Piper wasn't as strong as I was. There were times when she couldn't keep up with me. When she told me no and I knew she meant it, but I still didn't stop. She would whimper as I pressed against her opening and I knew it was on the tip of her tongue to tell me not to go any further, but each and every time I dived right on in. Within seconds she was always wet for me and on board, and the darkness deep down inside of me loved forcing her to obey my desires.

I got her drunk again the first night of our European PR dates. We had the following morning off to allow for jetlag and she was struggling to adjust to the time change, so I suggested a few drinks to help take the edge off. That way she could try and get some sleep, regardless of what her body was telling her. Piper fell right into my trap. The concierge brought us up a bottle of champagne in an ice bucket and this time; I joined her for a few before saying I was switching to the whiskey from the small chiller our rooms all came with. I poured myself miniscule shots over water and ice while Piper was giggling and falling about drunk before she'd even finished the first bottle. I knew it was time to do as I'd done the last night like this. I had to force myself into her mind. Make her think solely of me and be willing to do whatever it took to protect what we had.

"You'll stand by me through anything, won't you?" I asked, as I pulled her into my arms and began undressing her. "Be my rock. Have my back…"

"What do you mean, baby?" she replied with a frown.

"Like, if I did a bad thing. Would you join the others in persecuting me, or would you stand by me?"

"I don't know!" she cried, and I let her go, watching as she refilled her glass and took a swig. "What would you do that was so bad?"

"Nothing," my voice was low and hoarse. I stepped closer to her, capturing Piper in my grasp and in my stare. "And that's precisely my point. I could never do anything wrong or bad. That's what I mean, Piper. I need you to always believe it. To be ready to tell others the same."

"You're not the bad guy anyway," she said, swaying on her feet.

My whole body went tense, and I felt a wave of ice cold shudders trickle up and down my spine. She wasn't understanding what I was getting at, and it irked me to no end. I charged toward her and saw Piper flinch. Damn, that made me hard.

"I thought you said I wasn't the bad guy?" I croaked as I plucked the champagne flute from her hand and placed it down.

"You're not," Piper implored me, but I was having none of it. It was time she learned to stop thinking for herself and think the way I did. The way I let her think.

She then let out a gasp as I tore the rest of her clothes away and lifted her up into my arms, linking her ankles around my back. I shoved Piper against the wall and covered her mouth with mine.

"No, I'm not the bad guy," I then groaned against her lips. "You need to remember that always. Never forget it or deny the facts, because I love you and never want to leave you. No matter what… But right now, you're being a bad girl and bad girls need to be punished."

Piper flinched again, and this time, I saw real fear in her eyes. She was finally learning about my punishments and how I meant business when it came to administering them. But I wanted more. I needed for her to forget everything other than me. For her to think the same thoughts as I did. Have the same opinions as me and never deviate from whatever plan I dictated.

"What are you going to do?" she whimpered.

"I'm going to humiliate you somehow," I replied, after thinking on it for a second or two. I wasn't sure how or when, but I was going to make sure she understood just what it meant to follow not only my rules, but my unwritten and sometimes unspoken law to do as I said and please me without fail. Was this love? I couldn't know, but I did know I had to control her and exert that control over her any time I feasibly could.

"Why?" she replied timidly, and I shook my head.

"You know why." She peered up at me with doe eyes through her long blonde lashes and shook her head. Perhaps she wasn't quite there yet after all, which only made me surer that she needed her punishment. "Because you made me love you, dammit. You made me care, and that makes me weak. And I cannot be weak." I fixed Piper with a dark stare and shoved myself harder against her, taking her breath away—literally.

I kissed and stroked at her naked body for a while but could wait no longer and simply had to have her. Piper let me take her anyway I wanted. I threw her around that hotel room like a ragdoll and she loved every minute of it. My girl might've been a little unsure of whether she could handle my darkness, but she was certainly starting to embrace her own, and I loved her even more for it.

TWENTY-NINE

Piper

We woke late after our first night in London, but I felt reasonably rested despite the muscles in my legs and arms screaming as I stretched them. Tommy and I had been working out so hard between the sheets lately that I'd neglected my usual yoga routine, and in spite of the slight hangover churning my stomach, I decided to get up and do my sun salutation.

In nothing but my underwear, I climbed out of bed and began moving through the sequence I'd done hundreds of times since finding my favorite method of working out. It felt good, even when the top of my thighs smarted a little thanks to being sore.

I did the routine over and over and got steadily quicker, and by the time I was done, a light sheen of sweat covered me from head to toe. That was when I turned and found Tommy watching me from the bed. A memory of the night before snapped into the forefront of my mind, and part of me wanted to ask him about what he had in store for my punishment, but I also didn't dare. Knowing Tommy, he would make it ten times worse if I pushed him on the subject. I wasn't even all that sure why I was due a punishment, but I didn't ask him about that either. Instead, I simply smiled at him.

"How long have you been watching me?" I asked.

"I'm always watching, Piper. You know I like to watch. In fact, I believe you caught me once or twice," he replied, licking his lips as he eyed me up and down.

"Well, if I wasn't completely sure you made a habit of lurking in my bushes, then I am now," I teased, before checking my watch. "It's almost time to go."

"Ah yes, the joys of daytime television followed by some kind of comedy show," he said, following me into the bathroom. I laughed and turned to him.

"You've never seen it?" I asked, and he shook his head. "Well, I don't always get the British humor, but I have to admit, it's a damn funny show. They're gonna give you one hell of a time, baby."

Tommy didn't seem impressed with my offhand comment.

"What do you mean by that?" he demanded, but rather than cower timidly, something inside of me resisted the urge to let him dominate me. I knew I'd been letting him take charge more and more, but hadn't realized we'd gotten to the point where he really was becoming more than just overbearing. He was trying to intimidate me to where I felt I was no longer myself.

That wouldn't do, so I stood taller and met his hard stare.

"You heard me," I said. "They'll ask you the usual questions but be prepared to go off the scripted answers. They'll want to hear something funny or intriguing while trying to get you to slip up on something random for the fun of it."

Tommy shrugged and then backed off, much to my surprise. I then saw his cheeky grin return, and I was reminded of the first afternoon we'd spent together in his hot tub. I missed the banter we'd thrown one another's way that day. Before I'd seen that darkness flash behind his eyes and for some reason welcomed it with open arms. Part of me wondered if I'd live to regret that moment. If I'd come to see that, his demons were better to be locked away rather than coaxed to the surface.

I found myself constantly teetering back and forth on that thought. Sometimes I liked it and had forgiven Tommy for all the bad things he'd done, and then other times I felt rage boil beneath my skin towards him. I'd have walked away ten times already if I'd let myself, but there was always something that dragged me back. A force within him I was drawn to like a magnet.

He barely spoke for the rest of the afternoon and seemed thoughtful. Distant. I accompanied him during the interview on some sort of daytime show I can't say was a chore. The British hosts were lovely and had us both laughing as we chatted about the movie in a far less formal interview to the type I was used to.

That evening was the comedy show. I hadn't been invited to talk on that one, so I waited backstage, watching via a stream being fed directly into the greenroom as Tommy ran through his rehearsed lines and then played along when the host began to improvise.

"Come on, there had to have been one funny story from on set of any of your movies? An embarrassing anecdote you can exclusively reveal?" he asked, and Tommy positively beamed. My blood ran cold. I saw it coming before Tommy had even opened his mouth and reached for my cell, ready to call Janie and get myself booked onto the next flight out of London she could find.

Tommy was laughing, acting all coy as he squirmed under the host's scrutiny. He opened his mouth as though to answer, but then closed it again and shook his head.

"No, I can't," he replied, his face turning red. I'd think he was cute if I weren't already furious. Was this going to be my punishment he'd promised was coming my way for a crime I wasn't sure I'd even committed? It sure seemed like it. Even though he was playing it cool, Tommy was about to say something to incriminate me somehow. I just knew it. He was about to humiliate me like he'd promised.

"Ooh, this must be good! Look at you, you're practically bouncing in your seat!" the host teased again, playing with Tommy. But I knew how it was the opposite. Tommy was in control. It was my bad, bad man who had the upper hand. He knew exactly what he was doing, and something told me he'd probably planned it all along.

"Okay, but you're all gonna look at a certain someone a little differently afterwards…"

"Don't keep us in suspense," the man pleaded. I watched with bated breath as Tommy shuffled a little closer and lowered his voice, which didn't matter because he was mic'd up, but he knew that. It was all for effect.

"Well, I've done a few steamy scenes in my time and being a red-blooded man I can honestly say they got my blood pumping—if you know what I mean?" Tommy was met with a look of shock before the host then burst out laughing.

"So you… you know, were happy to see whichever female actress it was?" he asked, offering a wink to the audience.

"Oh yes!" Tommy joked. I let out a sigh, hoping that was going to be the end of it. I should've known better. "Put it this way, there was a bit of cleaning up to do after the director shouted cut."

"Oh my goodness, so what did you do?" the man then asked incredulously.

"Asked her to give me minute to calm down and then I got one of the crew to pass me a tissue." He cringed and made a wiping motion with his hand, looking embarrassed. I didn't buy it for a minute. Tommy wasn't even the slightest bit uncomfortable. He loved the attention and wouldn't have surprised me if he'd added more to the story for the fun of it.

Laughter broke out from both the audience and the other talk show guests. They'd clearly loved his story, and I just had to pray that was going to be the end of it.

"So, just which leading lady might it be who got you so hot under the collar, Mr. Darke?" he was asked, and thankfully Tommy shook his head and refused to say. Yes, he'd revealed more than he should, but as it stood, he wasn't in any dangerous territory. Anything more and he was liable to tarnish both our careers.

"All I can say is that she handled it with gentleness and a sense of grace that warmed me."

Wow, he was pushing his luck. He'd actually just given away who it was by outright saying my surname, and yet none of them seemed to have noticed.

Regardless of him having just paid me a compliment whilst still humiliating me, I was ready to throttle him. I had to hide all of this, of course, because the damn greenroom was full of other people either watching the show or waiting for it to be over so they could get out of there. I was beginning to feel that way, too.

I figured I didn't need to stay, though. My contractual obligation was to step in if Scarlet couldn't make it and there she was, sitting next to Tommy, all perfect and smiling sweetly while letting him do all the talking. She was probably only doing it because she couldn't understand the host's British accent. Yes, I was being decidedly petty, and I didn't care one little bit.

I stood and headed for the door, making some blasé comment about going for some air. One of the team escorted me outside and he hovered beside me, watching me like he thought I was about to light up or something.

"What?" I demanded, making him jump. "I just wanted some air, okay."

"Of course, Miss Grace," he replied, looking sheepish.

"Unless do you have a cigarette?" I hadn't smoked in years, but the urge to take a drag was suddenly good and strong. The young guy nodded and plucked a pack from his pocket, offering me one. I shook my head. "I just want a little bit. You have one and I'll steal a few drags."

"Sure," he said, seeming calmer around me in an instant. I eyed him up and down. He was kinda cute in an awkward, reserved way. His dark blond hair was swept to one side and brushed up into a quaff, and I could tell he'd taken the time in getting himself ready for the day's work. He didn't seem the type of guy to lie in until late and then throw on the first outfit he found while rushing out the door.

"What's your name?"

"Dylan."

"And what's your job here, Dylan?"

"I'm one of Mr. Washington's assistants. We're tasked with a bit of all sorts."

"Like accompanying strays?" I teased, earning myself a small laugh. He nodded, offering me the smoke. I took it and had a small puff. It hit my throat, and I inhaled, feeling the instant gratification as the euphoria hit. I had another drag before handing it back to him. "So, what's good to do around here, Dylan? Something I won't get noticed doing."

He hesitated, weighing my strange request up. Had I just asked for drugs? A place to get my rocks off? Dylan was clearly trying to figure out what, so I gave him a hint. "I like to party, Dylan. But I like it even more when people are naked. Is there anything like that in this city?" I don't know what came over me asking such a thing. Maybe it was the thrill of almost getting revealed as Tommy's on-screen paramour, but I wanted something else to give me a high. Something Tommy wasn't going to be in control of.

"There are a few places, yeah," Dylan said. He offered me the cigarette again, but I declined, and he took the last few drags before stubbing it out and then tossing it into a nearby pail already half-full of butts. "I'll make sure you get on the list, Miss Grace."

I thanked him and then followed him back inside with a coy smile. Dylan was fast becoming my new best friend.

THIRTY

Tommy

As we left the studio, I saw one of the assistants handed Piper something and whisper in her ear. The way he stared at her made my blood boil and my mind race. What had they been up to while I was on the set? I'd decided against public humiliation and gone with a close call instead, just enough to rile her up, and instead of being grateful it appeared she'd spent the time cozying up to the hired help.

"What did he want?" I demanded when I could finally get her alone.

"Nothing," she replied, grinning at me mischievously. Piper was playing games with me, and dangerous ones at that. That wasn't gonna fly.

"He handed you something. What was it?"

"A surprise…"

I let out a low growl. I didn't like surprises at all. "I'll tell you later. Well, more like show you."

Hmm, that sounded better. Had she arranged some kind of a date for us? I had to wonder. It wasn't like we were the dating type, but I figured we were slowly coming around. Perhaps it was also time to come clean about our relationship soon, too? I had so many secrets swirling in the back of my mind and couldn't deny it'd be a relief to rid myself of one.

We went back to the hotel, and it irked me when Piper refused my advances. It was late. I wanted to fuck and then fall asleep. But instead, she was getting changed into a skimpy black dress and kept telling me to put on my best suit.

After my dissatisfaction faded, my interest returned. Piper truly was intent on taking me out somewhere, and so I did as she asked. I obliged her small trial of dominance and let her take the lead. It was only a half hour before we were back downstairs and climbing into a sleek black car she'd evidently hired for the occasion.

Piper stayed quiet as the driver took us to our destination, but as soon as we pulled up, I knew what to expect inside. This wasn't my first rodeo, even though it clearly seemed to be hers.

I didn't want her to make a fool out of herself, so I took charge once she'd handed a piece of paper to the man on the door—presumably the same piece that boy had given her earlier—and he'd let us inside. It was just as I had expected. An underground S&M club catering for anyone from the fresh new types who were after just a little bit above vanilla to the hardcore pain fiends who wanted to either give it or take it at an extreme level.

"Why, Piper, you've outdone yourself," I whispered as we both took in the view. The place wasn't full by any means, but it was well turned out, and while people stopped and stared as we passed, none of them said a word. If they told their friends how they'd seen Tommy Darke and Piper Grace at an underground sex club, they'd have to reveal their dark sexual habits in the process, so I counted on their desire to remain out of the limelight to ensure we did the same.

"I told you I had a surprise for you," Piper told me when we came to a stop and watched a naked group of women who were casually playing with one another. Some were experimenting with nipple clamps and floggers, but I could tell they were either paid to be there or had been instructed on how to lure the lurkers in. There was no real spark between any of them. Not like if otherwise heterosexual women were touching another for the very first time. I wanted more than choreographed tantalization.

The sight still served its apparent purpose. I grew hard just thinking about how Piper would look with another woman's lips around her clit. Would she grow shy, or would she grab her hair and pull her closer? I found myself wondering about it while watching her as she watched them.

"Will you let me have you, Piper? Here, in front of whoever wants to see?" I whispered in her ear. I relished in the sound as her breath hitched. She stared up at me with those doe eyes of hers and bit her bottom lip nervously as she considered her response.

"Would you hurt me or punish me?" she asked in response. My girl was learning. She had to know what she was getting herself into before committing, and I loved how she was figuring out some of my intricacies at last. Piper knew I loved to torment her before tantalizing. Would she let me do it here? I couldn't tell. I decided to risk it.

"Yes," I said.

"How?" she replied, surprising me. Well, at least it wasn't a no. I thought of the film I'd frequented and how I wanted to recreate it somehow. Could it be possible? I was willing to try if she was.

"I'd like to blindfold you. Make it so you can't see a thing as I take you in my hands and then spank you with them. Maybe worse." She stiffened, and rightly so. I hadn't really given her a full answer, and we both knew how we were taking a risk being there at all, let alone if I started one of our punishment fuck sessions with a captive audience.

"Let me think about it," she answered, and I nodded. Again, it wasn't a no.

123

I led her deeper into the club so we could take in the sights. It came as no surprise to me that it wasn't like you'd see in the movies or read about in books. Not everyone there was a glorious Adonis, nor did they all ooze money or sex appeal. They were simply everyday people with a combined interest in fucking partners who also wanted something more than a bit of missionary and then snuggles.

We watched one couple going at it who had to both be in their forties. His body wasn't bad, and neither was hers, given her age, but I was put off by the slapping sound they were making as they thrust together. Far different from the sound of leather meeting flesh, theirs was purely natural and an extreme turnoff for me.

I took Piper into another room where we watched a dominatrix whip her submissive male lover as he cowered before her. Nothing about it made any sense to me, but Piper seemed intrigued and so we hovered there for a short while before I led her deeper into the dungeon. I wandered what scene we would happen upon next and found myself pleasantly surprised when we were presented with a woman who had been bound, gagged, and blindfolded. She was lying on a leather bed with her legs stretched open so that everyone could see every inch of her. She had nowhere to hide and the idea of strapping Piper to that same bed had me reaching for her.

"Can you imagine how she must be feeling?" I whispered in her ear. "Is she scared or anxious? Perhaps worried whether she looks good or is turning people on. Or does she like the attention?"

"I think she does," Piper replied, tilting her head up to look at me. "She's not shivering or trying to cover herself. Her breathing is even too, look." I did, noticing the same as Piper. The woman loved what was being done to her and wasn't about to put a stop to it anytime soon, as far as I could tell.

"How do you think you would feel in her place?"

Piper watched the couple for a moment, and I could see her eyes going to the hard-on the man approaching was sporting. When he touched the woman, she flinched, and he responded by pinching one of her nipples before forcing his way inside of her. Piper continued watching intently, and I hoped she might be coming around to the idea of me doing the same to her one day.

"I think I'd feel vulnerable. But then I'd like it once you started to touch me. Especially when you made me feel good," she finally answered.

"And what about before that, when you'd be at my mercy?"

Piper shook her head.

"I'd be scared."

Damn, she had no idea what she did to me with words such as those. Rather than put me off, she simply spurred my dark desire forwards. I wanted nothing more than for her to spend an evening at my mercy, having been scared and then pleasured in equal measure.

"Were you scared earlier when I told Washington how I came all over you on the set?"

"Yes," she replied with a laugh. "I also wanted to murder you."

My cock rocketed to life in my pants at hearing her say that. To even consider that she might be capable of that act had me wanting to bend her over and fuck her then and there. She couldn't know how what she'd said affected me. God, I was full of raw desire to not only take her, but to have another woman too. Not in the same way, of course. No, Piper had all of me now, but I still wanted to try to recreate what Marina had given me. Could I do it when it wasn't spur of the moment? Was I capable of premeditated murder?

Yes, came the voice from deep within me. Yes. I was.

THIRTY-ONE

Piper

Tommy went so quiet I had to turn and properly look into his face to make sure he was okay. He seemed lost in thoughts. Away with them and chasing something I couldn't be sure he'd ever tell me about. When he snapped back to reality and grinned at me, my heart leapt. And not in a good way. What I saw was ruthless and cold. Like when you saw the mug shots of serial killers after the police had caught them. I went cold too, but in fear.

Something about this club had stirred up something inside of him. Something I was quite convinced I wasn't going to like.

"Let's get out of here," he groaned, and for the first time, I didn't follow him. I didn't know what to expect when he got me alone, and I was growing more fearful of what awaited me back at the hotel.

"Tommy," I whimpered when I finally stepped out of the room and caught up to him in the hallway. "I'm, urm… I'm not feeling great. It just came over me all of a sudden, so I am gonna stay in my room tonight. Just in case I have the flu or something. I don't want to pass you my germs."

He didn't believe a word I was saying and tried to argue with me. He then resorted to pleading, but I stood my ground. I needed some space and wasn't going to change my mind. Eventually, Tommy seemed to realize he wasn't going to sway me, so he conceded, even though I could see he hated it.

"Sure. Whatever. You go get some rest. I'll see you tomorrow," he said with a blank expression, and I cringed. I'd expected him to leave with me, but he didn't. Tommy gave me a dark look of indifference and then sauntered back into the room we'd just left without so much as a backward glance in my direction.

Talk about a one-eighty. That guy was giving me whiplash with his ups and downs, but I figured I'd told him I was leaving and wanted to be alone, so did just that. I called the driver and left without another word.

I went back to the room I'd barely touched since arriving in London because I'd spent my nights in Tommy's bed rather than on my own. There, I busied myself by running a bath and then climbed into the hot suds with a sigh. It felt good to unwind after the hectic few weeks we'd been having, and I let myself slide beneath the surface to soak my hair.

I stayed there for a few seconds, holding my breath, and a thought came to me. A feeling of wonder. Many, in fact. I wondered how it would feel to fade away. Would I be missed? Passed off as some kind of poor, overworked soul who'd fallen asleep in the tub and drowned? Or would there be stories circulating about me while questioning my morals? People from the club might come forward and tell the story of how I was there but seemed off and then had left in a hurry. And then that boy, Dylan, he might tell them what I'd said. And of course, there was Tommy. Would he be incriminated?

I jumped up and out of the water. Tommy. What would he think if another woman close to him died in such a way? I was sure it would break him, and there was no way I could do that. Even hypothetically, the thought of leaving him that way broke my heart.

My thoughts then naturally turned to Marina and what she'd done. I started to imagine her there, lying in her own blood until Tommy had found her. It must've been awful.

In a bid to get my mind onto something else, I grabbed the waterproof control and turned on a small television set that'd been built into the wall down by my feet. God, I loved posh hotels and their randomly awesome added features. I flicked around the channels for a while and stopped as soon as I saw a movie that was playing on one of them. A young Tommy Darke was on the screen depicting yet another of his shadier roles. The movie had to be about ten years old and yet he'd hardly aged at all. He was violently beating a young woman and his coldness made me shudder, but I also couldn't take my eyes off him. There was a glint in his eye I had seen before. Why was I drawn to the bad guy? Where was my sanity? I was glued to the screen and even as I continued to watch him sink further into darkness, I liked what I saw. I liked him. The name truly matched him perfectly.

I hit the information button and read the blurb. He was portraying a ruthless gangster for the first but not last time. This one seemed far worse than George, though. He enjoyed beating the woman I'd caught him with on screen, but then the strangest thing happened. She began to whimper, begging him to stop. He refused, which was when she started to cry.

Tommy—or whatever character he was playing—stopped dead and glowered at her with a horrified expression on his cruel face. He seemed disgusted with the girl for daring to shed tears over what he was doing to her, but rather than discard her or send her away, his character murdered the poor girl in cold blood.

"You don't cry, Milly. Not in front of me. I told you, didn't I?" he then screamed at her lifeless body before spitting on her and then walking away with a growl.

My hand flew to my mouth. I knew it was just a movie and not real, but so much of it was scarily familiar. I recognized the actress and was sure she'd also had a number of hit movies since so was further reminded of how it was two actors playing out a scene. But it just felt so real.

It didn't take me long to realize why. I had seen that rage. I had felt those hands on me. But worst of all, I had been regarded with that same look of disgust. Tommy had told me himself how tears were a trigger for him, and I'd seen what my own had done to him. Was his trigger even real? Had it come from him or from the character? I had to know for sure because if that trigger was part of a character profile gone rogue, then there was something a lot more dangerous about Tommy than I'd realized.

I grabbed my cell and leaned over the side of the tub with it as I loaded my search engine and typed in the name of the guy Tommy was playing in the movie. I needed to know if the crying thing had been written in because it was real and if so, for whom.

Johnny McIntyre was a man no one dared mess with. He had an aversion to women in general and not only called them weak to their faces, but repeatedly beat any who foolishly tried to get close to him. He became famous for strangling his own sister at the age of fifteen because, in his words, she did nothing but cry all the time. After that, Johnny brutally punished any woman who dared shed a tear in front of him...

I could read no more, but it didn't matter, anyway. I'd seen more than enough to read between the blurred lines of Tommy's personality. He wasn't as brutal as this Johnny fellow, but damn, could he be as cold. He had other traits that were uncannily similar to his other characters, too.

I delved deeper over his movie history. As I read over his many movie hits and their plot summaries, I realized how so many of his roles had stayed with him. Like the hiker who had loved the solace of the mountains and was a skilled huntsman. Or the cocky playboy with a penchant for BDSM. And not to mention the manipulative drug lord who'd seduced women by drugging them and then brainwashing them.

They were all intense and had a dangerous side to them. And just like Tommy, they each hid it in front of everyone. But not the woman they loved. No, she was the only one who saw beneath the mask and had to live with what she found there. Because once she was under his skin, there seemed there was no way out.

I sympathized with each and every one of them. But I was different, wasn't I? This was real. Not a movie or a plot line someone had created, but my actual life. No one else had seen it or experienced first-hand how it felt to have to make amends with Tommy's dark side. But I had. He'd readily shown me, and I'd mistaken it for a bit of fun. But not anymore. This was real, and it was dangerous. I had to be careful, otherwise God only knew what he might do to punish me if I ever truly hurt him.

THIRTY-TWO

Tommy

After months of tormenting myself and going back and forth with my emotions and conscience, I'd finally chosen which side of the coin I wanted to rule me. I'd been desperate to explore that side of myself and had struggled with my conscience about doing so with Piper. But then she'd walked away from that club and left me to play with my demons rather than wrestle with them any longer.

One of the many nameless, faceless girls from the dungeon was in my keep. I'd gone back to her apartment after the night was over and now had her tied up with her cunt on full display before me. She wanted me to fuck her so badly I could practically smell it. The whore was lifting her hips off the bed, trying to entice my cock to fill her, but she wasn't getting anywhere near it. Instead, I decided to play a little longer. I took a mask from a travel pouch in her bedside unit and covered her eyes with it. Next, I used the earplugs that were also in the pack to block up her ears, rendering her both blind and deaf.

"Please," she whimpered, bucking against the restraints I'd put her in. "Please, master. Please fuck me."

I slapped her across the face and grinned as I saw the handprint I left behind. She didn't cry out and so I struck again. This time she let out a whimper and a sniffle that I presumed meant there were tears in her eyes. Thank fuck for the blindfold. At least that plan had worked.

After weighing up my options, I opted for checking out what else the girl had in her trusty bedside drawers and was pleasantly surprised by her array of toys and implements. I wasn't going to have sex with her myself, but this girl was certainly going to be fucked raw by the time I was done with her. I wanted to beat her, so I did.

First, I slapped her breasts. I then spanked her thighs and opened them wider, getting rougher and rougher every time I put my hands on her again. She had been trained to take it, and so I let my urges rule me. I did whatever I wanted, but only within reason. She was a masochist and could probably take more, but I had a reputation to uphold. A public persona to protect. She couldn't walk away in serious harm. And so, after I was done, I gave her what she'd begged me for, but never with the real me. She didn't deserve that. Only Piper.

"Don't take off the mask until I've left," I ordered when I was done, making her scream for me with both pleasure and pain. I was right to think I couldn't do anything more. It was too risky. I'd weighed up my options and knew people would've seen us leave together. There might also be surveillance cameras in her building or on the street outside showing me going up to her apartment. I would be caught if I indulged my murderer fantasy. If I was going to do it, I'd have to plan it meticulously in future, not on a whim.

"Thank you, master," she whimpered when I finally untied her.

I took a good look at my handiwork and took a mental picture. Her thighs and ass cheeks were red after my beatings, and she let out a soft moan as I rubbed my hands over them soothingly. Aftercare was a big thing in this scene, and I knew I had an obligation to make sure she was okay. Her ass still held the butt plug I'd filled it with, and I left it in place. She could deal with that later. Her pussy was still full, too. I'd found one of those double length dildos I'd seen lesbians use and had fucked her with it relentlessly. I could still see her clenching it from her final orgasm and carefully withdrew it. I wasn't sure if she'd known it wasn't my cock inside of her, but she hadn't asked and I didn't feel much like volunteering the info. I'd let her believe whatever she wanted to and didn't give a fuck what she assumed had happened between us.

Our time was over. I had to get back to the hotel and finally get my own rocks off. Piper had asked for privacy and she'd gotten it, for a few hours at least. I was about to burst her little bubble, and God help her if she tried to refuse me.

THIRTY-THREE

Piper

I woke with a start and looked around, finding nothing but the blackout darkness in my room. I began to wish I'd put on a little light somewhere before falling asleep, but I'd left my bath in such a tired state that all I'd wanted to do was crawl into bed and get comfortable. I'd been asleep moments later.

It was nothing; I told myself. Just a noise outside or someone out in the hallway. That was it. I had to be imagining things and managed to convince myself it was my mind playing tricks on me. I hadn't slept alone in weeks either, so was probably just on edge.

I turned onto my side towards the center of the bed and nestled back into the pillows, which was when I heard the footsteps approaching the bed. I stiffened for a split second and then told myself to run, or at the very least fight back.

By the time the covers were thrown off my naked body and I was exposed on the bed, I'd clambered up and was halfway turned, ready to do whatever I could to fend off whoever had snuck into my room in the dead of night. It was no use. He knew exactly where to strike me. His flattened palm hit me directly in the center of my chest, and the air rushed out of my lungs.

I fell back, gasping for breath, while my attacker quickly disrobed and then spread my legs. I hoped to God it was Tommy. I was going to be furious with him, of course, but at least if it was Tommy, I could handle being manhandled and tossed around like this. At least with Tommy, I kinda liked his heavy-handedness. At least with Tommy, I could let myself enjoy the consensual non-consent of it all.

"Stay down," he told me when I'd caught my breath and tried to squirm away. That was when I knew for sure it was him. I'd know that voice anywhere, and even with the doubts about his sanity still plaguing me, my carnal instincts took over. I wanted him and it was clear he wanted me too, but if we were playing this game, then I was going to properly go for it. I kicked him in the ribs when he got closer and, judging by his deep grunt, I had caught him nicely off guard. When I kicked again, he caught my ankle right before my foot connected with his chest.

I expected him to push it outwards and open my legs again, but instead he pushed it towards me, along with the other foot he had also grabbed while he was immobilizing me. Before I knew it, my knees were up by my ears, my ass and pussy facing the ceiling. Tommy knew how flexible I was thanks to the yoga so didn't stop pushing me and soon my hips were crushing against my stomach, which resulted in my stomach crushing my lungs.

I tried to push back but felt my strength waning thanks to the lack of oxygen. I thought I might pass out and was about to croak out a plea when Tommy climbed over me and plunged his cock inside of my pussy. He began pounding in and out, each plunge twisting me further in on myself, and at first I was struggling, but it wasn't long before the discomfort turned into pleasure. Like always, he overpowered me and did whatever the hell he wanted and, like always, I let him.

By the time we'd both climaxed and he let me go, I knew that despite the things I thought I'd learned about him, it'd would never change what was going on between the pair of us. It didn't matter the doubts I had or the questions that'd plagued me while lazing in that tub. I wasn't prepared to ask him about them or demand to know the truth, and until I was, I was doomed to forever wonder if I truly knew the man I'd fallen in love with.

I also had to wonder if I should cut my losses and run, but knew I was too scared to run from him. Too scared to be without him. Tommy owned me now, and there was nothing I could do about it.

THIRTY-FOUR

Tommy

Piper was huddling against her pillow by the time I'd finished with her and while I knew she wasn't happy with what I'd done, I refused to pander to her girlish whims and apologize. Thanks to the darkness of the room, I didn't have to see her face so brought no attention to her soft whimpering. I was sure to hold her, though, spooning her from behind. I even marveled at my ability to know she was upset and not let her get to me. Perhaps I was finally overcoming my obsessive aversion to the sight of tears? Or could it just be hers I was becoming untroubled by? Maybe not.

The main problem was that I didn't feel sorry for what I'd done. I'd used my keycard and invaded her private space even when she'd asked for a night by herself. I'd forced myself on her and crushed her body beneath mine so that she had no hope of fighting me back. Not a chance in hell of stopping me. And I'd loved every second of it.

That girl from the club had twisted me up so tightly that I'd been fit to burst and was surprised I'd even managed to last long enough for Piper to reach her orgasm.

As I listened to her tears slow, so did her breathing. I then felt her body calm and drift into sleep, and I tried to switch off but couldn't. All I could think about was that girl and how I'd wanted to take things further. Do more than just beat her.

I decided I needed some air so sneaked out of bed and pulled on my clothes. Piper didn't so much as stir as I crept away, and soon I was back out in the dim lights of the hallway.

Rather than go down to my own room, I headed for the stairs and followed them down and out a door at the bottom. There, I found myself standing out the back of the hotel and I didn't know what to do with myself or where to go.

That was when I saw him. There was a young man kneeling behind one of the dumpsters, and I could see the tourniquet around the top of his arm from my vantage point a few yards away. Fucking junkie. I approached cautiously, watching him as he watched me.

"Hey, back off, man," he croaked, but I simply slid down beside him.

"I'm not here for your stash, pal. Just checking you're okay."

"I'm fine," he said with a hiss as he pushed the needle filled with dirty brown shit into his vein. With a sigh, he let his head fall back against the grimy bins and his hand fall to the side, the needle clattering against the concrete floor. I reached for it on instinct but was sure to cover my hand with my hoodie when I did. There was still some heroin inside and I leaned forward, spying how there was more left on the guy's bent spoon as well.

Desire overwhelmed me. A need so strong I knew I was a slave to it. A willing accomplice. So, I refilled the syringe, not even bothering to tap the air bubbles away, and then injected him with a second dose. He jumped at first but was too out of it to react before he let out another sigh and his head rolled to one side, his lids closed.

I listened as his breathing became shallower and shallower and was beyond calm the entire time, even when he slipped away and stopped breathing completely. I watched him turn blue and even risked a closer look once I was sure he'd died. It was a curious sight, but one that fascinated me. Not as much as seeing a woman in the relative stages of death, but still interesting all the same.

And then, as though nothing was amiss, I put the needle back in the boy's hand and walked away. I was sure to keep in the shadows for as long as possible before then circling around and going back inside. The little junkie would be found before too long, and while this time around I knew there was nothing to link me with him, I was sure to head back to Piper's room to ensure I had an alibi.

As I lay there beside her, all I could think about was how I'd done it again. Not the same and certainly not as exciting or satisfying, but I'd done it. I'd killed someone. That made two people now, and I knew then and there how I wasn't stopping at that. I'd do it again. Hopefully, more and more. Next time I would have a woman at my mercy, like the girl from the club, but instead of untying her and leaving, I would slit her throat. Or squeeze it shut. Yes, that'd be good. To feel it crushing beneath my hands.

Damn, I was hard again. I grabbed my cock and started jerking off, the images so clear in my mind of what I had done and what I still wanted to do. I took myself close to the edge of my release and then stopped. It just wasn't good enough.

I curled my body around Piper's and teased the head of my cock inside her from behind. She stirred but didn't wake, so I pushed myself the rest of the way in and came. My darling girl had no idea, and I guessed she'd been so exhausted from my visit earlier that night she'd fallen into such a deep sleep and hadn't felt me penetrate her. I left my cock where it was until it'd gone down, and then I withdrew.

A quick clean up with a tissue and I was ready to catch some zzz's, so I turned away and closed my eyes. Sleep came to me quickly, and it was full of the best dreams. Girls lined up, ready for me to fuck them and then kill them. I did it over and over again and always with the same 'service with a smile' approach. Each of them were nameless and faceless, but they all screamed for me as they came and then screamed the same way as they died. It was heaven.

Of course, I woke the next morning with another raging boner, and I turned over to find Piper lying exactly where I'd left her. I nestled right back into position and started pushing myself inside. She groaned and tried to pull away, but I grabbed her hips and tucked another couple of inches into place. I could feel her tensing around me, resisting the intrusion, but it was no use. I had her exactly where I wanted her and was going to take what was mine.

"I'm sore from last night," she whimpered as I began rocking back and forth, my cock only coming out an inch or so rather than me fucking her the full length at a time.

"I'll be gentle," I replied as I pushed her onto her stomach and lifted her ever so slightly so that her ass and cunt were on full display as I climbed up on top of her. Piper whimpered as I began going for it, but she didn't tell me to stop, and I soon felt her begin to melt. She grew wetter around my cock and stopped fighting. She didn't even struggle when I licked one finger to moisten it and pushed it inside her ass. I couldn't help myself. It was far too appealing just sitting there on show and looking all inviting. She relaxed around me and that told me she'd done it before, so I slid in a second and began teasing her open, ready to accept my cock.

I didn't even ask. I simply withdrew from her pussy and plunged it into the hole above. Piper moaned into her pillow but still didn't fight, and I could see her hands gripping the bed beneath as I began sliding in and out.

Again, she didn't stop me. I took her compliance as an invitation and went for it, savoring every second I was inside of that sweet, tight hole. She soon came for me and I quickly followed, emptying into her ass without a care before slowly retreating.

Piper ran for the bathroom before I could even check her over, and a second later I could hear her using the facilities. "Are you okay?" I asked, thinking I'd better at least check.

Did I care? I thought so but wasn't overly sure at the same time. She was becoming something so wonderful to me. So... what was the word? Compliant? Perhaps. Piper was in a place where she did everything I wanted her to do and didn't fight me. Not since the day at the cabin when she'd learned how much joy I truly took from watching her squirm and wilt under the pressure of my humiliating tactics.

I heard no response, so opened the door and walked right on in. Piper flushed bright red and grasped in horror that I'd found her sitting on the toilet.

"Tommy!" she cried, but I refused to leave. Instead, I turned on the shower and climbed right on in. After a second, I poked my head out of the curtain and shot Piper a cool grin.

"You think I didn't know you'd have to squeeze my cum out? This isn't my first ride up the a-train," I told her, relishing in Piper's embarrassment.

"Doesn't mean you have to be here while I do it," she groaned, wiping herself and then flushing the toilet.

I put out my hand.

"Come here," I demanded. She hesitated for just a second and then did as I'd asked. I was glad, but also angry that there was even any hesitation at all. However, I let it slide. For now.

Piper climbed in with me, and I grabbed the soap and got to work on her pussy and asshole. She tried to stop me, but I was having none of it. I didn't go inside, nor was I rough, and soon she was putty in my hands. Piper welcomed my aftercare and let me trail suds all over her tender parts, and when I washed them away, she even let me shave her completely bald from her pubic bone to her coccyx. Then, with her legs wide, I inspected my handiwork while the shower water thundered down onto us like rain. I parted her lips and licked my way from her clit to her pussy, and then I slid a finger inside. I knew she wasn't ready for me to fuck her again, so simply fingered my way in and out while teasing her clit with my tongue. My girl came for me hard and by the time I'd finished, she had a fire in her eyes that drove me wild.

We switched places and Piper cleaned me up before sliding her mouth over my shaft and then forcing it to the back of her mouth. It was heaven, and I let myself moan and groan with pleasure as she licked and sucked me to the brink of another orgasm. But then she stopped.

With a cunning grin, Piper then stood over me and turned around. I was now lying on the floor of the bath and watched as she started to lower herself over me. I figured it was time for a sixty-niner, but it appeared she had other plans. Her soreness either abated or ignored, Piper pushed me inside her pussy and began to ride me. Reverse-cowgirl had never really been my thing before, but with Piper taking charge, I would happily be her steed, and she could ride me all day long.

I held my orgasm back and got a second wind as she arched her hips and moved back and forth atop me. I watched the muscles in her body contract and move with skilled precision and couldn't get enough. When she came again, it was a surprise to both of us and I could see her strength wane in the aftermath so let myself go.

Like a jackrabbit, I pushed up and down into her until I shot my load. She was trembling by the time she'd climbed free, and I watched her with fascination as she once again tried to hide her modesty from me as she clambered to the toilet and took a piss. From my vantage point, I could see it pouring out of her and refused to look away. "You're so fucking beautiful," I told her, and loved the smile Piper was overcome with.

She then started to giggle.

"Even when royally fucked and taking a piss?"

"Especially then."

THIRTY-FIVE

Piper

Tommy finished taking his shower while I shoved on a robe and headed back towards the bedroom to grab the room service menu in readiness to order some breakfast. I also snatched the remote from the center table and turned on the TV set, where I found an array of morning television shows to choose from. I stopped as soon as I saw Tommy's face plastered all over one of them and turned up the volume.

"*After reports that he visited an underground sex club last night, Hollywood star and movie bad boy, Tommy Darke was allegedly seen leaving with one of the other club visitors. In the aftermath of her night of passion with the notoriously private star his lover has agreed to sell her story to the highest bidder and went on record today as promising a sex story worthy of rivaling any you might've heard before. There's been no response from Tommy or his people, but we look forward to hearing both sides of the apparently sordid tale of BDSM and so much more. It looks like a certain someone is going to have to either answer to or accept his new reputation as a ladykiller...*"

I went cold. He'd gone home with another woman and given her the night of her life? And then he'd come to my room and had sex with me too? I wanted to throw up or scream the place down but opted instead to slump into the nearest chair.

I felt lost. Why hadn't I listened to myself before when I knew something was wrong? It had to be that I was blinded for my love for Tommy. There was no other explanation. Had he manipulated me? Brainwashed me somehow? It seemed the most logical reason for how I'd been acting and how often I had given him the benefit of the doubt when I ought not to have. When I'd covered for him and let him get away with hurting me because he'd convinced me it was all part of something I had brought to life within him. That his darkness was somehow my fault. My burden to bear.

All my instincts had slowly become wired to his actions. His ideas had seemed to mirror my own, but now that I was thinking about it more clearly, it was the other way around. I was mirroring him because he had gotten under my skin and influenced me into complying. Made me think it was my idea when he was the puppet master all along.

He'd broken me beyond repair. Taken my body and my heart, as well, having forced me to give up my freedom and free will because he'd infiltrated my mind and made me trust him. Tommy had manipulated me to believe the lies he'd woven between us while molding me into his perfect and willing slave.

But not anymore. My eyes were wide open, and I could see him for what he truly was. A monster. A master manipulator who was nothing but a fake smile and pretend promises. What I had discovered the night before was true. Each side of his personality was a ruse. A pretense so that all the world wouldn't see him for what he really was. But I could finally see.

Everything I thought I knew about Tommy was a lie. Was the man I thought I knew just another role he'd been playing? I believed so and had to presume it had been the same his adult life.

I grabbed my cell and checked out the online gossip pages. His name was everywhere. His face splattered over every one of them as they speculated about what'd happened between him and that woman. There wasn't so much as a mention of me having been at the club too and I breathed a sigh of relief for that one fact, but the rest of it made my blood boil.

How could Tommy do that to me? How could he be so incredibly callous and vile? I knew how. Because everything I thought he was and everything I thought he felt for me was a lie. A cruel, cruel myth he'd let me believe ever since that day in his goddamn swimming pool.

Tommy sauntered out of the bathroom without a care in the world, but then saw for himself how he was today's top story, and I couldn't say he even looked sorry for what he'd done.

"I want you to leave, Tommy. Get out of my room and don't ever come back," I told him in a cold voice I knew was purely for show. There was no I way I was truly that calm. Underneath the surface, I was losing my shit and knew it wasn't long until the façade would shatter along with my heart.

He frowned at me and then started to laugh, shaking his head.

"I didn't fuck her. I just roleplayed a little to satisfy some kinks I've been thinking about doing with you. I just shoved a dildo in her cunt a few times to make her think I was doing the deed. You know I'd never be with anyone but you now, Piper. I love you."

I couldn't believe he was daring to shrug off the story. That he was genuinely amused by my pain. I could tell by the stupid grin on his face that he truly thought he'd done no wrong. That I was being silly by letting it upset me.

I stood and glared at him. The mask really had now fallen, and I saw the real him. The man I'd been trying to deny was there all along. The monster. Not the person I thought I loved.

He truly believed in what he was saying. Honestly looked surprised that I had the audacity to call him out on what he considered to be reasonable behavior.

"You need to leave, Tommy," I tried again. "We're done. Do you hear me? Done!"

"You don't mean that," he tried, but I wasn't going to surrender to him. Not anymore. Not ever again. "You're just angry. Let's talk about this."

"I don't want to talk to you. I don't want to look at you. Now, get the fuck out of my room before I call security," I demanded, my voice turning shrill.

His smile dropped in a heartbeat, and he charged towards me. I did my best not to show him any fear but couldn't hide it when he fixed me with that awful stare of his. The one that meant I was going to incur his wrath. But it didn't matter anymore, because he wasn't going to be anywhere near me to deliver one of his fucked-up punishments ever again. I meant it when I'd said I wanted him to go away.

"You don't get to decide we're over," he ground. "We're done when I say so, Piper. I own you."

I slapped him across the face with all the strength I could muster and then quickly stepped back, realizing I'd made a rash choice and potentially huge mistake in doing so. He was unpredictable. And dangerous. And I'd just acted out rashly.

Tommy responded by picking up a nearby armchair as if it weighed nothing at all before then throwing directly at the still blaring TV set. The force of the throw ruined them both, and all I could do was stand there in shock and dismay.

"No one owns me," I eventually whimpered. "Least of all someone like you, Tommy Darke. You're a fraud and I know I won't even miss you, because I don't think I ever really knew you. Now get the fuck away from me." I went over to the door and opened it wide, hoping he'd just do as he'd been asked and leave me the hell alone.

He moved toward me in slow strides, his face seeming contorted and bereft after his outburst, and came to a stop beside me. I watched as every expression and emotion then disappeared from his face, leaving nothing but an utterly blank canvas. All I saw was darkness. And cold, cold eyes that I knew were the window to his empty soul.

I had been right about everything.

"If I don't have you, I'll do it again and again. I won't be able to stop myself," he told me, his voice barely more than a hoarse whisper.

"You should've thought about that before you cheated on me with that whore," I replied. "Do it again, for all I care. Do it over and over again while you think of me and realize what you've lost. I hope you die alone,

Tommy. I hope no one ever dares to love you again because I know now that you're not capable of love."

He walked out of my life that day and while it broke me, I hoped that would be the end of my love affair with Tommy Darke. I longed for the day that I could forget him and carry on with my life. But I also feared that I might never truly be free. No matter what lay ahead, he'd infected me, and I somehow knew that to some extent, I would always be Tommy's Girl.

To be concluded in part two…

Tommy's Girl
Part Two

By LM Morgan

Copyright LM Morgan
All rights reserved

DEDICATION

For all the people out there who feel lost and lonely.
For those who have someone to help pull them through those hard times,
and especially those who don't.
You are not alone.

ACKNOWLEDGMENTS

Thank you, as always, to the fabulous members of my group, Morgan's Minions.
Your encouragement and advice is the best. Thank you from the bottom of my heart, with a special shout out to Nadine for always promoting for me. And of course, to Sally and Laura for always offering to read for me and give advice whenever I need it xxx

PROLOGUE

Piper

I knew a man once.

He was sexy and powerful. Funny and alluring. He did things to my body and soul that no other person had done before, but I wanted him to.

Like an evil spirit, I'd invited him in. I'd welcomed him.

But it wasn't long until things had changed.

I learned the hard way that I was wrong to put my faith in someone so dark and dangerous.

After a whirlwind romance with the devil incarnate, my life is now nothing like it was before.

He became my entire world, but then broke me again. Turned me inside out and then failed to put me back together again in the aftermath.

He broke his promise to flip the switch.

He remained a tormentor rather than turn back into my protector.

But now I am free. I mended myself. Became my own protector and refused to let anyone torment like he did.

I'm myself again and Tommy is no longer part of my life.

I've not seen him in months and while I can't understand why he didn't fight for me, I'm glad.

I'm not his any longer. I'm me. Piper Grace.

Not Tommy's Girl.

ONE

Piper

We wrapped on set for my new movie after six weeks spent shooting on location in Thailand, and while everyone celebrated and looked forward to heading home, I felt sad to be leaving it all behind. I hadn't minded the long days spent trekking to remote locations while burning in the immense heat, or the dodgy food and even dodgier hotels. It'd been an adventure, and just what I'd needed after my awful breakup with Tommy three months before. He'd really done a number on me and just knowing he was somewhere in the city I knew was still my home made me not want to go back there. I didn't want to stand the risk of crossing paths with him out on the town or on any of the film sets he might be working on. I didn't want to be anywhere near him or his friends. Or those who represented him.

There was one saving grace, at least. As far as my relationship with Tommy had been concerned, no one other than Janie and Brad even knew we'd been together, so the breakup hadn't been public and awful. That was a blessing really and when he'd gone off the radar everyone had thought he was just keeping quiet until the allegations about that woman from London had blown over. But then, as far as I knew, he'd gone more than just off the grid, but out of the LA scene entirely. I hoped he'd stay that way even when I was back in the same city again.

At least this time, I would be living in a secure apartment building in the center of the city rather than in Beverly Hills. I'd ended my lease from my hotel room thanks to Janie's help and had placed my belongings in storage while I'd toured around Europe on my own like some backpacking hipster. The world had been my oyster, and I'd devoured the sights and then gone across into Thailand ready to begin filming a futuristic sci-fi adventure I'd signed up for called *Humankind*. The story was great and the team behind it even better, and so I'd arrived with a spring in my step and a new 'take no prisoners' attitude.

If anyone on my travels or on set had known I was a mess with a broken heart, they hadn't been quick to tell me so. In fact, I'd made a lot of new friends along the way and had some of the best times of my life staying in cities I'd never dreamed I'd visit with them. I felt like a whole new person, not the woman still pining after a man who'd broken her heart into a million pieces. I was ready for anything.

But then, just a few days into filming, our director had a heart attack. He'd been rushed off set, and we were left in limbo as to what was going to happen next. Most of us had thought it was all going to be over. That we would be going home empty-handed and have to let everyone down who was expecting us to come back with movie gold. But that didn't happen. By some kind of miracle, the show went on.

The production company flew in a new director and he turned the entire movie around. Edgar 'Eddie' Martin was a whole new breed of director. Young and with high hopes for our project, he seemed to knuckle down and take the bull by the proverbial horns from day one.

He kept the focus on me, the main character called Kyra, but he pulled the movie in a grittier direction than his predecessor had decided to go with. He wanted to see me huffing with genuine exertion during the scenes depicting the character's boot-camp style army training. I was to be covered in dirt and real beads of sweat during my fight scenes, while still being able to show a fresh-faced and softer side while out of the action and trying to convince the audiences I was on a mission for the good of mankind.

In a lot of ways, I was reminded of how Tommy had challenged himself for his roles. I felt consumed by Kyra. Like I was becoming her. I understood her quirks and the intricacies of her personality. I saw the world through her eyes when shooting my scenes and adored the way it felt to stop being myself for a little while and let someone else take over.

I mean, why not? Kyra was strong and determined. She was everything I wanted to be and more, and I connected with her. The scenes weren't hard to film, not even when I was pushing my body beyond its usual limits. And she wasn't tough to portray. I liked her. In fact, I never wanted it to end.

And then there was Eddie. He'd wanted a raw feel to the movie and had dared me to deliver it. His challenge was one I'd accepted, and so I worked hard to deliver the goods. In fact, I'd found myself wanting to do him proud. To please him. I'd liked his company on set and it wasn't long before he'd invited me to dinner so we could talk about what he expected of the end result.

We'd soon ended up spending a lot of time together. And, as these things often do, our relationship swiftly turned from colleagues to friends, and then friends to lovers. He was everything I'd needed and more and swiftly became my rock. Everyone knew about us and we didn't hide a thing, much to my delight. The other cast members and production staff saw us as we'd bicker on set and tease one another behind the scenes, and we let everyone watch as we'd dance the night away beneath the stars or while we stole kisses during the downtime. It was refreshing to be open and honest with one and all, but also freeing. I didn't have to lie to anyone about what we were doing, but most importantly, I didn't have to lie to myself.

There was finally a lot more making me happy than sad. The outlook was no longer bleak. I loved the direction the movie was going and, regardless of our relationship, Eddie was still as hard on me as he was anyone else and wouldn't stop until he got the ideal shots. He was certainly a perfectionist, but things seemed right with him on board, so none of us minded. We could all tell the finished film was going to be cutting edge. Something far from the usual Hollywood style. A revolutionary concept in movie artistry.

Eddie was well known for that kind of thing, and I soon came to respect him tremendously. To readily follow his direction and go to him in search of guidance without any embarrassment about the fact I was apparently still learning my craft. There was the age gap, sure. Eddie being fifteen years older than me felt odd at times, but that didn't stop us from flirting like lovesick teenagers and making love long into the nights when we both knew we should've been resting instead. But Eddie was exactly what I'd needed. He'd listened to me pour my heart out about Tommy and rather than stamp his feet and demand to defend my honor, he'd demonstrated his maturity by offering me advice and a shoulder to cry on instead. He promised he'd take care of me and build me back up, and as time went on, I began to believe him. To trust him.

With Eddie, I could be myself and not worry about the humiliation or torture. Not fret over tackling mood swings or oppressive tendencies. He was kind and gentle. He continued to be a generous lover and always made sure I knew he saw me as his equal. Eddie always made me feel like I mattered. It was one of the things he'd told me umpteen times during our time together, behind the scenes of our movie. Something that always made me feel better, no matter how shitty my mood was.

I guess it was obvious that I'd fallen in love again? That was not what I'd expected to happen.

When we returned to Los Angeles, Eddie didn't make light of our relationship, nor did he cast me away as some on-location fling. In fact, he knew I was heading for a hotel because I still had to find somewhere to live, so right before we'd disembarked the plane home he had asked me to move in with him.

So, I did. The first thing I arranged when I got out of the airport was for my belongings to come out of storage and be taken to his apartment building. My apartment building.

I was giddy with excitement just thinking about a future with him, so much so that it didn't matter how I hadn't seen his place yet. I would live in a tiny one-bedroom if I had to, just as long as we were together. We'd spent most nights sharing a room while in Thailand, so I knew we could make this work. I'd learned a lot and felt I'd come home a different person to the girl who had left the bright lights of Los Angeles months before.

My life was stress free and clutter free. My new outlook positive and without the dark clouds that had once been looming.

Of course, Eddie's apartment wasn't tiny at all. In fact, he had two floors of high ceilings and copious amounts of space in the roomy home. Eddie was a minimalist with his furnishings and I liked how calm his apartment was. Like he'd Feng Shui'd the crap out of it.

Part of me wondered how I was going to fit into his world. I didn't want to bring my own things into the mix and cause chaos and clutter, so I gave most of my old furniture to goodwill and kept only what I absolutely couldn't get rid of. I'd find a place for them eventually, I knew, but was in no rush to make my mark.

After my first night in the apartment, I woke up with a smile and performed my usual sun salutation yoga routine and then headed to the kitchen for a glass of water, only to find a maid cleaning up in there. A maid! He had a maid. I ran back to the bedroom before she could see me and intercepted Eddie on his way out of the shower.

"When were you going to tell me you had a maid?" I cried. "It's a good thing I didn't saunter out there naked, otherwise she'd have had a fun story to tell about our first meeting." Eddie laughed at me and shook his head as he toweled off.

"Firstly, she's *our* maid. But also, it's part of the way this building is set up. Didn't I tell you?" he replied, and I shook my head. I knew I would have remembered that conversation. "There are a handful of them who cover each of the apartments simultaneously. There are all sorts of hired helpers we can request the services of whenever needed. All we have to do is contact the front desk."

"Nice! So like, if we wanted some work doing or a dinner party catered?"

"They'd be able to help. I've used the service to hire caterers and servers for parties before, and a decorator. It saves us time so we can do the important things," he said, checking the clock on the wall. "Speaking of which, I've got to get to work on these edits. The quicker we get everything finalized the better. You gonna be okay without me?" I nodded. Of course I would, especially given the stunning apartment I was still yet to fully explore.

I then watched as Eddie got dressed in his designer suit and slipped on just one of his posh watches from the extensive collection in a drawer of his dresser. He looked so different in his LA gear, and I found myself missing the khaki shorts and shirts he'd worn every day in Thailand.

It was going to feel strange getting back to my old life, but I reminded myself I was still my own woman and would be absolutely fine on my own. I just had to get back into LA mode too. I had lots of unpacking to still do and planned to catch up with Janie over lunch, and so knew the day would fly by.

"I'm sure I'll cope," I answered with a playful smile I hoped Eddie could tell was genuine.

He then gave me a deep kiss, and I felt his longing. He wanted to stay home with me, but we'd already agreed not to let our relationship get in the way of our careers, so I wasn't going to tease him or beg him to stay. It wasn't fair when we both had people waiting on us. "And anyway, you get to go stare at me all day long. Lucky you…"

"Lucky me indeed," Eddie answered, and bit his bottom lip with a hiss as he took one more lingering look over me and my tight workout gear. "See you later," he then added before disappearing off to work.

I spent the morning unpacking, arranging, and the rearranging my stuff. It took forever for me to be happy with my efforts, but when it was done, it felt great to be moved in. Like I truly was home. My cell then chimed, and I checked it to find a text from Janie. She was demanding that I get ready and meet her down by the pier for cocktails and seafood. That sounded like an amazing plan to me. The perfect way to reacquaint myself with the city I'd once loved.

I got dressed, did my hair, and made myself wear makeup for the first time in weeks. I knew people would be watching me from the moment I set foot outside and wanted to look my best. I still had a wholesome image to uphold after all and knew there'd be no shying away when the paparazzi did their thing.

I couldn't falter. I had to be confident and ready to shine. To dazzle any audience—big or small. And I couldn't moan. *Wayward* had been a huge success, just like I'd hoped, but while it'd shot me to the level of fame, I had always hoped for, I would forever feel it was tainted by the memories of Tommy that were part and parcel of the George Ward experience. I hadn't been able to watch it again and when people asked me about the movie or the actors involved; I recited the same practiced lines and nothing more. In all honesty, I was more excited about the upcoming movie and could tell I'd gladly never revisit any semblance of the *Wayward* story again.

When I was all set, I checked the mirror and gave my dress a good swish to make sure no one would see my underwear should a gust of wind catch me off guard while at the beach. All good. No matter what, I still had my girl-next-door persona firmly in place and had to maintain it. Especially as I'd chosen to depict a younger woman in *Humankind* whom young adult readers across the world had loved and connected with on many levels. For the sake of the movie, I would remain covered up and respectful. I would mind my manners and smile sweetly for the paparazzi. I would behave.

On my way out, I found my new key on a hook by the door and grinned when I noticed Eddie had put an elephant keychain on it. A reminder of our time away together when we'd ridden on the backs of two mighty elephants, and I'd squealed with excitement the entire time. I'd crossed an item off my bucket list that day and Eddie knew they were my favorite animal. The chain was a heartfelt trinket and a sign of how much he listened to me and took it all in, and I loved him all the more for it.

I left the building with a huge smile on my face.

Life was good and things were only on the up.

I was stronger than ever and wasn't going to crumble.

I was finally happy and nothing was going to get in the way of it.

TWO

Tommy

Man, I wished I could blend in with a crowd better. I'd be able to get much closer, but instead the top-of-the-range digital SLR in my hand would have to do the job for me. Everything was planned out, down to my timing and positioning, and when the time came, I was ready.

It had been a long three months, but it'd all been worth it. The studying and perfecting of my new role. The research and preparation. The trial runs and near misses.

I caught my first proper glimpse of Piper as she left her new apartment building, and felt my pulse quicken as I took her in. She was stunning. Like a fucking goddess in the flesh. Her hair was blonder than before and her skin perfectly tan thanks to the sunshine she'd been getting while on her little jaunt across the world. And I liked it.

She had a kind of glow about her that appealed to my darker side. It was like she was taunting and goading me. Every sashay of those hips was a dare. Every soft smile a challenge. Did she know I was watching? God, I hoped so. If she did, then I was right. And this portrayal of independence she was trying desperately to convey was nothing but a lie. I chose to believe that idea to be true.

There was no way she could get over me so quickly.

I certainly hadn't gotten over her. I'd seen every single report about the movie she'd been working on. Kept abreast of her movements every step of the way since London. It didn't matter how long had passed or how many other women I'd taken; she was still the one. The only one that I wanted and who mattered. The one I was going to make mine again.

And so there I was. I had on a black wig, fake nose and a glued-on beard for the occasion and had blended in with the paparazzi without a single one of them noticing how I wasn't what I appeared. I had been trialing this same routine for months and had perfected the role in no time. I'd even used the same principle to pick up women, not that the sorts I'd had my eye on had been the type to play hard to get anyway, but it'd worked a treat to practice my anonymity. I'd had a different name and a different face anytime I wanted and had been having a great time the past three months preparing myself for when Piper would return to me.

I even had an accomplice. My trusty acolyte Miles had indeed been my kinda guy. When I'd returned from Europe, he'd come to my house and drank away an entire week with me. We'd talked about everything, even my penchant for hardcore porn and snuff films. We'd even watched some together, with a strict 'no jerking off' rule, of course, but Miles was into it. I mean, *really* into it. We'd then talked some more and had decided it was time we did some of that shit for real. My experience in London was just a taste, and I knew I wanted more.

With me in disguise, we'd then gone to a shitty club downtown and pulled a couple of chicks we took back to an even shittier motel the pair of us had rented for the night.

Miles had then beaten the crap out of one before fucking her, while I'd hate-fucked the other and then beaten her. Talk about scratching an itch I hadn't been able to get at. It was mind blowing, and so we did the same again and again, going to different parts of town and picking up women we didn't give a shit about so we could get our rocks off.

It was one of the best times of my life, and it'd only gotten better. Within a couple of weeks, we'd developed a faultless system, and it was working a treat. We never went to the same bar twice and not once used our real names. I loved letting off steam and had started ignoring the women's cries for mercy. Even their tears, and all without the need for a blindfold. I was just numb. Empty. The voices were quiet, and I was no one. Not Tommy. Not George.

Even the screams and cries that'd once haunted me, both asleep and waking nightmares were gone. I could close my eyes and remember her easily. Remember the pain I'd caused and the suffering. Remember her face, as I had choked the life out of her. My first real victim. Not Marina, like I'd thought back when I was still running from my past. No, there had been another long before her. Someone I'd forced myself to try and forget. Gwen. She had been like no one else. Someone I had loved since birth because I'd been forced to. Because it was expected of me as a big brother and her so-called protector. Even when she'd cried. All. The. Damn. Time.

Even as she'd taken her last breaths, she'd had tears streaming down her face. I could picture it now and rather than hate the memory, I drew strength from it. The courage to do it again. Over and over.

But now I was just a faceless, nameless brute that took what he wanted and then walked away. My aversion to tears had faded away and was gone now that I was utterly desensitized to the whores and their waterworks whenever they took my beatings and begged for me to leave them be. I was an animal. Nothing could stop me, especially not a few tears.

Miles was the same, too. He was an unfeeling, uncaring beast, like me.

And then, things had changed for us yet again. Miles had gone too far one night and had beaten this chick to death. He'd freaked and so did her friend, who I was balls deep in at the time. So, I shoved my hands around her throat and clamped down on her windpipe to silence her. I kept on fucking too and came right before she kicked the bucket. It was the most amazing feeling in the world, and Miles had watched me in awe. I didn't know if he was appalled or impressed but hadn't cared either way. If he didn't like it, what was he gonna do, call the cops? I didn't think so.

"Have you done this before?" he'd asked, and seeing as we were already accomplices enough, I told him yes. I'd half expected him to run, but he hadn't. He'd grinned. "Teach me," he'd then begged. "Show me."

And so, I had.

To date, we'd murdered more than twenty women between us. We'd become pros at doing the deed, clearing up evidence, and then dumping the bodies in the back alleys or waterways the city was blessed with. It was almost too easy and had become just another part of our lives. The perfect way for each of us to get our weekend kicks.

But then Piper had returned to Los Angeles and thrown me off my game. I couldn't escape her. I'd seen her face all over the news. Watched her walk out of the airport and jump in a cab with that fucker Eddie Martin. As soon as I'd rolled out of bed that morning, everything inside of me had started to churn. The voices were screaming and before I even understood why; I was out the door and getting in the shitty minivan I'd bought to drive around town in incognito. It had all my gear in the back for my disguises, and I knew right away which direction I was heading. To her new apartment, where she'd just spent her first night with that asshole.

I laid in wait and then watched him leave, and I even contemplated tailing him. Yeah, that'd be fun. I'd follow him down a dark alley somewhere and beat the shit outta him. Chop off his cock and feed it to him. Hmm, nice thought, but no. Not yet at least. Piper was first. As long as I got her back, I could see myself leaving Eddie alone, but his days were numbered if he got between the two of us. If he stopped me from getting my girl.

And so there I was. And there she was. Smiling to herself and looking utterly radiant, Piper jumped in a town car and it sped away. Myself and all the other paps quickly followed, and her driver made no attempt to shake us as it moved through the city towards the beach. She wasn't trying to escape the limelight in the slightest.

Fucking tease.

And in that dress, too. Red, like the one she'd worn when I'd all but fucked her over that kitchen counter. When we'd both come in front of a dozen onlookers and then billions of viewers. She was wearing it for my benefit. That was it. She had to know I was watching and had chosen that color on purpose to tempt me.

Yeah, she was going to get it all right.

When her car came to a stop, I used the crowd for cover and watched as she climbed out and went into one of the restaurants by the pier. I then spied through my lens and saw she was meeting with her agent. The woman I'd met a few times before. Janie.

I found my perch and waited, but while most of the other photographers opted to cover the main entrance, I walked up the pier and then turned back so I could see into the window of the restaurant from a different angle. And like a dream come true, I got the perfect view. Thanks to my trusty new camera lens, it was like I was seeing her for the very first time. In Technicolor when all my life I'd been living in black and white. She was sun-kissed, just like her hair. Did she have tan lines? I wondered. Had Eddie allowed her some naked sun worshipping time, or had he insisted she wear a bikini? I wanted to see. Needed to.

I had to know every little detail about how she'd spent the last three months without me.

I was forced back to reality when I saw Piper throw her head back and laugh. She and Janie were clearly chatting and giggling together. She was catching her friend up on how her summer abroad had gone and didn't stop from smiling even once. I loved seeing her so happy and didn't care that it was only because I was no longer in her life.

Nothing mattered but having her in my sights again, and so in that. At least I was back on a winning streak.

I then followed the two of them as they went from there to a bar and then another. Most of the paps kept a respectful distance, but not me. I changed into a different outfit and followed Piper and Janie inside. I then watched from a few tables away as they did some shots and giggled like teenagers at prom. I even risked getting closer and shoved right into Piper, just as she and her friend were trying to make their exit.

She said sorry and looked directly into my face, completely none the wiser as to who I was beneath the guise. Apparently, she thought I was just some random guy, and I smiled and told her it was no problem, adopting a simple southern twang that she still didn't see right through. This was too damn easy.

I was good at this disguise lark and decided to take it further next time. To engage her for real and see if I got away with it.

Yes, a voice in my head told me. *Become just another face in the crowd and then snatch her. Make her yours and never let her go again...*

THREE

Piper

I had the best day of catching up with Janie. It didn't matter that when we'd had enough of the bars, we took a car back to mine and both fell in the door of the apartment, tipsy and giggling. I didn't care that we were falling over each other as we clambered inside. Neither of us was there to judge the other, only to reignite our friendship and start anew. I'd loved our afternoon together and, even though we were already full of booze, had decided just one more drink would have to be had. She'd immediately accepted my invitation as she said she'd apparently been dying to see the new place, and so I gave her a little tour before popping open a bottle of sparkling wine and pouring it into two flutes.

"Wow, Piper. This place is stunning," Janie told me, staring out of the huge windows at the city below. "And Eddie really seems like the perfect guy. It's good seeing you so happy. You're like your old self again."

"He is perfect," I told her honestly. "Or he's perfect for me, at least. Every moment has been wonderful, and I just love him, Janie. I feel it so strongly."

"As strong as with, you know who?" she asked, and I didn't blame her. Of course, the conversation was going to turn to him sooner or later.

I had to think about it for a moment and couldn't lie to her. Things weren't the same with Eddie as they had been with Tommy. Just different, and I told her so.

We then talked about the new movie and how well things had gone during filming. We even discussed potential upcoming projects and Janie revealed how she had been inundated with offers for me.

It was happening at last.

I was becoming a real star and hoped to God it would continue.

Eddie came home to find me and Janie lazing on the sofa in our pajamas. Well, my pajamas. I'd loaned her a set to wear and invited her to sleep over rather than head back to her place alone. We were having far too much fun to call it a night yet and had even started to sober up when he got back. Eddie walked in to find the pair of us chatting and eating takeout while groaning that our hangovers were already starting to kick in. He didn't seem to mind at all though, and even joined us for something to eat before heading for a shower.

Damn, he truly was a perfect gentleman. I knew I was lucky to have found him. Or maybe he'd found me? I wasn't sure there was a difference, but either way, I felt safe with him. Like I mattered.

I instinctually followed Eddie into the bedroom when he got up to leave. He seemed distant, and it wasn't long before my stomach had begun to churn. I was scared I'd done the wrong thing and panic started to set in that I would have to make it up to him somehow.

Tommy's teachings were instilled in me, and I could suddenly tell it'd pissed Eddie off more to have to piece me back together than it had finding me drunk and truly making myself at home in the apartment so quickly.

"Don't do that, Piper. Don't give me those doe eyes," Eddie warned, but his tone was gentle and sincere. Almost soothing. "I'm not going to punish you because you've done nothing wrong."

He then pulled me close and ran his hand through my hair before letting out a sigh. "That guy and the things he made you do. You need to know that real people don't act that way or expect their partners to behave like this. He was just a foolish little boy throwing his weight around, Piper. You're with a big boy now," he added, making me laugh despite the seriousness of his reminder. We both knew it wasn't the first and wouldn't be the last time he had to say such things, but I still appreciated it. Still needed it.

"A real man," I replied, giving him a kiss. My smile returned in a flash, and I watched him stride to the bathroom, thinking about how I was the luckiest woman alive.

Janie stayed the night but got up and ready early the next day so she could get to the office. I told her to report back with scripts for me to read later that day, but then Eddie reminded me we still had work to do before I moved on to another project. We had to start working on the promos for *Humankind* so we agreed Janie would instead come and meet me at the studio that afternoon. There, Eddie promised he'd show us both some sneak previews of what he had so far, and neither of us could wait.

With the plans in place, I then waved them both off with a smile and set about my day.

First, I worked out and decided to really push myself hard in readiness for my upcoming photo shoot. I chose the hardest of my usual yoga routines and practiced my breathing as I went through the motions, forcing myself to remain in control even when I was dripping with sweat and panting as though I'd just run a marathon.

As I was going through the motions of my routine, a flash caught my eye from the apartment building just across from ours, and I did a double take when it then happened again. When I took a proper look, I realized it was something catching the sunlight on the roof opposite. I almost ignored it, figuring it must be a piece of glass or something on the rooftop. But then the sun went behind a cloud and revealed the truth about what was over there. I could see the figure of a man. He was tall and broad, and he had a cap on that covered his face. He was standing in plain sight, like he didn't care if he was caught, and he had a camera in his hands. A camera that was pointed directly at me.

I gave whoever it was the finger and stomped deeper into the apartment, feeling full of rage. How dare one of the press photographers stalk me like that? And in my own home too! I'd never had a problem with them tailing me, but this was crossing a line and I was pissed.

Yeah, I knew I shouldn't have flipped him the bird but hadn't been able to help myself. He'd deserved it.

I took another look. And he was still there, but then bolted a second later, so I decided to play him at his own game. I wanted that camera. Those shots. He wasn't going to make a dime off me.

I ran to the phone on the wall near the apartment door and called down to the front desk. After explaining the situation, the security team got to work, and I couldn't deny how I was more than impressed by how quickly they were on it. I then watched as a small team of people searched the rooftop. However, the photographer was long gone and had left nothing in his wake.

All I could do was admit he'd won this time and carry on about my day. I would pick my battles wisely. Take him down another day. The photos would surface and I'd have to deal with any backlash when the time came, but I wasn't going to let whoever that was ruin my good mood. Not when all he'd have was pictures of me working out and then maybe one of me flipping him off, but I doubted anyone could begrudge me that response to finding myself being spied on in my own home.

After then getting ready in more of a rush than I would've liked, I left the apartment and headed for the studio. There, I filled Eddie in on what'd happened. He wasn't happy but was glad I'd acted on it and assured me he'd have words with the security team to make sure nothing like that happened again.

His promises put me immediately at ease. Like always, Eddie took charge of the situation and had me smiling again in no time. He even cleared the room so we could be alone and didn't care that in doing so he'd had to give everyone an unscheduled break.

"All that matters is you're okay," he told me, kissing my lips gently.

"I am," I answered. "Thank you."

As it turned out, those pictures never did surface. I couldn't be sure if I had Eddie to thank for that, but I was glad either way that someone had squashed the scoop before it'd even hit. I often wondered who that photographer was. How he'd known to be there and just how long he was watching.

I spent the rest of the day looking over what Eddie and his team had so far before Janie took me to one side and we chatted over coffee.

"The writers and production company are all in agreement, Piper. You're the face of this franchise. They want to sign you up for the rest of the series. Four movies in total and potentially more, seeing as the books are still being written. This will be perfect for you, trust me. You've hit the big time, girl," she told me, her face glowing, while all I could do was stare at her in shock.

I knew this deal would benefit her too as the cut would be epic, but I also believed that wasn't the only thing exciting her about my offer to sign on for the rest of the series. She was pleased for me, I could tell, and I felt lucky to have such an amazing friend always in my corner.

"I can't believe it," I answered honestly. "This is all so amazing." I meant it, and even as I headed into makeup ready for my photo shoots so we could get some promo pictures right away, I was still pinching myself. This was really happening. I was front and center in every picture. The focal point of everything.

I had finally become the leading lady and was being treated like royalty by the team on set. Gone were the days of me being ushered on and off to accommodate the photographer or the needs of the starring actors. This time I was the lead. And the only one at that. Every other character was supporting me, and it was refreshing. I liked it up there on my cloud.

There was a full afternoon of photo shoots to be done for the movie promos, and I was more than ready. I then watched the huge mirror with a wide smile as my dark brown wig was pinned into place. I was transforming. Becoming someone new. Things were moving forward, and so I let myself stop fretting and was determined to enjoy every second of it.

***

The days that followed flew by and I was sure to enjoy every second of limelight that'd come hand in hand with my rise to stardom. When the promos for the movie were done and the edits finalized, we celebrated by throwing a party for our *Humankind* friends. Eddie insisted we do it at the apartment, and I agreed. It was the perfect way to show the team that they were more than just his colleagues. They were his friends. Mine too. We would be regrouping in just a matter of months to start filming the second movie in the series, and I could tell Eddie wanted to let the cast and crew know they were important to him. And letting them into his home was a great way to do it.

We all talked and drank copious amounts of booze. We ate canapés offered on trays by waiters and waitresses Eddie had hired via the trusty front desk service. We even had a private chef for the evening, and I was seriously impressed by everything he'd put together for us. The party had all the splendor I now associated with the lavish lives of the rich and famous in LA while also feeling homely and private. Like a family gathering. Eddie wasn't trying to show off. He had just wanted his friends around him and to have a good time, and we sure did.

When the party was over, we saw the last of the guests out and then I wandered over to the terrace to enjoy my wine in the cool night air while Eddie directed the cleanup operation inside. It was peaceful out there and somehow quiet, even with the city still bustling around us.

I closed my eyes and took deep, steady breaths. Any tension I might've had felt like it was leaving my body, and soon I was in a sleepy, tipsy daze. That was when I felt him behind me. His nose was in my hair, and his hands slid down my back before cupping my ass. I let out a sigh and then twisted on the spot to face him. But Eddie was gone, almost like he'd never even been there.

I frowned and looked around the terrace for him, but he was nowhere to be seen. I'd started to think I was imagining things and was about to go back inside when he appeared at the doorway with another glass of wine in his hand for me.

"Where'd you go?" I asked. Eddie just frowned and took a sip of his own drink before handing me mine.

"I was right here, babe. Just wanted to grab you another glass before the caterers left," he told me, and I nodded. So that explained it. He must've swung back inside quickly while I was still staring out at the city.

"And have they gone yet?" I asked, leaning back against the brick so that I pushed the tops of my breasts out over my low-cut dress. Eddie's eyes went straight to them, and I let out a small laugh. Men were so easy to lure into temptation.

"Not yet," he replied, stepping closer and closer until he was pinning me to the wall. He then slid one hand between my thighs and started caressing me in ways that had me panting for breath in seconds.

"What if someone sees?" I whimpered against him.

"They can't see a thing. Don't worry," he assured me, slipping one deft finger inside my core. I came quickly and had to force myself not to cry out. There were ten people still in our apartment and yet we were out on the terrace with his fingers in my pussy. It was a rush and by the time they'd all gone and the coast was clear, I was like a woman possessed.

Eddie was locking up and when he returned, I was lying naked on the couch in wait. He licked his lips and grinned at me and then let out a satisfied smile when I opened my legs and showed off my body without a care. I didn't need to ask or beg for what I wanted. He knew his mouth was like heaven against my pussy and that I could let him eat me all night long. I'd never massively enjoyed that with lovers in the past, but with him, I couldn't get enough.

He was soon going for it, and I had my head tilted back against the sofa, my eyes closed so I could enjoy what he was doing between my thighs. When I opened them again, I jumped right out of my skin and screamed, pulling the nearby throw blanket over me in a bid to cover up.

There was a man standing in the kitchen. From my angle I could see him perfectly and had caught him watching us. My sudden freak out surprised Eddie, of course, but as soon as I pointed toward the other side of the apartment, he knew something was up.

He charged for the kitchen and flung open the door, where I heard the man apologizing profusely inside. I could hear their raised voices and then Eddie finally came back, the man following quickly behind. He had his head down, but I recognized him as one of the servers who'd been working at the party earlier in the evening for us.

"Sorry, Mrs. Lady," he was saying to me in heavily accented English. His black beard and hair were thick and his skin darkly tan. He had to be Mexican or something, but I didn't care. I just wanted him out of our house. "Didn't mean to scare. No offense," he told me, but I looked away, feeling utterly ashamed at what he had to have seen while spying on us.

Eddie had him out the door before I could respond, and I was glad. I felt mortified and never wanted to have to deal with that man ever again.

"He said he was in the pantry when the others left and was going to come out but saw we were doing stuff," he explained after he'd checked the entire apartment for any other strays. "I think he genuinely just made a mistake. He didn't mean to scare you but didn't know what to do. Come on, let's go to bed."

I went but couldn't stop from shaking. I was embarrassed and furious. Talk about an awful end to an otherwise perfect evening. Eddie could tell I was on edge and hugged me tight as he led me to the bedroom, and I readily followed. At least in his arms I was safe.

FOUR

Tommy

I ditched the Mexican waiter costume the minute I was back in my van and grinned to myself as I thought about how humiliated Piper must be feeling. As far as she knew, a complete stranger had just seen her getting eaten out. I knew her and knew the shame would've killed her libido. Sorry Eddie, no more pussy for you tonight.

I let out a cackle and drove away, blending into the night traffic with ease. I'd spoken to her. Been right beside her. And still, Piper hadn't known it was me. And earlier than that, I'd hidden in the shadows and watched her on the terrace. I had even risked going right up behind her to smell her sweet scent and grab a handful of that ass I still dreamed about day and night. And still, I'd gotten away with it.

I hadn't planned to stick around but couldn't resist. I'd slipped into the kitchen after the rest of the workers had left and then watched her as that fucker had licked and sucked at the cunt that was still mine. Yeah, I was jealous, but not enough to take one of those knives and drive it through his heart. Don't get me wrong, the thought had crossed my mind, but I knew I had to wait. To toy with her some more. I wanted to play my game a little longer. To make her think she was going mad or being stalked.

My trick of taking pictures from the rooftop opposite had worked a charm too, and I knew without having to guess that she was already starting to grow paranoid. Paranoid about me? Yes, it had to be. Nothing else could shake her like I could. She was so terrified of me coming running back into her life that she hadn't noticed how was right under her nose. I was already back, and I had been since the moment she'd climbed off that airplane.

I texted Miles on my way back to the dingy apartment he'd rented for the week and arrived to find him balls deep in some slut he had picked up at a bar across town. She jumped with a start when I came in and took a seat and I simply smirked at her. There was no such thing as modesty in mine and Miles's world. He carried on fucking, and I watched the show, still reveling in my victory over Piper for yet another time. If I were keeping score, I'd be inclined to say I was winning ten-to-nothing. I also couldn't wait to tell her all about how I'd repeatedly gotten near and how she'd had no idea each time.

"Is he Tommy Darke?" the girl asked my partner in crime and as she broke my reverie and the silence, I immediately realized my mistake. I'd ditched the Mexican disguise but not adopted another, and then there I was sauntering into a dive of an apartment to play voyeur to my friend as he fucked some girl raw like I didn't have a care in the world. Yeah, like that'd go down well with whomever she decided to tell. But then again, this was us she was dealing with, and I knew she'd never get out of here alive. I grinned and nodded as I stood and stretched.

Miles withdrew his sheathed cock and flipped the girl over onto her front before pulling her up onto her knees. He then dived right back in and did her doggy style, while I unbuckled my pants and wandered over.

"Yeah, he's Tommy Darke, and he wants you to suck his cock," Miles informed her for me, but she already knew, and I could tell she wanted it. Superstar cock was attractive in its own right and I saw her eyes light up as I shoved it in her face. The girl went for it, taking me all the way to the back of her throat before sliding up and down with a smile. How sweet. A nice, vanilla blowjob that she probably thought was exactly how all the boys wanted it. But not me. I nodded to Miles, and we both gripped her hard before each of us began to pummel into her even harder.

She was gagging and groaning in a second and tears were streaming down her face, her mascara leaving lines of black to accentuate the torrents. But I didn't care. All I wanted was my fix, and I plowed on until I got it. Without thinking it through, I shoved my cock as far back as I could get it and came right down the back of her throat with a grunt. When I was completely done, I pulled out and cursed.

Miles was finished, too, and he discarded his condom before turning to me with a frown. "What the fuck, man?" he demanded, and I held up my hands. Yeah, I knew I'd messed up. He didn't have to tell me.

"I know, fucking DNA evidence. How long until it's out of her system?" I asked, supposing it was my mistake so I'd have to figure out a workaround.

"A few days, maybe? I dunno. But we can't exactly do it now, can we?"

"Do what?" the girl croaked as she clambered off the bed. We both ignored her. I was rubbing my chin in thought while Miles was standing there, his arms folded in anger and all of which was directed at me, and quite rightly so. I'd been somewhere else while fucking that girl's face and forgotten to be careful. Was I back out on the balcony with Piper? Or maybe back in that kitchen watching her build her climax? Either way, she was definitely to blame. Not me.

"Knock her out," I told him. "I'll deal with her later."

"What? No! Please…" the woman cried, but Miles was too quick. She didn't get the chance to utter another syllable or try and bargain with us again. His fist was up high, pulled back for maximum affect, and he sent it flying for her temple without a single care for how much he was going to hurt her or if he'd do serious damage. We needed her knocked the fuck out good and proper and Miles made quick work of it without even breaking a sweat.

The girl was a bloody mess by the time he was done but was still breathing, so I wrapped her in some sheets and carried her out to my van. With the coast clear, I then shut her in the trunk and went back to check on Miles.

"You heading for the cabin?" he asked, and I nodded. "Okay, I'll clear this place up and meet you there."

"Sure thing," I told him, and we clapped hands like the bros we were before I disappeared off into the night with our new hostage.

I arrived at my newly acquired cabin in the early hours of the next day and flung the now writhing bundle onto the bed. She kicked and cried out as I let the sheets cocooning her fall open. But it was no use. I'd chosen this cabin for many reasons, but mostly because it was even more remote than my previous abode. Plus, this one couldn't be traced to me should anyone come looking.

Using some rope I'd had at the ready, I tied the girl to the bed and ignored her pleas for mercy. I needed to think. To make plans. But she wouldn't stop begging to be set free. All I wanted was for her to shut the fuck up, so I decided a gag was in order. I left her tied by her wrists to the bed posts and went to the kitchen to look for a rag or something I could use to stuff her mouth with and came back to find her free of her restraints and running for the door.

With a cackle of mirth, I tackled the girl and threw her over my shoulder. She writhed and screamed. She even punched me in the back, but her attempts to fight back were purely laughable.

So, the bed couldn't hold her. The flimsy wood had broken easily, and she'd gotten free within minutes. This was good to know, so I decided I'd use her to help work out the kinks in my plan for when Piper came to stay. After scanning the room for more inspiration, we went for plan b—me handcuffing her to the radiator.

By that evening, she had pulled it off the wall and gotten free again. So I punished her by beating her and then chaining her to the balcony door—on the outside. After one night spent naked and freezing at the mercy of the elements, she was a little more compliant. But I didn't care. I was only using her. Biding my time before eventually ending her pitiful life, but only when I had my answers. There had to be some place I could tie her that wouldn't give. A method I could use to make sure she couldn't escape no matter what she tried?

By the time Miles had arrived, I'd found it. There was a thick pipe that fed water into the cabin and went through the wall behind the bed. It was fixed into the ground and went right down the mountain to its source and I knew it'd be ideal. The cabin was pretty much built around this thing, and I was sure it wouldn't budge no matter what the girl tried. So, with Miles keeping watch, I headed for the hardware store.

Wearing a generic disguise, I picked up all sorts of bits and pieces that I was sure would look like I was intending on using them for some home repairs and such. Amongst my haul were yards of thick metal chain and they were my real purchase. The rest was all for show. Well, apart from the huge hammer I needed so I could get behind the wooden walls and access the pipe properly. And the shovel for what was due to come after I was done testing my new setup.

After paying the cashier, I returned to the cabin and headed for the bedroom with purpose. Miles was in there and he had the girl bent over and taking him as he pummeled into her from behind. I was pretty sure she didn't want him to, but it didn't matter to either of us. She was just a plaything, and I think she knew it too because she was no longer putting up any kind of a fight.

Ignoring their antics, I unloaded my things and smashed my way into the wall cavity. Next, I made up her new restraints and secured the chain to her cuffs before looping it around that glorious pipe. Miles was just finishing up as I was and, with us both satisfied, we then left her curled in a ball on the bed.

Miles threw his used condom in the trash and then scoured the fridge, which I knew was pretty much empty, bar a few bottles of beer.

"You set up the game, I'll run to the store for food and more beer," he told me. I nodded and watched him go with a grin.

Damn, I had underestimated that guy. There was a time before that I'd thought I was a loner. That my urges weren't to be shared or indulged in. But Piper had teased them awake. Made me want to nurture these dark impulses within me, and boy, I really had. And then Miles had given me the courage to take it further. To do more and to take everything I wanted without caring for right or wrong. He was my best friend. I hadn't had one before, not really, but I knew he was it.

When he returned, I had the television on and a game loaded on the console I'd recently brought and installed in the cabin. For that night, we would be assassins worming our way through the streets of the many cities of the world while killing for honor. The next, we'd be footballers playing our way up a league table. The following day we might become part of a team of rogue secret agents infiltrating a government facility. We could be anything we wanted both in fiction and reality, and I knew this was just the beginning.

So much more was yet to come.

After a week of testing out my theories and trying different ways to secure my prisoner, we finally put the damn thing out of her misery and laid her to rest in a nice, deep grave in the woods. Sending her off was a pivotal moment for me. Like a spark of lightning, something exploded within me, and I felt truly alive.

It's time. Go to her... a voice inside my head said. *Yes,* was my answer.

For the first time, I agreed wholeheartedly and was going to do as my urges commanded.

FIVE

Piper

I woke early, feeling odd. I had that horrid sensation that someone was watching me again and rubbed my eyes, forcing myself to wake up properly. It was only a little after five in the morning, but I knew something didn't feel right. I just couldn't put my finger on what it was.

I peered around in the dim light. There was no one watching me. There couldn't be, and the rational part of my brain knew that. I'd talked to myself no end of times and forced my fears to abate, but something kept gnawing at me regardless and so I climbed up out of bed and pulled on my gym clothes. Eddie remained fast asleep which was actually unlike him as usually he was such a light sleeper, but I left him to rest, figuring I had woken earlier than usual. I was just going to work out and grab some breakfast. He could sleep a little longer and then I'd take him something to eat.

Stretching awake, I then walked through the apartment, heading towards my favorite spot by the window that caught the morning rays. I was almost there when I spotted a card on the small table next to the sofa. It was a greeting card, like you get on your birthday, and it'd been opened and propped on its end and on display.

At first, I thought it had to be Eddie's, but then the picture on the front made me do a double take and swallow a huge gulp. The picture was of me. I was a disheveled mess and was sitting cross-legged on a black leather sofa with a sign in my hands. A sign that said, *Please forgive me, Tommy. I'll never run away again.*

I took a sharp inhale and snatched up the card, staring at that awful picture in shock. With trembling hands, I then opened it, wondering what the hell I was going to see written inside. Had Tommy sent it to Eddie, and he'd left it out to punish me? No, he wouldn't do that. I knew he wouldn't. This was all Tommy's doing, and I was sure of it.

Inside the card in handwritten script were the words I'd been dreading reading for over four months. I was right. Tommy hadn't let me leave him. He'd just given me time enough for me to think I was free.

And now he was back.

'What was once mine will always be mine. I never set you free. I never let you go. You've been a bad girl, Piper. You need to be punished.

Meet me at the coffee shop on the corner behind your apartment building in five minutes, or else I'm coming to get you. And while I'm there, I'll pay your new friend Eddie a visit to show you just how much I mean it when I say you're mine…'

I didn't know whether to scream or cry but knew I didn't have long. I ran back to the bedroom and shook Eddie hard. But he wouldn't wake up. I carried on shaking him, but still, he slept on without so much as groaning. He was out cold. As if he'd been…

"Bastard!" I cried, and then I slid down onto the floor and began to rock back and forth in panic. Tommy was going to come for me if I didn't go to him first. He'd delivered me a promise, but also an ultimatum. If he did have to come get me, he'd hurt Eddie. I didn't doubt it. He'd clearly already been in my home that morning, so I knew he could slip in and out without being noticed, and I knew I had no chance against him if he came gunning for Eddie. I'd never been able to overpower him and figured he'd probably planned all of this so had plans B-Z all mapped out in his mind. The spectacle he'd performed so far showed me that much, and in my heart, I already knew he would win. I wasn't prepared. I had let myself believe I was safe and free, when I ought to have been planning ways to escape should Tommy do the exact thing he had done.

I shook Eddie again but got nothing. Not a single response.

My time was running out. I knew I had to go. To risk walking towards the danger rather than running from it. But I was going to leave some evidence behind. Some proof that I hadn't just upped and left in the early hours without a word. So, I stashed the card somewhere. I hoped Eddie would soon find it. And then I kissed him and said goodbye before grabbing my jacket and shades and taking off out the door without so much as a backward glance.

Rather than going out the front door, I took the back route, just like Tommy had directed. I bypassed security and left via the side door that took me out onto a thin delivery road behind the apartment building. There, I could see the coffee shop Tommy had told me to go to at the end of it. The baristas were just opening, and I ran toward them, only slowing to check the time on my watch.

That was when I passed a minivan on the side of the road. I hadn't noticed how the side door was open, at least not until it was too late.

As I turned my head to the right to look inside, someone collided with me on the left. They knocked me right off my feet like a footballer tackling the opposition and, as if I weighed nothing at all, bundled me straight into the back. The force had me bouncing off the seat and onto the floor of the van with a thud, and before I could say or do anything, I heard the door slam shut behind me.

Someone else was in the driver's seat and he took off a split-second later, while my attacker focused on subduing me and forcing me into submission. But I wasn't going to let him. I fought back with everything I had. I kicked out and screamed at the top of my lungs, but it was no use. He was one step ahead of me every time and soon had me facedown on the seat with my hands behind my back, which he zip-tied together. I turned my head and peered up at him. But it wasn't Tommy. The man was the same shape and size as him, but he was dark-haired and had a thick beard.

"Who the fuck are you?" I demanded, aiming a kick for his chest, which he caught with ease and flipped me over. Both him and the driver then started to laugh, and then my attacker peeled off his fake beard, prosthetic nose, and wig, revealing his true identity. It was Tommy after all, and the wild look in his eyes told me it wasn't only the face that'd changed. He had to have gotten worse since I'd last seen him. He wasn't the same man I'd known and seemed to have lost even more of his humanity. I realized then how I was royally screwed and, all fight in me gone, I started to wrack with sobs.

"What, didn't you recognize me?" he teased, feigning hurt feelings before pouting those lips I'd once loved kissing. "How about if I say, *sorry, Mrs. Lady*?" he then added, putting on a Mexican accent, and he just about fell over laughing when I groaned in recognition.

Tommy had been in my home while Eddie and I were there, and I was naked on the sofa. It wasn't some silly man who'd somehow gotten locked in behind his friends. He was the monster I'd run from months before and I'd been right to be paranoid because he hadn't left me be. He'd never been gone and the look on his face told me he was going to take great pleasure in telling me all the ways he'd infiltrated my life without me having had any idea.

"I hate you," I ground, but he didn't care. His eyes held nothing but urge-fueled desire that was burning scarily brightly for me.

Tommy finished laughing at my expense and then reached his hand towards me as though he might be about to stroke my face. Thinking twice, he then produced a small syringe from his pocket, which he tapped and pressed down on to release any air. I tried my best to move away, but he was quick and had the upper hand and so before I knew it the needle was in my thigh and I was drifting away into the black abyss of forced sleep.

SIX

Tommy

As I watched Piper succumb to the drugs I'd given her, I sunk back on my haunches and watched her with a heavy pang in my chest. Tears welled in my eyes and all I could do was stare at her unblinkingly as my emotions began to overwhelm me. I then balled my hands into fists and bit down on the knuckle of my right hand in a bid to silence myself as I began to cry.

I hadn't cried in years and didn't really understand why I was suddenly doing it, but when it was over and I forced myself to get a grip, I realized what it was—sheer fucking elation. Piper was back. She was mine. The plan had worked, and she was with me again.

I was overwhelmed with joy and love and clambered over to her so I could see her face up close. I kissed her lips and cheeks before then, pulling her into my lap on the floor of the van and cradling her like a baby. Man, I had it bad, but I couldn't help but worship her like some cult follower and their omnipresent leader. I would make her love me again. Piper had no choice because I would become her everything and take back all the power I'd once had over her. I'd manipulated her mind easily before and would do it again. I would have her with me forever.

I'd meant what I'd said, though. She had been naughty and needed to be punished. We'd get that over with and then I'd play nice.

Miles drove us straight to the cabin, where I bundled Piper's limp body into one of those huge backpacks hikers used and closed the zip. She was going to have a bumpy ride on my back, but it didn't matter if she had a few bruises in the aftermath. She wasn't going to leave the cabin for filming or photo-shoots this time. In fact, she'd never leave at all.

With her on my back, I waved goodbye to Miles and headed down the path that led to our den of iniquity. We'd cleaned up the place, and I'd laid everything out, ready for Piper's arrival. It was going to be perfect and so I found myself excited to get her there at long last.

"You're going to love it here, baby," I told her as I bounded over the roots and rocks. "It's perfect. Just like you. We're going to be happy again, you and me. I promise." God, I sounded soppy, but I just couldn't help it.

For the first time in months, I was excited and couldn't wait to share that excitement with the woman I loved.

We arrived, and I unzipped the bag before settling Piper on the bed. I carefully arranged her atop the covers and checked her pockets, removing her keys, the cell phone I'd already smashed up, and purse before stashing them back in the holdall, along with her sneakers and jacket. But there was something missing. Shit. She'd left the card behind. I was sure she'd be so mortified by it she would've shoved it in her pocket along with her other things, but I was wrong. I had underestimated her and felt myself flush with rage. It didn't matter that she was out cold. I still struck her. I slapped her soft face, leaving a handprint behind, and then ran my hand through my hair to stop myself from hitting her again.

It didn't matter. There was nothing Eddie could do and no way he could find her. So what that he'd see the photo I'd printed on the card. I hoped he'd hate her for being my special kind of slut. My dirty, deviant whore who had probably never given herself to him like she had to me.

Just thinking about it had me jonesing for a glimpse of her. I focused back on my task and peeled off her clothes. Fuck, she was still so perfect. Utterly beautiful and flawless. I couldn't wait to take her again and ripped my own clothes off as well, my dick rock hard as I continued to position her atop the bed. I started by shackling her ankles to one another via one of my trusty chains and then cuffed her right wrist and attached it to the chain that I'd secured around my good and sturdy friend Mr. Pipe. There was no escape. She was good to go.

I knew she'd fight me once she woke up though, so added a second pair of cuffs to the mix, securing her wrists to one another as well. Piper could scream and shout and fight all she wanted, but she wasn't going to get very far with her hands cuffed together and the chain between her ankles only giving a couple feet of slack. She couldn't run and was helpless. My captive. My perfect, perfect little slave.

I checked my watch and was both impressed and disappointed with how fast I'd completed the task of getting her settled in. I'd overestimated how long I'd need and realized I'd given Piper far too high a dose of the tranquilizer I'd opted for. She'd be out for at least another half hour or so.

She was cold too. I could tell thanks to the speckling of goosebumps all over her tanned skin and I climbed onto the bed so I could hold her. It didn't matter that she was out of it. Being close had the same effect as always and my cock was screaming at me to let it take the plunge into the pool it'd been left waiting for satisfaction in for far too long.

With just a tilt of my hips, I pushed up, coaxing my way inside. It took a few nudges, but then I was in. Coated in her gloriousness once more, and I began to weep all over again. By the time I'd come, my tears were dry and a different kind of need overcame me. I needed Piper to feel intimidated by me and know she'd been claimed. I could never show her that caring and loving side ever again. Only the dominant who owned her body and would take it whenever he damn well wanted.

I turned her onto her back and stretched her knees apart before sinking back inside. I took her harder than I ever had before and came quickly, but I didn't mind at all. I could go night and day now that she was with me, or at least that was how it felt. Nothing could stop me, and nothing would.

SEVEN

Piper

I felt like death warmed up when I came to and tried hard to fight the pounding headache that was clouding both my vision and my hearing. All I could hear was the thumping in my ears. But then, as it began to subside, it was replaced by another thudding sound. And a stinging, aching across my ass. As reality came swooping back, I realized what was happening and tried to move, but was held back in place by a heavy hand that bruised my skin it was holding me so damn hard. I was on my belly, my face pressed into a pillow, and my captor was over me, whipping me from behind.

"Please stop, Tommy. I don't deserve this," I croaked, but he didn't stop. He simply brushed the hair out of my face and kissed my cheek like he wasn't beating and hurting me.

Tommy then shushed me and kissed his way over the tops of my naked shoulders, and I realized then how he was using nothing more than his huge palm to deliver me his punishment.

"You can't lie to me, Piper. I warned you it was time for you to be punished. But who knew you'd so enjoy being woken this way? I never took you for a masochist. You've already come for me once, can't you feel it?" he moaned, and then delivered a slap to my exposed pussy, making me shriek in shock. "Our bodies were made to fit together, don't you agree?"

Tommy climbed up and positioned himself behind me, and I knew what was about to happen. I tried to move away, but he was too quick. He pushed his cock all the way inside me and I cried out, shaking my head as a barrage of tears cascaded from my eyes. He didn't care and left it exactly where it was as he continued to pin me down on the bed from behind.

And that was when I felt it. I could feel my pussy tensing. Sense the involuntary spasms that I knew could only mean one thing. He had to have been right, and I'd come for him even while knocked out. I wanted to be sick at the sheer thought.

"No, Tommy," I tried. "I don't want this. You can't just take it."

I felt my body spasm again and then could feel him emptying inside of me. I gagged and cried even harder. Tommy simply flipped me onto my back and watched me with a smile that turned my stomach even more.

"Okay, okay. You got me. I couldn't wait any longer, so I got started without you. But you can't blame me, baby. You're just too beautiful," he said, as if it was the most normal thing in the world to have fucked me like that. To have beaten me while I was out cold and then taken me against my will.

Oh, God. Reality struck at that thought. He'd taken me. Drugged me. Kidnapped me. I hated him more than I'd ever hated anyone before and glared at him.

"I'll just add it to your list, shall I?" I retorted. "Kidnapping, stalking, rape…"

Tommy simply continued to grin down at me, and he had the gall to nod his head as I reeled off his list of misdemeanors. Like he was proud of them.

"Don't forget murder," he then said, as though reminding me of something I ought to already know.

"M…murder?" I croaked.

"Oh yes," he replied as he climbed back and then began pacing up and down at the end of the bed. "It all started years ago, but I forced those urges away. I towed the line, but then Marina happened."

"No! You didn't murder that poor girl, did you?" I cried, feeling like such a damn fool for not having realized sooner. He'd never really cared that she was dead. Never showed any real empathy for what she'd been through. He'd always wanted to just brush the entire thing under the carpet, and I finally knew why. It wasn't because he felt bad for her or regretted not having been able to help her. It was because he hated not being able to brag and tell everyone the truth about what'd truly happened that day.

"Yes, of course. I mean, what else was there to do but put her out of her misery? It was a joint effort, but I did the hard part," he told me, still pacing. "I tried to stop myself from doing it again, but I couldn't, Piper. And then, when you left me, I told you I'd do it again. And you knew I had to keep going, didn't you?"

"I what?" I screeched. I'd done nothing of the sort.

"You remember," he told me, as though I was so cute for not recalling how I'd outright told him to go and murder people. *Do it over and over again while you think of me.* That's what you said. And I did, Piper. I thought of you every time I slit a woman's throat or beat them to death. I thought of you with every drop of blood I shed. You should be proud of me."

"I don't know what I am, but proud isn't it. You disgust me," I groaned, turning my face away from the man I couldn't believe I had ever loved. The man who was a monster. A monster I had apparently helped shape.

EIGHT

Tommy

My lady sure did protest too much. I could see that glint in her eye. The flush of her cheeks. The curl of her lip she was trying to hide. Piper was shouting it from the rafters, denying that what I'd done meant a thing at all. But I could see through her façade. She was proud of me. Of my chosen way of honoring her.

Women. Why couldn't they just let themselves be the person who was hiding within? Why were there always the fake smiles and the made-up faces? I didn't want any part of it anymore, and that was just another reason why the cabin was such an utterly perfect place for Piper and me to get reacquainted. She didn't have to play a role or maintain her golden-girl reputation. She simply had to let herself go and she'd be free. Like me. I would accept her only when she'd learned her lesson and accepted her fate.

Standing over her, she seemed so small. So insignificant in comparison to my own huge frame. And yet she meant the world to me. I needed her to see the truth. To understand. Even if I had to tear her to pieces just so I could put her back together how I designed.

She had to realize how I felt. That she was, and always had been, a part of me. An entity coursing through my veins. A voice inside my head that would never quit.

Surely I was the same for her?

Did she hear my voice night and day like I heard hers?

Did she wake up in the night drenched in sweat and screaming my name like I did hers?

Yes. She had to. If she didn't, then I would make her. Force her. She would become a part of me, no matter what.

I saw Piper shudder and had to admit; it was cold. Fall had arrived and with it, the chilled air, and darker nights. Being naked wasn't the best idea, but at least in my chilly cabin she was out of the elements. She wouldn't die of hypothermia or starve to death. Piper would stay with me until I decided otherwise, and so I didn't fret. Didn't rush.

She'd learn to please me and earn her rewards, and so I decided to play our first game to help her feel better acquainted with her new home and the rules I intended for her to follow there. It was a game Piper would easily win if she just did as she was told. Only her pride would get in her way, and I was determined to force her out of that timid shell, but for good this time.

"Are you cold?" I asked, "I'll give you a blanket if you play a game with me, Piper?" I offered and saw her eyes flash with both defiance and intrigue, but knew she was tempted. However, it appeared my girl wanted to negotiate first. She was having some kind of internal conversation with herself, as if she was deliberating over something. Probably trying to figure out what to say or do before she reacted, but I could see it all over her face.

I had expected her to beg for her freedom or barter with me for the chance to get free, but instead I saw the shutters go down behind her eyes and knew she'd forced her emotions aside. The first sign of her acceptance. Piper's head was in the game, and when she spoke, she was calm and collected. Nothing like a poor little captive, and I was pleased to see her succumbing to her true nature already, rather than continuing to play her good girl role.

"I don't care about being naked or cold, Tommy," she answered in a soft and timid voice. "What I care about is you not taking anything else from me without my consent. If I agree to play, it's for real rewards," she replied as she sat up on the bed and regarded me with an icy stare. Ooh. Now this was interesting.

"What kind of rewards?" I asked, feeling tempted myself. She knew I enjoyed toying with her, and I could tell she was using her knowledge of my inner demons to her advantage, but I loved how cunning she had decided to be rather than play the victim. We both knew that wouldn't work, so what was the point? It was fun watching her try, though.

"If I win, you can't touch me for say… twelve hours?" came her offer.

Never gonna happen, but I let her think it was a reasonable proposal.

"And if I win?" I countered.

"You can choose. I'll do you a favor or give you a space of time in which I won't fight back. You can do whatever you want to me and I'll take it." I thought about her offer for a moment. It was a good deal and one I was sure could be renegotiated should I lose our little bet. It was a risk I was willing to take and after all, she had more to lose than I did. She didn't even seem scared either, the silly little lamb.

"Deal," I told her. I then rummaged in my pocket for a quarter and flipped it in the air. The coin fell onto the ground and I covered it with my foot. "Nice and simple. Heads or tails?" Piper seemed awkward. As if the weight of what she was offering up suddenly dawned on her. If she lost, she would have to give me more than I'd already taken without her consent, and I wasn't all that sure she was totally ready for what I had in store.

NINE

Eddie

I woke late with a stinking headache and groaned as the bright sunshine streamed in through the large window beside our bed. Why was it hitting me by force this morning? It wasn't usually so bright. I turned and shoved my face into my pillow, groaning and forcing myself awake. My entire body was aching and after a few seconds spent trying to coax myself awake gently, I decided to do it by force. Rolling onto my side, I flung my legs off the bed and sat upright with a groan.

"Great. Flu, just what I need," I grumbled to myself, thinking how that had to be the reason for my sluggish body and all-round shitty feeling. Even my feet ached. Well, my left foot in particular. It felt like it was throbbing and as I stood and shuffled over to the en-suite, I cursed and walked on the heel of my foot to take some pressure off my toes. I tried to wrack my brains whether I'd stubbed a toe or trodden on something the night before, but everything was just too fuzzy.

When I hit the bathroom, I left the light off and just held the door open a crack while I took a piss and then splashed some water on my face. I guessed that made me feel a bit better, and so I did it again before padding back into the bedroom.

The clock on my nightstand told me it was almost noon, and I groaned again. I must've slept through my alarm and grabbed my cell to discover I'd also missed a bunch of calls. Shit.

Piper was nowhere to be seen too, so I tried her number, but it went straight to voicemail.

"Hey. I'm guessing you're out with Janie or something. I'm sorry I slept through you getting up, but I think I have the flu or maybe some kinda virus. I only just woke up and feel like crap," I said into the automated machine. "Call me when you can so I know everything's okay."

I turned and fell back onto the bed with a huff and was about to let myself fall back onto my pillow when I noticed a note tucked beneath my wallet and keys on the bedside table. Snatching it up, I stared at the note in shock. It took me a few reads before I fully comprehended what it was telling me and cursed as a wave of nausea washed over me.

'Eddie,

I can't do this anymore. I can't be who you want me to be, no matter how hard I try. I'm going away for a while by myself again and doubt I'll ever come back. Don't come looking for me because I don't want to be found.

Piper.'

My heart lurched, and I croaked out her name, hoping by some miracle she might be somewhere in the apartment and had changed her mind. This wasn't like her. None of it seemed the sort of thing she would've done, and I just couldn't believe that what she'd written was true. It looked like her handwriting all right, but those weren't her words. They couldn't be.

I jumped up, ignoring the pain in my foot or the flu-like symptoms that seemed to be abating, and checked her drawers. Some clothes were missing, as was her passport and the stash of money I knew she'd kept with it in case of emergencies. Even her toiletries had vanished from the bathroom and when I checked the kitchen for her purse, that too was gone. As if she'd packed a bag and disappeared into the night.

Could I really have misjudged her? Would she up and leave like that without talking things through with me first? The evidence told me yes, but a niggling sensation in the pit of my stomach was telling me otherwise. I couldn't shake the feeling that something was wrong.

I called up her manager and couldn't ignore the shakiness to her voice. She was worried too and agreed that the entire scenario didn't seem right. Piper would've at least gone to Janie about it if she wanted to run off and be alone. Even if she hadn't wanted to talk to me, she would've turned to her best friend for help and advice.

"I'm reporting her missing," I told Janie. "If she left us all and ran off for some alone time, then so be it, but at least we'll know we did everything we could before ignoring the fact that she upped and left in the middle of the night."

"I agree," she replied, which immediately made me feel better. "I'll come over and talk to the cops with you." I told her yes, thinking that'd be kinda great to have someone there who agreed with me, and then ended the call.

With hands that were shaking hard, I then pulled up the keypad and hit the number nine. I almost lost my nerve but then forced myself to press the number one in two quick successions.

I then heard the operator asking what my emergency was and quickly relayed the issue to her before being passed onto the missing persons department.

It took all day before anyone came to talk with me about Piper's disappearance. By that point Janie had been over for hours and we were both nervous wrecks.

"Listen, it honestly seems like she took off of her own accord," one of the police officers, Sergeant Fuller, told me after we'd been over the story what felt like fifty times. I knew he was right, but I couldn't let it go.

"Please, at least run her cards and check her cell GPS," I implored him.

"We're already doing that. There's been no activity on either," he answered.

With a huff, I stood and winced as my toe throbbed with pain again.

"What's with that?" a second officer asked me, and I shrugged.

"It's been hurting like a bitch all day," I answered.

"Only today?" Fuller jumped on the issue, and I frowned.

"Yeah..."

"Could we take a look?" he then asked. I nodded and lifted my foot, feeling around for the source of the pain. There was a small red lump right between my little toe and the one next to it. I guessed it was a bite or something, but Fuller didn't seem so sure. "I think we should run a tox-screen," he told his partner before turning back to me. "You definitely didn't have this before today?"

"No, definitely not. And, if it's relevant, when I woke up this morning it was way later than usual, and I felt like I had the flu."

"You don't seem feverish or sick now. So, your symptoms just stopped?" I nodded, and Fuller began to write furiously in his notebook. I hoped his reaction had to be a good sign. It finally felt like they were going somewhere, but I didn't quite know where. I just hoped we'd know more before too long.

TEN

Piper

All I could see was darkness. All I could hear was the trickling of rain overhead, and the only taste and smell I could distinguish was tangy and metallic. I knew without question that it was blood. My blood.

I'd won some of the coin tosses, which had resulted in thirty minutes of glorious peace and quiet each time, but the ones I'd lost had shown me just how far Tommy was willing to go with this horrible game of his. He'd fucked me the first time, and I'd done as I had promised and not fought back. But I hadn't enjoyed it. Not with him. Not anymore.

The next loss. It was apparently time for me to get a spanking, but the time after that Tommy decided a belt would be better and took that to my ass instead.

After losing another three consecutive coin tosses, I had fallen at Tommy's feet and begged him to stop playing. I'd promised him I'd be a good girl, and I'd even let my tears flow freely, thinking he might cave at the sight of them. He didn't so much as flinch. I knew he'd changed from just that act alone, but the beatings were entirely new between us, and he didn't stop there.

Tommy had slapped me across the face, sending me hurtling to the ground. And then, after he'd plucked me back up and thrown me on the bed, he'd punched me on my mouth and then blindfolded me.

"Heads or tails?" he asked me again, and I could hear the high-pitched ring of the coin in his hands. I refused to answer. Refused to play any longer. "Aww, you're no fun," he then demanded before climbing onto the bed behind me and pulling me close. I whimpered and tried to pull away, but he just gripped me tighter.

"What do you want from me, Tommy?" I whispered, hating that I couldn't see him thanks to the blindfold. "Did you bring me here to kill me?"

"Maybe," he answered, stroking my back so delicately it made me cry.

ELEVEN

Tommy

I let Piper sleep and found myself drifting off beside her in no time at all. I slept deeply and for a good eight hours, which was for the first night in weeks. I'd survived on a few hours' max for a long time and woke the next morning feeling refreshed and ready to conquer the world.

Piper was awake too, but I could tell she was trying to pretend otherwise, so I wrenched the blindfold off her eyes and looked her up and down in the morning light.

"You're a bit of a mess, baby," I told her honestly, eyeing her bruises and the bloody scabs I'd given her the day before. "Let's get you washed up and dressed for the day."

I unlocked each of her cuffs and lifted her up into my arms before then heading straight for the shower. Piper winced and let out small cries as I tended to her, but she was a good girl and let me wash her clean and take a razor to the few hairs that'd been left untended at the peak of her pussy.

She then stood pressed against the cold tiles while I washed myself too, and I was glad I hadn't had to warn her to behave. My girl just knew what was expected of her and I was pleased. I hadn't liked hurting her the day before, but she'd needed to see the new and improved me.

That was a lie. I'd loved it. She'd had to learn she couldn't turn on the waterworks and get away. That she couldn't talk her way out of my firm grasp on her or bargain for her life. It was all mine now, and she'd soon learn to accept her destiny and know that every moment of good or bad was because I'd allowed it. She wasn't in control any longer, and it was good to know she had begun to accept it.

After our shower, I dressed Piper in one of those stunning wispy dresses I knew she liked so much, and then blow-dried her hair. I enjoyed the process and continued to brush her long blonde locks for a while, even after they were dry. And then I took a good look at my handiwork and beamed down at her. "You're so beautiful, Piper," I said, delivering a gentle kiss to her lips. She flinched but didn't stop me.

After putting the shackles back on her ankles, I opted to handcuff her to me rather than leave her in the bedroom. I then directed Piper out into the small living area and kitchen, where I made her a bowl of cereal and we sat side-by-side at the table to eat our breakfast and watch the morning sunshine as it peered down at us from above the treetops.

This trip was turning out to be everything I'd wanted and more. So perfect, just the two of us, completely secluded and off the grid. Away from the noise of the city and the overbearing influences from other people. In the cabin, we could be ourselves again. We were free.

After breakfast we moved to the sofa, where we watched TV for a while and snuggled the entire time. Things were finally getting back to normal, and I loved being able to spend quality time with Piper so soon after having taken her. I expected more fight, but she'd succumbed to me easily and I knew it was because she understood there was no point in fighting. That we were meant to be.

After all, what was the point in fighting fate?

TWELVE

Piper

I kept quiet all day, having made a conscious decision earlier that morning to do everything I could to hopefully ensure I didn't incur any more of Tommy's wrath. But it was also in a bid to lure him into believing I was giving into him. That he was winning. I decided to play the timid captive if that was what he wanted, and it seemed to be working. He hadn't hurt me and that was a good start, at least.

He hadn't touched me sexually all day either, in fact, and it was nice not to have to endure his affections or rough lovemaking like we'd had the day before. We even snuggled and while I hated it, I forced myself to relax against him as I pretended to watch whatever show he seemed intent on binge watching.

He later unlocked the cuff securing me to his wrist and put it around the chain connecting my ankles. I was effectively tied to my own feet so knew I couldn't stand without being bent double, but thanks to the slack on the chain it wasn't too uncomfortable just sitting with my feet up on the sofa beneath me.

I was about to ask him why when he changed screen and grabbed a games controller from the nearby drawer and started playing some violent computer game. Tommy was quickly consumed by it and with his attention off me, I used the time to have a proper think about my situation. To take stock and try to come up with a plan of escape.

We were back in the mountains, but in a different cabin. One I was sure had no way of being traced back to Tommy, so knew that would be of no help. Next question on my list was whether I could get a message to the outside world somehow. There was no phone receiver on the wall and I'd not seen Tommy use his cell, so figured there'd be no reception either. But then again, he'd somehow managed to stream that TV show we'd just watched. How had he managed that? There had to be a hardline somewhere. A connection to the outside world I could try and use to get a message to the cops. A spark of hope ignited in my chest, and I found myself feeling lighter.

Tommy seemed to notice the change in the air, and I wanted to curse when he turned to me with a bright smile. Like I might be happy there with him or coming around. Not fucking likely, and if he thought so, then he truly was deluded.

I pretended to be watching his game, while really, I was enjoying being out from under his radar for a little while. I had hoped he might be one of those typical guys who would happily play their video games for hours and hours while ignoring their girlfriends, but it appeared I was shit outta luck on that front as he'd apparently had enough after just a short while.

"I like watching you play, Tommy," I lied. "What other games do you have?"

"I don't wanna play anymore," he answered with a roguish grin before plucking me up off the sofa and carrying me to the bedroom like I weighed nothing.

He placed me down on the bed, and I knew what was going to happen. I didn't fight him and let my body go limp when he lifted my dress and coaxed his way inside me. I even let him kiss me and I kissed him back in a bid to keep the sweet and gentle side of him out while doing the deed. I wouldn't be able to cope with it if my tormentor returned. The other guy would do quite nicely if that was the only other alternative.

But then, against my command, my body started to respond to him in other ways. Tommy was being so lovely, and before I could stop myself, I was moving in rhythm to his thrusts. I was letting out small gasps, and the only sensation coming from my core was one of pleasure. I even came for him. And it was good. Really good. So good that I didn't even try to stop him from carrying on when I came back down from my high.

God, I felt so confused. By the time he was done, we'd been at it for over an hour, and he hadn't hurt me or been too rough. I didn't even feel like I'd been forced into it. But I still wasn't going to let him win. I wasn't going to live the rest of my life as Tommy's slave.

It didn't matter that when he was nice he was so perfect, because when that other side of him came out, he was truly awful. And when that side was unleashed, there was a part of me that instinctually seemed to know that this would be how I eventually died. At the hands of the man who apparently loved me, but too much. So much so it'd turned him into a violent and devious monster.

THIRTEEN

Eddie

Piper had been gone another day, and I was going more and more stir crazy. I'd called up her folks and told them what was happening, and they hadn't heard from her either but revealed how they often didn't speak when she was busy with work so hadn't suspected a thing. They gave me nothing to go on, so I politely said my goodbyes and then set about searching the apartment from top to bottom again.

It was only when I decided to change the bed sheets that a clue finally revealed itself. Some kind of greeting card had been wedged between my bed and the mattress, and it came flying out the gap when I yanked the sheet clear.

I plucked it up off the floor and was almost sick right there. On the front of the card was my darling Piper. She'd been defiled and used like some cheap whore before being made to show a sign that I could tell was all for Tommy Darke's benefit. I didn't have to see what was inside to know the card had come from him. That it must have been his idea of some sick joke. The words inside were even more sinister. Everything finally added up. He'd threatened my life if she didn't go to him. And so, Piper must have gone, but it was clear to me how it couldn't have been willingly.

I grabbed my cell and called Fuller, who answered after the second ring.

"I've found something," I told him. "Something that proves she didn't go voluntarily."

He was at my apartment within twenty minutes and when I showed him the card, both Fuller and his partner Dobbs looked sour.

"You told us how she'd said things grew violent between her and Tommy before the end. Do you think this is what she was talking about?" he asked, indicating to the picture.

"It has to be," I replied. "She never gave me much in the way of details, but I was aware of how he manipulated and abused her for the fun of it. He liked to punish Piper and this screams his sick and twisted way."

"You can't know that for sure," Fuller reminded me. "You're only going on what Piper told you. By all accounts, she once told Janie that she enjoyed the rougher way Tommy had about him. That she toyed with his dark side. Maybe she liked being treated this way."

"It's not uncommon," Dobbs added, but I shook my head.

"She likes it rough sometimes, sure, but nothing like this," I demanded, pointing to the picture. "Never like this."

I felt like I was about to explode, but then Fuller's cell went off and everything went eerily quiet.

I watched as he listened intently to whomever was on the other end of the call. He barely said a thing until right at the end when he uttered the words I had been dreading, but which also put the case firmly beneath the right heading.

"We're coming in and I'm bringing Mr. Martin. Have the footage ready for when we get there," he said before ending the call and turning toward me with a frown. "Your tox-screen came back. You were drugged using a needle that was forced between your toes in an attempt to hide any marks. Whoever did it missed the vein, which is why the injection site was inflamed and sore."

I nodded in understanding and went cold and I began wringing my hands. "There's more," Fuller said, looking from me to his partner and back. "We've obtained footage from a side entrance to the apartment building at around five-am yesterday morning. It shows Piper as she's forced into a van before then being driven away."

"So he let himself in, drugged me, packed her bags and then delivered that card before waiting for her to follow the orders inside and head for the coffee shop so he could snatch her?"

"It appears so, yes," Fuller replied.

He then watched and didn't say a word as I stood, walked through to the kitchen, and then proceeded to vomit into the sink.

FOURTEEN

Tommy

Talk about the perfect day. Ours was epic on all proportions, and I found myself never wanting it to end. We stayed up late into the night making love and holding one another, and while there were times I wanted to talk and catch up, Piper was too tired. She would always listen as I spoke but not respond, and I'd soon given up and we'd both fallen deeply asleep.

When I woke up, Piper stirred but stayed asleep and so I handcuffed her, climbed out of bed, and pulled on some clothes before heading out the front door of the cabin. There, I turned a sharp right and descended a set of stairs that led to a secluded room built into the base of the house. Kind of like a basement. There had been nothing much inside when Miles and I had first taken over the place, but now it had been fully insulated and damp proofed. We had cables running into it from the pylons to the west and while primitive, we'd procured ourselves some Ethernet cabling and a couple megabytes of Internet connectivity. It was more than enough for what we needed. All I'd wanted was a small link to the outside world should we need it and both Miles and I had agreed from the start that if this place was to become our makeshift 'Man Cave' then we had to have TiVo and access to online gaming. We weren't cavemen after all.

I fired up the laptop we kept down there and accessed the gossip columns and news sites. Just as I thought, Piper's disappearance hadn't made the headlines at first, but now she'd been missing for a couple of days and her face was everywhere. That ass-hat Eddie Martin had called it in right away, but reports said it wasn't until evidence came into police possession the evening before that they'd truly thought anything sinister had happened to the young starlet. But now everyone knew Piper was gone, and not by choice. I wondered if I ought to have taken extra measures to make it look like she'd left of her own accord, but also knew I'd been too excited to finally take her that I had cut corners knowingly, and without a care. I'd gotten away with my prize, and that was all that mattered.

When I had seen enough, I shut down and locked back up and then headed up the stairs and into the cabin, where I was sure to take the lightest of steps so I could hardly be heard. Inside, I found Piper fiddling with her cuffs while pushing a hairgrip into the lock. She had no idea what she was doing, and I knew she'd never be able to get free that way. She was simply copying what she'd seen in the movies, and I let out a deep, rumbling laugh.

"While I find myself amused by your silly attempt at lock picking, I think you know what I have to do now," I told her with a cunning smile. Piper jumped out of her skin and held her hands up in defense, shaking her head and begging me not to. But it was no use. My girl just couldn't help herself, could she? She had to push the boundaries and break the rules. And now I was going to have to punish her for it.

"No, Tommy. Please," she tried, but it was already too late. Her tormentor was in the room. He was in control of every part of me and wouldn't stop until his hunger for retribution was quenched. Until her will was broken and her body his to command.

"Let's play a new game," I told her, and was surprised by how different my voice seemed to sound. Like I truly was someone else. Someone gruffer. Rawer. A feral mountain man. I rolled my shoulders and closed my eyes, acquainting myself with this persona I knew had always been there, but had laid dormant. Until now. He was tough enough to do what needed to be done without breaking, and with him in command, I was ready for anything.

I went to a set of drawers in which I'd stashed the backpack Piper had come in and stuck my hand in one of the side pockets. She watched in horror as I produced a small hunting knife and approached. She even scooted back on the bed and curled in around herself. Like that was going to save her from my wrath.

Silly girl.

Quickly, I lunged for her and grabbed the chain between her feet and then yanked hard. Piper seemed to forget she was light as a feather and a second later she was curled in a ball on the bed right in front of me. She cried out and tried to move back again. But I just curled the chain still in my grasp around my hand, the links tightening and pinching my flesh. Damn, that felt satisfying. More so than the knife, which I threw to one side.

Piper stopped fighting the inevitable and with my free hand I smoothed her hair out of her face, revealing the wide-eyed and understandably petrified girl beneath. If she thought her obvious fear and compliance would appeal to my better instincts, she would have to think again. All I wanted was to make her more scared of me, so I put my hand around her throat and gave it a little squeeze. Not enough to choke her, but enough to see to it that she knew I meant business. "One for you and one for me, Piper," I told her with a smile before letting go. "Even Stevens…"

And then I slapped her across the face, good and hard.

When she'd recovered, I was still standing over her, but I didn't strike. No, it was her turn.

Piper grasped the terms of our new game without any need for further explanation, and she offered me her still bound wrists.

"Then unlock these so I can do it properly," she demanded with a fire in her blue eyes that drove me wild.

I hesitated, wondering if I should refuse, but then I'd be breaking the terms of my own game. Things would never be even between us, but with her handcuffed, I had an even more unfair advantage. So, I reached into my pocket and pulled out the key, which I quickly used to remove the cuffs. I half expected her to hesitate when free of them. To not want to hurt me. But instead, she went right for it.

She punched me straight in the mouth and it hurt like a bitch but was the good sort of pain. The type of pain that fueled the rage bubbling within me rather than quash it.

I let out a small laugh and then licked the blood from my lower lip with a satisfied smile.

"That's one for you, which makes it my turn…"

As I stood in the kitchen later that afternoon, washing the blood from my hands, I watched the setting sun and breathed a deep sigh. I could hear Piper sobbing in the other room, but I wasn't sorry for what I'd done. She'd deserved it and I knew she'd come to understand the fundamentals just as she had before.

If she was naughty, I would punish her. End of story. And anyway, the blood on my hands was my own. She might have the bruises from where I'd hit her, but I would have the scars.

I finished cleaning up and found I couldn't stand her whimpering and whining any longer. I could feel myself growing angry again, so shut the bedroom door. I then fired up my discarded video game and grabbed a beer from the fridge before settling down for a few hours' gaming time. She could have a time-out while I took some time for myself, too.

I could never hate her, but that didn't mean I wanted to be around her all the time.

FIFTEEN

Eddie

We watched that awful surveillance camera footage over and over at the precinct. The picture was grainy, but it was obviously Piper charging down that street before being shoved into an awaiting minivan by one man before another drove them away. I'd expected to see Tommy Darke in all his glory on that screen, but it wasn't him at all. If anything, it looked kinda like that waiter from the other night.

"The waiter!" I cried, waving Sergeant Fuller over. He approached with a kind smile I saw right through. I knew he'd been growing tired of my presence at the precinct but was allowing me some respite of my forced alone time. It was paying off, though. I'd figured out another lead. "This man," I told him, pointing to the screen where I'd paused the awful footage. "He's not the same coloring but is the same height and build as this waiter we had a strange run-in with at our home a while ago."

"That's good," Fuller replied, and I was comforted to see that I might be able to help some more. "Tell me all about what happened and where you hired the people who came to work for you. We'll check their credentials and see if anything stands out."

We spent the next hour doing exactly that while his team scoured the records held at the apartment building for the hired helpers, they'd sent up to us that night. There wasn't a Mexican man who'd matched my description of the chef who had ended up staying behind. No one even remotely similar.

It was suddenly all too clear to me how it wasn't an accident at all. I had just been too trusting of the apologetic stranger, and all the while it'd been part of his ploy to get to Piper. To stalk her and infiltrate our lives.

I put my head in my hands and cursed. I should've believed her when she'd said she felt like someone was watching her. She hadn't been right since the moment we'd stepped off that plane and I'd forced her to let her guard down. Made her feel safe in a home that psycho had come into more than once.

"How did he get in and out unnoticed?" I eventually managed to ask Fuller, who opened a set of video files on his laptop to show me.

"Not unnoticed. He hid in plain sight, Mr. Martin," Fuller answered with a grim expression on his otherwise boyish face. He then pressed play on the files in turn, and I watched as an unassuming man strolled up and down the stairs and hallway to my apartment at different times over the past few days. He'd known where each and every camera was positioned. Had turned his face away and moved with such an air of authority, not a soul would've questioned his presence.

Even when he'd let himself into our apartment, Tommy had somehow made it look perfectly natural for a relative stranger to be gaining entry in the early hours. Plus, apparently, he'd had his own key too. Of course nobody would question him.

Nobody but Piper, who'd known something wasn't right.

SIXTEEN

Piper

I fell asleep lying on my belly with my arms tied above my head to the bedframe, courtesy of my captor, and was out cold in no time thanks to the pain and exhaustion keeping me just as captive as my binds.

God, I'd been so stupid. Tommy had crept up on me and caught me in the act, and there was nothing I could've said or done to try and deny the fact that I was clearly trying to escape. I'd found the hairpin in my toiletry bag and don't even know what I was thinking by attempting to magically unlock my cuffs using it.

Stupid. I was stupid and had spent the rest of the day paying for it.

Gone was my gentle lover from the day before. Tommy had flipped his switch and had gone into full tormentor-mode on me. He'd beaten me worse than anything I'd endured before and had then sat back and watched me struggle rather than comfort me. He'd watched as I had curled into a ball and cried my heart out with the pain. Like some sick show he was enjoying having front row seats to.

I had to wonder if or when he was going to flip the switch and become my protector again but hoped it would be soon. I couldn't handle more torture.

I woke early the next morning to discover I'd wet the bed. It wasn't a surprise really, given the fact that I'd been tied to the bed for an entire day so hadn't been able to relieve myself, but it didn't make me feel any less ashamed.

I stifled my gags at the smell and was overcome with a need to get away. To get off the disgusting mattress so I mustered my strength and yanked at the headboard, wincing with pain from my bruised body. But then the wooden pole holding me in place came loose. Loose enough that I could climb up off the dirty bed at last.

After standing by the bedside, trembling with both the cold and my fear, I then stripped the bed. When it was clear, I felt both surprised and disgusted to discover Tommy had thought ahead and put a mattress protector in place for this very eventuality. To catch whatever liquids might escape the person atop it.

I wanted to vomit.

Didn't he care about my needs at all? Would he just happily let me keep pissing the bed rather than give me the basic comforts everyone deserved?

"Good girl, cleaning up your mess," he told me from the doorway, and I jumped right out of my cold, bruised skin. He'd snuck up on me once again, the bastard, and I cringed. "I guess I can let it slide that you broke free."

I flinched when he charged toward me and was met with a satisfied snigger rather than any kind of apology. Tommy liked me being scared of him. It meant he was winning, but I wasn't strong enough to deny that he was. I had no strength to fight. Only to fear the cruelty I knew he was more than capable of.

"Can I please take a shower?" I asked. "And then I'll wash these sheets."

Tommy unlocked my handcuffs and each of my ankle shackles without a word. He then nodded to the small bathroom before gathering up the urine-stained sheets.

"I'll take care of these, baby. You go wash up," he finally answered, and I took tentative steps over to where I knew a glorious hot shower finally awaited me.

But I didn't trust that he was letting me out of his sight unshackled. Was this another game? A test? I turned back to ask him, but he was gone. So, I did as I'd been told and took a long shower, where I cried my heart out as I cleaned up my battered body.

When I finally emerged after brushing my teeth and braiding my wet hair, Tommy was nowhere to be seen. It felt cold in the cabin, so I headed for the dresser, where I picked out a pair of jeans and a shirt to wear. I hoped Tommy wouldn't begrudge me some warmth and a decent covering of clothing, but I didn't know. I knew nothing at all about what he wanted from me or where we were heading. All I could do was get myself ready and hope for the best.

When I was done, I waited in the bedroom, but Tommy didn't come back in. So, I took tentative steps out into the living area, where I found him lounging on the sofa watching the television like he didn't have a care in the world.

"Would… would you care for some breakfast?" I asked, and Tommy eyed me curiously. He seemed surprised to find me so timid and compliant.

Yeah, as if I'd dare risk shouting my mouth off and incurring more of his wrath. But the fact remained that I was starving. I'd downed a load of water from the bathroom taps, but my stomach was growling after a day of starvation, and I felt weak with hunger. I needed something to eat and so was being proactive about getting it, even if that meant playing nice.

I ambled over to the small kitchenette and made up two bowls of cornflakes, which I then took over to where Tommy was still sitting. He was fixated on the show in front of him and ate his meal without so much as a thank you or a word of warning to me. Nothing. Not even a 'good morning,' or a 'sorry I beat the shit out of you yesterday.' Just stone cold silence.

After I was finished, I took out our bowls and then washed them up, taking care to do a good job.

As I was standing there, the still silent Tommy flicked over to his games console and loaded up some loud video game that I didn't like the look of in just the first few seconds of footage that loaded. He was playing as some kind of gangster who shot people for the fun of it, and I had to wonder what kind of inspiration he'd gotten from games like this. Enough to go from being a loving and sexually domineering man to an all-out asshole who took the concept of a beast in the bedroom to a whole other level? Maybe.

As he sat engrossed in his game, I started cleaning up some more and didn't even think twice when I plucked up the garbage bag and took it outside in search of the trashcan.

I was standing there in the morning sunshine when realization hit me.

I was outside. Tommy was still playing his game in the living room, and I could hear him moving through the levels. He hadn't come after me. He hadn't chained me up or stopped me from leaving. He'd simply presumed I'd become his slave after the day before and was too afraid to dare try and leave him. Well, I wasn't going to stand for that. I was going to fight back. I was going to run.

All I had was socks on my feet, but I didn't let that stop me. I located what looked like a path and ran for it, not looking back for even a second.

I ran and ran until my lungs were screaming for air, and I only came to a stop when I ran out into a clearing by a small lake. A lake with a fisherman sitting right beside it with his fishing rods cast and his breakfast cooking on a small stove beside him.

He turned when he heard someone in the woods behind him, and I watched as his eyes opened wide and he took me in. Yes, I had to be a wreck, but I hoped that would just mean he would help me without question. That he could take me far away from here and maybe even deliver me back home. Back to Eddie.

"What's happened to you?" he asked as he stood and watched me approach. He was an older man who clearly enjoyed his food, judging by the roundness of him, but he seemed genuinely concerned for me. I could see it in his eyes and had to wonder, did he have a daughter my age?

Someone he likened me to just enough that it made him want to protect me? I sure hoped so.

I ambled closer, and I was so grateful at seeing his soft smile that I wanted to cry.

"Please…" I panted. "Please help me. I need to get away from here. I need to call the cops…"

The man nodded, and he pulled off his jacket, which he handed to me. I was so appreciative at the prospect of more warmth and reached for it, thanking him as I did. I'd just started to pull it from his grasp when I saw his eyes dart away from my face to something behind me. Or someone.

I knew before even looking that Tommy had followed my tracks away from the cabin. He'd caught up to us and wasn't going to take my attempt at freedom as anything other than personal.

I was left contemplating what to do next. Whether to explain who we both were and beg the man to help me escape, or perhaps turn and tell Tommy that enough was enough and how I was leaving. I was so close to freedom that I could taste it, and the thought of going back to that cabin made me want to scream.

I watched the fisherman squint as though he was looking at something far away, not just a few feet behind me on the path like I would've expected Tommy to be.

"What is that?" he asked, more to himself than to me, and he got his answer before I could even turn to check it out for myself.

The shot that echoed through the surrounding trees was deafening, and it took care of my new friend in one deathly move from farther up the mountainside. I jumped and stumbled forward, ready to grab hold of the fisherman's hand, but then screamed in horror when I saw how his face was no longer a face, but a skull shaped blob with a gaping and bloody hole in the center of it. It was the most disgusting thing I had ever seen. Nothing like in the movies or how I'd imagine it, but one hundred times worse.

He crumbled to the ground. And I knew I'd remember that awful sight until my dying day. Shame washed over me as I saw him fall, and while I hated knowing I'd been the cause of his untimely demise, I also knew I had two choices. Risk Tommy deciding my fate there and then, or go back to the cabin and my captivity.

I turned back, expecting to see him standing a short distance away, but he was nowhere to be found. So, I took a step back, thinking of keeping on running, when a bullet shot into the ground right by my foot. I followed its trajectory and spied him on his perch. Tommy could see me clearly in the wide open space beside the lake. I was his for the taking and it was his choice whether I'd leave dead or alive. Or maybe it was mine.

I let out a roaring scream, offloading some of my anger and fear as I came to terms with the decision I knew I had to make. To live or to die.

I went to step away again, and just like before, a bullet was fired right next to where I was standing. It appeared Tommy was more than just a deviant sexual predator. He was also an excellent marksman. And he was willing to keep on showing me just how good of a shot he was.

I moved toward the path back to the cabin and was rewarded for my efforts by not being shot at again. He was luring me back, I knew, and there was nothing I could do other than cave to another of Tommy's whims. To let him win in yet more of his games.

I knew I was going to pay for my insolence, but I didn't regret trying. My only regret was not having run faster.

After a slow walk back up the path, I passed Tommy at his perch and refused to so much as look at the smug smile I knew he wore. He was ugly to me now. His face had lost all its charm and cocky appeal. I hated him to his core and knew that it would never change.

I carried right on past him and trudged back up into the cabin, where I yanked off my dirty socks and threw them beside the washer.

"Oh, Piper," Tommy teased as he followed me inside. "You're such a bad girl."

"Yeah, I guess so. Let's just get this over with, shall we?" was all I replied before I shuffled into the bedroom and held my hands together in readiness for the cuffs I knew he was going to put back on me, whether I wanted him to or not.

What came next? I didn't dare wonder, but knew I was about to find out.

SEVENTEEN

Eddie

We had no leads. No witnesses. No ransom demands. That bastard Tommy had covered his tracks so well the police were left with nowhere else to look. No other avenues to pursue.

I left the station after another few hours spent watching the cops chasing their tails and jumped in a cab.

"Where to?" the driver asked me, and I was about to give him my home address, but the thought of going back to that apartment made my blood run cold. Instead, I directed him to the office. There, I could bury myself in work and try to get through the day without resorting to bugging Sergeant Fuller and his team any more than I already knew I had been.

I arrived at work and ignored the pitiful glances from my assistants and creative team. Yes, they hadn't expected me back to work while Piper was still missing, but what else was I meant to do? The police weren't getting anywhere and until she either escaped or Tommy let her go, Piper was gone and there was nothing any of us could do about it.

If Tommy resurfaced, then I just had to hope he'd be caught right away. However, given how he'd already disguised himself so expertly before, something told me he could've been right under our noses no end of times and we would've never known, so he could potentially do the same again and again.

I shut myself in my office and turned on the computer, where I loaded my emails and was met with nothing but her. There were questions and well wishes aplenty, all mixed in with people snooping and trying to get the gossip. And then there was something that made my heart sink. Piper's promo pictures for *Humankind* had been finalized and were sitting in my inbox. The edits were done, and she looked truly stunning, so much so that I broke down just looking at them.

With my head in my hands, I slumped to the ground, where I curled into a ball and cried like I hadn't done in years.

Where was she? What might my poor darling be going through, thanks to Tommy Darke and his obsessive infatuation with her? I didn't know, and I wasn't all that sure I'd ever be equipped to find out.

EIGHTEEN

Piper

I came around with a start and flinched when pain radiated down my spine that was so severe, I went cold and felt my mouth fill with saliva, as though I might be about to puke thanks to it. My cuffs were all back on and Tommy was nowhere to be seen but had well and truly taught me a lesson. One that I wouldn't easily forget. Even with my lame attempts at hurting him back, he'd beaten the shit out of me for daring to try and run. I'd expected that, but then he'd carried on even after I was a bloody mess and was screaming with all my might for him to stop. He'd never gone that far before.

I'd eventually passed out and had drifted in and out of consciousness a few times over the day and then had finally forced myself awake, only to discover I was lying on the cold and hard wooden floor of the cabin like some broken toy he'd had his fun with and then discarded.

The pain echoed again when I tried to move and I wondered if I might have broken bones or fractures, it was so strong. Every movement was torture, but I forced myself to carry on. All I wanted was to find some comfort. Perhaps a softer place to lie, or the warmth of a blanket I could find and put across my broken body. It would be worth it, or so I told myself over and over.

After a couple of attempts, I eventually managed to climb up onto my knees. I curled around myself, hugging my knees to my chest in a bid to stop from trembling, but it was no use. I was going into shock, I could tell, and needed to move. To find something good to hold on to.

With a final cry I eventually managed to stand, but then stood there fighting a head rush as the world around me started to spin. I focused on the sounds of the forest around us. On the birds and the wind rustling the trees. And then, as the dizziness began to subside, I focused on the here and now. The floor was rough beneath my bare feet, and I could feel dampness on the wooden boards. At first, I thought I might have wet myself again, but then I realized it wasn't moist from a liquid that'd been poured onto it, but from the forest itself. No wonder it was always so damn cold.

I clambered to the small bathroom, where I managed to get cleaned up despite my cuffs and the chain at my feet and then attempted to tend to my many wounds. The world closed in, and my panic threatened to return when I caught sight of myself in the mirror. I was a fucking mess and turned away immediately but couldn't stop from crying as I took care of business.

A hundred thoughts were whizzing through my head. Was this going to be my new life? The new me? A prisoner who would be beaten and abused by the man who supposedly loved her?

Yes. I believed it was, but I couldn't do it. I couldn't live like that. I knew I had to find a way to escape. A way out of this hellhole.

I promised myself I'd find it. Somehow. Some day. But first, I needed to play Tommy's game. I had to be a good girl so he wouldn't hurt me like this again. So I could get strong and be ready for when an opportunity eventually presented itself. And it would. He wasn't some mythical creature or a villain from a movie. This was real life, and in real life people made mistakes. They became complacent and let their guard down. I just needed to be patient and wait for Tommy to slip up. I'd learned a valuable lesson that morning and wasn't going to repeat it. I steeled my resolve and knew I couldn't be blinded by my anger or fear but strengthened by it.

I thought back to my questions just moments earlier and changed my answer. No. I wasn't going to be the girl who lived and died just to entertain the man who loved her, or whatever other sick thrill he was getting out of this. I was going to be cunning and clever. Play him at his own game.

The cabin was quiet by the time I'd finished pulling myself together and had finally emerged from the small bathroom. I wondered if Tommy had left, but then I heard the door slam and realized he was just coming back from somewhere. I then heard the television turn on so went to investigate. I peered around the open door to my bedroom just an inch and caught sight of him as he turned over to the sports channel and started peeling off his dirty clothes with his eyes glued to the screen. He was filthy. His boots were covered in thick mud and I could see blood on his hands.

I knew exactly what that meant.

Tommy had clearly just taken care of the mess down by the lake. My mess. The bloody sight of the fisherman being shot in the face right in front of me came whooshing back, and I had to grip the doorframe in front of me to stop from falling in a heap again. I had to wonder where that poor man's body now laid. Was he six feet under in an unmarked grave in which he might never be found? Or had Tommy carved him up and sent the pieces downstream? Either seemed entirely possible, and it made me sick just knowing I'd caused that man to die. It was my fault, and suddenly the beating I'd endured felt justified. As though I'd paid at least a little of the debt I now owed to that poor man.

I stayed silent as I turned away and climbed up onto the bed. The last thing I needed was to attract Tommy's attention again, and I also welcomed the solitude. It was time I started work on this new plan of mine. Time I started to heal. My sheets were still in the washer from before and the bare mattress felt rough against my tender skin, but it was that or the floor, so I made myself comfortable and it wasn't long at all until I'd succumbed to the sleep my body had been craving ever since I'd come to.

I woke early the next morning and unfurled my aching body with a groan, but I didn't cry or call out. I stayed perfectly silent. And I knew what I had to do. I had to stop being a victim and get my head in the game. Starting yesterday.

Tommy was fast asleep on the sofa when I peered around the doorjamb again. He looked peaceful, and there was a part of me that wanted to go to him. To have him hold me and tell me he still wanted me.

How fucked up was that? There I was, having been beaten black and blue by the man who supposedly loved me, and yet was still hoping he would continue doing so.

It was all part of my act, or so I told myself. I was forcing myself to remain warm with Tommy. I wouldn't be able to recoil from him or tell him no, not if I was hoping to fool him into believing I was going to behave. That I still cared for him. I had to force myself to want him. To love him, even after everything he'd done.

I turned away, retreating into the bedroom. The chain would only let me get as far as the doorway anyway so I couldn't have gone to him, but thankfully the small bathroom at the opposite end of the room was still available to me so I used the facilities without much bother and got washed up. It wasn't long before I realized I was starving but didn't dare wake Tommy to ask for something to eat.

Using my hands to cup the water flowing from the cold tap, I instead scooped handful after handful down my throat and gulped at it hungrily. My stomach was empty of food and was screaming for more than just water, but there was nothing else I could offer it, and so if I had this, I knew I could survive. I downed some more and then wiped my chin clean before heading back towards the bed with a sigh.

There, I climbed back onto it and curled into a ball again, willing myself to get some more sleep. It came quickly but wasn't without fretful dreams and a pain in my tummy that just wouldn't go away no matter what I tried.

When I woke again, I could hear the television blaring in the other room and knew Tommy was up and about. I sat up and looked around and immediately noticed how he had to have come into the bedroom while I was out of it again because the pile of my sheets was placed neatly on the chair at the other end of the room. I crept over to them and lifted the soft cotton stack into my arms. The sheets smelled nice and were so inviting I let out a small sigh.

I wasn't sure whether to call out to Tommy and thank him. Or did he want me to stay silent? The door to the living room was closed now, and I figured that had to be what he wanted, so went to it, leaning to one side so I could listen to what was going on through the other side.

I closed my eyes when I heard the sound of the news station wafting over to the doorway.

"The search continues and officers are still appealing for information that might lead to the whereabouts of Tommy Darke or his captive, Piper Grace…"

I covered my mouth as a cry threatened to erupt from my throat and had to force myself to step away from the door. Not to listen to anymore. But the fact remained that in spite of Tommy playing his games or wearing his masks, the police and press still knew it was him who'd taken me. They were onto him, and I just had to hope my ordeal would be over soon. That I'd be found and led to freedom before it would be too late.

I made the bed and then sat on it, my legs folded beneath me. And then I waited. I sat there for so long my stomach ached again, so I filled up on water just like I had the time before. I forced myself to think about anything other than my hunger and thankfully, it seemed to be working. Somehow, I was thinking of a million other things and while hard to bear, they were a welcome distraction. I thought about the outside world. My friends and family. They were out there and wanted me home. They were looking for me, so I used every ounce of strength I had and concentrated on remaining calm and keeping focused on the tasks I had given myself.

One – try not to make him angry.

Two – make him believe you still love him.

Three – avoid getting hurt again.

Four – find a way to escape.

Nighttime eventually came, and I'd seen neither hide nor hair of Tommy. I was restless after sitting still for so long with nothing to do, but my body was too broken to even contemplate doing my usual yoga routine and I didn't want to make any noise or get caught pacing the room. I felt too wired to sleep, but I forced myself to lie down and was glad when sleep finally took me. At least while asleep, I couldn't get myself in any more trouble.

***

When I woke up the next morning, someone was standing over me.

Watching me sleep. I jumped awake, startled by their presence, and hope spurred in my chest when I realized it wasn't Tommy. It quickly dissipated when I recognized my voyeur. It was Miles, Tommy's assistant. He was wearing a shit-eating grin and watching me with a sickening amount of amusement, which told me all I needed to know. He wasn't there to help me. Quite the opposite.

"My, oh my," he said, shaking his head as he eyed my many bruises. "You were a bad girl, weren't you?"

My hand instinctively reached up to my battered face, and I immediately shied away from his dark, lingering gaze. Miles made me feel uncomfortable, and for the first time I genuinely wished Tommy would return so he could shoo him away.

"What do you want, Miles?" I eventually asked him as I sat up, being sure to pull the duvet higher around me in a bid to cover up some more. He gave me a surprised smile and winked.

"You remember me? Nice," he said, as though I'd just paid him a compliment. "Tommy's just out grabbing some supplies from the car, so I thought I'd pop in and see how his little captive was doing. He told me all about how you tried to run…" Miles chastised, before he then added a couple of shakes of his head for added effect. "Such a silly, naughty girl."

I wished he'd stop doing that. Calling me things like *bad girl*, *silly girl*, and *naughty girl*. Tommy did that all the time, and I hated it. Especially whenever he called me *his girl*.

Miles continued to stare as he took a seat on the bed beside me and then ran a hand through his light brown hair. In other circumstances I might have thought he was good looking, but not now that I knew for sure he had helped Tommy kidnap me and, by the sounds of it, numerous other women. He was ugly on the inside, just like his mentor—or whatever Tommy was to him—and never would be handsome again. His darkness shone through his eyes, and I was sure anyone who truly looked into them would have to see it. They'd be blind not to miss it. Just like I had been with Tommy's. Shit, talk about telling yourself some hard truths.

"Please leave," I tried, but Miles simply continued to smile down at me, his eyes poring all over me. I felt vulnerable and exposed, naked in spite of the duvet covering me. Miles licked his lips and leaned closer, dropping his voice to a whisper.

"I told Tommy I was going to bring you some food, but he forbade me because you're being punished. How about I slip you some, anyway? He won't have to know," he asked with a cock of his head towards the front door.

I wasn't going to fall for his nice guy routine. No way was he going to help me without wanting something in return, and he didn't seem surprised when I didn't pounce on the offer.

"No, thank you," I replied in a forcibly timid tone, just in case this was a trap. For all I knew, Tommy could be standing just on the other side of the doorway, out of sight. He could be listening in and waiting for me to mess up so he could punish me again. Well, not this time. My stomach screamed yes but my head said no. I had promised myself I wasn't going to give Tommy any other reasons to hurt me and was sure this was the right way to do it.

"You can trust me," Miles urged, dropping his volume again. "It'll be our little secret. I'll do something nice for you and you can do something nice for me…"

"Oh, I see," I snapped back. "If I suck your cock, you'll bring me a sandwich?"

"Small price to pay for not starving, if you ask me," he replied with a shrug.

"I'll take my chances with starvation, thank you," I informed him with a scowl, and then our conversation was cut off completely when we heard footsteps coming up to the front door from outside.

Miles was up and out of the bedroom in a flash, and I could hear him chatting to Tommy out in the living room a few moments later, as though nothing was amiss. Like he hadn't just propositioned me.

I knew I'd have to watch my back with Miles there. He'd try something the moment Tommy's back was turned. I knew it. But he wasn't going to get a thing out of me. I was already playing one game of cat and mouse, and there was no chance I was up for a second.

NINETEEN

Tommy

I was cool, calm, and collected by the end of the second day I'd spent ignoring Piper, but that didn't mean I was ready to make things up with her. Oh no. Her torment wasn't over yet. She could wait a little longer to have my gentle side back. Learn to miss me just a little bit more.

Miles's arrival helped me stay away from her and together we let off a bunch of steam playing our favorite video games while devouring the case of beers and huge pair of T-bone steaks he'd turned up with for the barbeque. He'd also brought some much-needed supplies, and I found I liked knowing the cupboards were stocked up. It meant we were ready for however long a stay Piper and I could get in our little hideaway.

All I needed now was for her to be a good girl and not let me down or do anything stupid like she had the morning before.

I mean, just as I was beginning to trust her, she went and pulled a stunt like that. I'd had no choice other than to punish her, and at least she hadn't put up a fight. Things would've been a hell of a lot worse for her if she'd refused to play my game. At least her indulging me had quelled that fire within me somewhat. But still, because of her, I'd had to kill a man. I didn't care for the loss of innocent life, of course, but for the aggravation it had caused me. Cleaning up a dead body was messy, plus digging the grave and doing all the heavy lifting on my own had left me exhausted. And all of that'd come after having exerted myself teaching Piper a lesson, but I'd known the importance of covering my tracks.

Serial killer one-oh-one? Or something along those lines.

I'd even upturned the guy's boat and sent it downstream. Everyone would think his disappearance an accident and move on. They wouldn't come looking, but even if they did, I'd just kill them too. I'd kill anyone who dared get in my way. Mow down all who tried to take her from me. Cops. Friends. Family. She'd end up with no one but me.

I laughed to myself, just thinking about how she'd taken off in completely the wrong direction for any hope of escape, anyway. Piper had been heading further into the woods by running out the back door, so it was dumb luck she'd come upon anyone at all. I was all set to play a new game and let her keep on running just so I could track her for the fun of playing predator. I was going to follow from a distance until she'd exhausted herself and crashed somewhere in the woods, from which I could ensnare her again. But as it turned out, watching her turn away from the temptation of freedom and come trudging through the wilderness, and back into my clutches, was even more satisfying. And on so very many levels.

I'd won. She'd hated coming back to me, but she'd done it. She had caved. Swallowed her pride and admitted defeat. I just had to hope my girl would finally accept her fate.

She had broken down with every step she took, and I knew it had done its damage before I'd even laid a finger on her. In some ways, I didn't think the physical punishment was all that necessary, but I'd still done it, anyway. Still satisfied that urge within me. That voice which demanded I take more. Show her more brutality. More unending strength.

All that had been left afterwards was for Piper to endure her solitary confinement along with a bought of torturous starvation, and I knew she'd cave to my every whim. One more night and she would fall to my feet and worship me like the God I was. To her, I'd become life and death. Her judge, jury, and executioner. Or I could be her best friend. I could love her and treat her so well, if only she let me.

Deep down, I knew I didn't truly want to hurt her, but she'd made me do it. Well, maybe I did want to hurt her a little, but not to the extremes I'd been forced to so far. My beautiful girl deserved to remain that way, and as I settled down for another night of sleeping on the couch, I knew it was time we shook things up again.

I woke the next morning with the perfect idea of how to reward Piper for not having shouted or screamed at me to feed her. For staying in her room and doing as she knew I wanted despite her basic needs not having been met. She'd sensed I'd needed the alone time and left me to it, and I was pleased she hadn't tried to fool me either. Most girls would resort to playing nice when it might suit them, but instead Piper had left me alone and endured her punishment with more grace than I would've expected.

That in itself was worthy of my respect and admiration.

It was time I flipped the switch from tormentor to protector, but not just yet. I had an errand to run first.

TWENTY

Piper

I heard the front door close and waited, hoping that the sound symbolized the departure of our visitor Miles, but alas, I wasn't in luck. It was evidently Tommy who had left because Miles sauntered into the bedroom just moments later. At least this time I was dressed, albeit in not much more than a flimsy nightgown, but I was covered nonetheless.

I knew I had to play things carefully, otherwise he might get certain ideas about how to fill whatever time we had together while Tommy was gone, and something told me he might not take no for an answer.

"You must be so hungry, Piper," he told me as he produced a power bar from one pocket and a can of soda from the other. He opened both as he took a seat on the end of my bed and stared at me for a second before devouring both. "If only you'd let me help you…"

"Tommy would kill you," I informed him, turning my face away rather than watch him eat and drink when I was so very desperate for some. My stomach hurt so much and was churning thanks to me being so hungry. I was salivating like crazy and my head was foggy due to the lack of nourishment having made me start to shut down, but I was determined not to cave.

Miles finished his snack and continued to watch me for a moment before he then stood and headed over to the door. Just as he was about to walk through it, he looked back at me and shot me a devious smile.

"If you suck my cock, I'll feed you, Piper. But if you fucked me, I might even be persuaded to take Tommy out of the equation completely and set you free. Think about it, but get back to me sooner than later," he told me before casually leaving me alone again.

I was in shock and couldn't even fathom an answer. Would he really do it? Was he even capable? Or would he take what he wanted and then walk away with a smile while not intending to keep any of his promises? My instincts told me it was the latter of those outcomes, but I had to wonder if he might just do it. Perhaps Miles had been sick of Tommy for a while and was ready to go it alone? Perhaps not. I couldn't know for sure unless I took the risk and did as he asked, but the sheer thought of letting that vile man anywhere near me made me want to vomit. I'd stick with the devil I knew for now, thank you very much.

Tommy returned to the cabin within the hour, and he had with him another surprise, but a decent one this time. He had two more lengths of chain in his hands and, without a word to me, he set about securing it to the ten or so yards I already had attached to the cuff around my right wrist. With the previous length I could reach the doorway to the bedroom, but with the extra I was sure I could make it as far as the kitchen at the other end of the cabin. Maybe further.

"Thank you, Tommy," I whispered when he was done, and hated how timid I sounded. My voice was shaking, and I knew it was out of fear, but refused to acknowledge it. Not now. Not when I was doing so well at trying to be strong.

He didn't answer me and I couldn't be sure where he was at mentally, so I resisted the urge to jump up and test out how far I had to play with when it came to my new boundaries. All I could think to do was sit there and wait for him to tell me more when he was ready. To let me know my limits, but hopefully at least give me permission to go raid the kitchen cabinets. And I remained optimistic. This act of kindness on his part had to signify my punishment was over, surely?

"Your actions have consequences, Piper," he eventually answered before he stood and stepped back with a blank stare that seemed to go right through me. "If you run again, I'll find you and punish you just like this time, but I'll also send Miles after Eddie. And then the next time he'll pay your parents a little visit. Maybe even Janie. You won't be the only one who pays for your insolence. Don't make me warn you again."

My stomach lurched, and not because I was fearful at the prospect of him doing exactly as he'd cautioned. It was because I knew without a doubt that he'd follow through on his threat and that none of the people I loved would see it coming. Miles wasn't someone they knew to be wary of, and he could follow in Tommy's footsteps to easily disguise himself as necessary and get close to the people I loved. The people I had to keep safe at any cost.

There we had it. The winning move.

Touché motherfucker.

"I won't run again. Please don't hurt them," I cried. I couldn't do that to any of the people I loved and knew Tommy had me more than captive. He also had me completely cornered. He'd won. The game was over and I wasn't capable of playing another round. Tommy had seen to that.

"Then don't defy me," he demanded before he breathed a sigh and shook away his dark stare. It was as though he became another person right before my eyes. Someone I had once known. The Tommy from his poolside. The real one. And he regarded me with an almost gentle smile.

I wanted to weep.

God damn you, Tommy Darke, I thought.

He reached his hand out towards me and even though everything inside of me was telling me to get far away from him, I ignored my instincts and climbed up off the bed and then went to his side.

I put my hand in his and began to tremble when he pulled me into his embrace. There was no helping it, but he seemed to expect it, anyway.

I knew in my mind there was more I needed to do and say to make him believe he'd truly won me over, though. It was time I played the role of the doting and timid little slave. Time I did what I needed to do so that not only would I survive, but those I loved would, too.

"Please say it's over now, Tommy. Please let me get something to eat and come sit with you. I don't want to be alone anymore. I've missed you," I whimpered against him and then turned my face up to look into his eyes. I saw a satisfied smile spread across his features. Yes, this was perfect. I was saying and doing all the right things and knew I had to carry it on if I had any hope of getting through our time together in one piece.

Tommy offered me a simple nod before turning and leading me out of the bedroom. With my chain unwinding behind us, we went straight through the den and to the kitchen. Miles was lounging on the sofa as we passed, but he barely registered our presence, and Tommy ignored him, seemingly focused only on me.

When I reached the counter, I felt the chain tug and knew I was pretty much at the end of its reach, so I waited there while Tommy plucked two bowls from one of the cupboards. He then filled them with his chosen cereal before he then topped them off with milk. I didn't care what he delivered to me and devoured a bowlful after shoveling huge spoonfuls down my throat, one after another, in quick succession. It wasn't ladylike, and I knew I must look like a tramp, but I didn't care. My stomach went crazy over the first food I'd had in days and at I felt a bit sick initially, but then it quickly subsided, and I went into some kind of food coma, staring out of the window opposite with a satiated kind of high.

"Would you like something else?" Tommy asked me as he then cleared up the empty bowls and placed them in the sink. It appeared he was in one of his caring moods, and while on the inside I was still cursing his name, I forced myself to smile sweetly and nod, as though excited by the prospect of more.

"Coffee?" I asked, and Tommy immediately hopped to it. He delivered me a hot cup a minute later, and I cradled it in my hands, soaking up the delicious scent with a smile.

We sat there for a while and finished our drinks in silence. I liked it but had the feeling Tommy wanted to say something and was forcing himself to keep quiet. Part of me wondered if he might be about to apologize, but I didn't hold out for anything of the sort. He wasn't someone who ever said he was sorry.

When we were done, Tommy helped me stand, and then he pinned me to the counter before lifting me up onto it and pressing himself against me. I got my answer as to what he'd wanted and had been waiting for. There would be no telling him I didn't feel like it. No saying no.

I let him kiss me and did everything I could to persuade him I wanted his attention, even though deep down I wanted to scream at him to stop. But I couldn't. I had to be a good girl. I had to let him have his spoils.

Tommy then lifted my dress and unbuckled his pants, eyeing me in a way I knew all too well. He was going to take me then and there.

"Reminds me of our scene in *Wayward*," he groaned as he positioned himself at my entrance.

"We've got an audience again too," I told him, looking over his shoulder to where Miles was still sat. Tommy couldn't see him, but I could, and he wasn't watching the television anymore. There was a much better show on offer, and I cringed at the thought of him seeing us have sex.

"He's seen me do this a hundred times before, baby. Don't worry," he said, as if that'd make me feel any better. "And anyway, Miles knows you're off limits. Mine and mine alone. He wouldn't dare try anything with you."

Yeah, okay. That showed how much he knew.

I didn't correct him, but I knew Tommy was wrong on that front. If I'd been willing, Miles would've taken me twice already.

Tommy thrust and was inside me in a heartbeat. I let out a cry at the sudden intrusion but was surprised to find myself wet and at the ready for him. He began to move, and I cursed my body for wanting what he could so readily give me. For clenching around him with need and for letting him make me feel good after the awful few days that'd just passed. I closed my eyes and tried to clear my mind. Tried not to focus on what was happening and tell myself I was only doing this because I had to, and not because I liked it. Liked him.

My body refused to switch off, and I soon began to feel that winding ache twist in my belly. I told myself over and over not to do it. Not to come for him. Not to give him the satisfaction. Tommy didn't deserve to have me climax for him. He hadn't earned the right to love me and have me love him back. Not after the misery he'd put me through.

Stop, stop, stop, I thought, but he didn't, and I couldn't stop from climbing that wave of pleasure I knew I would come crashing down on any second. When I came, it was with a rush I felt from the tips of my toes to the top of my head. It overwhelmed me and I covered my face to stop him from seeing me come undone because I'd just lost another battle.

A battle not only with Tommy but also with myself.

TWENTY-ONE

Eddie

If another person asked how I was doing, I swear I was going to rip their heads off. Of course I wasn't doing well. The woman I loved had been kidnapped, and I'd been helpless to stop it. Thwarted by a goddamn needle in my foot, but what could I do other than let the police do their jobs? All I had left to do was wait for updates and sadly, no news had come my way in days. Fuller had done his best, I knew, but still we had nothing.

In fairness, I wasn't sure which lines of inquiry they'd pursued, but had given up asking. I was lost and stuck in limbo. All I could think to do was throw myself into my work.

In just a few days I'd done a fortnight's worth of editing and screen work. Watching Piper as she performed her epic leading role was bittersweet for me, but I couldn't get enough of it. I loved seeing her happy and healthy, and found it helped to stop me from imagining the potentially awful state of her now after a week of captivity at the hands of her obsessive ex-boyfriend. I dreaded to think about the things he must've made her do. Or the things she might have willingly done.

Would she come back to me in pieces? Metaphorically, of course. Would he break her so badly that the Piper I knew and loved might be gone? I couldn't let myself believe Tommy was capable of the alternative. Surely he couldn't bring himself to kill her. But I knew there were worse things than death. He could break her and mold her to whatever he wanted, and she would be powerless to stop him. She'd come back to me his broken toy, just like last time. But, like I'd always told her, she still mattered. Even in her darkest days. Piper meant everything to me and I wasn't going to let her down, no matter how hard it might be to pick up the pieces all over again.

I hoped she was staying strong, though. That she'd do what had to be done if the time called for action. I'd only been with her half a year, but I knew Piper wasn't capable of murder. I feared she wouldn't even take her chance and do it if the opportunity presented itself. That she would remain his captive until he set her free and, all the while, Tommy would continue to manipulate her and turn her into his perfect girl all over again.

My cell chimed, breaking yet another of my inner downward spirals, and I answered on the second ring.

"Yeah?" I demanded and was surprised to hear Sergeant Fuller's voice on the other end.

"Afternoon, Mr. Martin. It's Fuller here," he said, as if I didn't already know. "We've got a woman in custody who wants to speak with you. She says she has information that might help the investigation."

"That's great and all, but why does she want to speak with me?" I asked and could hear the terse tone of my voice.

"Because she says she's your ex-fiancée. Ingrid Wiseman?" I went cold at the sound of the name. The name of the woman who had broken my heart two years previously by leaving me at the altar and running off with my best man. Yeah, safe to say I hadn't seen either of them since, but I'd heard on the grapevine how they'd married and were living in Beverly Hills. The typical Los Angeles power couple, but still two people I hoped I'd never have to see again.

Shit. How might Ingrid be involved in this? In what universe might her and Billy have information that might help Piper's case? I figured I'd better swallow my pride and find out.

"I'll be right there," I told Fuller before ending the call and grabbing my jacket. I then left the office without a word to anyone, only my assistant, who now thankfully seemed adept at making up excuses for me without needing to be asked.

I arrived at the station in record time thanks to my driver for having put his foot down at my request. I had to know what Ingrid was up to and why she might've come forward. But I also wondered why had she waited so long? What had changed her mind?

When I reached the front desk, I was informed she was waiting in one of the rooms they interrogated suspects in, and I charged over to Fuller with a frown. He knew what I was about to ask, and quickly held up his hands.

"Whoa, Eddie. Calm down," he said, and I knew I must have been wearing a hard scowl so forced my features to relax. He wasn't the one who had me so riled. "She asked to be placed in there. Said she's too ashamed to tell you to your face so she just wants to make her statement with you behind the two-way glass."

"What?" I couldn't help but ask. I was beyond confused. "Then why couldn't I have just watched the tape afterwards?"

"I dunno, but she seems to think it's something big. Something that'll impact on you." I let out a groan and scratched roughly at my hair.

"Then let's go get this over and done with so I can figure out what the hell is going on."

TWENTY-TWO

Tommy

I no longer saw the bruises or the blemishes. My girl was utterly perfect in every way and was forgiven for all her wrongdoings. I had purged her first and then absolved her. I had fed and cared for her, before plummeting back into that pool of serene awesomeness that was her body.

Piper was resplendent. Such a beauty I wanted to weep, but I held my tears back. I couldn't let her see me so weak at the knees for her. She was allowed no victories. Only to be pursued, preyed upon, ensnared, and then kept locked away forever as my prize. And that's exactly what was happening.

After spending hours together back in the bed I'd left her in for days, she was now laid out beside me, fast asleep. She'd been so well behaved. So ready to do whatever I asked and had been rewarded by being so royally fucked that she had succumbed to her need for sleep, regardless of it not being nighttime yet. And all I could do was watch her. My heart was pounding in my chest, aching, and calling out to hers, which I knew was mine forever now that we'd sealed the deal, so to speak.

Her fate was in my hands, and Piper had finally learned to stop fighting me. Stopped trying to leave me. She could never leave. Not ever. I simply couldn't allow it and knew that if she ran again, I wouldn't hesitate to take her down if I had to because, as the cliché went, if I couldn't have her, then nobody would. But she wouldn't run. No, not now. She'd learned her lesson and listened to my warnings. She knew it was pointless to fight me. That I always won.

I climbed up off the bed and used the bathroom before pulling on my pants and going to find Miles, whom I knew from the sounds coming in from the living room had been playing video games all day long. I didn't mind. I didn't even want him to leave. He was part of my journey. Part of me, in many ways. My protégé and best friend, and I wanted to share in my victory with him.

"You finally had enough then?" he teased as I fell into the armchair beside him, not taking his eyes off the screen.

"Nah, I'll never have enough of her. You know that," I replied before grabbing the other controller and joining the game.

"Well, if the day ever does come, be sure and share. I don't care about partaking in your sloppy seconds," he joked, and it was all I could do not to lunge for him and rip his throat out.

Miles thankfully seemed to sense he'd overstepped the mark, and he turned to me with wide eyes. "I'm sorry, Tommy. I was just kidding. You know I'd never touch her."

"You're damn right you'll never touch her," I ground. "And if I ever found out you had, I'd cut your dick off and feed it to you in a hotdog bun. Understood?"

"Yeah, man. Understood…" he turned back to the game, and I continued to watch him for a few seconds, still seething.

Deciding against joining in after all, I stood and went back into the bedroom so I could take a load off and get some rest. I'd had nothing but broken sleep and anger-fueled days, but today had been different. Today had been wonderful, and I was determined that it ought to stay that way.

TWENTY-THREE

Eddie

I watched as Fuller took his seat opposite Ingrid at the table and then pointed to the mirror behind him.

"Eddie is here. He's listening, just like you asked," he told her, and I watched as she curled in on herself and began to cry. Despite my usually gentle nature, I didn't feel any pity for her. It was wrong of me to still carry such an enormous amount of hate for the woman, but the scars had taken a long time to heal and seeing her sat there only brought back the rage I'd felt when she'd left me stood waiting for her in the church. Our families and friends had been there to watch me be told the devastating news. They all saw me break down and have to be led away by my brother and father. It wasn't fair for me to have had to go through all of that. Ingrid shouldn't have been selfish enough to let us get all the way to our wedding day before finally revealing what a vile bitch she truly was.

"Just get on with it, whore," I whispered to myself before offering an apology to Dobbs, who had come in with me to watch their tête-à-tête.

"Don't worry, man. What'd she do, break your heart?" he answered.

"Yep. And then ripped it out and crapped on it," I told him with a frown.

Ingrid's voice then came in through the speakers, halting our conversation, and we both turned back to the mirror. Watching as she composed herself and started to explain why she'd even come forward at all.

"I'm not proud of the things I've done, but I couldn't sit back and do nothing when I knew that poor woman's life was at stake. Coming here was the least I could do," she said, wringing her hands. "I guess I'll start with the truth. I've been married to my husband, Billy Wiseman, for a year now and while I love him, I've not always been completely faithful."

"Shocker," I groaned, but then forced myself to shut the hell up and listen to what she had to say.

"He has this cousin on his mother's side, Miles Monroe. We met at our wedding and have hooked up a few times since. Usually at family parties and such," Ingrid carried on.

"The same Miles Monroe who used to work for Tommy Darke?" Fuller asked, flipping through his case file.

"Yes," she answered, and I was suddenly extremely interested in what she had to say. I'd seen Miles's statement from a few days before. He had an alibi for the morning of Piper's abduction and had told the cops he hadn't seen Tommy in months. That when he'd taken himself away from the limelight after the debacle in Europe and refused to take on any new scripts, he and Miles had gone their separate ways and that he hadn't heard from him since.

"Why do you believe this is of interest to the case, Mrs. Wiseman?" Fuller asked, urging her to reveal more.

"Because he told my husband how he and Tommy had ended their contract and he hadn't seen him in months, but I know different. I had been at Miles's place the day before he'd told Billy this and had spent the night with him while my husband was working nights. That morning, some guy turned up and let himself in and Miles didn't even bat an eye, like he'd told him to or something. It was Tommy Darke. He was wearing a disguise, but I knew it was him. I was a huge fan for years and spotted his dark hair poking out from behind his wig. After noticing that, it didn't take much to see beneath the fake beard and spot that it was him."

"And how did he react to your presence?" Fuller asked, writing notes as Ingrid spoke.

"I didn't let on that I knew, figuring he was in disguise because he wanted his privacy. I didn't even confront him when he asked if I'd like to fuck him." She blushed and shook her head, as though ashamed of herself. But I knew that bitch far too well. She would've reveled in revealing that fact. Not only to the police, but to me as well.

"And did you?"

"Yeah. Miles watched as he bent me over and took me on his couch. He was rough, violently so, but I liked it and didn't stop him," she added, making my stomach churn. Piper had liked it that way too, but I could only ever take it so far without feeling uncomfortable. It wasn't in me to beat or abuse women in the bedroom. Not even when they'd asked me to.

"And how long ago was this?"

"Three weeks…"

"Shit," both Dobbs and I said in unison.

"Miles has a dark edge to him I've seen more than a few times. I think he and Tommy realized somewhere down the line how they're the same and were working together on things that had nothing to do with scripts and movies. I think Miles was helping him stay under the radar and possibly helped plan Piper's kidnap, hence the disguises. Miles might even be the getaway driver from the video I saw on the news. He might know where Tommy has taken her."

Stunned silence descended and all I could do was stare at Ingrid. I might hate the woman, but she'd delivered a vital clue in figuring out where Tommy might have taken Piper. We had a lead at long last and I smiled for the first time in days.

"Thank you," Fuller told Ingrid, and I watched in wretched fascination as she lifted her gaze up to the mirror as though looking directly at me.

"Like I said, I'm not proud of the things I've done, but if I can help get her back, I'll do whatever it takes," she said and I had to admit, I was finally beginning to feel glad she'd turned up out of the blue and decided to come clean.

TWENTY-FOUR

Piper

It was barely evening when I woke from my nap, and I turned to find Tommy lying beside me. He had his arms folded beneath his head and he was staring up at the ceiling in thought.

"Hi," I said, watching his reaction in a bid to figure out what kind of mood he was in. I was famished again and hoped he had something planned for dinner. To be honest, I'd have happily devoured a power bar or a simple bowl of ramen. It didn't have to be anything fancy. Just food that wasn't being denied to me any longer.

He turned to me with a smile, and I mirrored it, thanking God for the good mood it appeared he was in.

"Hey," he replied, wrapping me in his arms and pulling me close. I felt him kiss my hair and smooth it behind me on the bed. So tender and like any other lover would in another place and circumstance. He continued to confuse the hell out of me, but in my heart, I still hated him. However, my body still wasn't getting the memo. I flushed with heat when he touched me, and my pussy welcomed his touch. I was so wet by the time I'd followed his lead and climbed on top of him that he slid right on in. Like he belonged. As though he was welcome.

But he wasn't. He was an invader. Someone pillaging what wasn't his, and yet I was powerless to stop him. To put an end to any of this.

And so, I closed my eyes and focused only on the act I was performing. Not who was beneath me, and I tried in vain not to think about our voyeur still eavesdropping from the other room. I mean, what the hell was Miles still doing at the cabin, anyway? Tommy wasn't going to share me with him, so he had to feel like a spare wheel here in our isolated hideaway. Why didn't he just leave?

I let out a small cry when I came, the force of it bringing me back to the present and out of my head. I hated how good it felt to ride Tommy. To have even a little bit of control in my otherwise dictated world was a rush in itself, and before I knew it, I was carrying on. My hips were gyrating and moving on glorious autopilot while my eyes were still closed, and I continue to try and block out who it was beneath me.

I then gave a shriek when Tommy lifted me off him by force and pushed me facedown onto the bed. He was back inside a second later and was rough as he pounded into me, eliciting another orgasm from me before I was even fully down from my previous high. I told him no. Begged him to stop, but we both knew I didn't mean it. Just like before, I wanted the roughness, and he was all too ready to give it to me.

It wasn't long before he joined me in his release and then fell back on the pillows while he caught his breath.

I did the same, lying there limply while I gathered my energy, swallowed my self-loathing, and hoped he wasn't about to instigate round two.

"Tommy?" I eventually croaked when he stood and I saw him pulling on some clothes.

"Yeah," he answered with a satisfied grin on his devilishly handsome face.

No. Scratch that. He wasn't handsome at all. He was evil and cruel, and I hated everything about him. I just had to remind myself at times.

"Can I please have something to eat?" I replied, having forced myself to be brave and just come out with it. I needed food if I had any hope of carrying on like we had been and was willing to beg if that was what it took to get it.

"Sure. Of course you can, Piper," he said, as though it was obvious I could go get something to eat whenever I liked. Yeah, like it was that easy. Nothing was as simple as that where Tommy Darke was concerned. "But first, I'm gonna run you a bath."

He left without another word, and I heard him go out through the living area to the main bathroom, where he turned on the taps. I could hear the water sloshing out of them and into the tub and clambered to my feet so I could follow him. The idea of getting in a nice warm bath was heaven, and I could only hope it wasn't going to come at some kind of price. I'd paid enough.

I was buck-naked so grabbed the only logical item I could find close at hand. It was a huge towel that I wrapped around my body and tucked up under the arm that was still cuffed to the lengthy chain. Using that hand, I held the cotton in place and took a few timid steps out into the main room.

Miles was watching television and pointedly ignored me, but I could see Tommy stomping around in the bathroom ahead. He kept turning the various knobs above and behind the metal basin. There wasn't any steam rising from the tub, so I guessed the hot water had to be off and I let out a sad sigh. Well, I wasn't going to take a cold bath. A wash would do for now, thank you very much.

As I approached the bathroom, he gave a loud curse and charged towards me with a face like thunder. I flinched and took a step to the side to let him pass, colliding with the sofa as I did so. But it was worth it. I didn't want to end up on his bad side. He didn't seem to see me though, and I breathed a sigh, managing to right myself before stumbling over the arm of the couch and straight into Miles's lap. I just stood completely silent and still while I tried to figure out what to say or do next without turning Tommy's mood even sourer and was about to turn back in the direction of the bedroom when Miles broke the tense silence.

"Try the generator. The hot water is wired differently in these old cabins," he informed him, and without so much as a word or a glance back in our direction, Tommy stormed out of the house. A second later I heard him bounding down the steps towards where I assumed a basement must be.

I was content to just stay where I was, thinking Miles was once again focused on the show he'd been watching, but it appeared he had other ideas. Quick as a flash, he had his hand off the remote control and between my legs, where he stroked at my pussy like he owned the damn thing.

I glared down at him and opened my mouth to shout at Tommy when Miles jumped to his feet and put his other hand over my mouth. He then leaned in close and whispered into my ear, his fingers still between my legs and clinging onto me, no matter how hard I tried to move away. "I told you, say the word and he's dead. Give me what I want and you'll be free, Piper."

He then took both hands away from where he was touching me and raised one eyebrow, as though daring me to answer him. To give him the word.

"And I told you no," I answered, watching in horror as he licked the fingertips he'd just used to stroke me with clean.

"No bother. It's just a matter of time before I take it anyway," he muttered as he returned to his seat on the sofa and turned his attention back to the TV.

Tommy returned moments later, and he charged past me again, heading for the bathroom. He tried the hot tap again, and this time was victorious, thank God.

I walked to him, eager to get away from Miles, but was yanked back by the chain at my wrist, which in turn caused the towel around me to fly open. Flushing bright red in both embarrassment and anger, I grabbed it back up and glowered at Miles again. He had gotten a good look and was clearly pleased with himself, and I saw him drop the chain from his hand, clearly having been the reason why it'd caught. "Oops, how'd that happen?" he joked, but we both knew damn well what'd happened.

He'd grabbed it with enough force to pull my hand away and make the towel drop. He was a devious little bastard who had to have known what he was doing. It was becoming more and more apparent that I'd have to tread carefully with him if I had any hope of avoiding having his vile hands on me again in the future. It was only Tommy who seemed oblivious to Miles's devious tactics, and I hoped he'd see his friend for what he truly was, and sooner rather than later. Or at least before it was too late.

TWENTY-FIVE

Eddie

Fuller and his team staked out Miles's house for days and saw a grand total of nothing. His firm said he was out of town on business but didn't hold much in the way of records as to which client he was supposedly visiting, and I realized very quickly how they also didn't seem to care. He was free and easy to do whatever he wanted, just as long as he scored a target amount of work for his handful of clients and got the bosses' fees paid on time. The perfect cover for a sinister character, or so I thought.

There'd been no activity on his cards or cell phone. No sight of him and the neighbors said they hadn't seen him come or go in over a week. It was like he too had dropped off the face of the earth, but we persisted. After all, we had nothing else. No other line of inquiry to pursue. Miles was our guy and Fuller had confided in me how he shared the same theory.

Tommy had to have employed an accomplice. The video footage from the alley had told us at least that much. All we had to do was ascertain whether Miles was the driver and follow him in the hope he led us to wherever Tommy was holding Piper hostage. Yeah, what a perfect world we would live in if that all actually happened. I was remaining pessimistically optimistic but was also on edge and could barely sit still waiting for Fuller's next update.

TWENTY-SIX

Fuller

After spending hours watching an empty apartment remain empty, I handed over to Dobbs and headed home for some rest. The drive seemed to take forever thanks to the morning traffic, and I cursed the entire way. Why wasn't anything going the hell right?

Our house was in one of the up-and-coming areas of Los Angeles, which to me just made clear how it'd used to be a shithole and was now getting better after a recent influx of money. That was thanks to the investors who, like them or not, had bought the run-down hovels once frequented by drug-lords and call girls and turned them into restaurants and wine bars instead. Those walls might now be covered in fancy wallpaper and modern art, but beneath the surface was the sort of grime and blood that would never wash off. Still, I'd take the façade over what once had been. All the better for me and my family to be around.

Just a few blocks away was my home. Mine and my wife's, Francine, and it was all ours. We'd bought it dirt-cheap and gotten married while still doing the place up. We had made two babies while still working double shifts and hardly seeing each other. I'd busted my ass to pay the bills and now, fifteen years after first signing the papers to buy the house, we had something I was proud of. A home I smiled at the sight of every time I turned the corner and saw it.

But today I couldn't smile, because it occurred to me how lucky I was to be returning home to my family. My thoughts had, of course, turned to the case. To the home Piper Grace had been trying to make with Eddie Martin when she was snatched up and taken against her will. To the choices she'd made in her previous life that had resulted in her having become the fixation of a man clearly prone to obsessive, compulsive behavior. She wasn't making her way in the world any longer. Not getting ready for her next adventure. She wasn't waking up with the man she'd chosen to spend her life with.

No, she would be waking up this fine and sunny morning in the clutches of Tommy Darke. A monster who'd outwitted us all and gotten away with it. I knew his type. Christ, we all did. Their legacies were sprawled in the history books and the headlines time and again. Murders, rapists, cult leaders, and crackpots. Master manipulators who cared only for what they could take without getting caught. I had a feeling we'd only scraped the surface of his true misdeeds so far. That Darke was more than just a name he had adopted, but a persona.

Fucking method actors. They should all be put on the LAPD watch lists.

I pulled up and looked over at my front door, debating whether to go in or not. Thinking about Piper again had made my cop impulses come alive. I wondered if I should go back to the precinct instead and trawl through what little we had in her file just in case I was missing something. But I knew, deep down, there was only one lead. The strange and lucky break that'd come to us in the form of an adulterous wife.

Thank God that some people in this town still had a conscience. Ingrid Wiseman had done a brave thing in coming to us with the information she had, and as much as I didn't want to be part of her deception, I would protect her at all costs. Miles Monroe might be playing nice with her right now, but something told me he would turn on her the minute he knew something wasn't right.

My days as a beat cop had shown me my fair share of the filth I knew was in my city and something told me Miles wouldn't be any different to the guys who'd readily beat their wives or girlfriends to a pulp the moment they stepped out of line. I'd never laid a hand on my wife and knew I never would, but that didn't mean I hadn't seen that blind rage with my own eyes.

I hated knowing there would never come a day when every man, woman, or child was safe. As a cop, you wanted to be the hero. To save the world one case at a time, but it wasn't feasible. Evil rose up no matter how many times you managed to quash it.

Tiredness overwhelmed me, along with my melancholy, and I trudged up to the house with my head down. I needed some shuteye. There was no denying or questioning it any longer. My wife was just getting our kids out the door for school as I hit the top step and, after fleeting hellos and goodbyes, I gave each of them a kiss before crawling into my pit and crashing.

I managed a few hours before my cell rudely rang and woke me up.

"Yeah?" I barked into it, rubbing the sleep from my eyes while trying to get my bearings. I'd never been a morning person.

"He's been spotted," Dobbs informed me from the other end.

"Who? Tommy?" I asked but knew better than to hope for that. Plus, Dobbs would be here banging my door down if that were the case.

"Miles," he corrected, but that was still good news. Information we could finally work on. "He didn't come back to his place but went to Ingrid Wiseman's. She just called the station in a panic and the clerk, Becky, told her to remain calm but not to let herself end up alone with him. He can't know anything is up."

"Yeah, because there is no way he's turned up at her house just to catch up with his cousin," I growled.

"Right," Dobbs groaned. "Billy Wiseman will be leaving for work any minute and I think we need to get over there so Ingrid isn't alone with Miles when he does."

"I agree. Get whoever is on duty to watch his apartment and you come pick me up. We'll go watch the Wiseman place," I told him, and Dobbs gave me a grunt of affirmation before ending the call. I knew he'd be here within minutes, so leapt out of bed and took a quick shower. Just about managing to be ready by the time Dobbs was on my doorstep.

I opened with a scowl and ushered him inside while I grabbed my essentials from the counter by the door and took my weapon from the safe I'd had built into the wall.

"Ingrid called again, and Becky put her straight through to my cell," Dobbs informed me as I gave myself the once over. "Told me Miles is in a good mood. She described him as clean and shaven, like he'd been staying somewhere, but she said his coat is damp and smells woody. Like he's been hiking or something."

"We checked out the cabin Tommy owns in the mountains, didn't we?" I checked and Dobbs nodded.

"There was no sign of life and it looked like there hadn't been in some time. It might be worth checking again though? Miles might've holed up there the past few days."

"Yeah, it's worth a shot," I agreed, and he scribbled a note on his to-do list.

We then left my house and headed across town and up into the Hills to where the Wiseman's lived. And just in time too, because as we pulled up down the street from their home, we saw Billy Wiseman get in his car and leave. His wife and cousin were at the window, waving him off with bright smiles. While the poor schmuck either had no idea they were cheating or he turned a blind eye to it. I hoped he had someone on the side too, just to even the playing field.

"What now?" Dobbs asked me, and I shrugged. Neither of us wanted to put Ingrid in any danger by getting closer, plus we wanted to stay as far away from Miles Monroe as we could. Just on the periphery so we could follow him to our prize. We also didn't wanna tip him off or let him out of sight, but that didn't mean it was okay to leave Ingrid to try and deal with him one-to-one. For all I knew, she might break down and reveal how she'd betrayed him to the cops and he could turn on her. I didn't need that kind of blood on my hands.

I grabbed my cell and dialed her number. She answered just before the voicemail kicked in and I breathed a sigh of relief.

"Mrs. Wiseman?"

"Yes," she replied, and I could tell she was on edge.

"This is Fuller. We spoke the other day," I clarified, withholding my rank just in case Miles could hear.

"Ah, yes. How can I help?" she replied, and I knew her guest must have been in earshot.

"I'd like you to get out of the house and stay away until I call you again. Is that understood? We're outside and intend to follow him but would like to know you're elsewhere first."

"Sure. I can come to the office now. Let me just grab my things and I'll be right over," she told me before ending the call.

Dobbs and I then watched as both she and Miles left the house, and she locked the door closed behind her. She waved him off and then climbed into her car before driving away. Her destination unknown to us, but we had other things on our minds. All that mattered now was that we had a suspect to follow and a case to piece together.

TWENTY-SEVEN

Tommy

Piper seemed far more relaxed after her bath and a long night's sleep. I woke early that morning and saw Miles off before making two coffees and taking them back to bed with me. It'd been oddly good to see him go if I were honest. I welcomed the quiet. He had things to do in the city and errands I needed him to run for me, but even more so I was ready for some alone time with my girl.

Things were finally starting to feel normal. Like the old days when she and I would spend every available moment together and make love all night long. Those were stolen moments out of the public eye, just like at the cabin now. But at least here, we had all the time in the world to just sit back, relax, and be together as one.

She smiled as she stirred and watched me as I placed her coffee down onto the bedside drawer. Her bruises were fading and her flawless body was on show for me, but all I could think about was holding her close. Nothing more.

And so, I did exactly that. I wrapped Piper in my arms and held on tight.

"Who are you beneath all the masks you wear?" she whispered timidly a short while later, clearly afraid she might anger me but also desperate to know more. "Who is the real Tommy Darke?"

"There's no such person, baby," I replied, and was surprised by my own honesty. "All I have are the pretenses."

"And the voices," she said, making me frown.

"You know about the voices?" I asked, peering down at her. Had I ever said about them to her? Ever revealed how often I'd let my other personas take charge? No. So how could she know?

"I know you're driven by urges you cannot control. But the voices can. They're the characters you've played and immersed yourself in, aren't they? They speak to you and you listen. You've adopted their mannerisms as well as their likes and dislikes. I can see it now…"

I felt anger simmering within me. Was Piper seriously trying to psychoanalyze me? What did she hope to gain by poking at the way my brain worked? I sensed her stiffen and knew I must've been giving off some serious bad vibes, but she couldn't take back what she'd said. Nothing could. "It's okay," she whimpered, catching me off guard again. And she didn't back off. Piper shuffled closer to me rather than move away. "I love them all. Each and every one," she finally added with a soft smile.

"You... you love them?" I asked, after taking a gulp in surprise.

"Of course, silly," she replied, her answer soothing my inner rage in a heartbeat. "I guess I never understood it all before, but now I do. And I love you. All of you."

"I love you, too," I told Piper in return, and then I showed her. I showed her all day long, stopping only for food and essentials. I let each side of me have their turn, showing her much they cared. How much they loved her, too. How every part of me was addicted to her and would be lost if she ever tried to discard us again.

TWENTY-EIGHT

Piper

Flattery and giving Tommy an ever-ready hole to shove his cock in. That was my new ploy to keeping him sweet and me in his good books, and by the grace of whatever God was watching over me, it was working. There was just one problem. He wanted more. Tommy kept trying to talk with me, but I hated it. I didn't want to talk about the future he wanted us to spend together, or the family he'd planned to have with me. In fact, I thanked my lucky stars I'd taken Janie's advice and had that implant fitted in my arm a year before so I wouldn't have to worry about being bloated or riddled with PMS while on set. It was still good for another few years and I knew the chances of me getting pregnant while it was in situ were slim to none. The last thing I wanted was to have Tommy knock me up. It wouldn't be the child's fault, but I was sure I would never love it. That I'd look into its eyes and see him, not an innocent young soul I was supposed to nurture and protect.

But that wasn't going to happen anytime soon, so as long as the situation was temporary, I relaxed and let my body take what he had to give while giving in to my own needs and desires for satisfaction. There was no denying the fact that I didn't hate all the sex we were having. In my head, I hated Tommy, but not what our bodies could do together in the right circumstances. There was nothing I hated about how he could make me feel. Not when it was just him and me wrapped up in our bubble of pure, raw, carnal desire.

And to make my day even better, Miles had left us alone. He'd gone back to the city, and I hadn't even had to say goodbye. No more playing nice while trying to fend off his advances whenever he got me alone. And thank goodness for that!

With us in isolation, it felt safer. I was far less on edge, and it seemed to resonate with Tommy, too. When we finally climbed out of bed, we spent the evening watching a trilogy of movies Tommy had chosen for us. They were thrillers I wouldn't have normally chosen to watch, but I happily sat through the five or so hours of footage because it gave me the headspace I needed to think and plan my next move.

I curled myself around Tommy, my eyes on the screen, but I wasn't taking it in. My mind was elsewhere. I knew there had to be something I could try. A means of escape Tommy might not have thought about. I kept looking at the cable television machine and his games console that were mounted below the huge set, wondering how they were wired up and if I could somehow use them to get a message out. Perhaps I could record myself on his computer and find a way to upload it to Eddie via email? Yeah, like I'd ever taken enough interest in technology to actually know how to do that on a normal day, let alone in my current predicament. Even if I did find a way onto the console, I had to assume Tommy had the settings locked tighter than I'd know how to work around. He didn't even seem to have a camera at all, much to my disappointment.

I began to despair. My mind was racing with all the potential outcomes, and it was the pessimistic ones which were winning. Maybe I just needed to face the truth. To admit to myself that my old life really might be over and had been for days. Could our arrival at the cabin have signified the end of everything I once had known? I wanted to believe it wasn't but had no surety. I couldn't bear it.

I wanted desperately to be free again and promised myself I would do whatever it took to find a way out. To bide my time and wait for Tommy to make a mistake, or to pounce whenever an opportunity presented itself later. There would come a time when he let his guard down. I just had to wait for it.

***

When I woke the next morning, Tommy was gone, and while I didn't feel like I missed him, the cabin was eerily quiet without him in it. In a bid to fill the void, I went out to the living room and turned on the television, where I flicked through the many different channels in a huff. I eventually found a news channel and watched, seeing how the world was doing without me in it. Much the same, apart from one interview at the end of the segment that made me start to weep.

My name was in thick letters at the bottom of the screen and Eddie was on the show being interviewed. He looked a wreck. As if he'd hardly slept in days, and I believed it might be the case.

Poor Eddie was someone who I knew loved with all his heart. He'd shown me that love, not only for me but for those who meant something to him, too. But now someone he loved had been taken from him, and it was clear to me that he wasn't dealing with it very well.

He was appealing for information on my whereabouts, while recent photographs of me were on show behind him via a green screen. He looked lost, and I sobbed harder at seeing his face after what felt like forever. Not just a couple of weeks.

"If anyone has seen Piper Grace or Tommy Darke in the past fortnight, please call the number on your screen. Any information you have, big or small, might help the police to track them down," the news anchor finished before turning to Eddie with a soft smile. "Was there anything you wanted to add?"

"Yes," he answered, before looking directly into the camera. "Piper, if you're out there, I want you to know that I won't stop looking for you. I'll never stop because you matter. Remember how I always said that to you? You matter so much to me and your friends and family that we won't rest until you're home safe. Don't ever forget it."

The camera then panned back to the anchor, who nodded and looked solemnly down the lens too.

"That's right. You matter, Piper. Don't give up."

"I matter..." I whispered to myself as I watched them move the show onto the next segment.

I broke down then, crumbling and curling in on myself protectively. I rocked back and forth on my knees and then I let out an angry roar into the nearby sofa cushion, screaming at the top of my lungs. "I fucking matter!"

TWENTY-NINE

Tommy

I heard screaming from my perch in the basement and lifted my head up, as if it might let me see through the floorboards and watch what she was doing up there. I could imagine the scene perfectly though. Piper was angry. I could hear it in her roars. And in emotional pain. There was a part of me that was annoyed with her for lashing out, but then again, I'd just watched the same news article on my laptop and could understand why she was upset. I mean, how dare Eddie do that to her? Pull at her heartstrings and try to make her feel bad for having left him behind. It wasn't fair on my poor, sweet girl and I wished he'd just give up already. She'd chosen me, after all. She loved me. Not him. Eddie was nothing to her but a filler. Someone who'd kept her busy while I was planning my next move. Putting all of this into motion.

Piper didn't want to go back to him. She was happy where she was, by my side. Ed just needed to get the damn memo.

With a frown, I then left her to her outburst and loaded up my encrypted email account. A message popped up from one of Miles's many anonymous accounts almost right away. As we'd previously agreed to do, he quickly filled me in on the current situation and what he was up to. The coast was clear, just what I liked to hear. He'd reportedly gone about his usual routine of dropping in to see Ingrid and try for a quickie, but then had hit the town. This morning he'd woken up in some random woman's apartment but told me it'd been worth it. He said she was the biggest nympho freak he'd ever met and was apparently majorly into slave roleplaying. A new kink I figured Piper and I had sparked in him. I wrote him back with a smile.

T:
Bring her to the cabin. Our slaves can play together.

M:
I can go one better than that. She's invited me to a party up the same goddamn mountain tomorrow night. Some rich guy's place who's into S&M in a serious way.

Apparently, they all get fucked up and do crazy shit at his hideout in the woods. She wants me to take her as my pet. In a gimp suit and the full works.

Well, fuck, if that didn't get my mind going. Was Piper ready yet? She was certainly broken in, and I wondered if I could get away with a little playtime of my own. I thought fuck it, why the hell not, so quickly typed a reply.

T:
Can I come?

M:
Yeah sure, man. There'll be plenty of filthy chicks there who'll be up for a bit of action.

T:
No, I'll be bringing P. Give her the chance to show me she's really learned her lessons. You'll have to buy her a full body suit and make sure the only holes in it are for breathing and fucking.

M:
Holy shit! You're serious?

T:
Since when do I ever tell you jokes?

M:
Never, especially about her. Okay, I'm on it. Will get her the works, T. I'll make sure no one will ever know it's her.

T:
Nice. Will check in with you later.

    I shut down and locked up, grinning from ear to ear. I was going to take Piper out on an actual date. We were going to party the night away, and not a single soul would know it was us. They'd all have seen the news and would know Piper was missing and how the dastardly Tommy Darke was her kidnapper, but they wouldn't know how those two same people were there in their midst. Only Miles would know, and he would join me in my revelry.
    When I hit the top step and sauntered into the kitchen via the back door, I found Piper straining against the chain around her ankle in a bid to reach for the coffee mugs. It was quite comical to watch, and I did so for a few seconds before she spied me and let out a huff. She was so endearing it was crazy. So sweet and innocent. And there was not a single sign of her

angst from just a few minutes before. It was as if nothing was amiss, and I was glad she'd decided to hide it. I wanted to talk about a hundred different things with her, but not Eddie or how his words had made her feel. No, I never wanted her to say that fucker's name to me again. I began to wish I'd just killed him instead of hitting him up with a tranquilizer. Would've been so much simpler.

"Please, Tommy. Don't just stand there," she cried, pulling me out of my reverie. Piper moved back into the house to get some slack on the chain. "I'm dying for a coffee."

"Go sit down, baby. I'll bring you one," I replied with a smile.

I then did as I'd promised and after brewing us up two perfect drinks, we sat together for a while chatting and watching the TV. Like a normal couple.

This was heaven. We were safe and secluded, just Piper and me. No one else to bother or disturb us. No one to interfere in the life we'd decided we were going to live here together. Nothing but peace and quiet. Endless days and nights ahead of us, and I intended to use every moment of it wisely. To enjoy her and our love to the max.

The voices were stirring in my head. The darker ones most prominent of all. They told me not to believe her. To hurt her again. To punish her for every minor indiscretion. I shushed them, or at least I tried. This wasn't the time for a fight. This was the honeymoon period. The aftermath of the punishments and the chance for both her and me to revel in our happiness—not to question it.

THIRTY

Fuller

"How the hell did you lose him?" I bellowed down the line to one of my junior officers. He stammered with his response. Something apologetic, I guess, but I was too livid to hear his excuses. He'd had one job to do and couldn't even manage that. All he and his partner had to do was tail Miles Monroe and keep tabs on him. How was it that hard?

"He left the bar with a woman named Jennifer Paulson and stayed the night at her place. His jeep is still parked in her driveway, but Monroe isn't there. We think he took a different car out, but she doesn't have a vehicle licensed in her name and no one saw him leave."

"So how the hell do you know he's not still in there?"

"Miss Paulson just left with two other women in a cab so I went and buzzed her apartment posing as a delivery driver but there was no answer. Plus, surely she wouldn't leave him there? They only met last night."

"Find out everything you can about the woman Monroe stayed the night with and keep watch over both the front and back of her place," I commanded. "I wanna know the minute either one of them returns."

"Sure thing, boss," he answered. "And sor—"

I cut the call short, not caring for his apologies. He'd messed up and let Miles slip away, but there was nothing that could be done about it now. My mind began spinning with the worst-case scenarios, though. Did that mean he was onto us? Or perhaps he was just another paranoid psychopath who was covering his tracks, regardless of whether he thought he was being watched or not? Maybe Tommy Darke had taught him well. Mentored him and taught him to watch his back while also hiding in plain sight?

But Miles wasn't as clever as his buddy Tommy. He'd had thirty years of perfecting this web of lies. I'd done my research on him and knew that he'd done this kind of thing over and over again when it came to women. There was a string of reports from his co-stars about his strange behavior while filming, but they'd always just put it down to his method acting. Never realized the extent of his depravities. It was rather clever of him to hide behind the character he'd immersed himself in. To let them believe it was all an act. But I could see it now. In black and white.

He had always been this way. Tommy had become obsessed with a girl in high school and had stalked her to the point where her father had filed for a restraining order, but being a minor, he'd gotten away with a warning. The girl's family had then moved away shortly afterward, but their testimony made for an interesting read. He'd broken into their home on numerous occasions, become obsessed with making her his and violently angry when she had refused him. That sounded familiar.

There was a history of violence and behavioral issues outside of that one case, plus the childhood trauma of him watching his father wither and die thanks to an aggressive form of lung cancer. Tommy had been just ten years old when he had become the man of the house, and he'd evidently taken the role very seriously. An only child, he'd looked after himself from that day and left his mother to her drinking habit. Tommy had liked things organized and clean. He was particular about every little detail, and his obsessive tendencies had sparked to life even then.

As far as his records suggested, he had eventually left home at eighteen and hadn't seen or contacted his mother since. Tommy had changed his name and started anew. He'd left it all behind and travelled across the country to pursue his dream of becoming a movie star. To play a role for a living. To be quirky in an industry where it welcomed the oddballs and outcasts.

I rubbed at my tired eyes and took another look at the case files strewn across my desk. My eyes landed on the most recently acquired information. They were the notes from a Dr. Steinberg who had been assigned to Tommy's case after he'd killed a neighbor's cat after an 'accident' with a BB gun the month before his father had died. Even his long since discarded therapist had questioned the possibility that Tommy might have some kind of dissociative identity disorder. However, he'd never had black outs or seizures associated with the changes in behavior. Tommy had always remained in control and had likened the experiences in his youth to letting an alter-ego take over. To find confidence in having another part of himself come through so he didn't have to feel self-conscious or shy. Or in the case of the cat, to act out on his behalf because he'd found himself curious about death.

Whatever the answer, he and his crony Miles had won for now, but we'd get back onto him.

Miles Monroe would surface sooner or later, and when he did, we'd have them both.

THIRTY-ONE

Piper

Tommy was quiet throughout the day, and it did nothing but put me more and more on edge. I couldn't read him and not knowing where I stood was scarier in some ways than having him at one end of his scale or the other. I didn't know if he was about to flip his switch on me and turn nasty or whether he was going to fall to his knees and profess his love for me. I knew I hadn't done anything wrong to deserve his wrath, but that hadn't stopped him before.

I couldn't stand it so forced myself to try and open the lines of conversation. He answered me and seemed okay but was distant and kept offering me vague responses to my simple questions, like he had other things firmly on his mind. I just hoped that whatever he was so engrossed in, it wasn't bad.

We talked a little about his childhood, and Tommy revealed how he'd had a sister who had died when they were younger. This surprised me because I'd never heard him speak about her in the past, but it was when he said the name, Gwen, that it occurred to me I'd heard it somewhere before. I tried to think back to where I remembered it from. Had he made some off-handed comment during our time together before? No, it felt like longer than that. A good deal longer. I closed my eyes and could picture Tommy standing with a girl named Gwen. A young girl whose sniveling and sobbing had then sent him into a blind fury and so he'd choked her to death.

Holy crap. It was from a movie! One of the ones I'd watched to get an insight into Tommy's acting style before working together on *Wayward*. Not a real memory or even a person, but a scene in which he had to have been so damn immersed he'd seen it as real. God, he really was messed up. Was that character another of those that'd manifested as urges inside of him? Were they like voices telling him what to do? I'd seen him change from one persona to the next and knew it might just be the case. He was never just one guy. Never just Tommy. He had to be snippets of them all, and foolishly I had coaxed them out that day in his hot tub. If only I could go back and tell myself not to accept that invitation.

I fell asleep on the sofa after a period of thoughtful silence, my head in Tommy's lap on a cushion while he played video games. My body felt tired from the non-stop beatings or fucking it'd taken the past few weeks and I let myself give in. I quickly wished I hadn't.

My feet were bare and covered in dirt, but I didn't stop running. Over the exposed roots of the forest floor and through the leaves of the trees that whipped my face as I passed them. But eventually, I hit a clearing. At first, I was so pleased. So happy to have found an open space amidst all the thickness of the woods. And then my heart leapt when I found a man sitting by the river's edge. He was fishing. I could see his rod in the water ahead and the tackle box by his feet, and as I approached, he turned to look at who had joined him at his retreat.

It wasn't the man I remembered. The round-faced stranger with the kind smile. No, it was Tommy. The evil Tommy. The one who always seemed to want to hurt me. He was grinning. Beaming from ear to ear. The smile seemed to stretch wider than humanly possible. Like a cold and unmoving mask rather than a real face. I wanted to scream and run from him, but I was rooted to the spot in fear. Even as he approached, his clown-like grin terrified me and I began to pant and mutter cries even I couldn't understand, but I remained glued to the spot. I let him come and take me. Let him put his hands around my throat and start to force the life from me. And all the while, his terrifying smile remained. It was the last thing I saw as the lightness around us began to fade...

And the first thing I saw when I woke up again.

"Hey," Tommy whispered, grinning down at me in that same awful way I'd just dreamt, and it was all I could do not to scream in his face.

I jumped up, panting for breath, and doused with sweat. That nightmare was going to haunt me. I knew it. Those cold and uncaring eyes. That wide, creepy smile. It was the face of my living and breathing captor and monster. And the one I was now staring into.

Tommy tried to question me about the dream, but I managed to convince him it was nothing. Just one of those things.

"Like when you feel as if you're falling in the dream and it's as if your heart skips a beat or something," I lied. Tommy just shrugged and went back to his game, while I sat up and as far away from him as possible without being obvious about it.

And all the while I was reeling. Shaken up by a dream so vivid it'd seemed real.

***

Later that afternoon, I tried again to reach the far side of the kitchen, hoping I could get my hands on the bar of chocolate I'd seen Tommy put in the fridge earlier that morning. I was craving different foods like mad and couldn't stop myself from obsessing over them when the desire struck. I figured my body was still replenishing itself and my cravings were nothing more than my body telling me what it needed. Okay, maybe it didn't need sugar per se, but I wanted the damn thing and almost pulled my arm out of its socket trying to stretch myself far enough to get it.

I heard Tommy laughing behind me and gave up my mission with a sulk before slumping down onto one of the stools beside the kitchen table we'd sat at during all our most recent meals.

"Please, can I have some chocolate?" I begged him before adding a pout.

He seemed to debate something before answering. Perhaps the pros and cons of giving into my request. Or maybe he was contemplating how best to tease and torment me with the object of my affections? I wouldn't put it past him to toy with me for the fun of it, but hoped he wasn't about to flip the switch and let that side of him come out to play.

With a devious smile, Tommy simply leaned toward me and reached for my hand. He then kissed my palm and, before I could ask him for anything else in the way of an answer, produced a key from around his neck on a chain. I'd seen it plenty of times during my captivity and knew exactly what it was. The key to my freedom. Quite literally.

"Go get it," he said as he pushed the key inside the lock on my cuff and turned it. I then watched in shock as it fell to the ground with a loud thud and then the cabin was plunged into the tense silence. I didn't know what to say or do. I knew I ought to play it cool and do as he'd just told me to, but there was also that small voice in the back of my head that was telling me to run. Screaming for me to fight him. To use whatever strength I had left to overpower my monster and take off again, but in the opposite direction this time, and not stop or look back. If he wanted to shoot me, so be it. But that inner voice was willing to risk it. To take that chance.

If only I was resilient enough to do it.

The punishment for crossing Tommy again would be torture beyond anything I'd known so far. He would take me to the edge. To the place where I would beg for him to kill me. And yet I was sure he never would.

As I battled with the decision I knew I'd already made, Tommy watched me, and it felt like he could read my damn mind. Like he knew exactly what inner turmoil was overwhelming me and was waiting patiently to see whether I went with fighting him or faking it.

I surprised both him and myself by reaching up tenderly and putting my hands on either side of his face. I had my freedom, even if just in the small space we now called home. It was glorious. A small victory, and one I would gladly accept.

I held Tommy in my palms and peered into his eyes and smiled, watching as he melted beneath my first genuine look of appreciation in months.

"Thank you," I whispered, and then I kissed him. It was the first kiss I had instigated since he took me. The first kiss I'd given him that wasn't unnatural or fake. It felt odd being so gentle with one another after all the roughness we'd endured, but I liked it. I wanted to keep kissing him like it all day. *No, no, no. Stop!* the voice inside my head was saying again, but I didn't stop. I chose not to listen of my own accord, which was when I realized things had taken a turn—for better or for worse. He was winning me over. Making me submit to him willingly, rather than by force.

The next morning, after half a day spent without chains and binds, I was walking on air. I woke to find Tommy fast asleep beside me and decided to get us both some coffee, so clambered out of bed and to the kitchen, where I brewed up a pot and poured some into two awaiting mugs. As I stood at the counter stirring the sugar into his, I found myself looking at the door. The same one I'd left via the last time he'd given me my freedom. I thought of all the potential outcomes should I creep out and away from the cabin in the hopes he'd continue to sleep until long after I was far away. Yeah, right. I knew he was more than likely already awake and listening for that lock to click open and signify my stupidity rearing its head all over again. I decided I wasn't going to give him any ammunition. I wasn't going to run. I was going to take Tommy his coffee and show him what a good girl I was being.

I'd barely taken a step into the living room when the lock on the front door of the cabin clicked, and the door was opened from the outside by someone who clearly had a key. I turned to watch as Miles appeared from around the doorframe and was about to offer him a fake greeting when Tommy came charging out of the bedroom like some kind of gorilla on the warpath. I'd never seen a man his size move so fast, as if he'd been coiled and waiting to spring to action the second he thought I was going to try something. Proved my earlier thought right, at least.

Tommy came to an abrupt stop when he saw Miles and me having our awkward standoff, and I found myself watching him with a confused frown. But then it dawned on me. He'd heard the door go and had thought it was me sneaking off. He was about to come charging after me, and it appeared he was more than ready to punish me for my insolence. But I hadn't done anything wrong. I hadn't tried to leave and hoped he could see that.

It was clear how I hadn't quite earned his trust after all, though. At least I'd done something right at last. I had made the right choice to stay and be a good girl.

"Tommy," I whimpered, looking from him to Miles, who was standing in the doorway watching the scene unfold with a scowl. "I wasn't.

I didn't," I stammered. "Miles opened the door just now. I had made us coffee and was coming back to the bedroom," I added, looking down at the two mugs in my hands that were shaking violently, so much so that I was close to sloshing the contents over the sides.

I put them down on the nearest surface and glared at Miles. "Tell him!" I screeched, desperate for him to back me up. I then watched as something vile flickered behind his eyes and knew before he'd even opened his mouth that he was going to throw me under the proverbial bus for the hell of it.

"I think she was going to escape but stopped when she saw me," he told Tommy, who turned to me with venom in his eyes.

"No-no-no," I was mumbling, my eyes wide.

"Go sit on the sofa," Tommy growled at me, but I was frozen to the spot in fear and couldn't make my feet move. I shook my head furiously and held up my hands in defense, desperately searching his face for a sign that he believed me. All I saw was cold, hard ice. "GO AND SIT ON THE DAMN SOFA NOW, OR SO HELP ME GOD!" Tommy then bellowed, and he was so huge and overbearingly domineering that I crumbled on the spot. For the very first time I felt true fear reverberate through me and I almost wet myself. I'd never been so scared before that I almost lost control over my bladder, but I felt that twinge down there and could sense it coming if I didn't get a grip, and pronto.

Before long, I was shaking from head to toe and began whimpering and crying, mumbling over and over about how I hadn't done anything wrong. My body began to shut down in fear, and I was nothing but a ball of jelly when Tommy physically lifted me up and flung me into the nearby armchair.

"Well, now that I come to think of it, she was carrying two mugs of coffee. Perhaps she was just coming back to bed after all," Miles then conceded with a shrug. He offered me no apology and his face held absolutely no remorse for having planted that seed of doubt between Tommy and me. I hated him even more than before.

I wanted to climb up out of my chair and beat the bastard black and blue. Or actually, I wanted Tommy to do it. I wanted to watch him inflict some of that rage on his horrible best friend rather than me. But then, what did he do? Sweet FA, that's what.

Tommy shrugged it off in a heartbeat and was back to his usual self almost immediately. He acted like nothing was amiss and with a huge grin he took a backpack Miles had just shimmied off his back and handed to him. I couldn't see what was inside, but it didn't matter, anyway. I was still in shock and could barely see a thing, least of all whatever purchases Miles had brought to the cabin with him.

THIRTY-TWO

Tommy

I still felt off as I began laying out the purchases Miles had made at my behest, but soon relaxed and began to feel positively giddy with excitement when I saw Piper's new outfit in all its glory. Miles had done as I'd told him and bought her a full body cat suit and mask to conceal her face, but then he'd added more to the outfit and gone the extra mile. There was a collar and leash so I could lead her around like a real slave. A ball-gag to silence her. More handcuffs, as if I didn't already have plenty?

"There are rules and passwords that'll get you through the gate and door. Without them or your slave behaving exactly as expected, you'll be asked to leave at once." He then handed me a piece of paper with the two passwords written on, as well as the address and time we were expected to arrive. "I'm going to stay here and meet Jennifer there, but we'll take separate cars, just in case you need to leave early."

I knew what that meant. If there was any kind of trouble or someone happened to notice something was up, I would take Piper and get out of there in a flash. But that didn't necessarily mean Miles had to also cut his night short.

"Sure," I answered, and then I gathered up the items he had brought me and took them into the bedroom.

I returned a couple seconds later and plucked Piper up into my arms, carrying her away so that I could work my magic and make her pliable to my wants and needs for the evening ahead. She had to be a good girl. The best, in fact. She had to do exactly as I told her and perform for me, otherwise I would hurt her. I would humiliate and torture her worse than anything before, and she needed to know it.

She whimpered and was still trembling even as I laid her down on our bed and began to soothe her.

"I wasn't going to run," she told me, over and over. "I saw the door and thought about what would happen if I ran, but I didn't do it. I didn't even get close."

"Yes, but you thought about it," I ground, climbing over her ominously. "You shouldn't even be thinking about leaving me. Not after all we've been through, Piper. All the lessons you've learned so well."

"No, I'll never forget. I'll never leave you," she tried, but it was already too late for her promises. I was going to use everything I could to my advantage. I was going to exploit every angle possible so that I could get my way.

"Of course you won't," I replied before peeling her nightdress off and leaving her naked before me on the bed. I then pushed open her thighs and eyed her body, wondering how ready she was for me. Whether she could take a beating and a good fucking before we headed out for the party. I wanted to so badly. I craved her tears, rather than loathe them, but promised myself it'd be so much sweeter if I just waited. If we played a little longer. "Miles, would you come help me?" I then shouted, reveling in the wide eyes she regarded me with. Piper shook her head and tried to close her legs, but I was too strong for her, and she could do nothing but lie there completely on show as my comrade joined us.

I turned to him with a smile. "Do you think she's ready?" I asked him.

"Ready for what?" Piper replied timidly, and it annoyed me to no end. I hadn't asked the question of her and hit out with a harsh backhander across her cheek to teach her to be silent.

"You have your answer," Miles replied, and then he came to her side, where he gripped Piper's face in his hand and wrenched her eyes back to mine. I saw rage and venom in them, as well as defiance that I knew needed snuffing out.

Had she been attempting to play me? Trying to make me think she was learning her lessons, when all along she was just being compliant in a bid to save her hide? My heart didn't want to think so, but my head was telling me yes.

Punish her, it said. *Show her who's boss.*

I nodded to Miles, who knew exactly what to do. We had played our game before, and it was far more fun than me playing both the tormentor and the protector alone. This time, Piper had two of us in both roles simultaneously and I undressed with a smile while Miles curled his hand around her throat and began to squeeze.

Piper let out a garbled cry, but it was useless. I was inside of her a second later and pounded in and out of her hard and without a care for if she might be sore from our previous endeavors in the bedroom.

Both Miles and I kept on going until she almost passed out and when he let go, I watched as she gathered herself with a vast amount of amusement. My girl was disoriented and scared, but her body was giving me everything I wanted and when she finally came, I could tell she was trying to fight her release. To ignore her pleasure. To deny me mine.

That simply wouldn't do. And by me bringing a third person into the mix, it'd thrown her off her game. I could see her coming undone with every passing moment and had to wonder why she was so ready to succumb.

Piper hated Miles. I already knew it, but it appeared I had touched on a nerve by inviting him into our bedroom. One she couldn't forget as easily as her darling Eddie or her desire for freedom, and I deliberated as to why she despised Miles so when they'd barely spent a moment together so far.

And I also vowed to find out.

THIRTY-THREE

Piper

As if Miles being there wasn't enough to humiliate me, Tommy had also made me endure having his hands on me while we fucked, or more accurately, while Tommy fucked me. There was no reciprocation. I simply lay there and took it while he did as he pleased, but the violation wasn't what was happening between my legs. No, it was what was happening at my head end.

Miles had climbed up onto the bed and cradled my head in his lap like some kind of human pillow, and I was far from happy knowing he was there and had gotten comfortable. When his hands wrapped around my neck and he began to squeeze tight, I wasn't surprised, but I had found myself glaring up at Tommy in shock and then pleading, hoping he might put an end to this awful punishment I knew I didn't deserve. Miles was chocking me and while I was no fool and knew it was how a lot of people got the orgasm of their lives, I also wasn't about to be a willing participant in their game.

I saw his eyes roving over me, darting up to Tommy, and then back to my pussy. Miles was taking in the view when he was able and was crafty enough to make sure his best pal wasn't aware of just how much he was coveting his girl. I wanted desperately to make Tommy see, but he was like a stranger to me. Shrouded in his own darkness and lost inside his head.

Miles held me tighter, and I felt his raging hard-on press into the back of my head.

"Never… gonna… happen," I croaked, staring him directly in the eye. I didn't care if I was heard by both men holding me hostage, but I got the impression Tommy was too busy doing his thing to notice I'd even spoken, which was kinda perfect.

Miles took my bait and pressed down harder against my windpipe, and I saw stars. I figured perhaps it'd be nice to pass out and leave Tommy to finish without me, but I was in no such luck. Miles let up just before I clocked out, and when my back immediately arched so I could take a breath, he shoved two fingers directly into my mouth and down my throat.

While Tommy carried on fucking me, so too did Miles, but in his own way. He had a glint in his eye as he regarded me, daring me to push him away or deny him, but I wasn't going to give him the satisfaction of seeing me be punished further. I opened my mouth and let him finger-fuck it to his heart's content and when Tommy was finally done with me, I pushed both of them away and ran for the small bathroom so I could finally be alone, where I sat on the toilet and cried into my hands, feeling used and more violated than ever before.

When I eventually returned, Tommy and Miles were chatting and laughing about something they seemed to both find highly amusing. I presumed it was me but refused to shout or scream at them for being so rude. I held my tongue and instead just stood there, my bathrobe wrapped around me in a tiny attempt at covering my modesty.

"Put this on," Tommy demanded, not even looking at me as he threw me a god-awful piece of latex I was apparently meant to wear. I went to refuse, but he gave me a look that meant serious danger should I hesitate or defy him. So, I swallowed my pride and pushed one leg into the strange feeling plastic, followed by the other.

I then rolled the suit up and over my hips, eventually covering my breasts and arms before all that remained was the zipper to do up at my back. I turned to Tommy, who immediately obliged, his demeanor seeming calmer already thanks to my compliance.

He left me in just the cat suit while he and Miles got ready. As I watched them get Tommy into one of his disguises, it quickly became apparent that we were going somewhere. Out of the cabin. Somewhere public, hence his need for a mask. This could be good. I couldn't help but wonder if maybe it was my chance to find help at long last, and so I swallowed my anger and pain. I promised myself it would be over soon. That I would figure out a way to get free, no matter what it might cost me.

All my plans were thwarted when Miles returned to the bedroom and showed me what else was in the bag in his hands. From inside, he pulled out a mask that I knew was meant for me because it would cover almost my entire face. There were just holes enough for breathing and seeing through, but at least the mouth had a zipper fastening I hoped I might be able to make use of at some point over the course of the night. With any luck, I could whisper my plea for help to someone at wherever our destination was, or at least ask them to call the cops?

He noticed me staring and let out a laugh before reaching into the bag again and then lifting out the small ball-gag I knew was going to make sure I remained silent, no matter what I decided to try with the zipper. It was made of hard plastic shaped like a pacifier and I knew how with that in place plus the hood, not a single soul would hear my voice no matter what I tried.

Miles was the one who put them both on me, his face mere inches away from mine as he worked slowly and almost tenderly to finish getting me ready.

Looking pleased with himself, he then checked me over and smiled to himself before leaning closer and pressing his lips over the taut latex where my mouth would've been if it weren't forced open via the gag. I tried to pull away, but he was too quick and had his hand around the back of my still tender neck before I could evade his strange advances.

"It won't be long now, Piper," he then whispered. "You see. He's already shared just a little bit of you, hasn't he? He let me come and choke you and take that glorious mouth, which he knows is my favorite. Next, he'll let me fuck it, and then your shy little cunt, just wait and see."

I let out nothing but moans because my words were swallowed thanks to his cruel setup. But Miles knew what I'd attempted to say. I'd tried to tell him to go fuck himself, and I knew I'd conveyed enough without needing the actual words.

And he wasn't delusional like Tommy. He saw through me and knew my days as his mentor's golden girl were numbered. One more slip up on my part, and Tommy might feed me to the wolves. And I knew one alpha-wannabe who would snap me up in no time at all.

THIRTY-FOUR

Fuller

We tailed Jennifer Paulson out of the city and up to a cabin in the mountains with some friends. It was obvious they were there for some kind of kinky affair, by just the remote location alone. But then Dobbs and I caught sight of the outfits they'd chosen to wear and each shook our heads in surprise.

"Don't get me wrong, they look good, but I couldn't be doing with all this," Dobbs told me, indicating to the party we could see was starting to come together a hundred yards ahead at the home of a filthy rich and notorious BDSM player named Roger Madsen. I had to agree, however we weren't there to ogle at the guests, we were there in search of one man in particular. Miles Monroe.

We simply had to get him back under our radar if we had any hope of finding a clue for Piper's whereabouts somewhere in the chaotic life we'd seen him lead in just the few days he'd been in our sights. The guy hadn't stopped and then had disappeared for a couple more days and done God only knew what, while we were left sitting on our asses. Yeah, I was still bitter about having lost track of him, but I was going to make it right.

Eddie Martin had called again that afternoon and I'd lied, telling him we still had nothing. I didn't want him to worry, plus I didn't need him calling every hour to ask what was going on. I liked the guy and could understand he was a wreck, but I had a job to do and that didn't mean holding his hand through every step of the way.

I focused back on the variety of partygoers making their way inside the huge, secluded mansion. There were businessmen and women who were accompanied by partners dressed in skimpy outfits and young women teetering on super high heels. That I was used to. It was the sex slave types I couldn't understand. The men and women who'd been covered in leather or latex from head to toe and whom their 'Master' was leading around like an animal. Some were forced to walk on their hands and knees across the grass, while others had seemingly been told to walk three steps behind and not speak to or look at anyone else. Who the hell found that sexy? Not me. I'd take missionary position and some snuggling with my wife any night of the damn week.

I knew we had to try and get closer, but the host had posted guards at both the entrance to his place and the door itself and we both knew it would be impossible to bribe our way inside without alerting at least some of the guests to the police presence. All we could do was wait. Keep watch from afar and hope no one spotted us. When it was over and Miles drove back to the city, we'd tail him and keep close this time. We wouldn't make the same mistake twice.

"There," I whispered to Dobbs, spotting a solitary figure who climbed out of a cab and sauntered up to the guard with such cocky swagger I wanted to go kick his ass. I didn't, of course, but I had to fight the urge to go and pull him in for questioning right then and there.

Miles was conceited, but I hoped that arrogance would pay off. That he'd make a mistake which would help us catch both him and Tommy. Help us find Piper and take her home. We had him again, so now all we had to do was be patient and let him lead us to our prize.

THIRTY-FIVE

Piper

We arrived at the party separately and ahead of Miles. Tommy had leaned close while we'd driven up the mountain to the isolated mansion that was our destination, telling me how he would make sure I paid for any insolence, and I didn't doubt it. I was then sure to do exactly as I'd been told as we walked up to the huge house to whatever awaited us. Nothing more and nothing less. There were rules I had to follow, but I was also determined to do whatever it took to flaunt them.

Tommy yanked me forward using a choke chain around my neck that he kept connected to him via a leash in his hand, further reiterating my instructions to remain three steps behind him at all times. I couldn't speak anyway but had nodded. Even when he'd said that if I tried to increase the gap between us or attempted any other kind of communication with a single soul, he'd string me up and whip me raw. And he'd let others watch, maybe even participate. I didn't believe it. Or, more likely, I didn't want to. I wanted to believe that somewhere in the crowd was my savior, but the longer we spent there, the more I realized my hopes were for naught.

There were slaves aplenty. Some were openly crying and begging to be released and saved, but not a single person paid them any care or attention. If anything, they seemed prepared to see them be punished for disobeying their Master. Like they were looking forward to seeing them get beaten and defiled. It appeared they enjoyed hearing their pleas and encouraged it, rather than act on their requests to be set free.

I wondered if it were all an elaborate act? Yes, that had to be it. They weren't truly in any danger or where they didn't want to be. I couldn't bring myself to think anything otherwise. I had enough shit to deal with thanks to my own captivity and wasn't about to let myself fret over the fates of others, no matter how convincing their stories seemed.

I knew I had to be selfish. To take it all in and not be fazed by a single moment. I had to be savvy and patient. My chance would come, I was sure of it.

The party was horrible, though. Tommy seemed to be enjoying the energy and openly sordid style of it and was soon chatting with people while watching the variety of sexual performances increasingly on offer, and yet all I could do was stand there like some little puppy following its Master around. My mouth and jaw ached from the gag, and I was desperate for a drink, but wasn't offered a thing, not even when the various Dom's had been served and it was the slaves' turn. Each one had been released from their various binds or shackles and was allowed to tend to themselves, but not me. I had to sit on my knees at Tommy's feet and endure being pointedly ignored by him, while also having to let the other Dom's ogle at me. The latex covering my body left little to the imagination, and I knew that every inch of my figure had shrunk since Tommy had starved me half to death, so hated that I most likely looked like a bag of bones. But the men and women eyed me, regardless. I figured they probably liked the emaciated captive look anyway, the filthy bastards.

"She's being punished," I heard Tommy tell one of his new friends when he was asked why I hadn't gone to the bar or the buffet. His fake southern accent was convincing enough, though, or it was good enough that the other guy didn't question it. "I'll grab her a doggy bag on the way out," he added, emphasizing the word *doggy* as though officially indicating how I was his pet. His fellow Dom didn't say anything else about it, seemingly an advocate for that kind of treatment too. I could feel them both staring, but kept my eyes on the ground, refusing to give Tommy the satisfaction of a reaction.

"And will you share her?" I caught the man ask and gulped when Tommy paused, as though he might actually be contemplating his answer.

"Not tonight," I heard him finally say, but my relief was short-lived. "But you are welcome to watch as I deliver her more punishments in a short while?" he offered. I shuddered and felt my body convulse against my will, earning myself a yank on the choke chain from Tommy.

"Better yet, we can let her and my slave entertain us," the other man countered. "Have you ever watched two women fight? And I mean, really fight?"

"No holds barred?" Tommy replied, and I had to resist the urge to turn around and glower at him for even entertaining the idea. I began to panic and could feel myself sweating inside my suit. If I had to try and fight someone I knew, I'd end up losing. I'd been starving for the better part of the past few weeks and hadn't worked out since Tommy took me, either. I could see and feel how diminished my muscles had become and how malnourished I was.

There was no way I could do it and still walk away in one piece. "I'll pass this time, but thanks for the offer," Tommy finally told him, and I felt him stand behind me and yank at my collar again. "Come, pet."

I did as I was told and followed him through the party and out into the huge garden, where Tommy came to a stop, turned, and pulled me into his arms. It was almost sensual, but I knew not to trust him for a second. Not even when he began to sway to the music, like we were dancing. "You're being such a good girl," he groaned in his normal accent, his hands stroking their way over my body as he held me.

I peered up into the face of a stranger and felt like frowning, but I knew it was him and realized how I didn't even see the disguise anymore. I saw Tommy staring back at me from behind his fake nose, colored contacts, and dark wig. How could no one see it? Wasn't it obvious? No one else seemed to have figured him out, though. He and Miles had put together something worthy of Hollywood itself and it began to dawn on me that I really was screwed. I was a fool to hope that I'd be able to use anyone at the party to help me get free.

Half of the people there would undoubtedly think it was just another type of role play should I try and ask for help. They wouldn't take pity on me. If anything, they'd probably be more inclined to help Tommy with the punishment side of things.

We then heard women giggling and turned to watch as Miles sauntered out of the party with a girl on each arm.

"Ladies, I'd like to introduce you to some friends of mine," he said, directing them over to us. "Bonnie and Clyde," he added with a smirk, making the women laugh even more.

"It's a pleasure," the blonde one who was wearing nothing, but a bikini told us, while the other simply nodded and smiled. She was darker skinned than her friend and was wearing a cat suit like me, but no hood, and hers opened at the front so that it framed her ample breasts. She had opened the zipper so low they were almost tumbling out, and I found myself staring.

"Clyde, it appears Bonnie likes the cleavage on my darling Jennifer," Miles told Tommy, having caught me staring.

"No, she's just jealous," he answered, with a spot of venom to his tone. I couldn't help myself and turned toward Tommy and peered up into his eyes as I glared to convey the 'what the fuck?' I was thinking. He'd never said anything like that to me before. He'd always claimed to adore me, not mock or scrutinize my body. It hurt. After all, that was the one thing I could always count on Tommy for—his unyielding sense of obsessive desire for me.

My little stunt of defiance earned me a backhander, followed by a harsh yank on the chain around my neck. Tommy then dragged me over to a large seating area and Miles followed, along with his pair of fuck buddies. They both pounced on him the moment he was seated and had his cock out in seconds, each licking one side while they knelt at his sides.

Sitting by Tommy's feet in the same submissive position as before, I sensed Miles's eyes on me, daring me to look. But I refused him, like every time before. Even when he made a grunting noise and came down the back of one of the girls' throats.

"Let's play a game," Miles then called, the mirth in his voice not even remotely hidden.

"I like games," one of the women said. I couldn't tell which one as I had my eyes on the ground, but it sounded like the same one who had spoken before.

"Okay, so it's simple. I pick three people and you have to tell me which you'd rather fuck, fetish indulge, or kill."

"Like kiss, marry, kill? Only in a kinky way?" the girl answered with a giggle.

"Yep, but with a twist. I'll make up some scenarios to add to the decision-making process," Miles answered. He then pointed to three guys who were talking inside the back door. "For example, let's pretend that blondie over there is married, but he only ever does it in her ass. The tall guy can only come if he's taken a shit on your chest first. The other guy is hung like a donkey but will only let you come once a night because he's an asshole…"

"Hmm," the blonde answered with another fake giggle. "I'd fuck the asshole, fetish indulge the blondie with a taste for sodomy and kill the guy with the shit fetish!" she exclaimed.

The three of them laughed and joked while playing their game, and I was just glad to have been kept out of it. But then I heard Miles as he directed his same question at Tommy.

"So, Clyde, how about you? Jennifer here is a nympho with daddy issues. She loves it when you dress her up like a little girl and fuck her hard. And Trudy here likes it when you slap her tits and call her a whore. Then there's your little pet down there. She's a bad little bitch who teases men relentlessly for the fun of it. Which one do you choose?"

I cringed, thinking how Tommy had to know Miles was talking from a place of truth, at least as far as I was concerned. I had to bet Miles thought I had teased him when I knew it was the exact opposite. I'd never wanted him to look at me or touch me. Never wanted his promises to give me a seeing to the moment Tommy's back was turned. He'd taken all of that upon himself without a shred of encouragement from my side.

"Hmmm," Tommy answered, and I felt him sit up in his seat behind me. "Well, I'd fuck Trudy and indulge Jennifer's daddy fetish. So that just leaves my darling girl…" He leaned down and spoke the rest directly in my ear. "She'd have to die."

I felt the air rush from my lungs and tears spring to my eyes.

I believed it, the bastard. I truly did.

With a sinister laugh, Tommy then sat back and continued chatting with Miles, having gone back to ignoring me. I tried to keep calm, but all I could think about was how I wanted to get out of there. Out of the horrid cat suit and away from Tommy, Miles, and all the awful people at the insane party they'd dragged me to.

Everywhere I looked people were having sex or partaking in whatever fetish play or fucked up fantasy was being indulged in, and I hated it. All hope of escape was lost, and I just wanted to go back to the isolation of the cabin. Back to where Tommy idolized and worshipped me. Where he loved me. I hated him when he was being violent and predatory, but I found myself loathing this nasty Dom side of him just as much.

I started to pant for breath, but wasn't getting nearly enough, and soon I began to panic. I reached up and tugged at the choker, somehow loosening it, which felt a little better at first, but then I wanted more. I unzipped the cover on my mouth and managed to suck in some fresher air around the gag, but again I wanted more. Needed it. Panic was rising within me, and I suddenly wanted to rip everything off my body and feel the air against my skin so I could breathe as deeply as possible.

I was clawing at the back of my head in search of how to open the hood when Miles suddenly noticed and alerted Tommy.

With a growl, he gripped my left wrist and twisted it away from the tiny hooks at the back of the hood I'd been slowly working open. I felt my wrist resist being turned against its natural bend and cried out as a crack, then emanated through it when Tommy didn't let go.

Pain overwhelmed every one of my senses and I tried to pull free, but he wrestled me to the ground and quickly secured my hands behind my back in a pair of cuffs he'd apparently had in his jacket pocket at the ready. He then zippered my mouth hole closed, put the chain firmly back in place, and stood.

As though nothing was remotely amiss, he then bid Miles and his two lovers farewell and dragged me from the party without a word to anyone.

THIRTY-SIX

Fuller

Dobbs and I watched as the first few groups and duos who we'd seen arrive then left the party. Most of them looked the same as they had going in, but there were a few who'd ditched their kinky outfits and were leaving either half-naked or in nothing much more than their underwear and a jacket draped over their shoulders. It wasn't hard to notice how most of the 'slaves' were the women, and they were the ones left in disarray, while their partners seemed to be without a hair or a piece of clothing out of place. I didn't want to believe their parties were full of women being put on display while the guys sipped bourbon and talked business, but the evidence seemed to be there. The girls were fodder. Eye candy. Nothing but a plaything to the men who cared very little for them or their welfare, or so I presumed.

As we continued to watch, I was further convinced that my suspicions were justified. I saw a Dom I recognized from earlier in the evening as he stalked from the house at a fair speed. He seemed to radiate with a sense of control and led his tiny companion away, still covered from head to toe in black latex and being pulled along by a leash around her neck. As they continued, I saw how she was also handcuffed behind her back, and I watched as she tripped over herself when he pulled her to where a cab sat idling at the side of the road. Part of me wanted to get out and stop them. To go and question the girl and make sure this was consensual.

"I still don't get it," I told my partner as I watched them. "Treating a woman that way isn't sexy or exciting. It's abusive. Do you think I should detain them?" I asked, pointing to the couple.

"Don't judge lest ye be judged," Dobbs replied with a shrug, and I understood where he was coming from so forced myself not to get out the car. Chances were she was here of her own accord and had wanted to be treated this way. Me coming between them would probably put a dampener on their evening, rather than me swooping in to save the day. Plus, we had an important task to complete first. Tommy's accomplice was inside that mansion, and he couldn't know we were here. It was our only lead. Our chance to gain the upper hand at long last.

"Only God can judge me," I ground in reply. "And he'll judge them too."

"Amen," Dobbs agreed before shaking off the deep and meaningful vibe I'd invited into the car with us. "But don't forget. This scene is massively oversubscribed these days, which means there is a large percentage of people who disagree with you, Fuller. If it's consensual and they're not getting hurt, who cares?"

"And what about the people who do get hurt?" I groaned in reply, watching as the cab sped down the mountain and out of sight.

Dobbs didn't have an answer for that one. We'd both seen our fair share of beaten wives and husbands. Half of the missing persons cases we'd had to deal with over the years had been runaways who'd left their abusive partners of their own accord, and it was hard to forget some of the stories those we caught up with had to tell.

What would Piper Grace's story be? I had to wonder, but also hoped, that wherever they were, Tommy was treating her kindly. After all, he loved her, right?

THIRTY-SEVEN

Piper

Tommy had the cab drop us outside some random cabin on the mountain and then he watched it go while pretending to fumble around in his pockets for the key. After the car had gone, he then hitched me up into his arms and carried me down the mountain via a narrow trail for what felt like an hour. Not once did he speak to me or set me down. All he did was thunder through the forest with his eyes set firmly on the horizon.

My wrist was aching from where he'd twisted it, but thankfully didn't feel broken, just bruised. I hoped there wasn't a fracture, but it was certainly sore after his rough treatment and with every step the handcuffs around my wrists dug in deeper.

I guessed I deserved it, though. I'd effectively tried to escape right in front of him and could've cursed myself for being so foolish, but that truly wasn't what I'd been after. All I'd wanted was some fresh air and a bit of space from the intense conversation Tommy and Miles had insisted on having. I'd freaked out and had tried my best to fend off my impending panic attack that'd threaten to overwhelm me. If he just let me down and removed the gag, I could've told him so. But my seething captor didn't appear interested in hearing what I had to say. He just carried on down the path in tense silence and I braced myself the moment the cabin came into view, because I knew what I was in for once we got inside. There wasn't a powerful enough word to describe what he was going to do to me. And no way I could stop him. No chance I could fight him off.

Once we were safely locked inside, Tommy flung me off him onto the hardwood floor and then ripped the hood from my head without opening the catches or a care for the clumps of hair he'd yanked away while he was at it. Tommy also ignored the scream that I'd managed to get out around the gag as he'd wrenched the hood from me. He just unbuckled the clasp at the back of my neck, holding the gag in place, and as soon as I felt it move, I spat the damn thing onto the ground before sucking deep breaths of air into my lungs.

My panic attack from earlier then returned, and I fell to the ground, hunching over my knees with weakness. My cheek hit the floor, and I sat there curled in on myself as I clutched at the precious oxygen I felt I had been denied for so long.

It was the first time since he'd taken me that I truly felt like a captive. My hair was all over the place and I knew I must look a mess, but all I could do was sit there and watch through the gaps in my tousled blonde hair as Tommy paced the small bedroom. My hands were still cuffed behind my back, but it didn't matter, anyway. I had a feeling I'd be too weak to do anything other than lie in wait for punishment regardless of still being bound. I certainly was in no position to fight.

So I told myself to breathe.

In…

Out…

In…

Out…

But they were coming too fast and too shallow. I felt dizzy and was starting to see stars, and so screwed my eyes shut in a bid to focus on my breathing again. My mantra began over, and I started counting my breaths in and out, each growing longer and longer until I somehow managed to steady it.

I wanted to steel my strength and face him, but instead the moment I felt strong enough to move, I broke down in tears and then freaked the hell out. I began screaming like a woman possessed. Tommy grabbed at me and shook me in a bid to shut me up, but I just kept on wailing, even when he slapped me around and kicked me in his rage.

"I can't do this anymore," I told him through my sobs, unable to help myself. All pretense was gone. The cards finally on the table. "I can't do it. Please just let me go. I can't be what you want me to be. I have a home and a life, and it doesn't revolve around you. Not anymore. I matter to someone and he's waiting for me."

I knew it was wrong to have said those things the second the words had tumbled from my mouth, but there was no taking them back now. I knew I'd have to suffer the consequences and was ready to accept my punishment. I was past caring. Past pretending.

Tommy roared in anger, and I watched his eyes widen, his pupils hugely dilated. It was as if I could see the red mist descending around him, and I started trembling violently with fear.

Had I actually hurt him? Had my words more than just incensed the monster who I was otherwise led to believe felt nothing? No remorse for the things he had done and no sorrow for what he'd taken from me? The look on his face told me yes, and while I was still terrified, I liked it.

I then heard the front door of the cabin unlock and open and breathed a sigh of miniscule relief when Tommy charged out to investigate.

"Miles," I heard him say, and I groaned to myself. Of course, it was just him. Who the hell else could it be? "I need some air. Sort her out or so help me, I'll fucking slit the bitch's throat," Tommy then added, making my blood run cold. I believed he'd do it, though. And there was a part of me that wanted it. At least then I'd be free.

I felt hands on me and lashed out when Miles lifted me up into his arms and threw me face down on the bed. He left me cuffed but unzipped the back of my cat suit and began peeling it off me as best he could around my squirming.

"Stop crying, bitch," he warned me before grabbing a handful of my right breast before pinching my nipple roughly. I howled with the pain, but he didn't stop. Of course he wouldn't. He was finally getting what he thought he deserved. What he'd been waiting for. "I told you he'd get bored and share. I said this was coming."

Miles let out a growl as he attempted to get the waist of the cat suit down but couldn't thanks to the sweaty latex that'd pretty much stuck to my skin. I tried again to scoot away but then heard a flicking sound and saw metal flash in the light from overhead as he opened up a knife he had to have had in his pocket. "I'm going to teach you a lesson you'll never forget, pretty girl. I'm going to show you what happens when he's had enough playing nice," Miles added, leaning over me from behind and pinning me to the bed.

"No!" I managed to cry when I felt him cut through the plastic suit and pulled away just enough of the cat suit to expose my ass. His hands were all over me and I heaved when I felt his fingers skim the opening to my pussy, attempting to gain entrance. "Don't, Miles. Don't!" I screeched.

"Yeah, I don't think so either." Tommy's voice pierced the chaos and both of us jumped in surprise. I didn't know whether to be relieved or not, and could hardly see a thing, but could feel the air around us turn to ice. I then felt it as he ripped Miles off me, like some kind of superhuman anti-hero.

I could hear every brutal sound as he then began beating the shit out of him. Every punch and garbled plea for mercy. The gurgling sound as Miles's mouth filled with blood and he choked on it.

I just about managed to climb up on my knees in time to see him fall and then could do nothing other than watch as Miles finally paid for what he was trying to do to me. At least Tommy could see at last what I'd had to put up with, and I was glad he'd exacted his revenge. That he'd taken away one of my threats, albeit the lesser of the two evils I'd had to learn to live with the past few weeks.

For the first time, I saw Tommy's inner darkness in all its violent glory. He was truly wild. An animal. He punched and kicked Miles to a pulp and only stopped when the guy was nothing but mush.

I felt like some sort of justice had somehow been served. I was glad to see him die. Miles had tormented and abused me, and at last he was gone. I might even have felt happy for a moment, although I was quickly reminded of how there were bigger issues at hand when Tommy turned to me with a spine-tingling grin, his face dripping with Miles's blood.

Was it my turn now? Or did I have to stay with the monster and endure his brutality again before hopefully having my protector back?

I guessed I'd just have to find out.

THIRTY-EIGHT

Tommy

There was only one voice. One overarching sound reverberating through my skull. All the others were silent and still, lying in wait while the alpha took charge.

I watched Piper whimper and cower before me, and rightly so. It didn't faze me. Didn't stop me.

I wanted so much from her. Everything. An eternity of everything.

Take it… the voice said, and it was only when she frowned that I realized I'd said it aloud.

"Tommy, please…" she tried, but it was no use.

"You've been a bad girl," I replied, stepping closer. I didn't need to say anything else. The light left Piper's eyes. The last ounce of hope was gone, and she was resplendent in her acceptance of my wrath as I closed the gap between us.

I hoped she was ready for this…

THIRTY-NINE

Fuller

Dobbs parked up, and I called it in while we waited a beat and then followed the path Miles had taken into the forest. But we had to stay back in case he had traps in wait, or worse, he himself was perched up high and had us in his sights. Without daylight or backup we could be sitting ducks, but at the same time we knew we couldn't wait.

We were just able to track his steps through the thick brush and I was about to turn back to Dobbs and suggest we try waiting for morning, when we heard a woman screaming in the near distance and knew we were on the right path. We both ran straight for the sound and ignored the tree branches that insisted on trying to block our path. It felt as if the forest was fighting us back, but eventually we prevailed.

Dobbs and I then found ourselves stood at the base of a set of steps leading up into a small cabin that'd been completely isolated and hidden from all sides thanks to the thick canopy of trees all around it we'd just had to penetrate. It was the perfect place to keep a captive.

We were cautious with our approach but knew we didn't have time to wait when a second wailing scream found our ears. I didn't even want to guess what was happening inside and worked on instinct rather than let my emotions get in the way.

I took out my weapon and tried the door. Blissfully unlocked. Yes, there was a God.

"Please, Tommy! I'm sorry," I heard the same woman cry and knew exactly who it was. Piper Grace. Dobbs and I crept inside, checking around for Miles Monroe, but he was nowhere to be seen. It was only when we slunk over to the bedroom door that we saw the carnage on the ground that was clearly all that was left of our unwitting informant, but knew the real threat was further inside the room.

"Tommy Darke, step away from the bed and hold your hands up where I can see them," I called as Dobbs and I went into the bedroom with our weapons raised. He responded by dragging the woman he'd been beating up off the bed and in front of him like a human shield. Goddamn coward.

It was Piper Grace all right, I could tell, but what churned my stomach was how I recognized her clothing from somewhere else that same evening—the party at the mansion. Her hands were cuffed behind her back, and her latex suit was off to her waist. But I knew without a doubt that they were the same couple we'd seen leaving the party just a couple hours earlier. We'd had them in our sights and hadn't known it. I could've kicked myself. My gut instinct then had been to stop the pair of them. If only I'd listened to it, poor Piper might've avoided the ordeal she'd clearly encountered since returning to their cabin.

Dobbs and I both aimed our weapons at Tommy, even as he continued to shield himself with Piper's battered and emaciated body. He grinned, assuming we were at some sort of standoff, and he might win, but I shook my head. There was no way we were walking out of there without her. "You've lost, Tommy. Hand her over and get down on your knees. Don't make this any worse than it already is."

His smiled faded in an instant and I nodded, watching as realization slowly dominated his features. There was no escaping this. No leaving with his captive still by his side. Tommy shook his head, clutching Piper tighter, and she whimpered but was in no state to try and fight his hold. All she could do was hang there limply, her feet not even holding her up off the floor, only Tommy and his strong grip.

"It's over," he croaked as he buried his face in Piper's tear-soaked hair and began to cry.

"It's over," Dobbs echoed when I couldn't seem to find the words to say. He then took a step forward and reached out the hand, not holding his gun at the ready. "Give her to me," he tried, but his advances only seemed to anger Tommy.

His tears stopped, and I watched in horror as absolute calm suddenly came over him. He looked at Dobbs blankly and then shifted Piper's weight so that he held her lower, like he might be about to set her down and let her go free. But then he evidently decided against it.

"Then neither of us have anything to live for," Tommy mumbled, and I saw as his face became devoid of not only emotion but also empathy. The profile we'd had made on him had been right. Tommy Darke was more than just an overly possessive ex-boyfriend. He was also a capable murderer, and I knew without any shadow of a doubt that Piper was going to become his next victim if we didn't stop him.

FORTY

Piper

Through my puffy eyes, I stared across at the two men and silently prayed for death. Not deliverance, but an ultimate end to my suffering. And an end to the chaos that had led us to this moment. I didn't care that I was half-naked in front of two strangers or that my body was a wreck. None of it mattered anymore. All narcissistic tendencies I might have once had were long gone.

I'd failed in my mission to stay strong.
I'd botched every chance I'd had to escape.
All hope was lost.
This was it.
The end…

FORTY-ONE

Fuller

It all happened so fast.

One second, Tommy was standing across from us, and he seemed to understand how he was out of options.

The next, he was wielding a flick knife he'd plucked up from the bed and held it to Piper's throat. At first, she didn't seem to care, but then emotion flashed across her eyes and I could see something snap. She started whimpering and crying, begging him not to hurt her, but that didn't stop Tommy from pressing it down against her jugular with real intent.

"Don't do it, Tommy!" Dobbs bellowed, but it didn't stop him.

He began slicing, and all I could think of was how I'd promised her parents I'd bring her home safely. How Eddie was waiting for her back home and that she wasn't allowed to die.

I trained my gun back on Tommy, forcing myself to ignore Piper's screams and the blood pouring from the wound he was making in her neck. It was too easy to panic and hesitate, but I wasn't going to let him take her life. Not today. Not ever.

After a steadying breath, I took the shot, sending a bullet directly into Tommy's forehead and killing him instantly. Both he and Piper fell towards the ground on impact, and I sprung forward so that I could catch her before she could hit the ground with a thud. I then turned Piper onto her back, pushing my hands down over the cut in her neck in a bid to stem the flow of blood pouring from her artery. It slowed but continued to flow up and over the barrier I was attempting to create with my palms, and so I pressed harder.

"It's okay," she whimpered. "I deserve this. It's all my fault…"

She went quiet then, as though resigning herself to death. But I couldn't let her go. Piper was breathing, and that flow of air meant everything to me. As long as I heard that sound, everything was going to be fine. Or so I kept telling myself.

Her hot blood pooled around me, and I began screaming and praying, begging for someone to help us. To come and help me. To make sure we saved her.

"Please, God. Don't take her. Don't you dare!" I cried over and over, peering down into Piper's increasingly vacant eyes. "You matter, and don't forget it. Eddie's waiting for you. Your family. Your friends. You matter, Piper. You matter to them, so hold the fuck on…"

EPILOGUE-ONE

<u>Six months later</u>

Eddie

Walking the red carpet just wasn't the same without her. I felt lost and had to force myself to do every single element of it. To pose and smile felt wrong. To conduct the interviews and talk with the fans was just awkward. Instead, I let her co-stars take the lead and share the glory. Who cared about the director, anyway? Or so I kept telling myself. I pushed the other actors to be the ones at the forefront of the campaign and give the premier of our amazing new movie the glory it deserved. And still, none of it seemed right.

I don't know what stopped me from heading straight inside. Maybe I was enjoying the red-carpet experience just a little? That didn't mean I missed Piper any less, though.

And then, out of the blue, there was a collective gasp. All I could hear was the raucous calls from the crowd of onlookers, as well as the reporters and the paparazzi who'd attended our small event. The night was suddenly lit up with their flashes as they took photograph after photograph in quick succession. I presumed the noise was because of the arrival of the heartthrob of our franchise and ambled over to greet him, but then the flashes didn't stop. The crowd was going mad, and that was when I saw her.

Piper. My darling woman was there, and she looked stunning. A vision in gold. She was the most beautiful woman there and I couldn't take my eyes off her. Everyone else was the same. They were calling her name and begging for a pose, but Piper just stood staring ahead as she basked timidly in their admiration. She had four heavily armed guards with her, and I didn't think anyone could begrudge her such overzealous protection. They all knew what she'd been through, maybe not all of it but the basics, and while she'd become a beacon of hope for other survivors, she still needed the reassurance that having an entire team of guards gave her.

I watched in awe as she took a few steps forward, admiring her strength and resilience in the face of all she had endured. And I was reminded of all that it'd taken to get her here. Piper had remained in hiding for months after leaving the hospital. She'd had surgery to reduce her scarring and the mark on her neck was barely even noticeable after the stellar work of the surgeon, but she still knew it was there. She fretted over it constantly, and even after the healing process was over, Piper always covered up. Her now long blonde hair was braided to one side and was swept down across her shoulder, but I could see her fiddling with it awkwardly. Aware and always fretting over the constant reminder of that awful night when we'd almost lost her.

She'd promised to try and come but had been doing the same thing for weeks and hadn't once left the apartment. I hadn't for a second thought she would be able to do it. Piper was paranoid and had been battling with her depression since almost dying by Tommy's hand, but she'd made it through and there she stood, doing her best to keep it together in front of the huge crowd.

I went straight to her side and then escorted Piper up the red carpet so that she wouldn't feel alone or intimidated. That was what I hoped she took from my presence, anyway. I'd been by her side every step of her recovery and knew she trusted me to take care of her how she needed. We'd gone through so much and her frailty and bashfulness only served to make me see how now, more than ever before, she had to stay with me. I would guide her through the rest of her life and couldn't wait for the new year to begin because we were going away to shoot on location, just like before. Into the futuristic world so she could transform once again and we could make our next movie together. The second of many.

But in the meantime, I would work on making her better. Making sure she knew she mattered. That she believed it, because in the end, wasn't that what we all needed?

EPILOGUE-TWO

Piper

Stepping out of that car was so hard. The hardest thing I'd had to do in weeks. The journey to the premier had been too short, though. Not long enough for me to steel myself against the attention I knew I was going to get the moment I climbed out of my heavily armed chariot of sorts. Yes, Cinderella would go to the ball, but this girl didn't feel like a princess. I felt like a fraud. And so, I'd asked the driver to go around the block again, just to give me some more time.

The few hours in the build up to leaving, I'd told myself over and over how I could change my mind if I'd wanted. Eddie had no idea I'd planned to attend the premier and while I'd done it as a surprise for him, I'd also used the element of secrecy to ensure I could back out at any given moment and not have to feel I'd let him down.

The stylists and makeup team had been briefed not to ask me questions or expect much in the way of conversation. Janie had been there through every step of the way and had directed them as needed, while my new security team had watched over it all from the doorways to the apartment and also inside. They had checked the bags coming and going, vetted each of the people who'd been invited into my home, and were the only thing that'd made me feel confident enough to finally walk out that door when the time came.

My days as a military kid hadn't been forgotten, and I thought back to how as soon as I was well enough, Janie had gone straight to an ex-special forces team to procure me a small army of guardsmen so that I could feel safe. They'd provided her with all the clearances and vetting she'd needed to convince me and as soon as I'd seen the list of their job histories' and where they'd all served in the past, I'd been convinced they were the guys for me. I'd slowly gotten to know each of them and had developed a rapport I knew was helping cure me of the agoraphobia that'd threaten to take hold since leaving the hospital.

It was funny really. All those days at the cabin when I'd wished to be free, but then I'd chosen solace over the outside world the moment I'd been able.

A shudder had gone down my spine while approaching the red carpet for the umpteenth time, and I'd closed my eyes, focusing on my breathing exercises. I remembered the words Sergeant Fuller had screamed at me in the cabin. How I mattered. Even as I'd drifted away, those words had been ringing in my ears and still I clung to them.

"Let's do this," I'd then told Brian, the biggest and burliest of my bunch of overseers. He'd smiled broadly and nodded before offering me a wink. His cheeky way always had me smiling again, and when the car had finally come to a stop, it was he who'd stepped out first and then offered me his hand.

I took it, and with another deep, steadying breath, I climbed up and faced the limelight for the first time in months.

I would go on to tell my story. I'd open up and let it all out eventually, but for the time being there was just one thing I had to do, and that was to keep on fighting. I had my friends to push me forwards, and I had Eddie to be my rock. I had my career to focus on and a path to greatness ahead of me in the job I loved. That was way more than some survivors got. There were blessings aplenty, and I counted them often.

All I had to do was cling to them tightly and not let myself look back.

But there are two sides to the tale, though. Two aspects I still struggle with.

Firstly, like I've said before, I had known a deeper love than any that'd come before it. I fell in love with the most fiercely passionate and darkly obsessive man I'd ever met. He'd swept me off my feet and had loved me so much he would do anything to make me his. It was wonderful in so many ways. But, on the other hand, I also became the object of a monster's affections and paid the price for his love. I was beaten and broken by it. Tortured and almost killed because he loved me too damn much to ever let me be free.

There are times when I miss it. I know I shouldn't, but I often dream of Tommy and how he made my body scream with pleasure. Those are the memories I'll keep. Not the others if I can help it. But I know he'll never leave me, though. He'll always be a voice in my head and a clawing in my heart. Not false memories like the ones he was plagued with, but real.

His darkness touched me and turned a part of my soul away from the light. That part of me craves the return of the knowing, aching pain and torment. The punishment.

The tormentor and the protector somehow rolled into one.

Maybe I'm going mad. I can't know for sure, but I do know I'll never be the same again.

And I also know I'll always, at least in some way, be Tommy's Girl…

The end.

About the Author

LM Morgan started her writing career putting together short stories and fan fiction, usually involving her favourite movie characters caught up in steamy situations and wrote her first full-length novel in 2013. A self-confessed computer geek, LM enjoys both the writing and creative side of her journey, and regularly seeks out the next big gadget on her wish list to help facilitate those desires.

She spends her days with her hubby looking after her two children and their cocker spaniel Milo, as well as making the most of her free time by going to concerts with her friends, or else listening to rock music at home while writing (a trend many readers may have picked up on in her stories.)

LM Morgan also loves hearing from her fans, and you can connect with her via the following:

www.LMauthor.com

If you enjoyed this book, please take a moment to share your thoughts by leaving a review to help promote LM's work.

LM Morgan's novels include:

The Black Rose series:
When Darkness Falls: A Short Prequel to the Black Rose series
Embracing the Darkness: book #1 in the Black Rose series
A Slave to the Darkness: book #2 in the Black Rose series
Forever Darkness: book #3 in the Black Rose series
Destined for Darkness: book #4 in the Black Rose series
A Light in the Darkness: book #5 in the Black Rose series
Don't Pity the Dead, Pity the Immortal: Novella #1
Two Worlds, One War: Novella #2

And her contemporary romance novels:
Forever Lost (gangster/crime)
Forever Loved (gangster/crime follow on from Forever Lost)
Rough Love (MC crime/mystery story. Can be read as a stand-alone)
Fly Away – (A short romance story – probably LM's sweetest story to date!)
Ensnared – A dark romance

LM also writes Science Fiction under the alias LC Morgans, with her new novels:
*Humankind: Book 1 in the Invasion Days series
Autonomy: Book 2 in the Invasion Days series
Resonant: Book 3 in the Invasion Days series
Hereafter: Book 4 in the Invasion Day series

*Yes! The movie Piper was filming is based on a real story. Humankind and the rest of the Invasion Day series are available on Amazon now!

Printed in Great Britain
by Amazon